Aesop's Fables

伊索寓言裡的人生真相

―― 405則故事，讀懂世道人心 ――

中英對照

伊 索 ―― 著
Aesop
盛世教育 ―― 譯

笛藤出版

序言

　　古希臘的《伊索寓言》是一部在全世界流傳最廣的寓言集。古希臘文化是歐洲文化的發源地，它在歐洲文化史上佔有特殊的地位，古希臘寓言地位也是不凡。

　　相傳《伊索寓言》是西元前 6 世紀一個名叫伊索的奴隸創作的。關於伊索的身世傳說不一。一說伊索是西元前 6 世紀巴爾幹半島上色雷斯地區的一個奴隸。他相貌雖醜，但天性聰慧，為主人賞識而獲得自由民的身份。西元 4 至 5 世紀編成的《伊索傳》，載有他的許多佚事趣聞，但這並非信史。也有學者懷疑伊索的存在，認為並無此人。更多的意見則把他視為古希臘寓言講述者和整理者的代表人物，所以後世的人們便把希臘寓言都歸於伊索名下。

　　西元前 4 至 3 世紀之交，雅典哲學家德米特里厄斯 (Demetrius Phalereus，西元前 345 至西元前 283) 編輯了第一部伊索寓言集《伊索故事集成》(Assemblies of Aesop's Tales)，搜集了近 200 則寓言，此本今已失傳。西元 1 至 2 世紀，費德魯斯 (Phaedrus) 和巴布里烏斯 (Babrius) 又分別用拉丁文和希臘文寫成兩部詩體的伊索寓言，但這兩個版本均流傳不廣。現在我們所說的《伊索寓言》，是後人根據 14 世紀初東羅馬帝國的僧侶學者普拉努得斯搜集的寓言和陸續發現的古希臘寓言傳抄本整理編輯而成。這個本子有 150 則寓言，1479 年首次印行。它成為後來《伊索寓言》刊印本的主要材料來源。

　　1484 年，威廉‧卡克斯頓 (William Caxton) 出版了伊索寓言的一個英文版本。羅傑‧愛思琴奇爵士 (Sir Roger L'Estrange) 於 1692 年對卡克斯頓的版本進行了更新。喬治‧法伊勒‧湯森 (George Fyler Townsend, 1814 至 1900) 的譯本則是最為流行的一個版本，本書採用的英文即基於此。班·E·佩里 (Ben E. Perry) 把伊索寓言按類別做了一個索引，這個索引對有興趣研究伊索寓言的人來說是不可或缺的。這些版本根據的底稿不同，收錄的故事也不盡相同。本書收錄湯森版本中的 312 個故事，另外在綜合比較的基礎上，刪去內容有重複的故事，從其他幾個英譯本中收錄了與湯森版本不同的一些故事，共收寓言故事 405 則。故事編排以寓言中出色的角色為線索，把同類角色歸納在一處，並以角色的英文譯名的字母順序先後排列，方便讀者查找。在每個故事下面，有故事的出處和在佩里索引 (Perry Index) 中的編號，方便讀者比較研究。如第一則下的文字 (Townsend 304 = Perry 357) 表示該故事出自 George Fyler Townsend 的版本第 304 個故事，在 Perry Index 中的序號為 357。書後的附錄也有湯森和佩里兩個版本的詳細目錄，便於讀者對照。

《伊索寓言》故事短小精悍，主人公雖然大多是狐狸、獅子、狼、小羊……卻睿智地折射出了人間百態，寓意深刻，讓人回味無窮。讀者在閱讀中文的同時亦可提高英語閱讀技巧，可謂一舉兩得。

盛世教育西方名著編譯組

Aesop's Fables

Αἰσώπου Μῦθοι

CONTENTS

一、ASS 驢 021

1. The Ass and the Charger
   驢和戰馬
2. The Ass, the Cock,
   and the Lion
   驢、公雞和獅子
3. The Ass and His Driver
   驢和他的車夫
4. The Ass and the Frogs
   驢和青蛙
5. The Ass and the Grasshopper
   驢和蚱蜢
6. The Ass and the Horse
   驢和馬
7. The Ass and the Lapdog
   驢和寵物狗
8. The Ass and His Masters
   驢和他的主人們
9. Asses to Jupiter
   向朱比特請願的驢
10. The Ass and the Mule
    驢和騾子
11. The Ass and the Old Shepherd
    驢和老牧羊人
12. The Ass and His Purchaser
    驢和買主
13. The Ass and His Shadow
    驢和他的影子

14. The Ass and the Wolf.
    驢和狼
15. The Ass's Brains
    驢的腦子
16. The Ass Carrying the Image
    馱著神像的驢
17. The Ass in the Lion's Skin
    披著獅子皮的驢
18. The Goat and the Ass
    山羊和驢
19. The Horse and the Ass
    馬和驢
20. The Mule
    騾子
21. The Mules and the Robbers
    騾子和強盜
22. The Playful Ass
    頑皮的驢
23. The Salt Merchant and His Ass
    鹽商和他的驢
24. A Wild Ass and a Tame
    野驢和家驢

二、BATS 蝙蝠 047

25. A Bat, Bramble,
    and Cormorant
    蝙蝠、荊棘與鸕鶿

26. The Bat and the Weasels
    蝙蝠和黃鼠狼
27. The Birds, the Beasts,
    and the Bat
    鳥、獸和蝙蝠

三、BIRDS 鳥 ················ 051

BIRDS OF VARIOUS KINDS 各種鳥

28. The Birdcatcher, the Partridge,
    and the Cock
    捕鳥人、山鶉和公雞
29. The Cage Bird and the Bat
    籠中鳥和蝙蝠
30. The Cock and the Jewel
    公雞和寶石
31. The Farmer and the Cranes
    農夫和鶴
32. A Fowler and a Blackbird
    捕鳥人與烏鶇
33. The Fox and the Crane
    狐狸和鶴
34. A Galled Ass and a Raven
    背受傷的驢和烏鴉
35. The Gamecocks
    and the Partridge
    鬥雞和山鶉
36. The Geese and the Cranes
    鵝和鶴
37. The Grasshopper and the Owl
    蚱蜢和貓頭鷹

38. The Hawk, the Kite,
    and the Pigeons
    鷹、鳶和鴿子
39. The Hawk and the Nightingale
    老鷹和夜鶯
40. The Hen and the Golden Eggs
    母雞和金蛋
41. The Hen and the Swallow
    母雞和燕子
42. The Jay and the Peacock
    松鴉和孔雀
43. A Kingfisher
    翠鳥
44. The Kites and the Swans
    鳶和天鵝
45. The Labourer
    and the Nightingale
    工人和夜鶯
46. An Ostrich, Birds, and Beasts
    鴕鳥、鳥與野獸
47. The Owl and the Birds
    貓頭鷹和鳥
48. The Partridge and the Fowler
    山鶉和捕鳥人
49. The Peacock and the Crane
    孔雀和鶴
50. The Peacock and Juno
    孔雀和朱諾
51. The Raven and the Birds
    渡鴉和鳥

52. The Raven and the Swan
渡鴉和天鵝

53. The Seagull and the Kite
海鷗和鳶

54. The Sick Kite
生病的鳶

55. The Sparrow and the Hare
麻雀和野兔

56. The Spendthrift
and the Swallow
敗家子和燕子

57. The Swallow
and the Other Birds
燕子和別的鳥

58. The Swallow, the Serpent,
and the Court of Justice
燕子、蛇和法庭

59. The Swan and the Goose
天鵝和鵝

60. The Swan and His Owner
天鵝和他的主人

61. The Thirsty Pigeon
口渴的鴿子

62. The Thrush and the Fowler
畫眉鳥和捕人

63. A Thrush and a Swallow
畫眉鳥和燕子

64. The Woman and Her Hen
婦人和她的母雞

CROW 烏鴉

65. A Crow and a Dog
烏鴉和狗

66. The Crow and Mercury
烏鴉和墨丘利

67. A Crow and a Tortoise
烏鴉和烏龜

68. The Crow and the Pitcher
烏鴉和水罐

69. The Crow and the Raven
烏鴉和渡鴉

70. The Crow and the Serpent
烏鴉和毒蛇

71. The Crow and the Sheep
烏鴉和綿羊

72. The Dove and the Crow
鴿子和烏鴉

73. The Swallow and the Crow
燕子和烏鴉

DAW 寒鴉

74. A Daw and Borrowed Feathers
寒鴉和借來的羽毛

75. A Daw with a String at Its Foot
腳上綁著繩子的寒鴉

76. The Jackdaw and the Doves
寒鴉和鴿子

77. The Vain Jackdaw
虛榮的寒鴉

78. The Eagle and the Arrow 鷹和箭	四、**BULL** 公牛 111
79. The Eagle and His Captor 鷹和捕鷹人	91. The Bull and the Calf 公牛和小牛
80. The Eagle, the Cat, and the Wild Sow 鷹、貓和野豬	92. The Bull and the Goat 公牛和山羊
	93. The Flea and the Ox 跳蚤和公牛
81. The Eagle and the Jackdaw 鷹和寒鴉	94. The Lion and the Three Bulls 獅子和三頭公牛
82. The Eagle and the Kite 鷹和鳶	95. The Heifer and the Ox 母牛和公牛
83. The Fighting Cocks and the Eagle 打架的公雞和鷹	96. The Oxen and the Axle-Trees 牛和車軸
	97. The Oxen and the Butchers 牛和屠夫
84. The Peasant and the Eagle 農夫和鷹	
85. The Serpent and the Eagle 蛇和鷹	五、**CAMEL** 駱駝 119
86. The Tortoise and the Birds 烏龜和鳥	98. The Camel 駱駝
87. The Tortoise and the Eagle 烏龜和老鷹	99. The Camel and the Arab 駱駝和阿拉伯人
LARK 雲雀	六、**CAT** 貓 123
88. The Lark Burying Her Father 雲雀葬父	100. The Cat and the Birds 貓和鳥
89. The Lark and Her Young Ones 雲雀和她的小鳥們	101. The Cat and the Cock 貓和公雞
90. A Lark in a Net 網裡的雲雀	102. The Cat and Venus 貓和維納斯

103. The Fox and the Cat
狐狸和貓

七、DEER 鹿 129

104. The Fawn and His Mother
小鹿和母鹿

105. The One-Eyed Doe
獨眼雌鹿

106. The Sick Stag
生病的雄鹿

107. The Stag in the Ox-Stall
牛圈裡的雄鹿

108. The Stag at the Pool
池邊的雄鹿

八、DOG 狗 137

109. The Bitch and Her Whelps
母狗和她的小狗

110. The Brazier and His Dog
銅匠和他的狗

111. A Dog and a Butcher
狗和屠夫

112. The Dog and the Cook
狗和廚師

113. The Dog and the Hare
狗和野兔

114. The Dog and The Lion
狗和獅子

115. The Dog in the Manger
牛槽裡的狗

116. The Dog and the Oyster
狗和牡蠣

117. The Dog and the Shadow
狗和影子

118. A Dog and a Wolf
狗和狼

119. The Dog's House
狗的家

120. The Dogs and the Hides
狗和牛皮

121. A Gardener and His Dog
園丁和他的狗

122. The Man Bitten by a Dog
被狗咬的人

123. The Man, the Horse, the Ox, and the Dog
人、馬、牛和狗

124. The Master and His Dogs
主人和他的狗

125. The Mischievous Dog
惡狗

126. The Old Hound
老獵狗

127. The Shepherd and the Dog
牧羊人和狗

128. The Thief and the Housedog
小偷和看門狗

129. The Traveler and His Dog
旅行者和他的狗

130. The Two Dogs
兩隻狗

九、FISH/OCEAN DWELLER
魚 / 海洋生物 159

131. The Crab and the Fox
螃蟹和狐狸

132. The Crab and Its Mother
螃蟹和牠的母親

133. The Dolphins, the Whales,
and the Sprat
海豚、鯨魚和鯡魚

134. The Fisherman Piping
吹長笛的漁夫

135. The Fisherman and His Nets
漁夫和漁網

136. A Fisherman's Good Luck
漁夫的好運

137. The Fishermen
漁夫們

138. Fishing in Troubled Waters
渾水摸魚

139. The Lion and the Dolphin
獅子和海豚

140. The Monkey and the Dolphin
猴子和海豚

141. A Tuna Fish and a Dolphin
金槍魚和海豚

十、FOX 狐狸 171

142. An Ape and a Fox
猿猴和狐狸

143. The Bear and the Fox
熊和狐狸

144. The Dog, the Cock,
and the Fox
狗、公雞和狐狸

145. The Dogs and the Fox
狗和狐狸

146. The Eagle and the Fox
鷹和狐狸

147. The Fox Who Had Lost His Tail
丟了尾巴的狐狸

148. The Fox and the Bramble
狐狸和荊棘

149. The Fox, the Cock
and the Dogs
狐狸、公雞和狗

150. A Fox and a Crocodile
狐狸和鱷魚

151. The Fox and the Crow
狐狸和烏鴉

152. The Fox and the Goat
狐狸和山羊

153. The Fox and Grapes
狐狸和葡萄

154. A Fox and a Hare to Jupiter
向朱比特請願的狐狸和野兔

155. The Fox and the Hedgehog
狐狸和刺蝟

156. The Fox and the Leopard
狐狸和豹子

157. The Fox and the Lion
狐狸和獅子

158. The Fox and the Mask
狐狸和面具

159. The Fox and the Monkey
狐狸和猴子

160. The Fox and the Partridge
狐狸和鷓鴣

161. The Fox and the Woodcutter
狐狸和伐木工

162. The Hares and the Foxes
野兔和狐狸

163. The Jackdaw and the Fox
寒鴉和狐狸

164. The Lion, the Bear, and the Fox
獅子、熊和狐狸

165. The Lion and the Fox
獅子和狐狸

166. The Lion and the Fox, and the Ass
獅子、狐狸和驢

167. The Quack Frog
青蛙庸醫

168. The Sick Lion
生病的獅子

169. The Swollen Fox
發胖的狐狸

170. The Wolf and the Fox
狼和狐狸

十一、FROGS 青蛙 ········ 201

171. The Boys and the Frogs
男孩和青蛙

172. The Frogs Asking for a King
青蛙想要一個國王

173. The Frogs and the Well
青蛙和井

174. The Two Frogs
兩隻青蛙

175. The Frogs' Complaint Against the Sun
青蛙抱怨太陽

176. The Lion and the Frog
獅子和青蛙

177. The Ox and the Frog
牛和青蛙

十二、GOAT 山羊 ············ 209

178. The Goat and the Goatherd
山羊和牧羊人

179. The Goatherd and the Wild Goats
牧羊人和野山羊

180. The She-Goats and Their Beards
母山羊和鬍子

181. TheWolf and the Kid
狼和小羊

十三、GODS 眾神 215

- 182. Apollo and the Snake
  阿波羅和蛇
- 183. Avaricious and Envious
  貪婪和嫉妒
- 184. The Bee and Jupiter
  蜜蜂和朱比特
- 185. The Camel and Jupiter
  駱駝和朱比特
- 186. The Goods and the Ills
  好事和壞事
- 187. Hercules and Pallas
  赫拉克勒斯和帕拉斯
- 188. Hercules and Plutus
  赫拉克勒斯和普魯托斯
- 189. Hercules and the Wagoner
  赫拉克勒斯和馬車夫
- 190. Hermes and the Earth
  赫爾墨斯和大地之神
- 191. The Image of Mercury and the Carpenter
  墨丘利木像和木匠
- 192. An Imposter to the Oracle
  到阿波羅神殿去的騙子
- 193. Jupiter and the Fox
  朱比特和狐狸
- 194. Jupiter and Fraud
  朱比特和欺騙
- 195. Jupiter and Modesty
  朱比特和謙遜
- 196. Jupiter, Neptune, Minerva, and Momus
  朱比特、尼普頓、密涅瓦和莫摩斯
- 197. Jupiter and a Serpent
  朱比特和蛇
- 198. Jupiter's Wedding
  朱比特的婚禮
- 199. Large Promises
  誇大的承諾
- 200. The Man and the Hero
  人和英雄
- 201. The Man and the Satyr
  人和薩提
- 202. Mercury and the Sculptor
  墨丘利和雕刻家
- 203. Mercury and Tiresias
  墨丘利和提瑞西阿斯
- 204. Mercury and a Traveller
  墨丘利和旅行者
- 205. Mercury and the Workmen
  墨丘利和工人
- 206. The Oath's Punishment
  誓言之神的懲罰
- 207. The Seller of Images
  賣神像的人
- 208. The Traveler and Fortune
  旅行者和命運女神
- 209. The Trees under the Protection of the Gods
  受到神靈保護的樹

- 210. War and His Bride
  戰爭和他的新娘
- 211. Zeus and the Jar of Good Things
  宙斯和存放好東西的罐子
- 212. Zeus and Man
  宙斯和人
- 213. Zeus and Prometheus
  宙斯和普羅米修士

十四、HARE 野兔 251

- 214. The Hare and the Fox
  野兔和狐狸
- 215. The Hare and the Hound
  野兔和獵狗
- 216. The Hare and the Tortoise
  龜兔賽跑
- 217. The Hare with Many Friends
  朋友眾多的野兔
- 218. The Hares and the Frogs
  野兔和青蛙

十五、HORSE 馬 259

- 219. The Charger and the Miller
  軍馬和磨坊主
- 220. The Horse and Groom
  馬和馬夫
- 221. The Horse and the Stag
  馬和鹿

十六、INSECT 昆蟲 263

- 222. The Ant and the Chrysalis
  螞蟻和蛹
- 223. The Ant and the Dove
  螞蟻和鴿子
- 224. An Ant Formerly a Man
  由人演變成的螞蟻
- 225. The Ants and the Grasshopper
  螞蟻和蚱蜢
- 226. The Cicada and the Fox
  蟬和狐狸
- 227. The Dung Beetle and the Eagle
  金龜子和老鷹
- 228. The Flea and the Man
  跳蚤和人
- 229. The Flea and the Wrestler
  跳蚤和摔角手
- 230. The Flies and the Honey-Pot
  蒼蠅和蜂蜜罐
- 231. The Fly and the Draught-Mule
  蒼蠅和拉車的騾子
- 232. The Gnat and the Bull
  蚊子和公牛
- 233. The Gnat and the Lion
  蚊子和獅子
- 234. The Scorpion and the Frog
  蠍子和青蛙
- 235. The Silkworm and Spider
  蠶和蜘蛛

236. The Wasp and the Snake
馬蜂和蛇

十七、LAMB 小羊 281

237. A Dog, a Sheep, and a Wolf
狗、綿羊和狼

238. The Stag, the Wolf,
and the Sheep
雄鹿、狼和綿羊

239. The Widow and the Sheep
寡婦和綿羊

240. A Wolf, a Lamb, and a Goat
狼、羊羔和山羊

十八、LION 獅子 287

241. Androcles
安德羅克勒斯

242. The Bowman and Lion
射手和獅子

243. The Doe and the Lion
母鹿和獅子

244. The Fox and the Lion
狐狸和獅子

245. The Hares and the Lions
野兔和獅子

246. The Kingdom of the Lion
獅子的王國

247. The Ass, the Fox, and the Lion
驢、狐狸和獅子

248. he Lion in a Farmyard
農場裡的獅子

249. The Lion in Love
戀愛中的獅子

250. The Lion and an Ass
獅子和驢

251. The Lion and the Boar
獅子和野豬

252. The Lion and the Bull
獅子和公牛

253. The Lion and the Eagle
獅子和鷹

254. The Lion and the Hare
獅子和兔子

255. The Lion, Jupiter,
and the Elephant
獅子、朱比特和大象

256. The Lion, the Mouse,
and the Fox
獅子、老鼠和狐狸

257. The Lion and the Shepherd
獅子和牧羊人

258. The Lion, the Wolg and the Fox
獅子、狼和狐狸

259. The Lion's Share
獅子的份額

260. The Lioness
母獅子

261. The Man and the Lion
人和獅子

262. The Old Lion
 老獅子

263. The Wild Ass and the Lion
 野驢和獅子

264. The Wolf and the Lion I
 狼和獅子（版本一）

265. The Wolf and the Lion II
 狼和獅子（版本二）

十九、MEN 人 313

MEN OF VARIOUS KINDS 各類人

266. The Aethiop
 黑僕人

267. The Bald Man and the Fly
 禿子和蒼蠅

268. A Bee-Master
 養蜂人

269. The Brother and the Sister
 兄妹

270. The Buffoon
 and the Countryman
 小丑和鄉下人

271. The Bull, the Lioness,
 and the Wild-Boar Hunter
 公牛、母獅和打野豬的獵人

272. The Charcoal-Burner
 and the Fuller
 燒炭人和漂洗工

273. The Cobbler Turned Doctor
 補鞋匠改行當醫生

274. The Laborer and the Snake
 工人和蛇

275. A Cunning Woman
 狡猾的女人

276. A Doctor and His Patient
 醫生和他的病人

277. The Doctor at the Funeral
 醫生和葬禮

278. The Two Men
 Who Were Enemies
 兩個仇敵

279. The Farmer and His Sons
 農夫和他的兒子們

280. The Father and His Sons
 父與子

281. The Father
 and His Two Daughters
 父親和兩個女兒

282. The King's Son
 and the Painted Lion
 國王的兒子與畫上的獅子

283. The Man
 and His Two Sweethearts
 男人和兩個情人

284. The Man and His Wife
 男人和他的妻子

285. The Man, the Pig
and the Miracle
人、豬和奇蹟

286. The Manslayer
殺人兇手

287. The Milk-Woman and Her Pail
擠奶姑娘和她的桶子

288. The Miller, His Son,
and Their Ass
磨坊主、他的兒子和他們的驢

289. The Miser
守財奴

290. A Musician
音樂家

291. The Old Man and Death I
老人和死神

292. The Old Woman
and the Physician
老婦人和醫生

293. The Old Woman
and the Wine-Jar
老婦人和酒罈

294. The Rich Man and the Tanner
富人和皮匠

295. The Thief and the Innkeeper
賊和客棧老闆

296. The Thieves and the Cock
小偷和公雞

297. The Three Tradesmen
三個工匠

298. The Trumpeter Taken Prisoner
被俘的號兵

299. Two Young Men and a Cook
兩個年輕人和一個廚師

300. The Widow
and Her Little Maidens
寡婦和她的小女僕

301. A Wife and a Drunken Husband
妻子和喝醉酒的丈夫

302. A Woman
and Her Two Daughters
一個女人和她的兩個女兒

BOY 男孩

303. The Boy Bathing
洗澡的男孩

304. A Boy and Cockles
男孩和文蛤

305. The Boy and the Filberts
男孩和榛子

306. The Boy and the Nettles
男孩和蕁麻

307. The Thief and His Mother
賊和他的母親

FARMER/HERDSMAN 農夫/牧人

308. The Farmer and the Fox
農夫和狐狸

309. The Farmer and the Snake
農夫和蛇

310. The Farmer and the Stork
農夫和鸛

311. The Herdsman
and the Lost Bull
牧人和走失的公牛

312. The Shepherd and the Sea
牧羊人和海

313. The Shepherd and the Sheep
牧羊人和羊

314. The Wasps, the Partridges,
and the Farmer
馬蜂、鷓鴣和農夫

HUNTER/FISHER 獵人 / 漁夫

315. The Boy Hunting Locusts
捉蝗蟲的男孩

316. The Fisherman
and the Little Fish
漁夫和小魚

317. The Hunter and the Horseman
獵人和騎馬者

318. The Hunter and the Woodman
獵人和伐木工

319. The Huntsman
and the Fisherman
獵人和漁夫

MILITARY MEN 軍隊人員

320. The Bald Knight
禿頭騎士

321. The Horse and His Rider
馬和騎兵

322. The Two Soldiers
and the Robber
兩個士兵和強盜

SEER 預言家

323. The Astronomer
天文學家

324. The Philosopher,
the Ants, and Mercury
哲學家、螞蟻和墨丘利

325. The Prophet
預言家

TRAVELER 旅行者

326. The Boasting Traveler
吹牛的旅行者

327. The Seaside Travelers
海邊的旅行者

328. The Shipwrecked Man
and the Sea
落水的人和海

329. The Travelers
and the Plane-Tree
兩個旅行者和梧桐樹

330. Truth and the Traveler
真理和旅行者

331. The Two Travelers and the Axe
兩個旅行者和斧頭

二十、MONKEY 猴子 381

332. The Apes
 and the Two Travelers
 猴子和兩個旅行者

333. The Dancing Monkeys
 跳舞的猴子

334. Jupiter and the Monkey
 朱比特和猴子

335. The Monkey and the Camel
 猴子和駱駝

336. The Monkey and the Fishermen
 猴子和漁夫

337. The Monkey and the Fox
 猴子和狐狸

338. The Monkeys and Their Mother
 猴子和牠們的媽媽

二十一、MOUSE 老鼠 391

339. Belling the Cat
 給貓繫鈴鐺

340. The Cat and the Mice
 貓和老鼠

341. The Lion and the Mouse
 獅子和老鼠

342. The Mice and the Weasels
 老鼠和黃鼬

343. The Mouse and the Bull
 老鼠和公牛

344. The Mouse, the Frog,
 and the Hawk
 老鼠、青蛙和鷹

345. The Town Mouse
 and the Country Mouse
 城裡老鼠和鄉下老鼠

346. The Weasel and the Mice
 黃鼠狼和老鼠

二十二、OBJECTS 各種物體 403

347. The Belly and the Members
 肚子和身體器官

348. The Lamp
 燈

349. The Mountain in Labor
 大山異動

350. The North Wind and the Sun
 北風和太陽

351. The Rivers and the Sea
 河與海

352. The Two Bags
 兩個袋子

353. The Two Pots
 兩個罐子

二十三、ODDS/ENDS 雜七雜八 411

354. The Bear and the Two Travelers
 熊與兩個旅人

355. A Hunted Beaver
被抓住的海狸

356. The Mole and His Mother
田鼠和牠的媽媽

357. The Panther and the Shepherds
豹子和牧羊人

二十四、PIG 豬 417

358. The Piglet, the Sheep, and the Goat
小豬、綿羊和山羊

359. A Sow and a Bitch
母豬和母狗

360. A Sow and a Dog
母豬和狗

361. The Wild Boar and the Fox
野豬和狐狸

二十五、SNAKE 蛇 421

362. The Fowler and the Viper
捕鳥人和毒蛇

363. The Serpent and the File
蛇和銼刀

364. A Snake and a Crab
蛇和螃蟹

365. The Woodman and the Serpent
樵夫和蛇

366. The Viper and the File
毒蛇和銼刀

二十六、TREES/PLANTS 樹 / 植物 427

367. Apples and Horse-Turds
蘋果和馬糞

368. The Fir-Tree and the Bramble
杉樹和荊棘

369. The Hart and the Vine
鹿和藤蔓

370. The Man and the Wood
人和樹林

371. The Oak and the Reeds
橡樹和蘆葦

372. The Oak and the Woodcutters
橡樹和伐木工

373. The Oaks and Jupiter
橡樹和朱比特

374. An Old Tree Transplanted
被移種的老樹

375. The Olive-Tree and the Fig-Tree
橄欖樹和無花果樹

376. The Peasant and the Apple-Tree
農夫和蘋果樹

377. The Pomegranate, Apple-Tree, and Bramble
石榴樹、蘋果樹和荊棘

378. The Rose and the Amaranth
玫瑰和不凋花

379. The Trees and the Axe
樹和斧頭

380. The Vine and the Goat

葡萄和山羊

381. The Walnut-Tree
核桃樹

二十七、WOLF 狼 441

382. The Blind Man and the Whelp
盲人和幼狼

383. The Kid and the Wolf
小羊和狼

384. The Lamb and the Wolf
羔羊和狼

385. The Mother and the Wolf
母親和狼

386. The Shepherd and the Wolf
牧羊人和狼

387. A Shepherd and a Wolf's, Whelp
牧羊人和小狼

388. The Shepherd's Boy and the Wolf
牧童和狼

389. The Wolf and the Crane
狼和鶴

390. A Wolf and a Fox
狼和狐狸

391. The Wolf, the Fox, and the Ape
狼、狐狸和猿

392. The Wolf and the Goat
狼和山羊

393. A Wolf, Kid, and Goat
狼、孩子和山羊

394. The Wolf and the Horse
狼和馬

395. The Wolf and the Housedog
狼和看家狗

396. The Wolf and the Lamb
狼和小羊

397. A Wolf and a Lion
狼和獅子

398. The Wolf and the Sheep
狼和羊

399. The Wolf in Sheep's Clothing I
披著羊皮的狼（版本一）

400. The Wolf in Sheep's Clothing II
披著羊皮的狼（版本二）

401. The Wolf and the Shepherd I
狼和牧羊人（版本一）

402. The Wolf and the Shepherds II
狼和牧羊人（版本二）

403. A Wolf and a Sow
狼和母豬

404. The Wolves and the Sheep
狼和綿羊

405. The Wolves and the Sheepdogs
狼和牧羊狗

| 附錄 1 |

Aesop's Fables: Townsend (1867)

| 附錄 2 |

Perry's Index to the Aesopica

1.
ASS
驢

ASS 驢

Townsend 304 = Perry 357

1. The Ass and the Charger

An Ass congratulated a Horse on being so ungrudgingly and carefully provided for, while he himself had scarcely enough to eat and not even that without hard work. But when war broke out, a heavily armed soldier mounted the Horse, and riding him to the charge, rushed into the very midst of the enemy. The Horse was wounded and fell dead on the battlefield. Then the Ass, seeing all these things, changed his mind, and commiserated the Horse.

♦　　Be content with your station.　　♦

1. 驢和戰馬

驢羨慕戰馬能吃到豐富的飼料，又可以得到精心的照顧，而自己不但草料匱乏，還得幹重活。但是當戰爭爆發時，全副武裝的士兵跳上戰馬，騎著他東拚西戰，衝入敵軍腹地。戰馬傷痕累累，戰死沙場。驢看到這一切，改變了先前的想法，反過來開始同情戰馬了。

♦　　要懂得滿足現狀。　　♦

Townsend 107 = Perry 82

2. The Ass, the Cock, and the Lion

An Ass and a Cock were in a straw-yard together when a Lion, desperate from hunger, approached the spot. He was about to spring upon the Ass, when the Cock (to the sound of whose voice the Lion, it is said, has a singular aversion) crowed loudly, and the Lion fled away as fast as he could. The Ass, observing his trepidation at the mere crowing of a Cock summoned courage to attack him, and galloped after him for that purpose. He had run no long distance, when the Lion, turning about, seized him and tore him to pieces.

♦ False confidence often leads into danger. ♦

2. 驢、公雞和獅子

驢和公雞在同一個圍欄中，這時一隻饑腸轆轆的獅子走了過來，就在獅子正要向驢撲過去的時候，公雞大聲鳴叫，獅子聽見後，以最快的速度跑掉了（據說獅子極其害怕聽見公雞的鳴叫）。驢看公雞的叫聲都可以把獅子嚇跑，勇氣倍增，跟在獅子身後窮追不捨，目的是為了教訓一下獅子。然而驢剛追了沒多遠，獅子突然轉過身來，一下子抓住驢，把他撕成了碎片。

♦ 盲目的自信常常導致危險。 ♦

Townsend 309 = Perry 186

3. The Ass and His Driver

An Ass, being driven along a high road, suddenly started off and bolted to the brink of a deep precipice. While he was in the act of throwing himself over, his owner seized him by the tail, endeavoring to pull him back. When the Ass persisted in his effort, the man let him go and said, "Conquer, but conquer to

ASS 驢

your cost."

♦ A willful beast must go his own way. ♦

3. 驢和和他的車夫

　　車夫趕著驢走在山路上，突然驢掙脫韁繩，一個箭步衝到了陡峭的山崖邊。就在驢將要掉下山的剎那，車夫一下子抓住了驢的尾巴，想盡力把他拉回來。但是驢不顧一切地掙扎，車夫只能鬆開手，讓驢摔下懸崖，他說道：「掙扎吧，最終會付出代價的。」

♦ 一意孤行的人總是鑽牛角尖。 ♦

Townsend 164 = Perry 189

4. The Ass and the Frogs

　　An Ass, carrying a load of wood, passed through a pond. As he was crossing through the water he lost his footing, stumbled and fell, and not being able to rise on account of his load, groaned heavily. Some Frogs frequenting the pool heard his lamentation, and said, "What would you do if you had to live here always as we do, when you make such a fuss about a mere fall into the water?"

♦ Men often bear little grievances with less courage than they do large misfortunes. ♦

4. 驢和青蛙

　　有頭驢馱著許多木料橫穿池塘。當他淌水過池塘時，不小心跌倒了，背上馱的東西太重，壓得他站不起身來，於是驢就大聲哀鳴起來。在池塘裡游來游去的青蛙們聽見了驢的呻吟，說道：「你不過是一跤跌進水中，就這樣大驚小怪，如果你得跟我們一樣在這兒長住，又會怎樣呢？」

◆　　**人在面臨小的挫折時，往往不像面臨巨大的災難時那麼無所畏懼。**　　◆

Townsend 3 = Perry 184

5. The Ass and the Grasshopper

An Ass having heard some Grasshoppers chirping, was highly enchanted; and, desiring to possess the same charms of melody, demanded what sort of food they lived on to give them such beautiful voices. They replied, "The dew." The Ass resolved that he would live only upon dew, and in a short time died of hunger.

◆　　Even a fool is wise—when it is too late!　　◆

5. 驢和蚱蜢

驢聽到蚱蜢在唱歌，為他們悅耳的歌聲而癡迷，自己也想唱出如此動聽的旋律，就問蚱蜢：「是什麼食物的滋養，讓你們有這樣美妙的歌喉？」蚱蜢回答說：「露水。」因此驢決心從今以後只喝露水，但不久之後就餓死了。

◆　　**傻瓜也會變得明智 ——但為時已晚。**　　◆

ASS 驢

Townsend 270 = Perry 571

6. The Ass and the Horse

An Ass besought a Horse to spare him a small portion of his feed. "Yes," said the Horse; "if any remains out of what I am now eating I will give it you for the sake of my own superior dignity, and if you will come when I reach my own stall in the evening, I will give you a little sack full of barley." The Ass replied, "Thank you. But I can't think that you, who refuse me a little matter now, will by and by confer on me a greater benefit."

◆ Without charity in the present, don't expect charity in the future. ◆

6. 驢和馬

驢懇求馬把他吃的東西分給自己一小部分，馬說道：「好吧，如果我現在吃的草料有剩下的就給你，這樣做是出於我既高貴又體面的身份。假如你晚上來我的馬廄，我可以送你一小袋裝得滿滿的大麥。」驢聽了，回答說：「謝謝了，但是現在你連一丁點兒草料都不願分給我，又怎麼會給我更好的東西呢？」

◆ 現在不會施恩，將來也不會。 ◆

Townsend 41 = Perry 91

7. The Ass and the Lapdog

A man had an Ass, and a Maltese Lapdog, a very great

beauty. The Ass was left in a stable and had plenty of oats and hay to eat, just as any other Ass would. The Lapdog knew many tricks and was a great favorite with his master, who often fondled him and seldom went out to dine without bringing him home some tidbit to eat.

The Ass, on the contrary, had much work to do in grinding the corn-mill and in carrying wood from the forest or burdens from the farm. He often lamented his own hard fate and contrasted it with the luxury and idleness of the Lapdog, till at last one day he broke his cords and halter, and galloped into his master's house, kicking up his heels without measure, and frisking and fawning as well as he could. He next tried to jump about his master as he had seen the Lapdog do, but he broke the table and smashed all the dishes upon it to atoms. He then attempted to lick his master, and jumped upon his back.

The servants, hearing the strange hubbub and perceiving the danger of their master, quickly relieved him, and drove out the Ass to his stable with kicks and clubs and cuffs. The Ass, as he returned to his stall beaten nearly to death, thus lamented, "I have brought it all on myself! Why could I not have been contented to labor with my companions, and not wish to be idle all the day like that useless little Lapdog!"

◆ To be satisfied with one's lot is better than to desire something which one is not fitted to receive. ◆

7. 驢和寵物狗

有個人養了一頭驢和一隻十分好看的馬爾濟斯寵物狗。驢住

ASS 驢

在牲口棚裡，有充足的燕麥和乾草吃，這和其他的驢並無不同。而那隻寵物狗特別會討主人的歡心，主人時常逗他玩耍，幾乎每次出去參加宴會，都會給寵物狗帶些美味的食物回來。

而驢，正好相反，每天都不辭辛苦地拉磨，還得到樹林中去運木頭，或者到農場去馱東西。驢時常感歎自己命運悲慘，希望過寵物狗那樣奢侈安逸的生活。終於有一天，驢脫去韁繩，像箭一般地跑到主人的屋子裡，又蹦又跳，還不斷地擺尾巴。他想像寵物狗那樣在主人跟前跳幾下，卻一腳踢倒了桌子，桌上的杯盤摔得粉碎。接著，驢想去舔他的主人，卻一下子竄上了主人的後背。

僕人們聽到怪異的喧鬧聲，以為主人遭遇危險，馬上跑過來救他。他們一路上棍棒交加、連踢帶踹地把驢弄回了驢舍。被打得奄奄一息的驢悲歎道：「我真是自討苦吃。我和夥伴們天天努力工作，不是挺好的嗎？為何偏偏想去做一隻整天虛度光陰、一無用處的寵物狗呢？」

◆　　　　滿足於現狀好過整天幻想。　　　　◆

Townsend 126 = Perry 179

8. The Ass and His Masters

An Ass, belonging to an herb-seller who gave him too little food and too much work made a petition to Jupiter to be released from his present service and provided with another master. Jupiter, after warning him that he would repent his request, caused him to be sold to a tile-maker. Shortly afterwards, finding that he had heavier loads to carry and harder work in the brick-field, he petitioned for another change of master. Jupiter, telling him that it would be the last time that he could grant his request, ordained that he be sold to a tanner. The Ass found that he had fallen into worse hands, and noting his master's occupation, said, groaning, "It would have been better for me to have been either starved by the one, or to have been overworked by the other of my former masters, than to have been bought by my present owner, who will even after I am dead tan my hide, and make me useful to him."

> He that finds discontentment in one place is not likely to find happiness in another.

8. 驢和他的主人們

驢的主人是個草藥販子，他總是讓驢吃得很少，卻要做很多工作。驢就請求朱比特給他換個主人。朱比特警告他道，他會為此感到後悔的，但還是設法把驢轉賣給了一個製瓦工。驢到了磚場後不久就發現，自己拉的車更加重，工作也更加多了。接著他又懇求朱比特給他再換個主人。朱比特告訴驢說，這是他最後一次同意驢的請求了，於是就下令又把驢賣給了一個皮匠。驢發現沒有比落到這個主人手裡更悲慘的了，於是悲哀地感慨道：「我不管在以前的主人那兒挨餓，還是在前一個主人那裡做粗工，也都比被如今的主人買來好得多，他在我死了以後還要剝掉我的皮來利用我。」

> 一處不滿意，處處不滿意。

ASS 驢

L' Estrange 191 = Perry 185

9. Asses to Jupiter

The Asses found themselves once so Intolerably Oppressed with cruel Masters and heavy Burdens, that they sent their Ambassadors to Jupiter, with a Petition for Redress. Jupiter found the Request Unreasonable, and so gave them this Answer, That Humane Society could not be preserved without carrying Burdens some way or other : So that if they would but join, and Piss up a River, that the Burdens which they now carried by Land might be carried by Water, they should be Eas'd of that Grievance. This set them all a Pissing immediately, and the Humour is kept up to this very Day, that whenever One Ass Pisses, the rest Piss for Company.

◆ Tis the uttermost degree of Madness and Folly ,to Appeal from Providence and Nature. ◆

9. 向朱比特請願的驢

從前，驢覺得自己再也無法忍受殘酷的主人和沉重的負荷，於是他們便派使者去見朱比特，請求朱比特免去他們的勞苦。對這個無理的要求，朱比特回答道，要是不用這樣或那樣的方式減輕人類的負擔，人類社會就會滅亡；所以，如果他們能夠團結起來撒尿成河，那麼到時候，他們現在在陸地上所背負的重荷就能用河水來運輸，他們也就能脫離苦海了。一聽這話，所有的驢馬上都撒了一泡尿。直到現在，只要看見有一頭驢撒尿，其餘的驢都會和他一起撒尿。

◆ 只有最愚蠢最不理智的人，才會求助老天或外界的力量來改變自己的命運。 ◆

Townsend 50 = Perry 181

10. The Ass and the Mule

A Muleteer set forth on a journey, driving before him an Ass and a Mule, both well laden. The Ass, as long as he traveled along the plain, carried his load with ease, but when he began to ascend the steep path of the mountain, felt his load to be more than he could bear. He entreated his companion to relieve him of a small portion, that he might carry home the rest; but the Mule paid no attention to the request. The Ass shortly afterwards fell down dead under his burden. Not knowing what else to do in so wild a region, the Muleteer placed upon the Mule the load carried by the Ass in addition to his own, and at the top of all placed the hide of the Ass, after he had skinned him. The Mule, groaning beneath his heavy burden, said to himself, "I am treated according to my deserts. If I had only been willing to assist the Ass a little in his need, I should not now be bearing, together with his burden, himself as well."

♦　　An ounce of prevention is worth a pound of cure.　　♦

10. 驢和騾子

有個趕騾子的車夫，驅趕著一頭驢跟一頭騾子上路，牲畜都馱著沉重的貨物。在平地上驢走得無比輕鬆，可是一旦爬上險峻的山路，驢就馱不動了。驢請求騾子替他馱一小部分東西，以便自己能馱著其他的貨物，接著往前走。但是，騾子對驢的請求不理不睬。過了一會兒，驢不堪重負，從山上跌落下去，摔死了。在那種荒山野嶺的地方，車夫別無他法，只得把驢馱的東西加在

ASS 驢

了騾子的背上,並且還把剝下的驢皮放在最上面。騾子被壓得喘不過氣來,對自己說道:「我真是自作自受!如果在驢需要的時候,我稍稍地幫他一下,如今就不至於既得馱著他的貨物,還得帶著他的皮了。」

◆　　　　預防一分勝於十分的補救。　　　　◆

Townsend 169 = Perry 476

11. The Ass and the Old Shepherd

　　A Shepherd, watching his Ass feeding in a meadow, was alarmed all of a sudden by the cries of the enemy. He appealed to the Ass to fly with him, lest they should both be captured, but the animal lazily replied, "Why should I, pray? Do you think it likely the conqueror will place on me two sets of panniers?"
　　"No," rejoined the Shepherd. "Then," said the Ass, "as long as I carry the panniers, what matters it to me whom I serve?"

◆　　In a change of government the poor change
nothing beyond the name of their master.　　◆

11. 驢和老牧羊人

　　有個牧人正看著他的驢在草地上吃草,突然傳來敵人的廝殺聲,牧人大驚失色,趕緊讓驢跟他一起逃跑,以免他們都被捉住。但是驢不急不徐地回答說:「為什麼我要逃?難道你覺得我被他們捉住之後,他們還會在我背上擱上兩副馱籃?」牧人說道:「不會。」驢說:「既然這樣,反正我是得背馱籃的,為誰背又有什麼關係呢?」

♦　　朝代更替之時，窮人改變的只是主人的姓名。　　♦

Townsend 255 = Perry 237

12. The Ass and His Purchaser

A man wished to purchase an Ass, and agreed with its owner that he should try out the animal before he bought him. He took the Ass home and put him in the straw-yard with his other Asses, upon which the new animal left all the others and at once joined the one that was most idle and the greatest eater of them all.

Seeing this, the man put a halter on him and led him back to his owner. On being asked how, in so short a time, he could have made a trial of him, he answered, "I do not need a trial; I know that he will be just the same as the one he chose for his companion."

♦　　A man is known by the company he keeps.　　♦

12. 驢和買主

有人想買頭驢，跟驢的主人商量好，在買之前得把牲口拉出去試一試。他把驢帶到了家裡，把他和自家的驢一塊關在圍欄裡。這驢不和其他的驢在一塊，卻馬上走過去和一頭最好吃懶做的驢站到了一塊。

發現是如此情形，買驢人給驢戴上轡頭，領回去交還給了他的主人。驢主人問道:「怎麼能在如此短的時間內試出驢的性情呢?」買驢人答覆道:「沒有必要試了,看他選擇了怎樣的朋友,就清楚他是什麼樣的了。」

♦　透過一個人所結交的朋友,就能知道此人的品行。　♦

Townsend 125 = Perry 460

13. The Ass and His Shadow

A traveler hired an Ass to convey him to a distant place. The day being intensely hot, and the sun shining in its strength, the Traveler stopped to rest, and sought shelter from the heat under the Shadow of the Ass. As this afforded only protection for one, and as the Traveler and the owner of the Ass both claimed it, a violent dispute arose between them as to which of them had the right to the Shadow. The owner maintained that he had let the Ass only, and not his Shadow. The Traveler asserted that he had, with the hire of the Ass, hired his Shadow also. The quarrel proceeded from words to blows, and while the men fought, the Ass galloped off.

♦　In quarreling about the shadow we often lose the substance.　♦

13. 驢和他的影子

有個人要去遠方旅行,租了一頭驢子當坐騎。天氣異常炎熱,熾熱的陽光曝曬著大地。旅行者停了下來,在驢的影子底下找陰涼處稍作休息。但是影子遮住的地方僅能容下一個人,旅行者跟驢的主人都聲稱這片陰涼是自己的，他倆就誰有權利享受這陰涼的問題，激烈地爭論起來。驢的主人說，他租出去的僅僅是驢，而不是驢的影子。旅行者堅持說，自己既然租了驢，也就自然把驢的影子一併租下了。兩人很快就由爭吵變成了廝打。正在他們打得不可開交的時候，驢一陣風似地溜掉了。

♦　　　　為影子而爭吵常常會連同實物一起失去。　　　　♦

Townsend 206 = Perry 187

14. The Ass and the Wolf

An Ass feeding in a meadow saw a Wolf approaching to seize him, and immediately pretended to be lame. The Wolf, coming up, inquired the cause of his lameness. The Ass replied that passing through a hedge he had trod with his foot upon a sharp thorn. He requested that The Wolf pull it out, lest when he ate him it should injure his throat. The Wolf consented and lifted up the foot, and was giving his whole mind to the discovery of the thorn, when the Ass, with his heels, kicked his teeth into his mouth and galloped away. The Wolf, being thus fearfully mauled, said, "I am rightly served, for why did I attempt the art of healing, when my father only taught me the trade of a butcher?"

♦　　　　　　　　Keep to your trade.　　　　　　　　♦

14. 驢與狼

一頭驢在草地上吃草時，看到狼走過來想抓住他，就立即裝成瘸腿的樣子。狼走到驢跟前，問他是怎樣變瘸的，驢回答說是過樹籬的時候，一根尖刺紮進腳裡了。驢勸說狼，讓狼幫他把刺挑出來，以免吃他時把刺卡在喉嚨裡。狼同意了驢的請求，抓住他的腿，認認真真地找那根刺。驢見勢用腳對準狼的嘴，使勁一踢，把狼的牙齒踢掉了，之後飛速地逃跑了。狼飽嘗其苦，於是說道：「這叫自討苦吃。父親只教我當屠夫，我為什麼偏偏改行做醫生呢？」

♦ 　　　　　要記得自己的身份。　　　　　♦

Jacobs 74 = Peny 336

15. The Ass's Brains

The Lion and the Fox went hunting together. The Lion, on the advice of the Fox, sent a message to the Ass, proposing to make an alliance between their two families. The Ass came to the place of meeting, overjoyed at the prospect of a royal alliance. But when he came there the Lion simply pounced on the Ass, and said to the Fox, "Here is our dinner for to-day. Watch you here while I go and have a nap. Woe betide you if you touch my prey." The Lion went away and the Fox waited; but finding that his master did not return, ventured to take out the brains of the Ass and ate them up. When the Lion came back he soon noticed the absence of the brains, and asked the Fox in a terrible voice, "What have you done with the brains?"

"Brains, your Majesty! it had none, or it would never have fallen into your trap."

♦ 　　　Wit has always an answer ready.　　　♦

15. 驢的腦子

　　獅子跟狐狸一起出去打獵。獅子聽從了狐狸的建議，去給驢送信，表示願意兩家結成同盟。驢高高興興地來到約定的地點，想像著獅子和自己結成神聖同盟之後的美好未來，樂昏了頭。但是驢剛到，獅子就撲上來把他抓住，接著對狐狸說：「這就是咱們今天的晚餐了。你在這裡守著他，我去小睡一會兒。假如你敢動一下我的獵物，你就會吃不了兜著走！」獅子走後，留下狐狸單獨看守著驢。狐狸趁著獅子不在，悄悄地取出了驢腦並吃光了他。獅子一回來就發覺驢的腦子沒有了，於是兇狠地問狐狸：「你對驢的腦子做了什麼手腳？」「驢的腦子？大王，驢本來就沒腦子，否則，他怎麼能落入您的陷阱呢？」

◆　　　　聰明人總是能找到現成的答案。　　　　◆

Townsend 117 = Perry 182

16. The Ass Carrying the Image

　　An Ass once carried through the streets of a city a famous wooden Image, to be placed in one of its Temples. As he passed along, the crowd made lowly prostration before the Image. The Ass, thinking that they bowed their heads in token of respect for himself, bristled up with pride, gave himself airs, and refused to move another step.

　　The driver, seeing him thus stop, laid his whip lustily about his shoulders and said, "O you perverse dull-head! it is not yet come to this, that men pay worship to an Ass."

◆　　　They are not wise who give to themselves the
credit due to others.　　　◆

16. 馱著神像的驢

有一次,一頭驢馱著一尊著名的木神像,被人趕著穿過城裡的大街小巷,去往安置祂的神廟。在街上,神像受到路人的頂禮膜拜,驢認為那是人們在對他表示景仰,就神色傲慢地端起了架子,再也不願往前邁一步。車夫見驢停留在原地不走,就拿鞭子狠狠地抽了驢一頓,罵道:「蠢貨,還沒到人向驢致敬的時候呢!」

♦　　借助他人的榮耀往自己臉上貼金是不明智的。　　♦

Townsend 244 = Perry 188

17. The Ass in the Lion's Skin

An Ass, having put on the Lion's skin, roamed about in the forest and amused himself by frightening all the foolish animals he met in his wanderings. At last coming upon a Fox, he tried to frighten him also, but the Fox no sooner heard the sound of his voice than he exclaimed,"I might possibly have been frightened myself, if I had not heard your bray."

♦　　Fine clothes may disguise, but silly words will disclose a fool.　　♦

17. 披著獅子皮的驢

一頭驢披上了獅子皮,在森林裡四處閒晃,碰見那些愚蠢的野獸就嚇嚇他們,拿他們尋開心。最後他遇見一隻狐狸,也想嚇唬嚇唬他。但是狐狸一聽見驢的聲音,就說道:「要是我沒聽見過你的叫聲,有可能也會害怕你的。」

♦　　**衣服也許能掩蓋傻瓜,但言語卻能使他原形畢露。**　　♦

Townsend 215 = Perry 279

18. The Goat and the Ass

A man once kept a Goat and an Ass. The Goat, envying the Ass on account of his greater abundance of food, said, "How shamefully you are treated: at one time grinding in the mill, and at another carrying heavy burdens"; and he further advised him to pretend to be epileptic and fall into a ditch and so obtain rest. The Ass listened to his words, and falling into a ditch, was very much bruised. His master, sending for a leech, asked his advice. He bade him pour upon the wounds the lungs of a Goat. They at once killed the Goat, and so healed the Ass.

♦　　Beware of envy.　　♦

18. 山羊和驢

有人養了一隻山羊跟一頭驢。山羊看到驢的食物比自己的豐富,很嫉妒,就對驢說:「主人對你真苛刻,一會兒讓你推磨,一會兒又讓你馱重擔。」他建議驢假裝患上癲癇病,不小心摔到水溝裡,這樣就能休息一下。驢聽從了山羊的建議,掉到了水溝裡,傷得很重。主人請醫生來為驢醫治,醫生建議他在驢的傷口處敷上山羊的肺。主人立即把山羊殺了,驢因此獲救。

♦　　**不要有嫉妒之心。**　　♦

ASS 驢

Townsend 222 = Perry 565

19. The Horse and the Ass

A Horse, proud of his fine trappings, met an Ass on the highway. The Ass, being heavily laden, moved slowly out of the way. "Hardly," said the Horse, "can I resist kicking you with my heels." The Ass held his peace, and made only a silent appeal to the justice of the gods. Not long afterwards the Horse, having become broken-winded, was sent by his owner to the farm. The Ass, seeing him drawing a dung cart, thus derided him, "Where, O boaster, are now all thy gay trappings, thou who are thyself reduced to the condition you so lately treated with contempt?"

♦ Better humble security than gilded danger. ♦

19. 馬和驢

馬配著體面的馬鞍，傲氣十足地在大路上走著，迎面碰見了一頭背上載滿了貨物的驢，驢走得很慢。馬對驢說：「我真想踢你一腳。」驢默不做聲，暗暗地祈求諸神維護公正。過了不久，馬得了氣喘病，主人把他賣到了一個牧場。驢看見拉著糞車的馬，就諷刺他說：「喂，愛吹噓的老兄，你那體面的馬鞍子在哪兒呢？先前你還看不起我，可是如今你不是也淪落至此嗎？」

♦ 謙卑的平安，好過趾高氣揚的危險。 ♦

Townsend 183 = Perry 315

20. The Mule

A Mule, frolicsome from lack of work and from too much

corn, galloped about in a very extravagant manner, and said to himself, "My father surely was a high-mettled racer, and I am his own child in speed and spirit." On the next day, being driven a long journey, and feeling very wearied, he exclaimed in a disconsolate tone, "I must have made a mistake; my father, after all, could have been only an ass."

◆　　　Be sure of your pedigree before you boast of it.　　　◆

20. 騾子

　　一隻騾子，因為沒有工作又吃了太多的玉米，所以就歡鬧嬉戲，放肆地亂跑，還自言自語地說：「我父親肯定是頭勇敢的賽馬，從速度和精神上來看，我都是他親生的。」第二天，騾子被趕著走了很長的路，感覺非常累，他鬱悶地叫道：「我一定是弄錯了，我的父親只能是頭驢。」

◆　　　　　自吹自擂之前，先要弄清自己的身世。　　　　　◆

Townsend 299 = Perry 491

21. The Mules and the Robbers

　　Two Mules well-laden with packs were trudging along. One carried panniers filled with money, the other sacks weighted with grain. The Mule carrying the treasure walked with head erect, as if conscious of the value of his burden, and tossed up and down the clear-toned bells fastened to his neck. His companion followed with quiet and easy step. All of a sudden Robbers rushed upon them from their hiding-places, and in the scuffle with their owners, wounded with a sword the Mule carrying the treasure, which they greedily seized while taking no notice of the grain. The Mule which had been robbed and wounded bewailed his misfortunes. The other replied, "I am indeed glad that I was thought so little of, for I have lost nothing, nor am I hurt with any wound."

♦ Flaunt wealth and thieves will know you have wealth. ♦

21. 騾子和強盜

兩頭騾子馱著袋子艱難地跋涉著。一頭馱著裝滿了錢的籃子，另一頭馱著沉甸甸的糧袋。馱著財寶的騾子昂著頭，好像知道他馱的東西的價值，上下甩著繫在脖子上的鈴鐺，發出清脆的聲音。他的同伴踏著安靜而輕鬆的步伐跟在後面。突然，強盜從藏身的地方衝了出來，與騾子的主人打成一團，他們用劍刺傷了馱著財寶的騾子，貪婪地抓起財寶，而對糧食毫不在意。剛剛被搶並受傷的騾子哀歎著他的不幸。另一頭騾子應道：「我雖然被忽視，卻為此感到很慶倖，因為我沒有失去什麼，也沒有受什麼傷。」

♦ 炫耀財富，強盜會很快上門。 ♦

Townsend 112 = Perry 359

22. The Playful Ass

An Ass climbed up to the roof of a building, and frisking about there, broke in the tiling. The owner went up after him and quickly drove him down, beating him severely with a thick wooden cudgel. The Ass said,"Why, I saw the Monkey do this very thing yesterday, and you all laughed heartily, as if it afforded you very great amusement."

♦ People that live by example need to look closely at the example they are following. ♦

22. 頑皮的驢

一隻驢爬上一間房子的屋頂，在上面蹦蹦跳跳，把瓦都踢壞了。主人追上來，很快把驢轟下來，並用一根粗木棒狠狠打了他。驢說：「哎呀！我昨天看見猴子做同樣的事，你們都哈哈大笑，好像這讓你們很開心。」

♦ 模仿前，要先搞清楚模仿的對象。 ♦

Townsend 54 = Perry 180

23. The Salt Merchant and His Ass

A Peddler drove his Ass to the seashore to buy salt. His road home lay across a stream into which his Ass, making a false step, fell by accident and rose up again with his load considerably lighter, as the water melted the sack. The Peddler retraced his steps and refilled his panniers with a larger quantity of salt than before.

When he came again to the stream, the Ass fell down on purpose in the same spot, and, regaining his feet with the weight of his load much diminished, brayed triumphantly as if he had obtained what he desired.

ASS 驢

The Peddler saw through his trick and drove him for the third time to the coast, where he bought a cargo of sponges instead of salt. The Ass, again playing the fool, fell down on purpose when he reached the stream, but the sponges became swollen with water, greatly increasing his load. and thus his trick recoiled on him, for he now carried on his back a double burden.

◆　　　You can fool someone only so many times.　　　◆

23. 鹽商和他的驢

一個小販趕著他的驢到海邊買鹽。在回家的路上有一條小河。驢馱著鹽過河，不小心腳下一滑，跌倒在河中。等他站起來時，頓時感到身上輕鬆了許多，因為袋子裡的鹽被河水給溶化了。小販只好原路折回，把馱籃重新裝滿，這可比先前裝的鹽要多很多。

小販再次來到了小河邊，驢有了上次的經驗，又故意在同一個地方跌倒，摔進河裡。等再站起來時，身上的負擔又減輕了，於是他得意地叫起來，好像他如願以償了一樣。

這一次小販看穿了驢的花招，再一次把他趕到海邊，但是這次卻沒有買鹽，而是買了許多海綿。驢依然裝傻，當他到河邊時又故意跌倒，但是他不知道海綿會因吸水而膨脹，這就大大增加了他的負擔。現在驢馱著比以前重兩倍的擔子。這就是聰明反被聰明誤，驢耍花招害的是他自己。

◆　　　　　騙人無法每次都得逞。　　　　　◆

L'Estrange 189 = Perry 183

24. A Wild Ass and a Tame

As a tame ass was airing himself in a pleasant meadow, with a coat and carcass in very good plight, up comes a wild one to him from the next wood, with this short greeting. Brother (says he) I envy your happiness; and so he left him. It was his hap some short time after this encounter, to see his tame brother groaning under a unmerciful pack, and a fellow at his heels goading him forward. He rounds him in the ear upon't, and whispers him, My friend (says he) your condition is not, I perceive, what I took it to be, for a body may buy gold too dear: and I am not for purchasing good looks and provender at this rate.

◆ The grass is always greener on the other side of the fence. ◆

24. 野驢和家驢

一頭體型健碩的家驢，在綠油油的草地上休憩，野驢看見了，就從旁邊的小樹林裡跑上前來，簡短地打了個招呼，說道：「兄弟，你過得這麼愜意，可真是讓我羨慕啊！」。野驢說完就走開了。這次見面後不久，野驢就看見家驢馱著沉重的貨物呻吟，後面還有個人在驅趕他。野驢就在家驢的耳邊對他說：「朋友，我覺得你的情況，並不是我之前想的那樣，你付出的代價太大了，我可不會為了追求那點享受，就付出這麼沉重的代價。」

◆ 籬笆另一面的草總是更綠，得不到的總是看起來更誘人些。 ◆

ASS 驢

2.
BATS
蝙蝠

L'Estrange 146 = Perry 171

25. A Bat, Bramble, and Cormorant

A bat, a bramble, and a cormorant entered into covenants with articles, to joyn stocks, and trade in partnership together. The bat's adventure was ready mony that he took up at interest; the bramble's was in cloaths; and the cormorant's in brass. They put to sea, and it so fell out, that ship and goods were both lost by stress of weather: but the three merchants by providence got safe to land. Since the time of this miscarriage, the bat never stirs abroad till night, for fear of his creditors. The bramble lays hold of all the deaths he can come at in hope to light upon his own again: and the cormorant is still sauntering by the sea-side, to see if he can find any of his brass cast up.

◆ Any notable misfortune will stick by a man as long as he lives. ◆

25. 蝙蝠、荊棘與鸕鷀

蝙蝠、荊棘和鸕鷀訂立了契約，決定合夥做生意。蝙蝠借了高利貸，荊棘購買了衣服，而鸕鷀則購買了銅。於是三人乘船出海，不幸的是，天公不作美，船和貨物都沉沒了；所幸三個商人還都安全地到了岸邊。從此以後，蝙蝠怕見到他的債主，只有在晚上才敢出來活動；荊棘纏住在他旁邊的每一具屍首，希望能從中發現他自己的衣服；而鸕鷀還在海邊徘徊，想看看他的銅能不能失而復得。

◆ 任何重大的不幸，都會跟隨人一輩子。 ◆

Townsend 2 = Perry 172

26. The Bat and the Weasels

A Bat who fell upon the ground and was caught by a Weasel pleaded to be spared his life. The Weasel refused, saying that he was by nature the enemy of all birds. The Bat assured him that he was not a bird, but a mouse, and thus was set free. Shortly afterwards the Bat again fell to the ground and was caught by another Weasel, whom he likewise entreated not to eat him. The Weasel said that he had a special hostility to mice. The Bat assured him that he was not a mouse, but a bat, and thus a second time escaped.

♦   It is wise to turn circumstances to good account.   ♦

26. 蝙蝠和黃鼠狼

一隻蝙蝠摔到地上，被黃鼠狼捉住了，蝙蝠苦苦哀求黃鼠狼放他一馬，但是黃鼠狼說自己跟鳥類是天生的仇敵，堅決不能放了蝙蝠。蝙蝠向黃鼠狼承諾，自己不是鳥類，而是一隻老鼠，於是黃鼠狼就把他放走了。不久以後，這隻蝙蝠再次摔到了地上，落到另一隻黃鼠狼手裡。蝙蝠求黃鼠狼別吃他，黃鼠狼說自己對老鼠特別仇恨。蝙蝠就對黃鼠狼發誓說，自己是一隻蝙蝠，絕對不是老鼠，因此再一次死裡逃生。

♦   化不利為有利，靈活應對，才算得上明智。   ♦

Townsend 239 = Perry 566

27. The Birds, the Beasts, and the Bat

The Birds waged war with the Beasts, and each were by turns the conquerors. A Bat, fearing the uncertain issues of the fight, always fought on the side which he felt was the strongest. When peace was proclaimed, his deceitful conduct was apparent to both combatants. Therefore being condemned by each for his treachery, he was driven forth from the light of day, and henceforth concealed himself in dark hiding-places, flying always alone and at night.

◆ He that is neither one thing nor the other has no friends. ◆

27. 鳥、野獸和蝙蝠

鳥類和野獸之間發生了一場戰爭,雙方各有輸贏。蝙蝠不確定戰爭的結果,就總是與他認為相對強大的一方為伍,不斷變換立場。當和平到來的時候,鳥獸雙方都發現自己受了蝙蝠的騙,共同聲討他的背叛行徑,不允許蝙蝠在大白天出門。自那之後,蝙蝠只好隱藏在黑暗的角落裡,孤獨地在夜裡飛來飛去。

◆ 立場不堅定的人,到最後連一個朋友也找不著。 ◆

3. BIRDS
鳥

BIRDS 鳥

BIRDS OF VARIOUS KINDS 各種鳥

Townsend 136 = Perry 361

28. The Birdcatcher, the Partridge, and the Cock

A Birdcatcher was about to sit down to a dinner of herbs when a friend unexpectedly came in. The bird-trap was quite empty, as he had caught nothing, and he had to kill a pied Partridge, which he had tamed for a decoy. The bird entreated earnestly for his life, "What would you do without me when next you spread your nets? Who would chirp you to sleep, or call for you the covey of answering birds?" The Birdcatcher spared his life, and determined to pick out a fine young Cock just attaining to his comb. But the Cock expostulated in piteous tones from his perch, "If you kill me, who will announce to you the appearance of the dawn? Who will wake you to your daily tasks or tell you when it is time to visit the bird-trap in the morning?" He replied, "What you say is true. You are a capital bird at telling the time of day. But my friend and I must have our dinners."

◆　　　　　Necessity knows no law.　　　　　◆

28. 捕鳥人、山鶉和公雞

捕鳥人正要坐定吃晚飯，突然一個朋友不請自來。捕鳥人因為當天沒有任何收穫，捕網空空如也，就打算殺一隻花斑山鶉，用來招待客人。這山鶉本來是他已經養大了，拿來誘捕獵物的。山鶉苦苦地哀求，希望捕鳥人放自己一條生路：「沒有了我，你下次再撒網捕鳥時，靠什麼呢？誰來唱著歌伴你入睡？誰來替你引出鳥兒呢？」捕鳥人聽完，就決定不殺山鶉，去捉那隻年輕漂亮的剛剛長出冠子的公雞。不料那公雞用可憐巴巴的語氣說道：「假如你殺了我，誰來為你通報黎明的到來呢？誰叫醒你開始一天的工作？誰在早晨告訴你是時候應該去看看捕鳥網了？」捕鳥人回答說：「你說得沒錯，你是一隻報時的鳥。但我跟我的朋友也總得吃晚餐啊！」

♦　　　　**迫不得已時，就沒有道理可言。**　　　　♦

L'Estrange 162 = Perry 48

29. The Cage Bird and the Bat

A singing bird was confined in a cage which hung outside a window, and had a way of singing at night when all other birds were asleep. One night a Bat came and clung to the bars of the cage, and asked the Bird why she was silent by day and sang only at night. "I have a very good reason for doing so," said the Bird. "It was once when I was singing in the daytime that a fowler was attracted by my voice, and set his nets for me and caught me. Since then I have never sung except by night." But the Bat replied, "It is no use your doing that now when you are a prisoner: if only you had done so before you were caught, you might still have been free."

♦　　　　Precautions are useless after the crisis.　　　　♦

29. 籠中鳥和蝙蝠

掛在窗外的一個鳥籠裡關著一隻會唱歌的鳥，但這隻鳥只在晚上其他鳥兒都睡著的時候才開口唱歌。有天晚上一隻蝙蝠飛來了，靠在鳥籠的柵欄上，問那隻鳥為什麼白天保持沉默，而晚上歌唱。「我這樣做有一個很好的理由。」鳥兒說道，「我曾經是在白天唱歌的，有一個捕鳥的人被我的歌聲所吸引，用他的網捉住了我。從那之後，我除了晚上其他時間就再也不唱歌了。」蝙蝠說：「你現在這樣做是沒用的，因為你已經成了囚徒了。在你被人捉住之前就這樣做的話，你現在可能仍然是自由的呢。」

◆　　　　危機發生以後再戒備是沒有用的。　　　　◆

Townsend 8 = Perry 503

30. The Cock and the Jewel

A Cock, scratching for food for himself and his hens, found a precious stone and exclaimed, "If your owner had found thee, and not I, he would have taken thee up, and have set thee in thy first estate; but I have found thee for no purpose. I would rather have one barleycorn than all the jewels in the world."

◆　　Precious things are for those who prize them.　　◆

30. 公雞和寶石

有一隻公雞，在為自己和妻子刨東西吃的時候，發現了一枚貴重的寶石，公雞大聲叫道：「如果是你的主人而不是我找到你的話，他一定會把你從地上撿起來的，放在一個最合適的地方。可是我找到你也沒用；比起世界上所有的寶石，我寧願要一粒大麥。」

◆　　　珍貴的東西在，重視它們的人眼中才有價值。　　　◆

Townsend 30 = Perry 297

31. The Farmer and the Cranes

Some Cranes made their feeding grounds on some plowlands newly sown with wheat. For a long time the Farmer, brandishing an empty sling, chased them away by the terror he inspired; but when the birds found that the sling was only swung in the air, they ceased to take any notice of it and would not move. The Farmer, on seeing this, charged his sling with stones, and killed a great number. The remaining birds at once forsook his fields, crying to each other, "It is time for us to be off to Lilliput: for this man is no longer content to scare us, but begins to show us in earnest what he can do".

♦   If words suffice not, blows must follow.   ♦

31. 農夫和鶴

一群鶴在剛剛播下小麥種子的農田裡覓食。很長一段時間以來，農夫揮舞著空彈弓想把他們嚇走，但是當鶴群發現農夫的彈弓只是在空中揮來揮去後，他們就不再理會農夫的恐嚇，不管農夫怎麼嚇唬都原地不動。農夫看到這個情況，就在彈弓裡裝上了石頭，打死了很多隻鶴。剩下的幾隻鶴立刻飛離他的農田，大聲地叫喊著：「我們該離開這裡去小人國了！這人已經不再滿足於嚇唬嚇唬我們，他開始來真的了！」

♦   如果語言發揮不了作用，那就用拳頭說話。   ♦

BIRDS 鳥

L'Estrange 97 = Perry 193

32. A Fowler and a Blackbird

As a fowler was bending his net, a black-bird called to him at a distance, and asked him what he was a doing. Why says he, I am laying the foundations of a city; and so the birdman drew out of sight. The black-bird mistrusting nothing, flew presently to the bait in the net, and was taken; and as the man came running to lay hold of her; Friend, says the poor black-bird, if this be your way of building, you'll have but few inhabitants.

♦ There is no glory in tricking those easy to trick. ♦

32. 捕鳥人與烏鶇

捕鳥人正在張網，烏鶇遠遠地看見了，便問他在幹什麼。「哦，沒什麼！」他說，「我正在建城市。」說完捕鳥人就走開了。烏鶇對此信以為真，很快飛進網裡吃捕鳥人留下的誘餌，於是被逮住了。捕鳥人跑過來抓住她的時候，這隻可憐的烏鶇對他說：「朋友，要照你這麼個建法，這個城市是不會有什麼人住的。」

♦ 欺騙那些容易上當的人並不是什麼光榮的事。 ♦

Townsend 251 = Perry 426

33. The Fox and the Crane

A Fox invited a Crane to supper and provided nothing for his entertainment but some soup made of pulse, which was poured out into a broad flat stone dish. The soup fell out of the long bill of the Crane at every mouthful, and his vexation at not being able to eat afforded the Fox much amusement. The Crane, in his turn, asked the Fox to sup with him, and set before his a flagon with a long narrow mouth, so that he could easily insert his neck and enjoy its contents at his leisure. The Fox, unable even to taste it, met with a fitting requital, after the fashion of her own hospitality.

◆　　　　One bad turn deserves another.　　　　◆

33. 狐狸和鶴

一隻狐狸邀請一隻鶴吃晚飯，結果卻只給他一些盛在平底大石盤裡的豌豆湯。鶴每次用他長長的喙喝湯時，湯就會從她的嘴裡流出來，結果什麼都吃不到，害得他很著急，而狐狸卻在一旁看得非常開心。輪到鶴請狐狸吃飯時，他把食物放在一個又細又長的瓶子裡，這樣鶴就可以輕而易舉地把自己的長脖子伸進瓶子裡，享受裡面的美味，而狐狸卻因為自己對鶴的「好客」，沒有嚐到任何東西，得到了應有的回報。

◆　　　　　　　　惡有惡報。　　　　　　　　◆

L'Estrange 194 = Perry 190

34. A Galled Ass and a Raven

As an ass with a galled back was feeding in a meadow, a raven pitched upon him, and there sate, jobbing of the sore. The ass fell a frisking and braying upon it, which set a groom that saw it at a distance, a laughing at it. Well! (says a wolf that was passing by) to see the injustice of the world now! A poor wolf in that ravens place, would have been persecuted, and hunted to death presently; and 'tis made only a laughing-matter, for a raven to do the same thing would have cost a wolf his life.

♦　　　　　Not everyone is treated alike.　　　　　♦

34. 背受傷的驢和烏鴉

驢在草地上吃草,他的背已經磨傷了。烏鴉看見了,就落在他身上,戳他背上的傷口。驢痛得又跳又叫。馬夫遠遠地看見了,大笑起來。經過的狼歎氣道:「唉!看看這都什麼世道!要是有哪頭狼敢像那隻烏鴉那樣,肯定很快就會受到圍攻,立即被處死。雖然是做同樣的事,但狼會因此喪命,而烏鴉只是成為了笑談。」

♦　　　　　每個人的待遇是不同的。　　　　　♦

Townsend 234 = Perry 23

35. The Gamecocks and the Partridge

A man had two Gamecocks in his poultry-yard. One day by chance he found a tame Partridge for sale. He purchased it and brought it home to be reared with his Gamecocks. When the Partridge was put into the poultry-yard, they struck at it and followed it about, so that the Partridge became grievously troubled and supposed that he was thus evilly treated because he was a stranger. Not long afterwards he saw the Cocks fighting together and not separating before one had well beaten the other.

He then said to himself "I shall no longer distress myself at being struck at by these Gamecocks, when I see that they cannot even refrain from quarreling with each other."

♦ Some people quarrel just for the sake of quarrelling. ♦

35. 鬥雞和山鶉

有個人在他的養雞場裡養了兩隻鬥雞。有一天，他偶然看到一隻家養的山鶉要賣，就把他買下來了，帶回家跟他的鬥雞一起飼養。山鶉剛一出現在養雞場，兩隻鬥雞就衝過來，四處追趕著他又啄又咬。山鶉為此痛苦不堪，心想被公雞這樣虐待，肯定是因為自己是個新來的。然而沒過多久時間，他時常看見那兩隻鬥雞鬥成一團，不打個你死我活決不罷休。於是山鶉對自己說：「看來這兩隻鬥雞，也經常互相鬥個不停，我只是被他們咬幾下，大可不必為此傷心了。」

♦ 有些人總是莫名其妙地爭吵。 ♦

Townsend 224 = Perry 228

36. The Geese and the Cranes

The Geese and the Cranes were feeding in the same meadow, when a birdcatcher came to ensnare them in his nets. The Cranes, being light of wing, fled away at his approach; while the Geese, being slower of flight and heavier in their bodies, were captured.

♦ The more vulnerable need to watch more closely. ♦

BIRDS 鳥

36. 鵝和鶴

　　一群鵝和一群鶴在同一塊草地上進食，這時走過來一個捕鳥人，張開網想捕住他們。鶴見捕鳥人走近，張開輕盈的雙翅飛走了；然而鵝本來飛得就慢，加上身體又重，結果被捉住了。

◆　　　　　　越弱小的，越需要謹慎從事。　　　　　　◆

Townsend 264 = Perry 507

37. The Grasshopper and the Owl

　　An Owl, accustomed to feed at night and to sleep during the day, was greatly disturbed by the noise of a Grasshopper and earnestly besought her to stop chirping. The Grasshopper refused to desist, and chirped louder and louder the more the Owl entreated. When she saw that she could get no redress and that her words were despised, the Owl attacked the chatterer by a stratagem. "Since I cannot sleep," she said, "on account of your song which, believe me, is sweet as the lyre of Apollo, I shall indulge myself in drinking some nectar which Pallas lately gave me. If you do not dislike it, come to me and we will drink it together." The Grasshopper, who was thirsty, and pleased with the praise of her voice, eagerly flew up. The Owl came forth from her hollow, seized her, and put her to death.

◆　　　Don't be unreasonable against greater force.　　　◆

37. 蚱蜢和貓頭鷹

　　貓頭鷹習慣於晚上出去捕食，白天睡大覺。白天被蚱蜢的叫聲搞得心煩意亂，懇請蚱蜢別再叫個不停。但蚱蜢拒絕了貓頭鷹，貓頭鷹越懇求，蚱蜢叫的聲音就越大。貓頭鷹見蚱蜢不理會，就決定想辦法來制止這個傢伙。貓頭鷹說：「既然我也睡不著，你的聲音又像阿波羅神彈奏的琴聲那般悅耳，不如我去飲一口智神帕拉斯最近送給我的花蜜。如果你不反對，那就跟我一同去喝吧！」蚱蜢正好唱得很口渴，又聽見貓頭鷹讚美自己的聲音，滿心歡喜，就迫不及待地飛了出來。蚱蜢剛伸出頭，貓頭鷹就一下子從她的洞裡衝出來，抓住蚱蜢，吞到了肚子裡。

◆　　　　面對強大的對手，不要蠻不講理。　　　　◆

Townsend 98 = Perry 486

38. The Hawk, the Kite, and the Pigeons

　　The Pigeons, terrified by the appearance of a Kite, called upon the Hawk to defend them. He at once consented. When they had admitted him into the cote, they found that he made more havoc and slew a larger number of them in one day than the Kite could pounce upon in a whole year.

◆　　　Avoid a remedy that is worse than the disease.　　　◆

38. 鷹、鳶和鴿子

　　鴿子因為鳶的出現十分恐懼，到鷹那裡去尋求保護。鷹一口就同意了。鴿子讓鷹進入鴿棚之後才發現，老鷹比鳶更兇殘，他在一天之中吃的鴿子，比被鳶一年抓去的還要多。

◆ 切忌飲鴆止渴 ◆

Townsend 211 = Perry 4

39. The Hawk and the Nightingale

A Nightingale, sitting aloft upon an oak and singing according to his wont, was seen by a Hawk who, being in need of food, swooped down and seized him. The Nightingale, about to lose his life, earnestly begged the Hawk to let him go, saying that he was not big enough to satisfy the hunger of a Hawk who, if he wanted food, ought to pursue the larger birds. The Hawk, interrupting him, said, "I should indeed have lost my senses if I should let go food ready in my hand, for the sake of pursuing birds which are not yet even within sight."

◆ A bird caught is better than more uncaught. ◆

39. 老鷹和夜鶯

一隻夜鶯在高高的橡樹枝頭唱歌，被饑腸轆轆的老鷹發現了。老鷹衝下來一下子捉住了他。夜鶯眼看就要命喪黃泉，懇求老鷹放他一馬，說自己的身體太小了，不足以讓老鷹填飽肚子。如果老鷹想找食物，應該去捉大隻點的鳥才對。老鷹插話道：「如果我為了去抓幾隻到如今還不見蹤影的鳥，就放棄早已到手的肥肉，那樣才是傻子呢！」

◆ 一隻到手的鳥兒，好過很多隻未到手的。 ◆

Townsend 163 = Perry 87

40. The Hen and the Golden Eggs

A cottager and his wife had a Hen that laid a golden egg every day. They supposed that the Hen must contain a great lump of gold in its inside, and in order to get the gold they killed it. Having done so, they found to their surprise that the Hen differed in no respect from their other hens. The foolish pair, thus hoping to become rich all at once, deprived themselves of the gain of which they were assured day by day.

♦　　　　　Greed often overreaches itself.　　　　　♦

40. 母雞和金蛋

農夫和他的妻子有一隻每天下一枚金蛋的母雞。他們認為母雞的肚子裡面必然藏有許許多多的金蛋，為了得到金子，他們把母雞宰了，但是驚訝地發現，這隻雞跟其他的母雞並無不同。這對愚蠢的夫妻希望馬上富裕起來，最終卻失去了本來每天都能夠獲得的錢財。

♦　　　　　貪婪的人將會自食其果。　　　　　♦

Townsend 275 = Perry 192

41. The Hen and the Swallow

A Hen finding the eggs of a viper and carefully keeping them warm, nourished them into life. A Swallow, observing what she had done, said, "You silly creature! why have you hatched these vipers which, when they shall have grown, will inflict injury on all, beginning with yourself?"

◆ A good natured man will often assist his own destruction. ◆

41. 母雞和燕子

一隻母雞發現了毒蛇下的蛋,就小心翼翼地暖著它們,並期待著新生命的降臨。燕子看見母雞的所作所為,對她說:「你真是傻瓜!為什麼要暖這些毒蛇蛋呢?一旦這些小蛇破殼而生,它們會對所有的人造成傷害,肯定從你開始下手!」

◆ 善良的人總會害了自己。 ◆

Townsend 251 = Perry 472

42. The Jay and the Peacock

A Jay venturing into a yard where Peacocks used to walk, found there a number of feathers which had fallen from the Peacocks when they were moulting. He tied them all to his tail and strutted down towards the Peacocks. When he came near them they soon discovered the cheat, and striding up to him pecked at him and plucked away his borrowed plumes. So the Jay could do no better than go back to the other Jays, who had watched his behaviour from a distance; but they were equally annoyed with him, and told him: "It is not only fine feathers that make fine birds."

◆ Pretending to be some else with a false appearance will not gain recognition. ◆

42. 松鴉和孔雀

有隻松鴉冒失地闖進孔雀常散步的院子裡，看見了很多孔雀換毛時掉下的羽毛。松鴉把所有的羽毛捆在自己的尾巴上，昂首闊步地朝孔雀走過去。他剛剛走近孔雀，孔雀就發現了這個騙局，大步走過去啄他，把他的假羽毛都啄掉了。松鴉無奈之下，只能回到松鴉群去。其他的松鴉遠遠地觀望之後，也對他的行為感到惱怒，告訴他：「高貴的鳥兒憑藉的不單單是漂亮的羽毛。」

◆　　用虛偽的外表冒充別人，是無法得到認同的。　　◆

L'Estrange 168 = Perry 25

43. A Kingfisher

The kingfisher is a solitary bird that wonts commonly by the water-side, and nestles in hollow banks to be out of reach of the fowlers. One of these birds happened to be foraging abroad for her young ones, and in the interim, comes a raging torrent, that washes away nest, birds and all. Upon her return, finding how 'twas with her, she brake out into this exclamation: Unhappy creature that I am! to fly from the bare apprehension of one enemy, into the mouth of another.

◆　　Many a wise man will provide against one danger but fall into another.　　◆

43. 翠鳥

翠鳥天性孤僻，常年在水邊活動，並把巢築在捕鳥人搆不到

BIRDS 鳥

的凹岸裡。有一隻翠鳥出去為她的孩子們覓食，這時候，海上起了暴風雨，鳥巢和小鳥都被水沖走了。她回來後，看見這慘狀，不禁驚呼：「我真命苦啊！才出虎穴，又落虎口。」

♦　　　　　　智者千慮，必有一失。　　　　　　♦

Townsend 170 = Perry 396

44. The Kites and the Swans

The kites of olden times, as well as the Swans, had the privilege of song. But having heard the neigh of the horse, they were so enchanted with the sound, that they tried to imitate it; and, in trying to neigh, they forgot how to sing.

♦　　The desire for imaginary benefits often involves　　♦
the loss of present blessings.

44. 鳶和天鵝

古時候的鳶和天鵝一樣，也有歌唱的天賦。可是當他們聽到了馬的嘶鳴聲之後，就為此著迷並試圖模仿。在他們模仿馬嘶鳴的時候，卻忘了如何歌唱。

♦　　渴望想像中的好處，常會失去現有的幸福。　　♦

Jacobs 58 = Perry 627

45. The Labourer and the Nightingale

A Labourer lay listening to a Nightingale's song throughout the summer night. So pleased was he with it that the next night he set a trap for it and captured it. "Now that I have caught you," he cried, "you shall always sing to me."

"We Nightingales never sing in a cage." said the bird.

"Then I'll eat you." said the Labourer. "I have always heard say that a nightingale on toast is dainty morsel."

"Nay, kill me not", said the Nightingale; "but let me free, and I'll tell you three things far better worth than my poor body." The Labourer let him loose, and he flew up to a branch of a tree and said, "Never believe a captive's promise; that's one thing. Then again: Keep what you have, and third piece of advice is: Sorrow not over what is lost forever." Then the song-bird flew away.

◆ Not everything of value is material: True worth can lie in things like beauty, joy, or wisdom. ◆

45. 工人和夜鶯

夏天的一個夜晚,有個工人躺著徹夜聽夜鶯歌唱。他聽得如此入迷,以至於第二天晚上佈下陷阱,捉住了夜鶯。「既然我捉住了你。」他喊道,「你就要一直為我歌唱。」

「我們夜鶯從來不在籠中歌唱。」夜鶯說。

「那樣的話我就吃了你。」工人說,「我總是聽人說,烤夜鶯是美味佳餚。」「別,別殺我,」夜鶯說,「放了我,我就告訴你三件事,那可遠比我有價值多了。」工人放了夜鶯。夜鶯飛上枝頭,說道:「絕對不要相信俘虜的承諾,這是一件。再者,保住你現有的東西。第三條勸告是:永遠不要為失去的東西傷心。」說完,夜鶯就飛走了。

◆ 並非所有有價值的事物都是物質的:真正的價值可以存在於美麗、喜悅或智慧之中。 ◆

L'Estrange 42 = Perry 418

46. An Ostrich, Birds, and Beasts

The ostrich is a creature that passes in common reputation, for half--bird, half-beast. This amphibious wretch happened to be taken twice the same day, in a battle between the birds and the beasts, and as an enemy to both parties. The birds would have him to be a beast, and the beasts concluded him to be a bird; but upon showing his feet to prove that he was no bird, and upon showing his wings, and his beak, to prove that he was no beast, they were satisfied upon the whole matter, that though he seemed to be both, he was yet in truth neither the one, nor the other.

♦　　　　Sometimes a half-truth is necessary.　　　　♦

46. 鴕鳥、鳥與野獸

鴕鳥一般都被認為是介於鳥與野獸之間的一種生物。有一天，在一鳥獸間的戰爭中，這隻可憐的傢伙在一天之內被抓了兩次，不管哪一方抓到他都認為他是他們的敵人。鳥把他當成獸，獸把他當成鳥；但是，鴕鳥讓野獸看他的腳，證明他不是鳥，又給鳥看他的翅膀和喙，證明他不是野獸。雖然他看起來既像鳥又像野獸，但是實際上他不屬於任何一方。對此，大家都感到非常滿意。

♦　　　　半真半假的陳述，有時候是必要的。　　　　♦

Townsend 242 = Perry 437

47. The Owl and the Birds

An Owl, in her wisdom, counseled the Birds that when the acorn first began to sprout, to pull it all up out of the ground and not allow it to grow. She said acorns would produce mistletoe, from which an irremediable poison, the bird- lime, would be extracted and by which they would be captured. The Owl next advised them to pluck up the seed of the flax, which men had sown, as it was a plant which boded no good to them, and, lastly, the Owl, seeing an archer approach, predicted that this man, being on foot, would contrive darts armed with feathers which would fly faster than the wings of the Birds themselves. The Birds gave no credence to these warning words, but considered the Owl to be beside herself and said that she was mad.

But afterwards, finding her words were true, they wondered at her knowledge and deemed her to be the wisest of birds. Hence it is that when she appears they look to her as knowing all things, while she no longer gives them advice, but in solitude laments their past folly.

◆　　Destroy the seed of evil, or it will grow up to your ruin.　　◆

47. 貓頭鷹和鳥

一隻很有智慧的貓頭鷹勸鳥兒們，說當橡樹第一次開始發芽時，就把橡樹從地裡全拔出來，不能讓它生長。他說橡樹會生出槲寄生，從槲寄生中能提煉出一種無藥可解的毒物——黏鳥膠，能被用來抓鳥。貓頭鷹又勸鳥把人們播下的亞麻種子刨出來，因

BIRDS 鳥

為這是一種對鳥類來說預示著不祥的植物。有一次，貓頭鷹看見一個弓箭手走近，預言這個人會製造出帶有羽毛的飛箭，飛得比鳥還快。鳥不信這些警告的話，卻認為貓頭鷹神志失常，說他瘋了。

但是後來，鳥發現貓頭鷹的話是真的，他們對他的預言表示驚奇。認為他是鳥類中最聰明的。因此，當他出現的時候，他們就指望他預言一切，而貓頭鷹卻不再給他們忠告了，只是獨自哀歎他們的愚蠢。

◆　要把邪惡的力量及時剷除，否則會後患無窮。　◆

Townsend 289 = Perry 265

48. The Partridge and the Fowler

A Fowler caught a Partridge and was about to kill it. The Partridge earnestly begged him to spare his life, saying, "Pray, master, permit me to live and I will entice many Partridges to you in recompense for your mercy to me." The Fowler replied, "I shall now with less scruple take your life, because you are willing to save it at the cost of betraying your friends and relations."

◆　A traitor undermines the foundations of society.　◆

48. 山鶉和捕鳥人

一個捕鳥人抓住了一隻山鶉，要殺了他。山鶉懇求捕鳥人饒命，說：「大人，請饒了我吧，我會引來很多山鶉來報答你對我的仁慈。」

捕鳥人回答,「我現在更不會猶豫取你性命了,因為你想要以背叛你的親戚和朋友為代價,保住你的命。」

◆　　　　　**背叛者會毀了社會的根基。**　　　　　◆

Townsend 179 = Perry 294

49. The Peacock and the Crane

A Peacock spreading its gorgeous tail mocked a Crane that passed by, ridiculing the ashen hue of its plumage and saying, "I am robed, like a king, in gold and purple and all the colors of the rainbow; while you have not a bit of color on your wings."

"True," replied the Crane, "but I soar to the heights of heaven and lift up my voice to the stars, while you walk below, like a cock, among the birds of the dunghill."

◆　　　**Fine feathers don't make fine birds.**　　　◆

49. 孔雀和鶴

一隻開屏的孔雀譏諷從旁經過的一隻鶴,嘲笑鶴的灰色羽毛,說:「我像個國王,穿著金色、紫色和彩虹一樣七彩的禮服;而你翅膀上一點顏色都沒有。」

「你說的沒錯。」鶴回答,「但是我能飛到天上,對著星星大聲叫喊,而你卻在下面像隻公雞,在糞堆上的鳥群裡,走來走去。」

◆　　　　**有好的羽毛不一定是好的鳥。**　　　　◆

BIRDS 鳥

Townsend 210 = Perry 509

50. The Peacock and Juno

The Peacock made complaint to Juno that, while the nightingale pleased every ear with his song, he himself no sooner opened his mouth than he became a laughingstock to all who heard him. The Goddess, to console him, said, "But you far excel in beauty and in size. The splendor of the emerald shines in your neck and you unfold a tail gorgeous with painted plumage."

"But for what purpose have I," said the bird, "this dumb beauty so long as I am surpassed in song?"

"The lot of each," replied Juno, "has been assigned by the will of the Fates—to thee, beauty; to the eagle, strength; to the nightingale, song; to the raven, favorable, and to the crow, unfavorable auguries. These are all contented with the endowments allotted to them."

◆ Be content with your lot; one cannot be first in everything. ◆

50. 孔雀和朱諾

孔雀向朱諾抱怨說夜鶯用他的歌取悅每一個人，而他自己一開口就會成為所有聽到他聲音的人的嘲笑對象。女神為了安慰他，說：「但是你更美麗，身量也更好。你的脖子閃爍著翡翠的光芒，你開屏時人們能看到美麗的羽毛。」

「但是……」這隻鳥說，「我為什麼擁有的是這種比不上歌聲的無聲的美麗呢？」朱諾回答：「每個人的命運都是按照命運女神的意願指定的——對你，是美麗；對鷹，是力量；對夜鶯，是歌聲；對渡鴉,是討人喜歡；而對烏鴉,則是令人不快的預兆。這些動物都滿足於分配 給他們的天賦」

♦　　　**要滿足命運的安排,人不能樣樣都得第一。**　　　♦

Caxton 4.11 = Perry 577

51. The Raven and the Birds

The raven pretended that it was his birthday and invited the birds to a party. Once the birds were inside, he locked the door and began to kill them one by one.

♦　**This fable is meant for people who rush off to some merry feast but who find that things are the opposite of what they expected.**　♦

51. 烏鴉和鳥

有一天,烏鴉騙其他的鳥說,那天是他的生日,並邀請他們到他家參加生日聚會。等鳥都到齊了,烏鴉就把門鎖上,並把他們都殺了。

♦　**有些人也是這樣：跑去湊熱鬧,卻發現事情並不總像他們期望的那樣。**　♦

Townsend 36 = Perry 398

52. The Raven and the Swan

A Raven saw a Swan and desired to secure for himself the

same beautiful plumage. Supposing that the Swan's splendid white color arose from his washing in the water in which he swam, the Raven left the altars in the neighborhood where he picked up his living, and took up residence in the lakes and pools. But cleansing his feathers as often as he would, he could not change their color, while through want of food he perished.

♦　　　Change of habit cannot alter Nature.　　　♦

52. 渡鴉和天鵝

一天渡鴉看到了一隻天鵝，希望自己也能夠獲得像天鵝一樣美麗的羽毛。他認為天鵝一定是常在水中游泳，才能把羽毛洗得如此潔白無瑕，因此渡鴉離開了他賴以生存的祭壇，住到湖邊和池塘邊。一有時間，渡鴉就洗滌自己的羽毛，可是羽毛的顏色沒有發生任何變化。然而，他卻因為缺乏食物餓死了。

♦　　　這個故事告訴我們，本性是不會隨著習慣而改變的。　　　♦

Townsend 144 = Perry 139

53. The Seagull and the Kite

A Seagull having bolted down too large a fish, burst its deep gullet-bag and lay down on the shore to die. A Kite saw him and exclaimed, "You richly deserve your fate; for a bird of the air has no business to seek its food from the sea."

♦　　Every man should be content to mind his own business.　　♦

53. 海鷗和鳶

　　一隻海鷗吞吃了一條很大的魚，把他的氣管脹破了。海鷗只能奄奄一息地躺在岸邊等死。一隻鳶看見後叫起來：「你真是自作自受啊！本是天上的飛鳥，為什麼要到海裡覓食呢？」

◆　　　　　　**每個人都應該安分守己。**　　　　　　◆

Townsend 102 = Perry 324

54. The Sick Kite

　　A Kite, sick unto death, said to his mother, "O Mother! do not mourn, but at once invoke the gods that my life may be prolonged." She replied, "Alas! my son, which of the gods do you think will pity you? Is there one whom you have not outraged by filching from their very altars a part of the sacrifice offered up to them?"

◆　　**We must make friends in prosperity if we would have their help in adversity.**　　◆

54. 生病的鳶

　　一隻快要病死的鳶對他的媽媽說：「親愛的媽媽，不要悲傷了，現在趕緊去懇求神靈延長我的生命吧！」母鳶回答道：「唉！我的兒子啊！你想想還有哪位神會可憐你呢？幾乎每一位神靈都被你惹怒過，還有哪位神靈祭壇上的供奉品沒有被你偷過？」

◆　　**若要在患難時，得到朋友的幫助，就必須在順利時與別人締結友誼。**　　◆

BIRDS 鳥

Townsend 245 = Perry 473

55. The Sparrow and the Hare

A Hare pounced upon by an eagle sobbed very much and uttered cries like a child. A Sparrow upbraided her and said, "Where now is thy remarkable swiftness of foot? Why were your feet so slow?" While the Sparrow was thus speaking, a hawk suddenly seized him and killed him. The Hare was comforted in her death, and expiring said, "Ah! you who so lately, when you supposed yourself safe, exulted over my calamity, have now reason to deplore a similar misfortune."

♦   Misery loves company.   ♦

55. 麻雀和野兔

一隻野兔遭到老鷹的襲擊，嚇得哽咽不止，最後竟像個孩子一樣，放聲大哭起來。一隻麻雀飛來，對此不以為然，他訓斥兔子道：「你那飛一般的速度哪兒去了？你的腿為什麼跑得這麼慢？」麻雀正訓著，一隻老鷹突然從天空中撲下來，抓住麻雀，瞬間麻雀就丟了性命。看見麻雀被老鷹吃掉，兔子心裡感到好受多了，便說起了風涼話：「唉！剛剛你還自以為很安全，對我的不幸遭遇還幸災樂禍，現在自己也遭到同樣不幸的命運了吧！」

♦   禍不單行。   ♦

Townsend 240 = Perry 169

56. The Spendthrift and the Swallow

A young man, a great spendthrift, had run through all his

patrimony and had but one good cloak left. One day he happened to see a Swallow, which had appeared before its season, skimming along a pool and twittering gaily. He supposed that summer had come, and went and sold his cloak. Not many days later, winter set in again with renewed frost and cold. When he found the unfortunate Swallow lifeless on the ground, he said,"Unhappy bird! what have you done? By thus appearing before the springtime you have not only killed yourself but you have wrought my destruction also."

♦ Don't draw a conclusion based on a single observation. ♦

56. 敗家子和燕子

有一個年輕人揮金如土，把傳下來的祖業都揮霍一空，最後只剩下身上的一件考究的大衣。一天，他偶然看見一隻提早回來的燕子繞著池塘不停地飛舞，唧唧喳喳地歡叫著，以為春天到了，就把大衣賣掉，不久，冬天再次來襲，凜冽的寒風捲來霜凍，寒冷刺骨。當他發現那隻不幸的燕子凍死在地上時，說道：「不幸的鳥兒啊！看看你都幹了些什麼啊？春天還沒來到，你就趕著回來，害死了你自己不說，還把我也給拖累了。」

♦ 不要因為簡單的觀察，草率地下結論。 ♦

L'Estrange 17 = Perry 39

57. The Swallow and the Other Birds

It happened that a Countryman was sowing some hemp

BIRDS 鳥

seeds in a field where a Swallow and some other birds were hopping about picking up their food. "Beware of that man," quoth the Swallow. "Why, what is he doing?" said the others. "That is hemp seed he is sowing; be careful to pick up every one of the seeds, or else you will repent it." The birds paid no heed to the Swallow's words, and by and by the hemp grew up and was made into cord, and of the cords nets were made, and many a bird that had despised the Swallow's advice was caught in nets made out of that very hemp. "What did I tell you?" said the Swallow.

◆　　Destroy the seed of evil, or it will grow up to your ruin.　　◆

57. 燕子和別的鳥

　　一個農民往田裡種下了一些大麻籽，被田裡蹦蹦跳跳覓食的燕子和其他鳥看見了。「一定要當心那個人。」燕子警告。「為什麼呢？他在幹什麼？」其他的鳥好奇地問道。「他往田裡種的可是大麻籽啊！你們一定要細心地啄掉每一粒種子，否則到時候後悔就來不及啦！」但是別的鳥並沒把燕子的警告當回事。漸漸地，大麻長大了，人們採下它並製成了繩索，又把繩索編織成網放在田裡。那些沒有聽取燕子告誡的鳥，正是被從那塊地裡長出的大麻所織成的網捉住的。「我是怎麼警告你們的？」燕子歎息道。

◆　　若不及時把邪惡的種子扼殺在搖籃裡，而任其發展，終將引禍上身。　　◆

Townsend 83 = Perry 227

58. The Swallow, the Serpent, and the Court of Justice

A Swallow, returning from abroad and especially fond of dwelling with men, built herself a nest in the wall of a Court of Justice and there hatched seven young birds. A Serpent gliding past the nest from its hole in the wall ate up the young unfledged nestlings. The Swallow, finding her nest empty, lamented greatly and exclaimed, "Woe to me a stranger! that in this place where all other's rights are protected, I alone should suffer wrong."

♦　　　　　　Justice is fickle.　　　　　　♦

58. 燕子、蛇和法庭

一隻從海外回來的燕子，特別喜歡和人類住在同一個屋簷下，她在法庭的圍牆上築了一個巢，並在裡面孵出七隻雛燕。一條住在牆洞裡的蛇知道了，他順著牆爬進燕子的小巢，把七隻雛燕全吃掉了。看見巢裡空空的，若不及時把邪惡的種子扼殺在搖籃裡，而任其發展，終將引禍上身。

小雛燕全沒了，燕子悲痛欲絕，她聲嘶力竭地喊道：「我這個悲慘的外來者啊！在這個所有人的權益都能得到保護的地方，唯獨我卻要遭受這麼大的不幸。」

♦　　　　　　公平是多變的。　　　　　　♦

BIRDS 鳥

Townsend 133 = Perry 399

59. The Swan and the Goose

A certain rich man bought in the market a Goose and a Swan. He fed the one for his table and kept the other for the sake of its song. When the time came for killing the Goose, the cook went to get him at night, when it was dark, and he was not able to distinguish one bird from the other. By mistake he caught the Swan instead of the Goose. The Swan, threatened with death, burst forth into song and thus made himself known by his voice, and preserved his life by his melody.

◆ A man cannot be too careful of what he does, where the life of any creature is in question. ◆

59. 天鵝和鵝

一個有錢人從市集上，買了一隻鵝和一隻天鵝。他養天鵝是因為天鵝歌聲美妙，而養鵝的目的則純粹是為了吃肉。終於有一天，到該宰鵝的時候了，他們家的廚子就到鵝棚裡去抓鵝。可是時值夜晚，棚裡的光線極其昏暗，廚子根本就分不清到底哪隻是鵝。他就隨手一抓，結果天鵝被當作鵝抓了出去。在這生死攸關之際，天鵝立刻引吭高歌，用美妙的歌聲讓廚子認出了自己，才使倖免於難。

◆ 每個生命都有自己的特點，人往往忽略了這一點。 ◆

Chambry 174 = Perry 233

60. The Swan and His Owner

They say that swans sing when they are about to die. A certain man chanced upon a swan that was for sale and bought him, since he had heard that swans sing very beautifully. At the man's next dinner party, he came and got the swan, expecting that the bird would serenade his guests at dinner. The swan, however, was completely silent. Later on, when the swan realized that he was about to die, he began to sing his funeral dirge. When his owner heard him, he said, "Well, if you are going to sing this song only at the moment of your death, then I was a fool for having commanded you to do it. I should have ordered you to be butchered instead!"

◆ Some people are the same way: they will agree to do things under compulsion that they are not willing to do as a favour. ◆

60. 天鵝和他的主人

據說，天鵝在臨死前會唱歌。某天，有個人聽說天鵝的歌聲非常美妙動聽，就買了一隻。第二天，這個人舉行晚宴的時候，他就請天鵝為他的賓客們演唱。但是，天鵝卻悶不作聲。直到後來有一天，天鵝意識到自己的生命就要結束了，就開始為自己唱起輓歌來。他的主人聽到後，說：「好吧，我之前請你唱歌真是愚蠢至極，既然你只在臨死前才唱歌，我當時就應該命人把你給宰了！」

◆ 這則寓言適用於那些敬酒不吃吃罰酒的人。 ◆

BIRDS 鳥

Townsend 35 = Perry 201

61. The Thirsty Pigeon

A Pigeon, oppressed by excessive thirst, saw a goblet of water painted on a signboard. Not supposing it to be only a picture, she flew towards it with a loud whir and unwittingly dashed against the signboard, jarring herself terribly. Having broken her wings by the blow, she fell to the ground, and was caught by one of the bystanders.

♦ Zeal should not outrun discretion. ♦

61. 口渴的鴿子

有隻鴿子正口渴得厲害，看見看板上畫著一杯清水，便以為是真的。她將翅膀揮得嗡嗡作響，不假思索地猛衝過去，不料卻重重地撞到看板上。鴿子折斷了雙翅，摔在地上，被旁觀者抓住了。

♦ 不要一時亢奮沖昏頭失去判斷力。 ♦

Townsend 310 = Perry 86

62. The Thrush and the Fowler

A Thrush was feeding on a myrtle-tree and did not move from it because its berries were so delicious. A Fowler observed her staying so long in one spot, and having well bird-limed his reeds, caught her. The Thrush, being at the point of death, exclaimed, "O foolish creature that I am! For the sake of a little pleasant food I have deprived myself of my life."

♦ Men fell worst when they contribute to their own undoing. ♦

62. 畫眉鳥和捕鳥人

一隻畫眉鳥正在香桃木上覓食，樹上甘甜可口的漿果實在是太好吃了，所以牠一直待在上面。一個捕鳥人發現，畫眉鳥整天都待在那棵樹上，很容易地就用塗有黏鳥膠的蘆葦桿捉住了牠。畫眉鳥在臨死前大聲叫喊：「我真是太愚蠢啦，就因為貪吃那一點美味的食物，到頭來把自己的命都給賠上了！」

♦ 人們在自己釀成大禍時感覺最糟。 ♦

L'Estrange 68

63. A Thrush and a Swallow

"Ah my dear mother!" says the thrush, "never had any creature such a friend as I have, of this same swallow." "No," says she, "nor ever any mother such a fool to her son as I have, of this same thrush; to talk of a friendship between people that cannot so much as live together in the same climate and season. One is for the summer, the other for winter, and that which keeps you alive, kills your companion."

♦ Know the nature of those you deal with. ♦

BIRDS 鳥

63. 畫眉鳥和燕子

「啊，親愛的媽媽！」畫眉鳥說，「沒有誰像我一樣有這麼好的朋友，看！我說的就是這隻燕子。」、「當然沒有了。」她說，「也沒有哪個母親像我一樣，有個這麼蠢的兒子，看！我說的就是這隻畫眉鳥。生活環境完全不一樣，怎麼可能做朋友呢？你們一個住在夏天，一個住在冬天，你賴以為生的東西，對他來說卻是致命的。」

◆　　　要了解你交往對象的本性。　　　◆

Townsend 168 = Perry 58

64. The Woman and Her Hen

A woman possessed a Hen that gave her an egg every day. She often pondered how she might obtain two eggs daily instead of one, and at last, to gain her purpose, determined to give the Hen a double allowance of barley. From that day the Hen became fat and sleek, and never once laid another egg.

◆　Set bounds to our desires and content ourselves when we are well.　◆

64. 婦人和她的母雞

有個婦人養了一隻雞，那隻雞每天只下一個蛋。她常常想怎樣才能讓它一天下兩個蛋，而不是下一個蛋。最後，為了達到這個目的，她決定每天給母雞餵兩份燕麥。結果從那天起，那隻母雞越長越胖，羽毛也越來越油光發亮，卻再也不下蛋了。

◆　　要求要有限度，要懂得滿足於所擁有的一切。　　◆

CROW 烏鴉

L' Estrange 180 = Perry 127

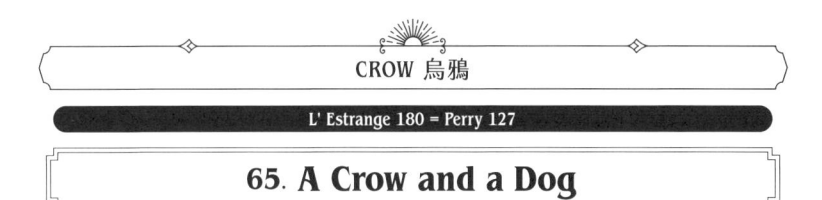

65. A Crow and a Dog

A crow invited a dog to join in a sacrifice to Minerva. That will be to no purpose (says the dog) for the goddess has such an aversion to you, that you are particularly excluded out of all auguries. Ay, says the crow, but I'll sacrifice the rather to her for that, to try if I can make her my friend.

♦ Men turn to religion out of fear or interest instead of affection. ♦

65. 烏鴉和狗

一隻烏鴉勸說一條狗和她一起為密涅瓦獻身。狗說，密涅瓦女神很討厭你，不允許你出現在任何占卜儀式中，所以這樣做是沒有意義的。烏鴉說，但我還是會為她這樣做的，為了爭取成為她的朋友。

♦ 人信教不是出於喜愛，而是恐懼或興趣。 ♦

Townsend 231 = Perry 323

66. The Crow and Mercury

A Crow caught in a snare prayed to Apollo to release him, making a vow to offer some frankincense at his shrine. But when rescued from his danger, he forgot his promise. Shortly afterwards, again caught in a snare, he passed by Apollo and

BIRDS 鳥

made the same promise to offer frankincense to Mercury. Mercury soon appeared and said to him, "O thou most base fellow? how can I believe thee, who hast disowned and wronged thy former patron?"

◆　　　Lie once and you may not be believed later.　　　◆

66. 烏鴉和墨丘利

　　一隻落入陷阱的烏鴉懇求阿波羅神放了他，發誓向他的神殿供奉乳香。可是當他從危險中逃脫後，就忘記了自己的諾言。之後不久，他又再次陷入了陷阱，這次他不再求阿波羅了，而是轉向墨丘利神，許諾為他供奉乳香。墨丘利不久就出現了，對他說道：「你這個卑鄙的傢伙！你欺騙了你的恩人，又背叛了他，讓我如何信任你呢？」

◆　　　一旦撒謊，就永遠不被人相信。　　　◆

L'Estrange 12 = Perry 490

67. A Crow and a Tortoise

　　There was one of your royston-crows, that lay battering upon a tortoise, and could not for his blood break the shell to come at the flesh. A carrion-crow, in this interim, comes up, and tells him, that what he could not do by force, he might do by stratagem. Take this tortoise up into the air, says the crow, as high as you can carry it, and then let him fall upon that rock there; his own weight, you shall see, shall break him. The royston took his advice, and it succeeded accordingly; but while the one was upon wing, the other stood lurching upon the ground, and flew away with the flesh.

♦ Most people are kind to their neighbors for their own sake. ♦

67. 烏鴉和烏龜

一隻黑冠松鴉，精疲力竭地蹲在一隻烏龜旁邊，不知道怎樣把殼打開吃到裡面的肉。這時一隻食腐肉的烏鴉過來，告訴他用暴力不能解決的問題，可以用計策來解決。他說，可以把烏龜叼到高空，要儘量高，然後鬆開口，讓他自己掉下來摔到石頭上，這樣他自身的重量就可以將其打開。黑冠松鴉採納了這個建議，成功摔碎了烏龜殼，可是當他還在空中的時候，那隻在地面的烏鴉叼起肉就跑掉了。

♦ 很多人為了自己的好處卻使他人得利。 ♦

Townsend 186 = Perry 390

68. The Crow and the Pitcher

A Crow perishing with thirst saw a pitcher, and hoping to find water, flew to it with delight. When he reached it, he discovered to his grief that it contained so little water that he could not possibly get at it. He tried everything he could think of to reach the water, but all his efforts were in vain. At last he collected as many stones as he could carry and dropped them one by one with his beak into the pitcher, until he brought the water within his reach and thus saved his life.

♦ Necessity is the mother of invention. ♦

BIRDS 鳥

68. 烏鴉和水罐

　　一隻口渴得半死的烏鴉,看到一個水罐,這水罐曾經裝滿了水。當他到了水罐跟前,不幸發現瓶裡只剩下了一點兒水了,他根本就不可能喝到它。烏鴉嘗試了他能想到的一切辦法來喝水,但到頭來,他所有的努力都徒勞無功。最後,烏鴉找來了很多小石子,用嘴銜著一塊接一塊地丟進瓶裡,最後終於喝到了水,因此救了自己的性命。

◆　　　　　　　困境激發創造力。　　　　　　　◆

Townsend 165 = Perry 125

69. The Crow and the Raven

　　A Crow was jealous of the Raven, because he was considered a bird of good omen and always attracted the attention of men, who noted by his flight the good or evil course of future events. Seeing some travelers approaching, the Crow flew up into a tree, and perching herself on one of the branches, cawed as loudly as she could. The travelers turned towards the sound and wondered what it foreboded, when one of them said to his companion, "Let us proceed on our journey, my friend, for it is only the caw of a crow, and her cry, you know, is no omen."

◆　　Those who assume a character which does not
　　　belong to them, only make themselves ridiculous.　　◆

69. 烏鴉和渡鴉

　　有一隻烏鴉非常嫉妒渡鴉，因為渡鴉被人們看作是祥鳥，總是能吸引注意，人們透過觀察他的飛行，來預測將來的運程。烏鴉看到幾個旅行者正走過來，就飛到一棵樹上，站在枝頭上，竭盡全力地叫起來。旅行者循聲望去，不知道這叫聲預兆著什麼，其中一個人對他的同伴說：「讓我們繼續旅程吧！我的朋友，那不過是一隻烏鴉在叫，你知道的，她的叫聲並不是什麼徵兆。」

◆　　**那些沒有能力，還要冒充內行的人，到頭來只會讓自己變得荒唐可笑。**　　◆

Townsend 277 = Perry 128

70. The Crow and the Serpent

　　A Crow in great want of food saw a Serpent asleep in a sunny nook, and flying down, greedily seized him. The Serpent, turning about, bit the Crow with a mortal wound. In the agony of death, the bird exclaimed, "O unhappy me! who have found in that which I deemed a happy windfall the source of my destruction."

◆　　**Desire things you don't understand and you accept the consequences.**　　◆

70. 烏鴉和毒蛇

　　有一隻正在急切尋找食物的烏鴉，看到一條毒蛇正曬著太陽在一個偏僻的角落裡睡覺，就猛撲下來，貪婪地抓住了蛇。毒蛇回過頭來，咬了烏鴉一口，那可是致命的一口。垂死的烏鴉歎道：

「我真是不幸啊!原以為是一筆橫財的東西,竟是導致我毀滅的源頭。」

◆　　　　　　渴求未知的東西會害了自己。　　　　　　◆

Townsend 284 = Perry 553

71. The Crow and the Sheep

A troublesome Crow seated herself on the back of a Sheep. The Sheep, much against his will, carried her backward and forward for a long time, and at last said, "If you had treated a dog in this way, you would have had your deserts from his sharp teeth." To this the Crow replied, "I despise the weak and yield to the strong. I know whom I may bully and whom I must flatter; and I thus prolong my life to a good old age."

◆　　　　　　Pick your enemies.　　　　　　◆

71. 烏鴉和綿羊

一隻討厭的烏鴉站在一隻綿羊的背上。那隻羊,很不情願地馱著烏鴉前前後後地走了很長時間。最後他終於對烏鴉說:「如果你是用這種方式對待一隻狗,他一定會讓你嚐嚐他鋒利牙齒的厲害。」聽到這句話,烏鴉回答道:「我是欺軟怕硬的,我知道自己該欺負誰,又該去奉承誰,因此我才長壽。」

◆　　　　　　選擇立場時要慎重。　　　　　　◆

Townsend 248 = Perry 202

72. The Dove and the Crow

A Dove shut up in a cage was boasting of the large number of young ones which she had hatched. A Crow hearing her, said,"My good friend, cease from this unseasonable boasting. The larger the number of your family, the greater your cause of sorrow, in seeing them shut up in this prison-house."

♦ Many children are a great blessing;but a few good ones are a greater. ♦

72. 鴿子和烏鴉

有一隻被關在籠子裡的鴿子,誇耀自己養育過很多很多的小鴿子。一隻烏鴉聽到了她的話,就對鴿子說:「我親愛的朋友,快別亂吹牛了。你家裡的成員越多,看到他們都被關在籠子裡面,就會勾起你越大的悲傷。」

♦ 孩子多是福氣,孩子少但是都好,才是更大的福氣。 ♦

Townsend 24 = Perry 229

73. The Swallow and the Crow

The Swallow and the Crow had a contention about their plumage. The Crow put an end to the dispute by saying, "Your feathers are all very well in the spring, but mine protect me against the winter."

♦ Fair weather friends are not worth much. ♦

73. 燕子和烏鴉

　　燕子和烏鴉為了各自的羽毛而爭論起來，烏鴉的一句話結束了這場口舌之爭：「春天你的羽毛固然很美麗，但是我的羽毛卻能讓我抵禦嚴寒。」

♦　　　　　　漂亮的羽毛不一定有用。　　　　　　♦

DAW 寒鴉

L'Estrange 33 = Perry 472

74. A Daw and Borrowed Feathers

　　A Daw that had a mind to be sparkish, tricked himself up with all the gay Feathers he could muster together: and upon the credit of these stolen or borrowed Ornaments, he valued himself above all the Birds in the Air beside. The Pride of this Vanity got him the Envy of all his Companions, who, upon a Discovery of the Truth of the Case, fell to pluming of him by Consent; and when every Bird had taken his own Feather, the silly Daw had nothing left him to cover his Nakedness.

♦　We steal from one another in all manner of Ways, and to all manner of Purposes; Wit, as well as Feathers; but where Pride and Beggary meet, People are sure to be made Ridiculous in the Conclusion.　♦

74. 寒鴉和借來的羽毛

　　有隻寒鴉想讓自己變漂亮，於是就用所有他能找到的漂亮羽毛來打扮自己；在這些偷來的或是借來的羽毛的裝扮下，他自認為比世界上其他的鳥都漂亮。這種虛榮的驕傲，使他的同伴都非常嫉妒。但是，他們一發現事情的真相，就一起飛到他身上，拔他的羽毛，就連他自己原本的羽毛也都被他們拔光了。這隻愚蠢的寒鴉只得赤身裸體。

♦ **出於各式各樣的目的，我們千方百計地在彼此身上進行盜竊，比如智慧，還有羽毛；但是驕傲與貧窮的結合，最終會使人們變得荒謬可笑。** ♦

L'Estrange 183 = Perry 131

75. A Daw with a String at Its Foot

A country fellow took a daw and tied a string to his leg; and so gave him to a little boy to play with. The daw did not much like his companion, and upon the first opportunity gave him the slip, and away into the woods again, where he was shackled and starved. When he came to die, he reflected upon the folly of exposing his life in the woods, rather then live in an easy servitude among men.

♦ The mind is responsible for our happiness. ♦

75. 腳上綁著繩子的寒鴉

有個鄉下人抓到了一隻寒鴉，在他的一隻腳上綁了條繩子，把他送給一個小男孩玩。可是，寒鴉並不怎麼喜歡這個玩伴，於是乘機從他身邊逃跑了，又回到了樹林。但是，綁在腳上的繩子使他的行動頗為不便，他不得不忍饑挨餓。在他臨死前，他才意識到回到樹林的決定有多麼愚蠢，還不如當初乖乖地當人類的奴

BIRDS 鳥

隸呢,至少還不愁吃喝。

♦ 　　　我們的想法,決定我們幸福與否。　　　♦

Townsend 192 = Perry 129

76. The Jackdaw and the Doves

A Jackdaw, seeing some Doves in a cote abundantly provided with food, painted himself white and joined them in order to share their plentiful maintenance. The Doves, as long as he was silent, supposed him to be one of themselves and admitted him to their cote.

But when one day he forgot himself and began to chatter, they discovered his true character and drove him forth, pecking him with their beaks. Failing to obtain food among the Doves, he returned to the Jackdaws. They too, not recognizing him on account of his color, expelled him from living with them. So desiring two ends, he obtained neither.

♦ 　　He that trims between two interests, loses himself with both ,but is true to neither.　　♦

76. 寒鴉和鴿子

有隻寒鴉,看見鴿籠裡幾隻鴿子的食物很豐盛,就把自己渾身都塗白鑽到鴿籠裡,跟鴿子共用豐盛的美食。寒鴉不說話,鴿子也就當他是自己的一員,允許他到鴿籠裡去。

一天,寒鴉忘了自己的身份,開始大叫,鴿子此時才發現了他的真實身份,就驅趕他,對他又啄又咬。寒鴉在鴿籠中吃不著東西,就回到寒鴉群中。寒鴉們看他遍體通白,同樣不認識他並驅趕他,不允許他跟寒鴉們再一同生活。

♦　　　　　　兩頭都想得到,就會兩者都失去。　　　　　　♦

Townsend 57 = Perry 101

77. The Vain Jackdaw

Jupiter determined, it is said, to create a sovereign over the birds, and made proclamation that on a certain day they should all present themselves before him, when he would himself choose the most beautiful among them to be king.

The Jackdaw, knowing his own ugliness, searched through the woods and fields, and collected the feathers which had fallen from the wings of his companions, and stuck them in all parts of his body, hoping thereby to make himself the most beautiful of all.

When the appointed day arrived, and the birds had assembled before Jupiter, the Jackdaw also made his appearance in his many feathered finery. But when Jupiter proposed to make him king because of the beauty of his plumage, the birds indignantly protested, and each plucked from him his own feathers, leaving the Jackdaw nothing but a Jackdaw.

♦　　　　A fine bird is more than fine feathers.　　　　♦

77. 虛榮的寒鴉

傳說朱比特決定挑選百鳥之王,於是他傳諭眾鳥,定下了他們朝覲的日期。屆時，他會親自挑選出最美麗的鳥，並把他封為百鳥之王。

寒鴉自知相貌醜陋，就到樹林和田野到處尋覓，收集從同伴們身上掉落下來的羽毛，把那些羽毛插滿全身，希望能成為最美麗的鳥兒。

朝覲的日子終於來臨了，所有的鳥兒齊集在朱比特面前，寒鴉插著各式各樣花俏的羽毛亮相了。然而當朱比特因為欣賞寒鴉全身漂亮的羽毛而提議立他為王時，眾鳥紛紛抗議，他們都從寒鴉身上啄走屬於自己的羽毛，寒鴉恢復了他的本來面貌，什麼也沒有得到。

◆　　　好的鳥兒不僅僅要有漂亮的羽毛。　　　◆

Townsend 101 = Perry 276

78. The Eagle and the Arrow

An Eagle sat on a lofty rock, watching the movements of a Hare whom he sought to make his prey. An archer, who saw the Eagle from a place of concealment, took an accurate aim and wounded him mortally. The Eagle gave one look at the arrow that had entered his heart and saw in that single glance that its feathers had been furnished by himself. "It is a double grief to me," he exclaimed, "that I should perish by an arrow feathered from my own wings."

◆　　We often give our enemies the means for our own destruction.　　◆

78. 鷹和箭

鷹站在一塊高高的岩石上，觀察著一隻野兔的行動，打算去捕捉他。一個在隱蔽處觀察的射手精確地瞄準，並給了鷹致命的一箭。鷹看了一眼那隻射入他心臟的箭，匆匆一瞥看見了那支箭上鑲著自己的羽毛。「這對我真是加倍的傷痛啊！」他感歎道，「我竟被鑲有自己翅膀上羽毛的箭給殺死了。」

♦　　　　　人們經常幫助敵人傷害自己。　　　　　♦

Townsend 305 = Perry 275

79. The Eagle and His Captor

An Eagle was once captured by a man, who immediately clipped his wings and put him into his poultry-yard with the other birds, at which treatment the Eagle was weighed down with grief. Later, another neighbor purchased him and allowed his feathers to grow again. The Eagle took flight, and pouncing upon a hare, brought it at once as an offering to his benefactor. A Fox, seeing this, exclaimed, "Do not cultivate the favor of this man, but of your former owner, lest he should again hunt for you and deprive you a second time of your wings."

♦　　　　Favor those who do you kindness.　　　　♦

79. 鷹和捕鷹人

有一次，有個人抓住了一隻鷹，馬上就剪掉了鷹的翅膀，把他放進養雞場裡面，與其他的鳥類關在一起。鷹受到這樣的對待，因為憂傷而過度憂鬱。後來，一個鄰居買下了這隻鷹，允許鷹的羽翼重新長出來。鷹展翅高飛，突襲了一隻野兔，便馬上拿來送給自己的恩人。有一隻狐狸看到了，大聲說道：「先別忙著培養這個人對你的好感了，而應該先去討好你原來的主人，以免他再次抓住你，讓你第二次失去翅膀。」

◆ 要懂得感恩。 ◆

Townsend 181 = Perry 488

80. The Eagle, the Cat, and the Wild Sow

An Eagle made her nest at the top of a lofty oak; a Cat, having found a convenient hole, moved into the middle of the trunk; and a Wild Sow, with her young, took shelter in a hollow at its foot. The Cat cunningly resolved to destroy this chance-made colony. To carry out her design, she climbed to the nest of the Eagle, and said, "Destruction is preparing for you, and for me too, unfortunately. The Wild Sow, whom you see daily digging up the earth, wishes to uproot the oak, so she may on its fall seize our families as food for her young."

Having thus frightened the Eagle out of her senses, she crept down to the cave of the Sow, and said, "Your children are in great danger; for as soon as you go out with your litter to find food, the Eagle is prepared to pounce upon one of your little pigs." Having instilled these fears into the Sow, she went and pretended to hide herself in the hollow of the tree. When night came she went forth with silent foot and obtained food for herself and her kittens, but feigning to be afraid, she kept a lookout all through the day.

Meanwhile, the Eagle, full of fear of the Sow, sat still on the branches, and the Sow, terrified by the Eagle, did not dare to go out from her cave, and thus they both, along with their families, perished from hunger, and afforded ample provision for the Cat and her kittens.

◆ Don't let fear paralyze you. ◆

80. 鷹、貓和野豬

鷹在一棵高大的橡樹樹冠上搭了一個巢；貓在樹幹中段發現了一個方便舒適的洞，便在那裡安了家；野豬帶著她的小豬們，住在樹根的洞裡。狡猾的貓一心想要獨占這棵樹。為了實現這個陰謀，她爬到鷹的巢裡，對她說：「我們可真是不幸啊！就要大難臨頭了。你看看那隻野豬，天天在下面挖土，存心想把橡樹連根拔起，這樣她就可以在橡樹倒的時候，輕而易舉地抓住我們兩家人，去餵她的孩子了。」

把老鷹嚇得魂飛魄散之後，貓又爬到樹根的野豬洞裡，對她說：「你的孩子們危險了！你一帶他們出去覓食，老鷹就準備叼走你的小豬。」這樣嚇唬了野豬一番之後，貓就回到家裡，裝模作樣地躲在樹洞裡。到了晚上，她就悄悄溜出去給自己和孩子們找食物，但是白天的時候，她又裝出一副擔驚受怕的樣子，整天躲在洞裡張望。與此同時，老鷹擔心野豬要推倒大樹，就整天待在樹枝上，而野豬又擔心老鷹突襲，也不敢走出洞口半步。就這樣鷹和野豬兩家都餓死在家裡，成了貓一家人的美食。

◆ 不要被恐懼冲昏了頭腦。 ◆

BIRDS 鳥

Townsend 250 = Perry 2

81. The Eagle and the Jackdaw

An Eagle, flying down from his perch on a lofty rock, seized upon a lamb and carried him aloft in his talons. A Jackdaw, who witnessed the capture of the lamb, was stirred with envy and determined to emulate the strength and flight of the Eagle. He flew around with a great whir of his wings and settled upon a large ram, with the intention of carrying him off, but his claws became entangled in the ram's fleece and he was not able to release himself, although he fluttered with his feathers as much as he could. The shepherd, seeing what had happened, ran up and caught him. He at once clipped the Jackdaw's wings, and taking him home at night, gave him to his children. On their saying,"Father, what kind of bird is it? "he replied, "To my certain knowledge he is a Daw; but he would like you to think an Eagle."

◆　　Don't take on more than you can accomplish.　　◆

81. 鷹和寒鴉

鷹從高處岩石上的窩裡俯衝下來，用他的利爪抓住一隻小羔羊，然後騰空而起。寒鴉看見這一幕後，非常嫉妒，決定和鷹較量一下力氣和飛行技巧。他奮力地拍動著翅膀，衝向一頭大公羊，想要把他抓起來。但是寒鴉的爪子和羊毛纏了起來，儘管他用盡全力扇動翅膀，還是無法讓自己脫身。牧羊人看見這一切後，跑過來一把抓住寒鴉，剪斷了他的翅膀。他晚上回家的時候把寒鴉帶給他的孩子們。孩子們問道：「爸爸，這是隻什麼鳥啊？」牧羊人回答道：「我可以確定他是一隻寒鴉，但他更喜歡別人叫他老鷹。」

♦ 不要承擔自己能力範圍之外的事。 ♦

Townsend 308 = Perry 574

82. The Eagle and the Kite

An Eagle, overwhelmed with sorrow, sat upon the branches of a tree in company with a Kite. "Why," said the Kite, "do I see you with such a rueful look?" "I seek" she replied, "a mate suitable for me, and am not able to find one." "Take me" returned the Kite, "I am much stronger than you are." "Why, are you able to secure the means of living by your plunder?" "Well, I have often caught and carried away an ostrich in my talons."

The Eagle, persuaded by these words, accepted him as her mate. Shortly after the nuptials, the Eagle said, "Fly off and bring me back the ostrich you promised me." The Kite, soaring aloft into the air, brought back the shabbiest possible mouse, stinking from the length of time it had lain about the fields. "Is this" said the Eagle, "the faithful fulfillment of your promise to me?" The Kite replied, "That I might attain your royal hand, there is nothing that I would not have promised, however much I knew that I must fail in the performance."

♦ Some people will do anything to what they want. ♦

82. 鷹和鳶

一隻鷹滿心哀傷地站在樹枝上，旁邊的鳶問她：「你為什麼

BIRDS 鳥

看起來這麼傷心啊？」鷹回答說：「我在尋找一位適合我的伴侶，但卻一直都沒找到。」鳶說：「你可以找我啊，我比你要強壯多了。」「真的嗎？你可以靠捕獵來維持我們的生計嗎？」「當然，我常常用爪子抓鴕鳥。」

　　鷹相信了鳶的話，接受他做自己的伴侶。婚禮一結束，鷹就對鳶說道：「你去抓一隻鴕鳥來吧！你許諾過要給我的。」鳶飛上天空，卻帶回一隻小得不能再小的老鼠，而且這老鼠因為長時間暴屍荒野，還散發著一陣惡臭。鷹質問道：「這就是你對我履行的承諾嗎？」鳶回答道：「為了得到高貴的你，無論什麼事情我都敢答應，即使我很清楚自己無法兌現諾言。」

◆　　　　有些人會不擇手段達到目的。　　　　◆

Townsend 66 = Perry 281

83. The Fighting Cocks and the Eagle

　　Two Game Cocks were fiercely fighting for the mastery of the farmyard. One at last put the other to flight. The vanquished Cock skulked away and hid himself in a quiet corner, while the conqueror, flying up to ahigh wall, flapped his wings and crowed cxultingly with all his might. An Eagle sailing through the air pounced upon him and carried him off in his talons. The vanquished Cock immediately came out of his corner, and ruled henceforth with undisputed mastery.

◆　　　Pride goes before destruction.　　　◆

83. 打架的公雞和鷹

　　兩隻鬥雞為了爭奪農場大院，進行了激烈的搏鬥，最後其中一隻被打得落荒而逃。戰敗的公雞躲到一個安靜的角落裡，而勝利者則飛上高牆，拍拍翅膀，扯開嗓子得意地大聲啼叫。這時一隻老鷹從空中衝了下來，用爪子一把抓住這隻公雞，把他帶走了。那隻戰敗的公雞立刻從角落裡跑出來，從此在大院裡當起了統治者，無人能否認他的地位。

◆　　　　　　　驕者必敗。　　　　　　　◆

Townsend 148 = Perry 296

84. The Peasant and the Eagle

　　A Peasant found an Eagle captured in a trap, and much admiring the bird, set him free. The Eagle did not prove ungrateful to his deliverer, for seeing the Peasant sitting under a wall which was not safe, he flew toward him and with his talons snatched a bundle from his head. When the Peasant rose in pursuit, the Eagle let the bundle fall again. Taking it up, the man returned to the same place, to find that the wall under which he had been sitting had fallen to pieces; and he marveled at the service rendered him by the Eagle.

◆　　　　　　　Return favors.　　　　　　　◆

84. 農夫和鷹

　　一個農夫發現一隻鷹落入陷阱，他非常喜歡鷹，就把鷹放了。

鷹沒有對他的解救者忘恩負義，他看見這個農夫坐在一面危牆下面時，就朝他飛過去，用爪子抓走了他頭上的包裹。當農夫站起身去追的時候，鷹又把包扔了下來；撿起包裹，這個人回到原來的地方，結果發現自己剛才一直靠坐的那堵牆已經倒塌了；他對鷹的報恩行為非常驚歎。

♦　　　　　　　好人有好報。　　　　　　　♦

Townsend 185 = Perry 395

85. The Serpent and the Eagle

A Serpent and an Eagle were struggling with each other in deadly conflict. The Serpent had the advantage, and was about to strangle the bird. A countryman saw them, and running up, loosed the coil of the Serpent and let the Eagle go free. The Serpent, irritated at the escape of his prey, injected his poison into the drinking horn of the countryman. The rustic, ignorant of his danger, was about to drink, when the Eagle struck his hand with his wing, and, seizing the drinking horn in his talons, carried it aloft.

♦　　　　　　Help those who help you.　　　　　　♦

85. 蛇和鷹

蛇和鷹正在進行殊死的搏鬥。蛇占據了上風，想要把鷹活活纏死。一個農夫見狀，急忙跑過去，將死死纏在鷹身上的蛇，使勁拽下來，鷹得到了自由。看著到手的獵物就這樣跑掉了，蛇被農夫激怒了，他把毒液注入了農夫的角杯裡。不知情的農夫，拿起角杯正準備喝水，鷹猛撲過來用翅膀打掉農夫手上的杯子，隨即抓起杯子竄上了雲霄。

♦ 　　　　　　要懂得知恩圖報。　　　　　　♦

Townsend 225 = Perry 278

86. The Tortoise and the Birds

A Tortoise desired to change its place of residence, so he asked an Eagle to carry him to his new home, promising her a rich reward for her trouble. The Eagle agreed and seizing the Tortoise by the shell! with her talons soared aloft. On their way they met a Crow, who said to the Eagle, "Tortoise is good eating." "The shell is too hard," said the Eagle in reply. "The rocks will soon crack the shell," was the Crow's answer; and the Eagle, taking the hint, let fall the Tortoise on a sharp rock, and the two birds made a hearty meal of the Tortoise.

♦ 　　Never soar aloft on an enemy's pinions.　　♦

86. 烏龜和鳥

有隻烏龜要搬新家。他請求鷹把自己帶到新居，並且許諾事成之後會給他豐厚的報酬。是鷹同意了烏龜的請求，用爪子抓住龜殼，展開翅膀飛到雲端。半路，他們遇見了一隻烏鴉。那隻烏鴉悄悄地對鷹說：「你知道嗎？烏龜的肉可好吃啦！」「可是龜殼實在是太硬了。」鷹回答道。烏鴉笑著說道：「用石頭把它砸開肯定是輕而易舉的事。」鷹領會了烏鴉的暗示，突然狠狠地把烏龜摔到鋒利的石塊上。隨後，鷹和烏鴉地享用了一頓烏龜大

BIRDS 鳥

餐。

◆　　　絕對不要幻想借助敵人飛黃騰達。　　◆

Townsend 27 = Perry 230

87. The Tortoise and the Eagle

A Tortoise, lazily basking in the sun, complained to the seabirds of her hard fate, that no one would teach her to fly. An Eagle, hovering near, heard her lamentation and demanded what reward she would give him if he would take her aloft and float her in the air,"I will give you," she said,"all the riches of the Red Sea." "I will teach you to fly then," said the Eagle; and taking her up in his talons he carried her almost to the clouds suddenly he let her go, and she fell on a lofty mountain, dashing her shell to pieces. The Tortoise exclaimed in the moment of death, "I have deserved my present fate; for what had I to do with wings and clouds, who can with difficulty move about on the earth?"

◆　　If men had all they wished, they would be often ruined.　　◆

87. 烏龜和老鷹

一隻烏龜懶洋洋地躺著曬太陽，向海鳥抱怨自己命苦，說沒有人肯教他飛行。一隻在附近盤旋的老鷹聽到了這番話，問烏龜，如果自己把她帶到空中飛一圈，會有什麼好處。「我會給你……」烏龜說，「紅海中的所有財富。」，「好，那我教你。」老鷹說。老鷹用爪子抓著烏龜，飛雲中時突然放開了爪子，烏龜摔到了一座山上，殼都摔碎了。烏龜臨死前呻吟道：「我真是自作自受，在陸地上移動都困難，幹嘛還想著飛入雲中呢？」

◆ **如果人得到了想要的一切，很可能馬上就會徹底毀滅。** ◆

LARK 雲雀

Townsend 259 = Perry 447

88. The Lark Burying Her Father

The Lark (according to an ancient legend) was created before the earth itself, and when her father died, as there was no earth, she could find no place of burial for him. She let him lie uninterred for five days, and on the sixth day, not knowing what else to do, she buried him in her own head. Hence she obtained her crest, which is popularly said to be her father's grave-hillock.

◆ Youth's first duty is reverence to parents. ◆

88. 雲雀葬父

古代的傳說中，雲雀是先於地球被創造的。她的父親死於一場大病，那時因為沒有地球，她找不到地方來埋葬父親。她就停喪五天，到了第六天，實在別無他法，就將父親葬在自己的頭上。因此，她頭上就有了冠毛，人們都說那是她父親的墳山。

◆ **青年人的首要責任就是孝敬父母。** ◆

BIRDS 鳥

Townsend 202 = Perry 325

89. The Lark and Her Young Ones

A Lark had made her nest in the early spring on the young green wheat. The brood had almost grown to their full strength and attained the use of their wings and the full plumage of their feathers, when the owner of the field, looking over his ripe crop, said,"The time has come when I must ask all my neighbors to help me with my harvest." One of the young Larks heard his speech and related it to his mother, inquiring of her to what place they should move for safety. "There is no occasion to move yet, my son," she replied; "the man who only sends to his friends to help him with his harvest is not really in earnest."

The owner of the field came again a few days later and saw the wheat shedding the grain from excess of ripeness. He said, "I will come myself tomorrow with my laborers, and with as many reapers as I can hire, and will get in the harvest." The Lark on hearing these words said to her brood,"It is time now to be off, my little ones, for the man is in earnest this time; he no longer trusts his friends, but will reap the field himself."

♦ Self-help is the best help. ♦

89. 雲雀和她的小鳥們

早春的時候，一隻雲雀在嫩綠的麥田裡築了個巢。當雛鳥們力氣快要長足，羽翼逐漸豐滿快要會飛時，那塊田地的主人看著他那成熟的莊稼，說道：「時候到了，我一定要去請所有的鄰居來幫我收割。」一隻小雲雀聽到他的話，便講給他的媽媽聽，問她他們該搬到什麼地方才安全。「現在還不是搬的時候呢！我的兒子。」她答道，「那人只是傳信要請他的朋友來幫忙收割，並不是真的很急切。」幾天過後，田地的主人又來了，看到麥子熟過頭，穀粒都在脫落，說道：「明天我要開始收割了，我要多僱些人來一起幹活。」雲雀聽到這些話後，對她的小鳥們 說：「現在我們該搬家了，我的小傢伙們，因為那人這次真的要行動了，他不再信賴他的朋友，而要親自動手收割這塊麥田了。」

◆ **自助是最好的幫助。** ◆

L'Estrange 143 = Perry 251

90. A Lark in a Net

A poor lark entered into a miserable expostulation with a bird-catcher, that had taken her in his net, and was just about to put her to death. Alas (says she) what am I to dye for now? I am no thief; I have stolen neither gold, nor silver; but for making bold with one pitiful grain of corn am I now to suffer.

◆ The story shows that people are willing to risk their lives for the sake of Some petty profit. ◆

90. 網裡的雲雀

有個捕鳥人網住了一隻雲雀，剛要殺她，這隻雲雀可憐兮兮地向捕鳥人哀求道：「唉！為什麼我現在就得死呢？我又不是小偷，我沒偷什麼金銀財寶，只不過擅自要了一顆玉米，現在就要受這種苦。」

◆ **人總是冒著生命危險，去追求一些微不足道的東西。** ◆

BIRDS 鳥

4.
BULL
公牛

BULL 公牛

Townsend 177 = Perry 531

91. The Bull and the Calf

A Bull was striving with all his might to squeeze himself through a narrow passage which led to his stall. A young Calf came up, and offered to go before and show him the way by which he could manage to pass. "Save yourself the trouble," said the Bull,"I knew that way long before you were born."

♦　　　　Some people just won't change.　　　　♦

91. 公牛和小牛

一隻公牛用盡全力，想透過一條狹窄的通道，進入他的牛欄。一隻小牛犢走了過來，主動要走在公牛前面為他帶路，這樣他就能成功地穿過通道。「你省省力氣吧！」公牛說道，「早在你出生之前，我就知道那條路了。」

♦　　　　　　有的人總是固執己見。　　　　　　♦

Townsend 150 = Perry 217

92. The Bull and the Goat

A Bull, escaping from a Lion, hid in a cave which some shepherds had recently occupied. As soon as he entered, a He-Goat left in the cave sharply attacked him with his horns. The Bull quietly addressed him,"Butt away as much as you will. I have no fear of you, but of the Lion. Let that monster go away and I will soon let you know what is the respective strength of a Goat and a Bull."

♦ It shows an evil disposition to take advantage of a friend in distress. ♦

92. 公牛和山羊

一隻正在逃避獅子追捕的公牛，躲進了牧羊人最近待過的一個洞穴裡面。公牛剛走進去，一隻留在洞裡的雄山羊就用他的羊角猛烈地攻擊公牛。公牛平靜地對山羊說：「你想怎麼頂就怎麼頂吧！我可不怕你，我怕的是獅子。等那個怪物走了，我很快就會就讓你知道，山羊和公牛誰更厲害。」

♦ 這個故事揭露了朋友有難時還欺負他的卑劣行為。 ♦

Townsend 246 = Perry 273

93. The Flea and the Ox

A Flea thus questioned an Ox, "What ails you, that being so huge and strong, you submit to the wrongs you receive from men and slave for them day by day, while I, being so small a creature, mercilessly feed on their flesh and drink their blood without stint?" The Ox replied, "I do not wish to be ungrateful, for I am loved and well cared for by men, and they often pat my head and shoulders." "Woe's me!" said the flea; "this very patting which you like, whenever it happens to me, brings with it my inevitable destruction."

♦ A reward for one might be destruction for another. ♦

BULL 公牛

93. 跳蚤和公牛

　　一隻跳蚤這樣問一頭公牛：「你可真悲哀啊！你的體格那麼大，身體又那麼強壯，卻要聽從於人類的驅使，天天為他們辛苦勞作，而我這種小小的昆蟲，都敢毫不留情地咬人，大口大口地吸他們的血。」公牛回答道：「人們愛惜我，把我照顧得很好，而且他們還常常用手拍拍我的頭和肩膀呢！我可不會忘恩負義。」，「我太可悲了！」跳蚤說，「你喜歡他們拍你，可是如果他們這樣拍我，那我可就死定了。」

　　◆　　　　一個人的榮耀可能是另一個人的災難。　　　　◆

Townsend 220 = Perry 372

94. The Lion and the Three Bulls

　　Three Bulls for a long time pastured together. A Lion lay in ambush in the hope of making them his prey, but was afraid to attack them while they kept together. Having at last by guileful speeches succeeded in separating them, he attacked them without fear as they fed alone, and feasted on them one by one at his own leisure.

　　◆　　　　　　　　Union is strength.　　　　　　　　◆

94. 獅子和三頭公牛

　　有三頭公牛在一塊吃草已經很長時間了。一隻獅子埋伏一旁，想要獵捕他們，但是他們在一塊的時候又不敢襲擊。最後，獅子用花言巧語成功地把公牛離間開來，當他們獨自吃草時，他就毫無畏懼地襲擊他們，輕而易舉地將他們一個個吃掉了。

♦　　　　　　　**團結就是力量。**　　　　　　　♦

Townsend 82 = Perry 300

95. The Heifer and the Ox

A Heifer saw an Ox hard at work harnessed to a plow, and tormented him with reflections on his unhappy fate in being compelled to labor. Shortly afterwards, at the harvest festival, the owner released the Ox from his yoke, but bound the Heifer with cords and led him away to the altar to be slain in honor of the occasion. The Ox saw what was being done, and said with a smile to the Heifer, "For this you were allowed to live in idleness, because you were presently to be sacrificed."

♦　　　　Be careful how you make fun of anyone.　　　　♦

95. 母牛和公牛

母牛看見套上挽具的公牛，在辛辛苦苦地犁地，就嘲諷公牛命運悲慘，得做勞動工作。不久之後，收穫的季節到了，主人把公牛身上的牛軛卸下，把母牛用繩子捆住帶到祭壇上去，打算把她殺了作祭品。公牛目睹這一切，面帶微笑對母牛說：「人們允許你虛度光陰，是因為不久後，就要宰殺你來獻祭了。」

♦　　　　　　　**不要取笑別人。**　　　　　　　♦

BULL 公牛

Townsend 34 = Perry 45

96. The Oxen and the Axle-Trees

A heavy wagon was being dragged along a country lane by a team of Oxen. The Axle-trees groaned and creaked terribly; whereupon the Oxen, turning round, thus addressed the wheels, "Hullo there! why do you make so much noise? We bear all the labor, and we, not you, ought to cry out."

♦　　　　Those who suffer most cry out the least.　　　　♦

96. 牛和車軸

一隊牛正拉著一輛沉重的大車沿著鄉間小路前進。車軸嘎吱作響，發出可怕的聲音；於是牛轉回頭對車輪說：「嗨！你們為什麼這麼吵？我們幹了所有的活，該抱怨的是我們，而不是你們。」

♦　　　　吃苦最多的，抱怨最少。　　　　♦

Townsend 55 = Perry 290

97. The Oxen and the Butchers

The Oxen once upon a time sought to destroy the Butchers, who practiced a trade destructive to their race. They assembled on a certain day to cany out their purpose, and sharpened their horns for the contest. But one of them who was exceedingly old (for many a field had he plowed) thus spoke, "These Butchers, it is true, slaughter us, but they do so with skillful hands, and with no unnecessary pain. If we get rid of them, we shall fall into the hands of unskillful operators, and thus suffer a double death: for you may be assured, that though all the Butchers should perish, yet will men never want beef."

♦   Do not be in a hurry to change one evil for another.   ♦

97. 牛和屠夫

從前，牛群想要殺了屠夫，因為屠夫做的這一行對他們的破壞很大。一天，他們聚集在一起，磨尖了角，為戰鬥做準備。可是一頭非常老的牛（他犁過許多地）這樣說：「說實話，這些屠夫是屠殺我們，可是他們手法嫻熟，不會給我們帶來不必要的痛苦。如果我們除掉了他們，就會落到生手的手裡，死得會更加痛苦：因為你們要相信，即便所有屠夫都死了，人也決不會不吃牛肉。」

♦   不要草率地改變一種災難去換來另一種災難。   ♦

BULL 公牛

5. CAMEL
駱駝

CAMEL 駱駝

Townsend 174 = Perry 195

98. The Camel

When Man first saw the Camel, he was so frightened at his vast size that he ran away. After a time, perceiving the meekness and gentleness of the beast's temper, he summoned courage enough to approach him. Soon afterwards, observing that he was an animal altogether deficient in spirit, he assumed such boldness as to put a bridle in his mouth, and to let a child drive him.

♦ Use serves to overcome dread. ♦

98. 駱駝

有個人第一次見到駱駝的時候，看到駱駝巨大的體形，非常害怕，以至於拔腿就跑。過了一段時間，他察覺到駱駝脾氣溫順，就鼓起勇氣靠近駱駝。這之後不久，他注意到駱駝是個一點脾氣都沒有的動物，於是就大著膽子，把一個籠頭套在了駱駝的嘴上，然後讓一個小孩子趕著他。

♦ 利用經歷可以克服恐懼。 ♦

Townsend 282 = Perry 287

99. The Camel and the Arab

An Arab camel-driver, after completing the loading of his Camel, asked him which he would like best, to go up hill or down. The poor beast replied, not without a touch of reason, "Why do you ask me? Is it that the level way through the desert is closed?"

♦ Forsake the hard when an easier way is available. ♦

99. 駱駝和阿拉伯人

有個趕駱駝的阿拉伯人,把貨物放到駱駝背上,然後問駱駝喜歡上山還是下山。這可憐的牲畜不無理由地回答道:「你為什麼這麼問我呢?難道穿過沙漠的那條平路被關閉了嗎?」

♦ **解決問題要用最簡單的方法。** ♦

CAMEL 駱駝

6.
CAT
貓

CAT 貓

Townsend 75 = Perry 7

100. The Cat and the Birds

A Cat, hearing that the Birds in a certain aviary were ailing dressed himself up as a physician, and, taking his cane and a bag of instruments becoming his profession, went to call on them. He knocked at the door and inquired of the inmates how they all did, saying that if they were ill, he would be happy to prescribe for them and cure them. They replied, "We are all very well, and shall continue so, if you will only be good enough to go away, and leave us as we are."

◆　　　　　　Know your enemies.　　　　　　◆

100. 貓和鳥

有一隻貓，聽說某個飼養場裡的鳥生病了，就裝扮成一個醫生，還拿著醫生用的手杖和一個提包的器械，去拜訪那些鳥。他敲了敲門，詢問裡面的鳥兒都怎麼樣了，說如果他們病了話，他將很高興為他們開處方治病。裡面的鳥兒們回答道：「我們都很好，如果你能善良點兒走開，就讓我們這樣待著的話，以後也會繼續好下去。」

◆　　　　　　要看清敵人的本質。　　　　　　◆

Townsend 44 = Perry 16

101. The Cat and the Cock

A Cat caught a Cock, and pondered how he might find a

reasonable excuse for eating him. He accused him of being a nuisance to men by crowing in the nighttime and not permitting them to sleep. The Cock defended himself by saying that he did this for the benefit of men, that they might rise in time for their labors. The Cat replied,"Although you abound in specious apologies, I shall not remain supperless"; and he made a meal of him.

♦　　　　　Tyrants need no excuse.　　　　　♦

101. 貓和公雞

　　有一隻貓，抓住了一隻公雞，考慮找一個什麼合理的理由，吃掉公雞。於是，他指責公雞在夜裡的時候啼叫，不讓人們睡覺，對人來說是個討厭的東西。公雞為自己辯解說，他這樣做是為了人好，這樣的話，他們就會及時去工作。貓回答道：「儘管你有很多似是而非的辯解，也不能讓我不吃晚飯。」於是，貓就把公雞吃了。

♦　　　　　殘暴的人不講道理。　　　　　♦

Townsend 280 = Perry 50

102. The Cat and Venus

　　A Cat fell in love with a handsome young man, and entreated Venus to change her into the form of a woman. Venus consented to her request and transformed her into a beautiful damsel, so that the youth saw her and loved her, and took her home as his bride. While the two were reclining in their chamber, Venus wishing to discover if the Cat in her change of shape had also altered her habits of life, let down a mouse in the middle of the room. The Cat, quite forgetting her present condition, started up from the couch and pursued the mouse, wishing to eat it. Venus was much disappointed and again caused her to return to her former shape.

♦ Nature exceeds nurture. ♦

102. 貓和維納斯

有一隻貓愛上了一位英俊的青年人,懇求維納斯把她變成一個女人。維納斯答應了她,把她變成了一個美麗的年輕女子。青年人看到她後,就愛上了她,並把她帶回家做自己的新娘。正當兩人步入臥室的時候,維納斯想要看看改變了外形的貓,是不是也改變了生活習性,就把一隻老鼠放到了屋子中間。那隻貓,完全忘了她目前的身份,從睡椅上跳起來去追趕老鼠,想要吃掉牠。維納斯非常失望,把她變回了原來的樣子。

♦ 本性難移。 ♦

Jacobs 38 = Perry 605

103. The Fox and the Cat

A Fox was boasting to a Cat of its clever devices for escaping its enemies. "I have a whole bag of tricks," he said, "which contains a hundred ways of escaping my enemies."

"I have only one," said the Cat; "but I can generally manage with that." Just at that moment they heard the cry of a pack of hounds coming towards them, and the Cat immediately scampered up a tree and hid herself in the boughs. "This is my plan," said the Cat. "What are you going to do?"

The Fox thought first of one way, then of another, and while he was debating the hounds came nearer and nearer, and at last the Fox in his confusion was caught up by the hounds and soon killed by the huntsmen. Miss Puss, who had been looking on, said,"Better one safe way than a hundred on which you cannot reckon."

◆ In times of crisis, haring one reliuoble method is more valuoble than having many impractical plans. ◆

103. 狐狸和貓

狐狸對貓自吹自擂，說自己有很多聰明的方法可以避開敵人：「我有一個錦囊，裡面裝滿一百種可以從敵人面前逃跑的妙計。」

「我只有一個辦法。」貓說，「但一直都很管用。」就在這時，一群獵狗叫著跑向他們，貓迅速地爬上了樹，躲在樹幹後面，「這就是我逃跑的辦法。」貓說，「你準備怎麼辦呢？」

狐狸想了一種又一種方法，就在他舉棋不定的時候，獵狗已經越來越近了。最後，稀裡糊塗的狐狸被獵狗抓住，很快就被獵人宰了。貓看到了這一幕，說道：「一種安全的方法，要勝過千百種不可靠的辦法。」

◆ 知道得多，不如知道得精。功夫要用在刀口上。 ◆

CAT 貓

7.
DEER
鹿

DEER 鹿

Townsend 22 = Perry 351

104. The Fawn and His Mother

A young Fawn once said to his Mother, "You are larger than a dog, and swifter, and more used to running, and you have your horns as a defense; why, then, O Mother! do the hounds frighten you so?" She smiled, and said, "I know full well, my son, that all you say is true. I have the advantages you mention, but when I hear even the bark of a single dog I feel ready to faint, and fly away as fast as I can."

◆　　No arguments will give courage to the coward.　　◆

104. 小鹿和母鹿

有一天，一隻小鹿問他的媽媽：「你的體型要比狗大，動作要比狗敏捷，比狗更善於奔跑，而且你頭上還有角來自衛，可是媽媽，為什麼你還要這麼怕獵狗呢？」母鹿笑了笑，說：「我的孩子，媽媽知道你說的都對，媽媽也有你說的這些優點，但即使只聽到一隻狗汪汪地叫，我就會嚇得幾乎昏過去，拚命地拔腿跑。」

◆　　不論什麼話，都無法讓膽小懦弱的人鼓起勇氣。　　◆

Townsend 105 = Perry 75

105. The One-Eyed Doe

A Doe blind in one eye was accustomed to graze as near to the edge of the cliff as she possibly could, in the hope of securing her greater safety. She turned her sound eye towards the land that she might get the earliest tidings of the approach of hunter or hound, and her injured eye towards the sea, from whence she entertained no anticipation of danger. Some boatmen sailing by saw her, and taking a successful aim, mortally wounded her. Yielding up her last breath, she gasped forth this lament,"O wretched creature that I am! to take such precaution against the land, and after all to find this seashore, to which I had come for safety, so much more perilous."

♦ You cannot escape your fate. ♦

105. 獨眼雌鹿

一隻瞎了一隻眼睛的雌鹿，習慣在離懸崖盡可能近的地方吃草，希望能使自己更安全。她把那隻好眼向著陸地，這樣她可以儘早得到獵人或獵狗走近的消息，而她那隻受傷的眼睛則朝向大海，她從沒想過那裡也會有危險。有幾個經過的船員看到了她，於是準確地瞄準她，給了她致命的一擊。在雌鹿咽氣時，她發出這樣的哀歎：「唉！我是個可憐的傢伙！這樣防備著陸地，卻根本沒發現，我前來尋求安全的海岸卻要危險得多。」

♦ 不能逃避現實。 ♦

Townsend 53 = Perry 305

106. The Sick Stag

A sick Stag lay down in a quiet corner of its pasture-ground. His companions came in great numbers to inquire after his health, and each one helped himself to a share of the food which had been placed for his use; so that he died, not from his sickness, but from the failure of the means of living.

♦   Evil companions bring more hurt than profit.   ♦

106. 生病的雄鹿

有隻雄鹿生病了，躺在牧場上一個安靜的角落養病。他的許多同伴紛紛前來探望他。但是每隻來探望他的鹿，都毫不客氣地把原本為病雄鹿準備的食物吃掉一些。過了沒多久，生病的雄鹿死了，但是可悲的是他並不是因病而死，而是因為缺少食物被餓死了。

♦   交友不慎，貽害非淺。   ♦

Townsend 97 = Perry 492

107. The Stag in the Ox-Stall

A Stag, roundly chased by the hounds and blinded by fear to the danger he was running into, took shelter in a farmyard and hid himself in a shed among the oxen. An Ox gave him this kindly warning, "O unhappy creature! why should you thus, of your own accord, incur destruction and trust yourself in the house of your enemy?" The Stag replied, "Only allow me, friend, to stay where I am, and I will undertake to find some favorable opportunity of effecting my escape."

At the approach of the evening the herdsman came to feed his cattle, but did not see the Stag; and even the farm-bailiff with several laborers passed through the shed and failed to notice him. The Stag, congratulating himself on his safety, began to express his sincere thanks to the Oxen who had kindly helped him in the hour of need. One of them again answered him,"We indeed wish you well, but the danger is not over. There is one other yet to pass through the shed, who has as it were a hundred eyes, and until he has come and gone, your life is still in peril."At that moment the master himself entered, and having had to complain that his oxen had not been properly fed, he went up to their racks and cried out,"Why is there such a scarcity of fodder? There is not half enough straw for them to lie on. Those lazy fellows have not even swept the cobwebs away."While he thus examined everything in turn, he spied the tips of the antlers of the Stag peeping out of the straw. Then summoning his laborers, he ordered that the Stag should be seized and killed.

◆ Nothing escapes the master's eye. ◆

107. 牛圈裡的雄鹿

　　一隻雄鹿被獵犬窮追不捨，嚇得暈頭轉向，一頭栽進一個農家庭院，惶恐不安地鑽進牛棚混在牛群中，躲藏起來。一頭牛好心地告誡他：「喂，你這個不幸的傢伙！你為什麼要這樣做，居然跑到敵人的家裡來？這不是自投羅網嗎？」雄鹿回答：「朋友，就允許我待在這兒吧！我一定會找到合適的機會逃跑的。」

　　到了傍晚，牧人來餵牛，他並沒有發現雄鹿，甚至管家帶著幾個工人經過牛棚時，也沒有注意到他。雄鹿暗自慶倖自己安然無恙，便向在他危難時刻提供幫助的牛友們，表示衷心的感謝。其中一頭牛回答他：「我們真心希望你能平安無事，但危險並沒有就這樣過去,還不能完全放心。還有一個人沒有來,他對萬事都十分留心,只有在他來過之後,你才能確保無恙。」此時,主人親自來到牛棚,他一邊抱怨工人沒給他好好餵牛,一邊走近乾草架,然後大聲叫了起來:「怎麼搞的,只有這麼一點點飼料?還有這乾草。這麼少,怎麼給牲口墊在地上躺的乾草,連一半也不到呀?這些懶蟲連蜘蛛網也不打掃乾淨。」他就這樣在牛欄裡走來走去,依次查看每樣東西,此時,雄鹿卻從藏身的乾草堆裡偷偷向外張望,被主人逮了個正著。他發現了尖尖的鹿角,於是喚來工人,命令他們抓住雄鹿,並將他殺掉。

◆　　　　什麼都逃不過主人的眼睛。　　　　◆

Townsend 257 = Perry 74

108. The Stag at the Pool

A Stag overpowered by heat came to a spring to drink. Seeing his own shadow reflected in the water, he greatly admired the size and variety of his horns, but felt angry with himself for having such slender and weak feet. While he was thus contemplating himself, a Lion appeared at the pool and crouched to spring upon him. The Stag immediately took to flight, and exerting his utmost speed, as long as the plain was smooth and open kept himself easily at a safe distance from the Lion. But entering a wood he became entangled by his horns, and the Lion quickly came up to him and caught him. When too late, he thus reproached himself, "Woe is me! How I have deceived myself! These feet which would have saved me I despised, and I gloried in these antlers which have proved my destruction."

◆　　What is most truly valuable is often underrated.　　◆

108. 池邊的雄鹿

　　一隻雄鹿酷熱難耐，跑到泉邊喝水。望著自己在水中的倒影，雄鹿對自己美麗多姿的大角，感到非常滿意；但是卻對自己纖細瘦弱的腿，感到十分失望。正當他看得入神的時候，一頭獅子悄悄潛伏到了泉邊，隨即一躍而起撲向雄鹿，雄鹿用最快的速度拔腿就逃。只要是在空曠的平原上，雄鹿總能和獅子保持一大段距離，但是當他跑進樹林時，雄鹿美麗的雙角被樹枝掛住了，獅子很快趕上來捉住了他。在臨死之前，雄鹿自責不已：「我真是太可悲了！竟然自欺欺人！我輕視的雙腿能拯救我生命，但是我引以為榮的雙角，卻斷送了我的性命。」

◆　　　　往往越是珍貴的東西，越容易被低估。　　　　◆

DEER 鹿

8.
DOG
狗

DOG 狗

Townsend 261 = Perry 480

109. The Bitch and Her Whelps

A Bitch, ready to whelp, earnestly begged a shepherd for a place where she might litter. When her request was granted, she besought permission to rear her puppies in the same spot. The shepherd again consented. But at last the Bitch, protected by the bodyguard of her Whelps, who had now grown up and were able to defend themselves, asserted her exclusive right to the place and would not permit the shepherd to approach.

◆ Those to whom you give kindness may turn on you. ◆

109. 母狗和她的小狗

一隻母狗馬上要生小狗了，她懇求牧人借給她一片地方，好讓她能夠把小狗生下來。在得到牧人的允許後，母狗又求牧人讓她在這兒把小狗帶大，牧人也答應了。到小狗都長大了，有能力自我保護之時，母狗倚仗小狗們的護衛，居然聲稱這片土地唯她獨有，不准牧人接近。

◆ 好心不一定有好報。 ◆

Townsend 124 = Perry 415

110. The Brazier and His Dog

A brazier had a little Dog, which was a great favorite with his master, and his constant companion. While he hammered away at his metals the Dog slept; but when, on the other hand, he went to dinner and began to eat, the Dog woke up and wagged his tail, as if he would ask for a share of his meal. His master one day, pretending to be angry and shaking his stick at him, said, "You wretched little sluggard! what shall I do to you? While I am hammering on the anvil, you sleep on the mat; and when I begin to eat after my toil, you wake up and wag your tail for food. Do you not know that labor is the source of every blessing, and that none but those who work are entitled to eat?"

◆ All creatures naturally look to the business of food and propagation. ◆

110. 銅匠和他的狗

銅匠養了一隻小狗，這隻小狗是他的寵兒，也是忠實的夥伴。當銅匠鍛造銅器的時候，小狗就在一邊呼呼大睡；但是另一方面，當銅匠開始吃晚飯的時候，小狗也睡醒了，搖著尾巴，彷彿在請求分享他的晚餐。有一天，他的主人假裝生氣，揮舞著棍子對狗說道：「你這個惡劣的小懶鬼！我該拿你怎麼辦呢？我在鐵砧上錘錘打打的時候，你卻在墊子上睡大覺；當我辛苦過後，開始吃飯，你也睡醒了，還搖著尾巴討吃的。難道你不知道，工作是所有幸福的來源，只有工作的人才有資格吃飯嗎？」

◆ 所有生物都把生存和繁衍，當作基本任務。 ◆

L'Estrange 59 = Perry 254

111. A Dog and a Butcher

As a butcher was busy about his meat, a dog runs away with

DOG 狗

a sheep's heart. The butcher saw him upon the gallop with a piece of flesh in its mouth, and called out after him, "You haven't stolen my heart; indeed, I have taken heart from this lesson! So if you ever come back in here again, I will give you the reward you deserve for this act of robbery !"

◆ If you've learned something by a loss, it really wasn't a loss. ◆

111. 狗和屠夫

屠夫正忙著切肉，狗趁機叼走了一塊羊心。屠夫看見狗嘴裡叼著一塊肉飛奔而去，就在後面喊道：「你還沒有偷走我的心，我已經從中得到教訓！所以，如果我在這裡再看到你，我會讓你為這次的搶奪行為，受到應得的懲罰！」

◆ 如果你能從損失中吸取教訓，那麼它就不算是什麼損失了。 ◆

Townsend 292 = Perry 328

112. The Dog and the Cook

A rich man gave a great feast, to which he invited many friends and acquaintances. His Dog availed himself of the occasion to invite a stranger Dog, a friend of his, saying, "My master gives a feast, and there is always much food remaining; come and sup with me tonight." The Dog thus invited went at the hour appointed, and seeing the preparations for so grand an entertainment, said in the joy of his heart, "How glad I am that I came! I do not often get such a chance as this. I will take care and eat enough to last me both today and tomorrow."

While he was congratulating himself and wagging his tail to convey his pleasure to his friend, the Cook saw him moving about among his dishes and, seizing him by his fore and hind paws, bundled him without ceremony out of the window. He fell with force upon the ground and limped away, howling dreadfully. His yelling soon attracted other street dogs, who came up to him and inquired how he had enjoyed his supper. He replied, "Why, to tell you the truth, I drank so much wine that I remember nothing. I do not know how I got out of the house."

◆ Some respect is due the servant for the sake of the master. ◆

112. 狗和廚師

有一個富人設下豐盛的宴席，請來許多朋友和熟人。他養的狗，也趁此機會邀請了一隻流浪狗，那是他的一個朋友，他說：「我的主人設宴，總是會有很多食物剩下來的，今晚過來和我一起大吃一頓吧！」流浪狗如約前往，看到這家人正在準備一場非常盛大的娛樂表演，心裡不禁樂開懷：「真高興我來了啊！這麼難得的機會，可不是經常能碰到的，我能吃得飽飽的，到明天都不餓。」

正當他暗自慶幸，搖著尾巴，向他的朋友表達自己的喜悅時，廚師看見這狗在自己的碗碟附近走來走去，就抓住他的頭和尾巴，毫不客氣地把他從窗子裡扔了出去。狗重重地摔在地上，悲慘地嚎叫著，跛著腳走了。他的慘叫聲很快就引來了街上的其他野狗，那些野狗們紛紛跑來問他晚飯吃得怎麼樣。他回答道：

「嗯,說實話吧!我酒喝得太多了,以至於什麼都記不起來了,我甚至連自己是怎麼從屋子裡出來的都忘了。」

◆ 　　有些尊敬是狗仗人勢得到的。　　◆

Townsend 176 = Perry 136

113. The Dog and the Hare

A Hound having started a Hare on the hillside pursued her for some distance, at one time biting her with his teeth as if he would take her life, and at another fawning upon her, as if in play with another dog. The Hare said to him, "I wish you would act sincerely by me, and show yourself in your true colors. If you are a friend, why do you bite me so hard? If an enemy, why do you fawn on me?"

◆ 　No one can be a friend if yon know not whether to trust or distrust him.　◆

113. 狗和野兔

有一隻獵犬在山坡上發現了一隻野兔,追了他一段距離,一下用牙齒咬住野兔,彷彿要奪走她的生命;一下又奉承野兔,彷彿是在與一隻狗玩耍。野兔對獵犬說:「我希望你對我表現得真誠一點,讓我看看你的真面目。要是你是我的朋友的話,為什麼要那麼兇狠地咬我呢?要是你是我的敵人的話,又為什麼要奉承我呢?」

◆ 　★如果你不知道該不該信任一個人,就不要跟他成為朋友。　◆

Aesop's Fables
伊索寓言

Chambry 187 = Perry 132

114. The Dog and The Lion

A dog was chasing a lion with all his might when the lion turned around and roared at him. The dog abandoned his pursuit, turned tail, and ran. A fox happened to see the dog and said, "Why on earth would you chase after something when you cannot even stand the sound of its voice?"

♦ It is a foolish man who wants to rival his superiors. He is doomed to fail, and becomes a laughing-stock as well. ♦

114. 狗和獅子

一隻狗正拚盡全力追趕一頭獅子。但是，當獅子轉過身來，朝他大吼一聲的時候，狗立馬就停止追逐，轉身逃命，能跑多快就跑多快。這個情景，剛好被狐狸看見了，狐狸就對狗說：「你究竟為什麼要去追趕那些一出聲，就能把你嚇跑的傢伙呢？」

♦ 只有傻瓜才會想要挑戰比自己強大的對手，因為他不但注定要失敗，還會成為別人的笑柄。 ♦

Townsend 31 = Perry 702

115. The Dog in the Manger

A Dog lay in a manger, and by his growling and snapping prevented the oxen from eating the hay which had been placed for them. "What a selfish Dog!" said one of them to his companions;

143

"he cannot eat the hay himself, and yet refuses to allow those to eat who can."

♦ People often begrudge others what they cannot enjoy themselves. ♦

115. 牛槽裡的狗

一隻狗躺在牛槽裡，對來吃草的公牛又咆哮，又猛咬，不讓公牛們吃原本為他們準備的乾草。「多麼自私的狗啊！」其中的一隻公牛對他的同伴說道，「他自己吃不了乾草，還不讓我們這些能夠吃草的來吃。」

♦ 有些人自己得不到想要的，也不讓別人得到。 ♦

Townsend 287 = Perry 253

116. The Dog and the Oyster

A Dog, used to eating eggs, saw an Oyster and, opening his mouth to its widest extent, swallowed it down with the utmost relish, supposing it to be an egg. Soon afterwards suffering great pain in his stomach, he said,"I deserve all this torment, for my folly in thinking that everything round must be an egg."

♦ Thy who act without sufficient thought, will often fall into unsuspected danger. ♦

116. 狗和牡蠣

一條喜愛吃雞蛋的狗看見了一個牡蠣，就使勁張開嘴，一口就把它吞了下去，而且吃得津津有味，還以為它是個雞蛋。沒多久，狗感到胃裡一陣劇痛，就說道：「我真是活該受到這樣的折磨，誰讓我愚蠢地認為，每個圓的東西都是雞蛋呢！」

♦　　**做事欠缺考慮的人，往往會陷入意想不到的危險。**　　♦

Townsend 15 = Perry 133

117. The Dog and the Shadow

A Dog, crossing a bridge over a stream with a piece of flesh in his mouth, saw his own shadow in the water and took it for that of another Dog, with a piece of meat double his own in size. He immediately let go of his own, and fiercely attacked the other Dog to get his larger piece from him. He thus lost both: that which he grasped at in the water, because it was a shadow; and his own, because the stream swept it away.

♦　　If you covet all, you may lose all.　　♦

117. 狗和影子

有一隻狗，嘴裡銜著一塊肉，走上小溪上的一座橋，看到了自己在水中的影子，誤以為那是另外一隻狗，嘴裡也銜著一塊比自己的那塊還大一倍的肉。他馬上就扔掉了自己嘴裡的那塊肉，惡狠狠地就去攻擊那隻狗，想要從那隻狗口中得到那塊更大的肉。他因此失去了兩塊肉：一塊是他在水中抓住的那個，因為它是個影子；還有他自己的那一塊，因為溪水把它給沖走了。

♦　　**什麼都想要，什麼都得不到。**　　♦

DOG 狗

L'Estrange 120 = Perry 134

118. A Dog and a Wolf

A wolf took a dog napping at his master's door, and when he was just about to worry him, the poor creature begged hard, only for a reprieve. Alas (says he) I'm as lean at present as canyon; but we have a wedding at our house within these two or three days, that will plump me up you shall see with good cheare. Pray have but patience 'till then, and when I'm in a little better case, I'll throw my self in the very mouth of you. The wolf took his word, and so let him go; but passing some few days after by the same house again, he spied the dog in the hall, and bad him remember his promise. Heark ye, my friend, says the dog; whenever you catch me asleep again, on the wrong side of the door, never trouble your head to wait for a wedding.

◆ Take the meal at hand instead of waiting for better. ◆

118. 狗和狼

狗在主人的門邊打盹，卻被狼抓住了。正當狼要吃他的時候，這個可憐的傢伙拚命地哀求，說他只是想請狼過幾天再殺他。他說：「唉！我現在瘦得皮包骨頭；但是，在這兩三天，我們家就要舉行一場婚禮，到時候那些大魚大肉，就會把我餵得圓滾滾的。請你耐心點，到那時，等我變得比現在豐滿的時候，我就任由你宰割。」狼相信了他說的話，把他放走了；但是，之後，狼再次經過同一戶人家，發現狗在門廳裡，就讓狗遵守自己的諾言。「你聽好了，我的朋友！」狗說，「不論你下次什麼時候，在門外邊趁我睡著的時候再抓到我，千萬別想著要等什麼婚禮。」

♦ 　　到手的食物要儘快享用，不要期望等到更好的。　　♦

Townsend 237 = Perry 449

119. The Dog's House

In the wintertime, a Dog curled up in as small a space as possible on account of the cold, determined to make himself a house. However when the summer returned again, he lay asleep stretched at his full length and appeared to himself to be of a great size. Now he considered that it would be neither an easy nor a necessary work to make himself such a house as would accommodate him.

♦ 　　It's easy to put off today what can be done tomorrow.　　♦

119. 狗的家

冬天時，有一隻狗由於寒冷，盡可能地把身子縮成一團，他下決心一定要為自己蓋一所房子。可是當夏天到來的時候，狗伸直了身子躺著睡覺，把身體盡可能伸展開。現在他覺得為自己蓋個適合自己的房子來住實在是不容易，也沒有那個必要。

♦ 　　人們總是把今天應做的事拖到明天。　　♦

Townsend 262 = Perry 135

120. The Dogs and the Hides

Some Dogs famished with hunger saw a number of cowhides

DOG 狗

steeping in a river. Not being able to reach them, they agreed to drink up the river, but it happened that they burst themselves with drinking long before they reached the hides.

♦   Attempt not impossibilities.   ♦

120. 狗和牛皮

有一群極度饑餓的狗，看到有幾張牛皮浸泡在河裡面。他們搆不到，於是決定把河水喝乾。但是直到狗們因為喝河水撐破了肚皮，還是沒有搆到牛皮。

♦   不要去嘗試不可能之事。   ♦

L'Estrange 150 = Perry 120

121. A Gardener and His Dog

A gardener's dog dropped into a well, and his master let himself down to help him out again. He reached forth his hand to take hold of the dog, and the cur snapped him by the fingers: for he thought it was only to duck him deeper. The master went his way upon it, and e'en left him as he found him. Nay (says he) I'm well enough served, to take so much pains for the saving of one that is resolved to make away himself.

♦   Benefits are refused by those who don't understand them.   ♦

121. 園丁和他的狗

園丁的狗掉進了井裡，他的主人親自下井想把他救上來。園丁伸出他的手想抓住狗,但那條惡狗卻突然咬了他的手指頭,因為他以為園丁伸手是想把他壓入水底。於是,主人就上去了,讓狗就那麼在井裡待著。他說:「不,我已經受夠了。他想死就讓他死吧!我也省得費這麼大力氣救他。」

◆　　★不知好歹的人總是拒絕別人的好意。　　◆

Townsend 88 = Perry 64

122. The Man Bitten by a Dog

A man who had been bitten by a Dog went about in quest of someone who might heal him. A friend, meeting him and learning what he wanted, said,"If you would be cured, take a piece of bread, and dip it in the blood from your wound, and go and give it to the Dog that bit you."The Man who had been bitten laughed at this advice and said,"Why? If I should do so, it would be as if I should beg every Dog in the town to bite me."

◆　Benefits bestowed upon the evil-disposed increase their means of injuring you.　◆

122. 被狗咬的人

有個人被狗咬傷,四處求醫問藥。一個朋友遇見他,知道了他的需要後便說:「你要想治好,就拿上一片麵包,浸上你傷口裡流出來的血,再扔給咬你的狗吃。」被咬的人聽到這個建議,不覺笑起來說:「為什麼?如果我這麼做,不就是在求鎮上的每隻狗都來咬我嗎?」

◆　　惡人若受益,就會更加為所欲為地傷害你。　　◆

DOG 狗

Townsend 198 = Perry 105

123. The Man, the Horse, the Ox, and the Dog

A Horse, Ox, and Dog, driven to great straits by the cold, sought shelter and protection from Man. He received them kindly, lighted a fire, and warmed them. He let the Horse make free with his oats, gave the Ox an abundance of hay, and fed the Dog with meat from his own table.

Grateful for these favors, the animals determined to repay him to the best of their ability. For this purpose, they divided the term of his life between them, and each endowed one portion of it with the qualities which chiefly characterized himself. The Horse chose his earliest years and gave them his own attributes: hence every man is in his youth impetuous, headstrong, and obstinate in maintaining his own opinion. The Ox took under his patronage the next term of life, and therefore man in his middle age is fond of work, devoted to labor, and resolute to amass wealth and to husband his resources. The end of life was reserved for the Dog, wherefore the old man is often snappish, irritable, hard to please, and selfish, tolerant only of his own household, but averse to strangers and to all who do not administer to his comfort or to his necessities.

♦ The profound meaning of this fable lies in encouraging people to cherish life, understand the value of each stage, and face the challenges and responsibilities of life with a balanced mindset. ♦

123. 人、馬、牛和狗

　　馬、牛和狗被寒冷逼入困境，向人求庇蔭和保護。人親切地接待了他們，生上火讓他們取暖。他讓馬隨意地吃燕麥，給牛弄來許多乾草，還用他自己桌子上的肉餵狗。

　　動物們對這些幫助很感激，決定盡最大能力報答他。因此，他們把人的一生分成幾段，分別把自己的特質賦予人生某一階段。馬選擇了人最早的幾年，把自己的特質送給他們，因此每個人在他的青春時代，都是浮躁、輕率並且固執己見的。牛把自己的特質賦予人生接下來的一個階段，因此人在中年時代，是埋頭工作、全力以赴來積累資產。最後的一段則留給了狗，於是老年人常常脾氣暴躁、易怒、挑剔、自私自利，只容得自己的家人，而厭惡生人，和所有不給他帶來安逸或必需品的人。

◆　　**讓人們珍惜生命，理解每個階段的價值，並以平衡的心態面對生活中的挑戰與責任。**　　◆

Townsend 114 = Perry 52

124. The Master and His Dogs

　　A certain man, detained by a storm in his country house, first of all killed his sheep, and then his goats, for the maintenance of his household. The storm still continuing, he was obliged to slaughter his yoke oxen for food. On seeing this, his Dogs took counsel together, and said,"It is time for us to be off, for if the master spare not his oxen, who work for his gain, how can we expect him to spare us?"

◆　　He is not to be trusted as a friend who mistreats his own famify.　　◆

DOG 狗

124. 主人和他的狗

有個農民，因暴風雪被困在家裡。為了養活家人，他先是殺掉了綿羊，後來又殺了山羊。暴風雪仍然刮個不停，最後，他不得不宰殺掉了耕地用的公牛來裹腹。他的幾條狗看到這種情形，聚在一起商量，說：「現在是我們應該離開的時候了。主人連辛辛苦苦為他工作的牛都不放過，還能指望主人放過我們嗎？」

♦　　薄待自己家人的人，是不能被當作朋友來信賴的。　　♦

Townsend 59 = Perry 332

125. The Mischievous Dog

A Dog used to run up quietly to the heels of everyone he met, and to bite them without notice. His master suspended a bell about his neck so that the Dog might give notice of his presence wherever he went. Thinking it a mark of distinction, the Dog grew proud of his bell and went tinkling it all over the marketplace. One day an old hound said to him: " Why do you make such an exhibition of yourself? That bell that you carry is not, believe me, any order of merit, but on the contrary a mark of disgrace, a public notice to all men to avoid you as an ill mannered dog."

♦　　Notoriety is often mistaken for fame.　　♦

125. 惡狗

一條狗不管遇到誰，總是悄悄地跑到這個人的腳邊，然後突然咬一口。他的主人在他脖子上繫了一個鈴鐺，這樣不論狗去哪兒，別人都知道。狗以為戴鈴鐺是與眾不同的標誌，於是為他的鈴鐺而變得驕傲了起來，還叮叮噹噹地跑遍了市場。一天，一隻老獵狗對他說：「你為什麼這樣炫耀你自己？相信我，你戴的那鈴鐺不是什麼榮譽勳章，正相反，那是恥辱的標記，是一種公告，要所有的人都把你當成不守規矩的狗來躲著。」

♦　　　　　惡名常常被誤認為是美譽。　　　　　♦

Townsend 120 = Perry 532

126. The Old Hound

A Hound, who in the days of his youth and strength had never yielded to any beast of the forest, encountered in his old age a boar in the chase. He seized him boldly by the ear, but could not retain his hold because of the decay of his teeth, so that the boar escaped. His master, quickly coming up, was very much disappointed, and fiercely abused the dog. The Hound looked up and said,"It was not my fault, master: my spirit was as good as ever, but I could not help my infirmities. I rather deserve to be praised for what I have been, than to be blamed for what I am."

♦　　　The spirit is willing but the flesh weak.　　　♦

126. 老獵狗

有一隻獵狗，他年輕力壯的時候，從不向森林中的任何野獸低頭。他老了之後，在狩獵時遇到一頭野豬。他大膽地咬住了野豬的耳朵，可是因為牙齒不夠鋒利而沒咬住，結果野豬逃跑了。他的主人很快跟了上來，非常失望，狠狠地將獵狗罵了一頓。獵狗抬起頭來說：「這不是我的錯，主人。我的精神還和過去一樣好，但是擋不住年老體衰。我應該為我以前的表現受到讚揚，而不應為現在的情形遭到責備。」

♦ 　　　　　　壯志仍在，身體已老。　　　　　　♦

Townsend 158 = Perry 365

127. The Shepherd and the Dog

A Shepherd penning his sheep in the fold for the night was about to shut up a wolf with them, when his Dog perceiving The Wolf said, "Master, how can you expect the sheep to be safe if you admit a wolf into the fold?"

♦ 　　　　Be watchful or all be will be lost.　　　　♦

127. 牧羊人和狗

夜裡牧羊人要把羊群趕進圍欄裡，不小心把一隻狼也趕了進去。牧羊人正要關上圍欄時，狗發現了羊群裡的狼，他趕緊對牧羊人說：「主人，你要是把狼也關進圈裡，那羊又怎麼能安然無恙呢？」

♦ 　　　　　凡事要小心，否則會全盤皆輸。　　　　　♦

Townsend 197 = Perry 403

128. The Thief and the Housedog

A Thief came in the night to break into a house. He brought with him several slices of meat in order to pacify the Housedog, so that he would not alarm his master by barking. As the Thief threw him the pieces of meat, the Dog said,"If you think to stop my mouth, you will be greatly mistaken. This sudden kindness at your hands will only make me more watchful, lest under these unexpected favors to myself you have some private ends to accomplish for your own benefit, and for my master's injury."

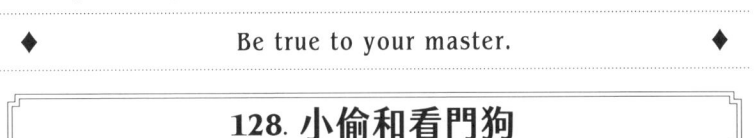

♦　　　　　Be true to your master.　　　　　♦

128. 小偷和看門狗

　　一天夜裡，小偷悄悄潛入一戶人家行竊。為了不讓屋裡的看門狗發現他後向主人報警，他特意帶了一些肉片來安撫這隻狗。當小偷正要把肉投給狗時，狗說話了：「如果你覺得這麼做可以讓我閉嘴的話，那你可就大錯特錯了。這種沒有理由的施捨只會使我更加警惕，省得你借著給我的好處收買我幫助你謀取私利，到最後受到傷害的只是我的主人。」

♦　　　　　　　對主人應當忠誠。　　　　　　　♦

Townsend 14 = Perry 330

129. The Traveler and His Dog

　　A traveler about to set out on a journey saw his Dog stand at the door stretching himself. He asked him sharply,"Why do you stand there gaping? Everything is ready but you, so come with me instantly."The Dog, wagging his tail, replied,"O, master! I am quite ready; it is you for whom I am waiting."

♦　　The loiterer often blames delay on his more active friend.　　♦

DOG 狗

129. 旅行者和他的狗

　　一個人打點好行裝準備出門旅行,卻看到他的狗正蹲在門邊打哈欠伸懶腰,於是旅行者就嚴厲地責問他:「你為什麼還蹲在那裡打哈欠?我都已經把一切準備妥當了,就只等你了,趕快跟我出發。」狗搖了搖尾巴,回答道:「噢,我的主人,我早已經準備好了,我這是在等您啊!」

◆　　　　效率低的人倒常責備高效率的同伴誤事。　　　　◆

Townsend 96 = Perry 92

130. The Two Dogs

　　A man had two Dogs: a Hound, trained to assist him in his sports, and a Housedog, taught to watch the house. When he returned home after a good day's sport, he always gave the Housedog a large share of his spoil. The Hound, feeling much aggrieved at this, reproached his companion, saying,"It is very hard to have all this labor, while you, who do not assist in the chase, luxuriate on the fruits of my exertions."The Housedog replied," Do not blame me, my friend, but find fault with the master, who has not taught me to labor, but to depend for subsistence on the labor of others."

◆　　Children are not to be blamed for the faults of
their parents.　　◆

130. 兩隻狗

　　有個人養了兩隻狗：一隻獵犬和一隻看家狗。他馴養獵犬狩獵，而讓看家狗守門。每當他打完獵，滿載而歸時，他總會把一大份戰利品賞給看家狗。獵犬對此感到十分委屈，便去指責看家狗說：「打獵要東奔西跑，四處奔波，你知道有多苦多累嗎？你什麼事情都不用做，卻坐享其成，分了我不少的勞動成果。」看家狗對獵狗說，「朋友，這不能怪我啊！要怪只能怪我們的主人。他不教我勞動，卻只教我坐在家裡，享受別人的勞動成果。」

◆　　　　孩子不應該承擔由父母造成的過失。　　　　◆

DOG 狗

9.
FISH/OCEAN DWELLER
魚／海洋生物

Townsend 167 = Perry 116

131. The Crab and the Fox

A Crab, forsaking the seashore, chose a neighboring green meadow as its feeding ground. A Fox came across him, and being very hungry ate him up. Just as he was on the point of being eaten, the Crab said,"I well deserve my fate, for what business had I on the land, when by my nature and habits I am only adapted for the sea?"

♦   Contentment with our lot is an element of happiness.   ♦

131. 螃蟹和狐狸

有一隻螃蟹,徹底離開了海邊,選擇鄰近的一片綠草地安家。一隻非常饑餓的狐狸碰到了他,想把他吃掉。就在要被吃掉的瞬間上,螃蟹說道:「我真是活該得到這樣的命運。我的天性就只適合住在海裡,為什麼要跑到陸地上來呢?」

♦   滿足於你現有的一切,是快樂的要素之一。   ♦

Townsend 81 = Perry 322

132. The Crab and Its Mother

A Crab said to her son,"Why do you walk so one-sided, my child? It is far more becoming to go straight forward. "The young Crab replied,"Quite true, dear Mother; and if you will show me the straight way, I will promise to walk in it." The Mother tried in vain, and submitted without remonstrance to the reproof of her child.

♦ Example is more powerful than precept. ♦

132. 螃蟹和牠的母親

　　一隻螃蟹對她的兒子說：「你為什麼總是橫著走呢？我的孩子，應該向前直著走才是啊！」小螃蟹回答道：「你說得很對，親愛的媽媽。如果你能讓我看看怎樣直著走，我發誓我一定會直著走的。」螃蟹媽媽徒勞無功地試了試，從此不再糾正兒子走路的方法了。

♦ 榜樣的力量勝過言教。 ♦

Townsend 116 = Perry 62

133. The Dolphins, the Whales, and the Sprat

　　The Dolphins and Whales waged a fierce war with each other. When the battle was at its height, a Sprat lifted its head out of the waves and said that he would reconcile their differences if they would accept him as an umpire. One of the Dolphins replied, "We would far rather be destroyed in our battle with each other than admit any interference from you in our affairs."

♦ Some would rather fight than not. ♦

133. 海豚、鯨魚和鯡魚

　　海豚和鯨魚之間爆發了一場激烈的戰爭。正當戰爭進行到高峯時，一條鯡魚從水波中探出頭來，說如果鯨魚和海豚願意讓他做裁判的話，他可以來替他們和解。其中的一隻海豚回答道：「我們寧可在戰爭中同歸於盡，也不願讓你來干涉我們的事情。」

◆　　　　★有時候，戰爭是有必要的。　　　　◆

Townsend 11 = Perry 11

134. The Fisherman Piping

A Fisherman skilled in music took his flute and his nets to the seashore. Standing on a projecting rock, he played several tunes in the hope that the fish, attracted by his melody, would of their own accord dance into his net, which he had placed below. At last, having long waited in vain, he laid aside his flute, and casting his net into the sea, made an excellent haul of fish. When he saw them leaping about in the net upon the rock he said, "O you most perverse creatures, when I piped you would not dance, but now that I have ceased you do so merrily."

◆　　People or things respond according to their
　　inherent tendencies, not external whims.　　◆

134. 吹長笛的漁夫

有一位精通音律的漁夫帶著自己的長笛和漁網來到海邊。他站在一塊岩石上，吹了好幾首曲子，希望魚兒能被他的笛聲吸引，自動游進他放在岩石下的漁網裡。他等了很長時間都一無所獲，最後他放下笛子，將漁網撒入大海，捕到了很多魚。當看到魚在岩石上的漁網中活蹦亂跳時，他說：「你們這些固執的傢伙，我吹笛子時你們不跳，現在我不吹了，你們卻跳得這麼歡心。」

◆　　人或事物，會根據其固有的本性作出反應，而非隨
　　　　　外界的任意影響改變。　　　　◆

Townsend 92 = Perry 282

135. The Fisherman and His Nets

A Fisherman, engaged in his calling, made a very successful cast and captured a great haul of fish. He managed by a skillful handling of his net to retain all the large fish and to draw them to the shore; but he could not prevent the smaller fish from falling back through the meshes of the net into the sea.

♦ To be small is a way to stay safe and avoid problems, whereas you rarely see a man with a big reputation who is able to keep out of danger. ♦

135. 漁夫和漁網

有一位漁夫，一生都在捕魚，每次撒網都非常成功，一網可以打到很多魚。他熟練地拉著網，留住網裡所有的大魚，然後把它們扔到岸邊，但是卻無法阻止小魚從網眼裡逃回大海。

♦ 小有小的好處，可以迴避問題，保護自己。很少能看到很出名的人，又能置身危險之外。 ♦

L'Estrange 110 = Perry 21

136. A Fisherman's Good Luck

A fisherman had been a long while at work without catching any thing, and so in great trouble and despair, he resolved to take up his tackle, and be gone: but in that very instant a great fish leapt into the boat, and by this providence he made a tolerable day on it.

♦　　　　　Patience has its own reward.　　　　　♦

136. 漁夫的好運

　　漁夫已經很久沒有捕到魚了，因此，他又愁又絕望，決定收拾工具，然後離開；但是，就在這個時候，一條大魚一躍掉進了船裡。承蒙上天的眷顧，他得到了這條魚，這一天過得還算不錯。

♦　　　　　只要耐心等待，總會有所收穫。　　　　　♦

Townsend 219 = Perry 13

137. The Fishermen

　　Some Fishermen were out trawling their nets. Perceiving them to be very heavy, they danced about for joy and supposed that they had taken a large catch. When they had dragged the nets to the shore they found but few fish: the nets were full of sand and stones, and the men were beyond measure cast down so much at the disappointment which had befallen them, but because they had formed such very different expectations. One of their company, an old man, said, "Let us cease lamenting, my mates, for, as it seems to me, sorrow is always the twin sister of joy; and it was only to be looked for that we, who just now were over-rejoiced, should next have something to make us sad."

♦　　　　　Life has its ups and downs.　　　　　♦

137. 漁夫們

　　幾位漁夫在拉漁網時，發現漁網非常重，以為抓到了很多魚，高興得手舞足蹈。哪知漁網被拉上岸後，他們發現裡面全是沙子和石頭。發生了這樣的事，他們感到很失望，這結果與他們期待的相差太遠。他們中的一位老漁夫說道：「夥計們，別難過，在我看來，快樂和悲傷，本來就是一對孿生姐妹，只是因為我們剛才過於高興，現在才會覺得傷心難過。」

◆　　　　　　生活總有起起伏伏。　　　　　　◆

L'Estrange 171 = Perry 26

138. Fishing in Troubled Waters

　　A fisher-man had ordered his net, for a draught, and still as he was gathering it up, he dashed the water, to fright the fish into the bag. Some of the neighbourhood that looked on, told him he did ill to muddle the water so, and spoil their drink. Well (says he) but I must either spoil your drink, or have nothing to eat my self.

◆　　Some never understand the actions of others.　　◆

138. 渾水摸魚

　　漁夫撒開漁網，網進了一網的魚。他邊收網邊擊打水面，魚受到驚嚇紛紛跳進袋子裡。有些人在旁邊觀看的說，他不該這樣攪和水，把他們喝的水都弄髒了。漁夫說：「好吧！但是，要是不弄髒你們喝的水,我就只有餓肚子了。」

♦ 　　　有些人永遠不明白別人的做法。　　　♦

Townsend 103 = Perry 145

139. The Lion and the Dolphin

A Lion roaming by the seashore saw a Dolphin lift up its head out of the waves, and suggested that they contract an alliance, saying that of all the animals they ought to be the best friends, since the one was the king of beasts on the earth, and the other was the sovereign ruler of all the inhabitants of the ocean. The Dolphin gladly consented to this request.

Not long afterwards the Lion had a combat with a wild bull, and called on the Dolphin to help him. The Dolphin, though quite willing to give him assistance, was unable to do so, as he could not by any means reach the land. The Lion abused him as a traitor. The Dolphin replied,"Nay, my friend, blame not me, but Nature, which, while giving me the sovereignty of the sea, has quite denied me the power of living upon the land."

♦ 　　The spirit may be willing, but the flesh may be unable.　　♦

139. 獅子和海豚

一隻獅子在海邊閒蕩,看見一隻海豚從波浪間探出頭來,便勸他和自己結盟。獅子說在動物裡面,他們倆應該是最要好的朋友,因為一個是陸地百獸之王,一個是海中動物之王。海豚欣然同意。

不久以後，獅子與野牛打仗，請海豚助戰。海豚雖然很願意幫助他，但是卻不可能這樣做，因為他怎麼也不能上岸來。獅子指責他背信棄義。海豚回答說：「不，我的朋友，你別責怪我，還是去責備自然吧！自然給予我海裡的霸權時，我便失去了陸地上的權力。」

♦　　　　　　心有餘而力不足。　　　　　　♦

Townsend 191 = Perry 73

140. The Monkey and the Dolphin

A Sailor, bound on a long voyage, took with him a Monkey to amuse him while on shipboard. As he sailed off the coast of Greece, a violent tempest arose in which the ship was wrecked and he, his Monkey, and all the crew were obliged to swim for their lives.

A Dolphin saw the Monkey contending with the waves, and supposing him to be a man (whom he is always said to befriend), came and placed himself under him, to convey him on his back in safety to the shore. When the Dolphin arrived with his burden in sight of land not far from Athens, he asked the Monkey if he were an Athenian. The latter replied that he was, and that he was descended from one of the most noble families in that city. The Dolphin then inquired if he knew the Piraeus (the famous harbor of Athens). Supposing that a man was meant, the Monkey answered that he knew him very well and that he was an intimate

FISH/OCEANDWELLER 魚 / 海洋生物

friend. The Dolphin, indignant at these falsehoods, dipped the Monkey under the water and drowned him.

◆ Bragging, lying, and pretending, has cost many a man his life and estate. ◆

140. 猴子和海豚

一個水手馬上要遠航，他帶了一隻猴子，到船上去給自己解悶。當他駛離希臘海岸時，一場猛烈的暴風雨降臨，船在暴風雨中失事了，他、猴子和全體船員，被迫游泳逃命。

一隻海豚看見猴子在與波浪搏鬥，以為猴子是人（據說海豚總是善待人類），他過來鑽到猴子身下，要把他安全地馱到岸上。當海豚馱著猴子到達距雅典不遠的陸地附近時，他問猴子是否是雅典人。猴子回答說是，而且說他出身於雅典城中最高貴的家族之一。然後海豚問他是否知道比雷埃夫斯（雅典的著名海港）。猴子以為指的是一個人，回答說，他跟比雷埃夫斯很熟，而且他是比雷埃夫斯的一位親密朋友。海豚被這些謊言激怒了，把猴子浸在水下淹死了。

◆ 人因為吹噓、撒謊、裝模作樣，失去了很多時間和財產。 ◆

L'Estrange 93 = Perry 113

141. A Tuna Fish and a Dolphin

A tuna fish gave chace to a dolphin; and when he was just ready to seize him, the tuna fish struck before he was aware, and the dolphin, in the eagerness of his pursuit, ran himself a ground with him. They were both lost; but the tuna fish kept his eye still upon the dolphin, and observing him when he was just at last gasp: Well, says he, the thought of death is now easy to me, so long as I see my enemy go for company.

♦ There is satisfaction in taking one's enemy along if one has to die. ♦

141. 金槍魚和海豚

一條金槍魚追捕一條海豚，馬上就要抓到時，金槍魚迅速出擊，被追得無處可逃的海豚遊到了地面上，二者都擱淺了，但是金槍魚一直看著海豚，直到他喘最後一口氣。金槍魚說，既然已知死亡就要到來，那麼有敵人的陪伴，會讓死亡更容易接受。

♦ 一個人死時，如果有敵人的陪伴，他會心滿意足的。 ♦

FISH/OCEANDWELLER 魚 / 海洋生物

10.
FOX
狐狸

L'Estrange 50 = Perry 533

142. An Ape and a Fox

An ape that found many inconveniences by going bare-arse, went to a fox that had a well-spread, bushy tail, and begged of him only a little piece on't to cover his nakedness: For (says he) you have enough for both, and what needs more than you have occasion for? Well, John (says the fox) be it more, or be it less, you get not one single hair on't; for I would have ye know, sirrah, that the tail of a fox was never made for the buttocks of an ape.

◆　　　　Be content with your station.　　　　◆

142. 猿猴和狐狸

猿猴發現光著屁股到處走有許多不便，就跑去找一隻尾巴上長著又濃又密的毛的狐狸，請求他給他一點點毛，好遮掩他裸露的屁股。他說：「你的毛都夠我們使用了，你要這麼多毛，又有什麼用呢？」狐狸 說：「嘿！小子，不管我的毛多還是少，我一根都不會給你的。你要知道，小子，狐狸的尾巴永遠不可能長在猴子屁股上。」

◆　　　　悅納你自己的處境吧！　　　　◆

Townsend 23 = Perry 288

143. The Bear and the Fox

A Bear boasted very much of his philanthropy, saying that of all animals he was the most tender in his regard for man, for he had such respect for him that he would not even touch his dead body. A Fox hearing these words said with a smile to the Bear, "Oh! that you would eat the dead and not the living."

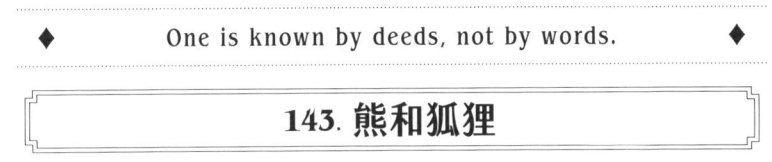

♦　　　　One is known by deeds, not by words.　　　♦

143. 熊和狐狸

一隻熊炫耀自己的好心腸,說是在所有的動物中,他對人類是最溫柔可親的,因為他對人非常地尊重,甚至連人的屍體都不碰一下。熊的話被一隻狐狸聽著了,他笑著對熊說:「喔!你真應該吃死人而不是吃活人!」

♦　　　　行動而非話語揭露一個人的內心。　　　♦

Townsend 212 = Perry 252

144. The Dog, the Cock, and the Fox

A Dog and a Cock being great friends, agreed to travel together. At nightfall they took shelter in a thick wood. The Cock flying up, perched himself on the branches of a tree, while the Dog found a bed beneath in the hollow trunk.

When the morning dawned, the Cock, as usual, crowed very loudly several times. A Fox heard the sound, and wishing to make a breakfast on him, came and stood under the branches, saying how earnestly he desired to make the acquaintance of the owner of so magnificent a voice. The Cock, suspecting his civilities, said, "Sir, I wish you would do me the favor of going around to the hollow trunk below me, and waking my porter, so that he may open the door and let you in."When the Fox approached the tree, the Dog sprang out and caught him, and tore him to pieces.

♦   Cunning often outwits itself.   ♦

144. 狗、公雞和狐狸

　　一隻狗和一隻公雞成為了很好的朋友，決定一起結伴去旅行。夜幕降臨時，他們在一片茂密的森林中找了個避身之處。公雞飛起來，棲息在樹枝上休息，同時狗就在下面的樹洞裡休息。

　　第二天拂曉時，公雞像往常那樣大聲啼叫了幾次。一隻狐狸聽到了公雞的叫聲，想要把他捉來當早飯吃，就跑過來在樹下對公雞說，自己誠摯地渴望結識一下擁有如此宏亮聲音的主人。公雞懷疑狐狸的禮貌，就說道：「先生，我希望你可以幫我到下面的樹洞裡去，叫醒我的守門人，那樣他就會把門打開，讓你進來的。」狐狸果然向樹洞靠過去，狗猛撲出來，抓住狐狸，把他撕成了碎片。

♦   聰明反被聰明誤。   ♦

Townsend 226 = Perry 406

145. The Dogs and the Fox

　　Some Dogs, finding the skin of a lion, began to tear it in pieces with their teeth. A Fox, seeing them, said,"If this lion were alive, you would soon find out that his claws were stronger than your teeth."

♦   It is easy to kick man that is down.   ♦

145. 狗和狐狸

有幾條狗,找到了一張獅子皮,想用牙齒把它給撕碎。一隻狐狸看見了他們,就說道:「如果獅子還活著的話,你們就會很快發現,獅子的爪子比你們的牙齒要有力多了。」

♦　　　　欺負潦倒的人總是比較容易的。　　　　♦

Townsend 253 = Perry 1

146. The Eagle and the Fox

An Eagle and a Fox formed an intimate friendship and decided to live near each other. The Eagle built her nest in the branches of a tall tree, while the Fox crept into the underwood and there produced her young. Not long after they had agreed upon this plan, the Eagle, being in want of provision for her young ones, swooped down while the Fox was out, seized upon one of the little cubs, and feasted herself and her brood. The Fox on her return, discovered what had happened, but was less grieved for the death of her young than for her inability to avenge them.

A just retribution, however, quickly fell upon the Eagle. While hovering near an altar, on which some villagers were sacrificing a goat, she suddenly seized a piece of the flesh, and carried it, along with a burning cinder, to her nest. A strong breeze soon fanned the spark into a flame, and the eaglets, as yet unfledged and helpless, were roasted in their nest and dropped down dead at the bottom of the tree. There, in the sight of the Eagle, the Fox gobbled them up.

♦　　　　God is the ultimate judge.　　　　♦

146. 鷹和狐狸

鷹和狐狸成了親密無間的好朋友,並決定做鄰居。鷹在一棵大樹的樹枝上,建了個巢孵育後代,狐狸則鑽進灌木叢中安了家,生兒育女。沒過多久,鷹為了找食物給她的孩子們吃,就趁狐狸不在家的時候,飛下來叼走了一隻小狐狸,和孩子們飽餐了一頓。狐狸回來之後發現了老鷹的所作所為,不僅為自己孩子的死而傷心,更為自己無力給小狐狸報仇而痛心。

不過老鷹很快就遭到了報應。有一天,村民們正在用山羊祭祖,在祭壇上空盤旋的鷹,忽然飛下來叼走一塊肉,連同一塊燃燒著的木炭,一起帶回了她的巢中。一陣狂風吹過,木炭上的火星變成了熊熊火焰。窩裡著了火,羽翼未豐的小鷹無力逃跑,從巢裡掉下來,摔死在樹下。狐狸當著老鷹的面,把小鷹全都吞進了肚子。

♦ 　　　　老天會做出正確的裁決。　　　　♦

Townsend 60 = Perry 17

147. The Fox Who Had Lost His Tail

A Fox caught in a trap escaped, but in so doing lost his tail. Thereafter, feeling his life a burden from the shame and ridicule to which he was exposed, he schemed to convince all the other Foxes that being tailless was much more attractive, thus making up for his own deprivation. He assembled a good many Foxes and publicly advised them to cut off their tails, saying that they would not only look much better without them, but that they would get rid of the weight of the brush, which was a very great inconvenience. One of them interrupting him said,"If you had not yourself lost your tail, my friend, you would not thus counsel us."

◆　　　Distrust advice from someone who stands to gain.　　　◆

147. 丟了尾巴的狐狸

一隻狐狸掙脫了捕獸器,但是卻被夾斷了尾巴。從此之後,他因為變成了這個樣子,而遭到了羞辱與奚落,他深感壓力,於是計畫讓其他所有狐狸都相信,沒有尾巴更有魅力,這樣一來就能掩蓋自己的缺陷。他召集了很多狐狸,建議他們割掉尾巴,說沒有尾巴,不僅看起來更加帥氣,而且也少了尾巴的負擔,這東西確實很不方便。這時候一隻狐狸插嘴說:「朋友,如果你自己沒有把尾巴弄丟,就不會這麼勸我們了。」

◆　　　不要聽從已經得到結果的人的建議。　　　◆

Townsend 285 = Perry 19

148. The Fox and the Bramble

A Fox was mounting a hedge when he lost his footing and caught hold of a Bramble to save himself. Having pricked and grievously to the soles of his feet, he accused the Bramble because, when he had fled to her for assistance, she had used him worse than the hedge itself. The Bramble, interrupting him, said,"But you really must have been out of your senses to fasten yourself on me, who am myself always accustomed to fasten upon others."

◆　　　To be selfish all are selfish.　　　◆

148. 狐狸和荊棘

一隻狐狸在爬越籬笆的時候失足摔了下去,幸好抓住了一根荊棘,才得以保住性命。但是他的腳底卻被紮到,非常痛,於是他埋怨荊棘說,自己本來是向她求救的,結果她卻比籬笆還要壞。荊棘打斷了狐狸的話,說道:「我自己常常會黏著東西不放,而現在卻是你拚命抓著我不肯放手!」

♦　　　　　在自私的人眼裡,人人都是自私的。　　　　　♦

Townsend 20 = Perry 425

149. The Fox, the Cock and the Dogs

One moonlight night a Fox was prowling about a farmer's hencoop, and saw a Cock roosting high up beyond his reach.

"Good news, good news!" he cried.

"Why, what is that?" said the Cock.

"King Lion has declared a universal truce. No beast may hurt a bird henceforth, but all shall dwell together in brotherly friendship."

"Why, that is good news," said the Cock; "and there I see some one coming, with whom we can share the good tidings."and so saying he craned his neck forward and looked afar off.

"What is it you see?"said the Fox.

"It is only my master's Dog that is coming towards us. What, going so soon?" he continued, as the Fox began to turn away as soon as he had heard the news. "Will you not stop and congratulate the Dog on the reign of universal peace?"

"I would gladly do so," said the Fox, "but I fear he may not have heard of King Lion's decree."

♦　　　　　**Cunning often outwits itself.**　　　　　♦

149. 狐狸、公雞和狗

在一個明月當空的夜晚，一隻狐狸悄悄地潛入了農夫的雞舍，遠遠地看到一隻公雞站在高處休息，於是他大聲叫道：「好消息，好消息！」

「怎麼了，是什麼好消息？」公雞問道。

「獅子大王已經宣佈世界和平，從此以後，任何野獸不得襲擊鳥類，所有人都要住在一起，相親相愛。」

「是嗎？這可真是個好消息。」公雞說，「我看到有人來了，我們把這個好消息跟他分享一下吧！」公雞一邊說著，一邊伸長了脖子朝遠處望去。

「你看到什麼了？」狐狸問道。

「是我家主人養的狗，正朝我們這兒走過來呢！咦！你怎麼那麼快就走了啊？」狐狸一聽到這消息，立馬轉身就跑，公雞接著說：「你不想留在這裡，和狗一起慶祝這個世界和平的好消息嗎？」

「非常樂意啊！」狐狸說，「但我怕他還沒聽說獅子大王的命令呢！」

♦　　　　　**狡詐的人總是自作聰明。**　　　　　♦

FOX 狐狸

L'Estrange 102 = Perry 20

150. A Fox and a Crocodile

There happened Contest betwixt a Fox and a Crocodile, upon the Point of Blood and Extraction. The Crocodile amplified wonderfully upon his Family, for the Credit of his Ancestors. Friend (says the Fox, smiling upon't) there will need no Herald to prove your Gentility; for your carry the Marks of your Original in your very Skin.

♦ Great Boasters and Liars have the Fortune still some way of other to disprove themselves. ♦

150. 狐狸和鱷魚

狐狸和鱷魚在爭論，誰的血統更尊貴。鱷魚非常詳盡地述說了他們家的光輝史，頌揚祖先們的豐功偉績。狐狸對此置之一笑，說：「朋友，就算你不說，人們也能知道你的出身，因為你的皮膚上，不就留有你祖先的印記嗎？」

♦ 在吹牛的人和說謊的人身上，總能找到自相矛盾之處。 ♦

Townsend 95 = Perry 124

151. The Fox and the Crow

A Crow having stolen a bit of meat, perched in a tree and held it in her beak. A Fox, seeing this, longed to possess the meat himself, and by a wily stratagem succeeded. "How handsome is the Crow," he exclaimed, in the beauty of her shape and in the fairness of her complexion! Oh, if her voice were only equal to her beauty, she would deservedly be considered the Queen of Birds!" This he said deceitfully; but the Crow, anxious to refute the reflection cast upon her voice, set up a loud caw and dropped the flesh. The Fox quickly picked it up, and thus addressed the Crow,"My good Crow, your voice is right enough, but your wit is wanting."

♦　　　　　　　Do not trust flatterers.　　　　　　　♦

151. 狐狸和烏鴉

一隻烏鴉偷到了一塊肉，叼著它站在樹上。狐狸看見了，很想把肉占為己有，他馬上就想到了一條妙計。狐狸大聲地喊道：「這隻烏鴉可真美啊！她的身材多麼勻稱，她的羽毛多麼亮麗啊！如果她的歌聲能和她的外表一樣有魅力，她自然就是當之無愧的鳥中之王嘍！」這些都是狐狸的謊言，但是這隻烏鴉，急切地想要改變大家對她嗓音的看法，於是大聲地叫起來，而那塊肉也跟著掉在地上。狐狸趕緊把肉撿起來，然後對烏鴉說：「我的好烏鴉，你的歌聲還可以，不過你的腦子實在是太笨了。」

♦　　　　　　　不要相信阿諛奉承者。　　　　　　　♦

Townsend 32 = Perry 9

152. The Fox and the Goat

A Fox one day fell into a deep well and could find no means of escape. A Goat, overcome with thirst, came to the same well, and seeing the Fox, inquired if the water was good. Concealing his sad plight under a merry guise, the Fox indulged in a lavish praise of the water, saying it was excellent beyond measure, and encouraging him to descend.

The Goat, mindful only of his thirst, thoughtlessly jumped down, but just as he drank, the Fox informed him of the difficulty they were both in and suggested a scheme for their common escape. "If," said he, "you will place your forefeet upon the wall and bend your head, I will run up your back and escape, and will help you out afterwards." The Goat readily assented and the Fox leaped upon his back. Steadying himself with the Goafs horns, he safely reached the mouth of the well and made off as fast as he could. When the Goat upbraided him for breaking his promise, he turned around and cried out, "You foolish old fellow! If you had as many brains in your head as you have hairs in your beard, you would never have gone down before you had inspected the way up, nor have exposed yourself to dangers from which you had no means of escape."

◆　　　　　Look before you leap.　　　　　◆

152. 狐狸和山羊

有一天，一隻狐狸掉進了一口深井裡，他想盡了辦法也無法逃出來。這時，一隻口渴的山羊來到這口井邊，發現了裡面的狐狸，就問他井水的味道如何。為了掩蓋自己的窘境，狐狸就裝出一副開心的表情，極力誇獎這井水好，說它甘甜無比，讓山羊也下來嚐一嚐。

山羊只知道自己口太渴，想也沒想就跳了下來。但就在山羊喝水的時候，狐狸告訴他，他們倆都陷入了困境，並提出了一個逃生的辦法。他說：「如果你能把前腿搭在井壁上，把頭低下，我就可以踩著你的背逃出去，然後再把你救上來。」山羊欣然同意了。狐狸跳上山羊的背，扶著羊角，安全地到達井口，然後飛快地跑走了。山羊在井底大罵狐狸不守承諾，狐狸聽到了便轉過頭來對他說：「你這個老糊塗！如果你的腦子有你的鬍子那麼多，就不會在找到上來的路之前就跳下去，也不會讓自己落入無法逃脫的困境之中。」

◆　　　　　三思而後行。　　　　　◆

Townsend 208 = Perry 15

153. The Fox and the Grapes

A Famished Fox saw some clusters of ripe black grapes hanging from a trellised vine. She resorted to all her tricks to get at them, but wearied herself in vain, for she could not reach them. At last she turned away, hiding her disappointment and saying, "The Grapes are sour, and not ripe as I thought."

◆　　It is easy to despise what you cannot get.　　◆

153. 狐狸和葡萄

一隻非常饑餓的狐狸，看到好幾串熟得發紫的葡萄，掛在高高的葡萄架上。她用盡各種辦法想要搆到它們，結果卻白費力氣，累得筋疲力盡。最後，狐狸只好走開，為了掩飾自己的失望，她自言自語道：「這葡萄是酸的，肯定沒有我想像的那麼甜。」

◆　　　人們往往輕視得不到的東西。　　　◆

FOX 狐狸

L'Estrange 81 = Perry 17

154. A Fox and a Hare to Jupiter

A fox and a hare presented a petition to Jupiter. The fox prayed for the hare's swiftness of foot, and the hare for the fox's craft, and wilkness of address. Jupiter told them, that since every creature had some advantage or other peculiar to it self, it would not stand with divine justice, that had provided so well for every one in particular, to confer all upon any one.

♦ Do not pray for more than your due. ♦

154. 向朱比特請願的狐狸和野兔

狐狸和野兔向朱比特請願。狐狸請求朱比特賜予他野兔奔跑如飛的速度,而野兔則想要狐狸的聰明和口才。朱比特告訴他們說:「既然每種生物都具有獨一無二的某種優勢,而這優勢對不論哪種生物的生存都至關重要,那麼,為了保證上天的公平,我不能把所有的優點都集中在隨便哪一種生物身上。」

♦ 不要貪求不應得的東西。 ♦

Townsend 180 = Perry 427

155. The Fox and the Hedgehog

A Fox swimming across a rapid river was carried by the force of the current into a very deep ravine, where he lay for a long time very much bruised, sick, and unable to move. A swarm of hungry blood-sucking flies settled upon him. A Hedgehog, passing by, saw his anguish and inquired if he should drive away the flies that were tormenting him. "By no means," replied the Fox; "pray do not molest them." "How is this?" said the Hedgehog; "do you not want to be rid of them?" "No," returned the Fox, "for these flies which you see are full of blood, and sting me but little, and if you rid me of these which are already satiated, others more hungry will come in their place, and will drink up all the blood I have left."

♦　　Consider carefully before changing your situation.　　♦

155. 狐狸和刺蝟

　　狐狸在渡過一條水流湍急的河時，被沖進了一座深谷。狐狸遍體鱗傷地在地上躺了很久，一動都不能動。一群饑餓的吸血蠅撲在狐狸身上。這時，一隻刺蝟路過這裡，看到狐狸這麼痛苦，就問他需不需要趕走這些害人的蒼蠅。狐狸說道：「千萬不要，求你別打擾牠們。」「這是為什麼？」刺蝟好奇地問道，「難道你不想趕走牠們嗎？」狐狸回答說：「是的，你看到的這些蒼蠅都已經喝飽血了，雖然我很痛苦，但已經好了很多，如果你趕走了這些已經吸飽血的蒼蠅，那麼就會有更多饑餓的蒼蠅來這裡，吸乾我全身的血。」

♦　　　　　考慮清楚再做出改變。　　　　　♦

Townsend 152 = Perry 12

156. The Fox and the Leopard

The Fox and the Leopard disputed which was the more

beautiful of the two. The Leopard exhibited one by one the various spots which decorated his skin. But the Fox, interrupting him, said, "and how much more beautiful than you am I, who am decorated, not in body, but in mind."

♦   Liars and boosters will undo themselves.   ♦

156. 狐狸和豹子

狐狸和豹子爭論誰長得更漂亮。豹子一個勁地向狐狸炫耀，裝飾在自己皮毛上的那些五彩斑斕的斑點，但狐狸打斷了他，說道：「我可比你漂亮多了！我修飾的不是自己的外表，而是頭腦。」

♦   ★吹牛和說謊者都會拆穿自己。   ♦

Townsend 203 = Perry 10

157. The Fox and the Lion

When first the Fox saw the Lion he was terribly frightened, and ran away and hid himself in the wood. Next time however he came near the King of Beasts he stopped at a safe distance and watched him pass by. The third time they came near one another the Fox went straight up to the Lion and passed the time of day with him, asking him how his family were, and when he should have the pleasure of seeing him again; then turning his tail, he parted from the Lion without much ceremony.

♦   Familiarity breeds contempt.   ♦

157. 狐狸和獅子

狐狸第一次見到獅子的時候,被嚇得半死,跑進樹林裡躲了起來。但是當第二次見到這萬獸中之王時,狐狸遠遠地站在一邊,看著獅子走過去。第三次見面時,他們挨得更近了,狐狸直接走上前去問好,問他家裡是否安好,什麼時候能有幸再見到他。然後狐狸毫不客氣地告別了獅子,大搖大擺地轉身走了。

◆　　　　　　　熟悉滋長輕蔑。　　　　　　　◆

Townsend 223 = Perry 27

158. The Fox and the Mask

A Fox entered the house of an actor and, rummaging through all his properties, came upon a Mask, an admirable imitation of a human head. He placed his paws on it and said,"What a beautiful head! Yet it is of no value, as it entirely lacks brains."

◆　　Outside show is a poor substitute for inner worth.　　◆

158. 狐狸和面具

一隻狐狸闖進了演員家,翻遍了家裡所有的道具,發現了一個做得惟妙惟肖的人頭面具,他拿起這個面具說道:「多漂亮的腦袋啊!可就是沒長腦子,一點用處都沒有。」

◆　　　　　　外表遠遠比不上內在重要。　　　　　　◆

Townsend 196 = Perry 14

159. The Fox and the Monkey

A Fox and a Monkey were traveling together on the same road. As they journeyed, they passed through a cemetery full of monuments. "All these monuments which you see," said the Monkey, "are erected in honor of my ancestors, who were in their day freedmen and citizens of great renown." The Fox replied, "You have chosen a most appropriate subject for your falsehoods, as I am sure none of your ancestors will be able to contradict you."

♦　　　A false tale often betrays itself.　　　♦

159. 狐狸和猴子

狐狸和猴子結伴同行，途中經過一片滿是墓碑的墓地。猴子說：「你看到的這些墓碑，都是為紀念我的祖先而立的，當年他們可都是聲名遠揚的自由人和公民。」狐狸回答道：「你說瞎話還真會找對象，我肯定你的這些祖先沒有一個會站出來反駁你。」

♦　　　謊言往往都會不攻自破。　　　♦

Caxton 5.3 = Perry 562

160. The Fox and the Partridge

A partridge had seated herself high on a perch when a fox came up to her and said, "How beautiful you are to look at: your legs are so red! your mouth is like coral! Ah, if only you were sleeping, you would be even more lovely..." The partridge believed the fox and closed her eyes, and the fox immediately grabbed her. In a voice choked with sobs, the partridge said to the fox, "I beg you, in the name of all your artful wiles, please say my name before you eat me up." As the fox's mouth opened to pronounce the word "partridge", the partridge flew out and escaped. The fox said sadly, "Woe is me, what need was there for me to speak?" The partridge likewise said, "Woe is me, what reason was there for me to close my eyes, when I wasn't even sleepy?"

◆ For people who speak when there is no reason to do so and who go to sleep when they should be on their guard. ◆

160. 狐狸和鷓鴣

鷓鴣在高高的樹枝上歇息，狐狸看見了，走上前來對她說：「看，你多美啊；多麼紅的腿啊！還有你的嘴巴就像珊瑚一樣！不過，我敢說，你睡覺的時候肯定更漂亮。」鷓鴣信以為真，就閉上了雙眼，說時遲那時快，狐狸一下子就抓住了她。鷓鴣用悲慘的聲音對狐狸說：「求你在吃掉我之前，先叫一下我的名字吧。」狐狸剛開口，鷓鴣立馬抓住機會，飛出來逃走了。狐狸歎氣道：「唉！我剛才幹嗎要開口說話呢？」鷓鴣同樣也說道：「唉！我剛才明明沒睡覺，為什麼要閉上眼睛呢？」

◆ 這個故事是要告誡那些在不該說話的時候說話的人，和在本該提高警惕的時候卻鬆懈偷懶的人。 ◆

Townsend 135 = Perry 22

161. The Fox and the Woodcutter

A Fox, running before the hounds, came across a Woodcutter felling an oak and begged him to show him a safe hiding-place. The Woodcutter advised him to take shelter in his own hut, so the Fox crept in and hid himself in a corner.

The huntsman soon came up with his hounds and inquired of the Woodcutter if he had seen the Fox. He declared that he had not seen him, and yet pointed, all the time he was speaking, to the hut where the Fox lay hidden. The huntsman took no notice of the signs, but believing his word, hastened forward in the chase.

As soon as they were well away, the Fox departed without taking any notice of the Woodcutter: whereon he called to him and reproached him, saying,"You ungrateful fellow, you owe your life to me, and yet you leave me without a word of thanks. " The Fox replied,"Indeed, I should have thanked you fervently if your deeds had been as good as your words, and if your hands had not been traitors to your speech."

◆　　Conscience is as answerable actions as words.　　◆

161. 狐狸和伐木工

　　一隻被一群獵狗追趕的狐狸，遇到了一個正在砍橡樹的伐木工，便求他給自己一個安全的藏身之處。伐木工建議狐狸去自己住的小屋躲一下，於是狐狸鑽了進去，躲在角落裡。

　　很快獵人就帶著獵狗趕到這裡，問伐木工有沒有見到一隻狐狸。雖然伐木工嘴上一直說自己沒見過，手卻指著狐狸藏身的小屋,可是獵人相信了伐木工的話,並沒有注意到他的手勢,急急忙忙地繼續追趕。

等獵人一夥兒走遠,狐狸便離開這裡,什麼話也沒跟伐木工說。為此伐木工叫住了狐狸,並責備道:「你這個忘恩負義的傢伙,我救了你一命,可你卻連聲謝謝都沒說就走了。」狐狸回答說:「是啊,如果你言行一致,如果你的手勢沒有背叛你的言語,那我是應該由衷地謝謝你。」

◆ 真正有正義感的人應當言行一致。 ◆

Townsend 172 = Perry 256

162. The Hares and the Foxes

The Hares waged war with the Eagles, and called upon the Foxes to help them. They replied, "We would willingly have helped you, if we had not known who you were, and with whom you were fighting."

◆ Count the cost before you commit yourselves. ◆

162. 野兔和狐狸

野兔和老鷹之間爆發了戰爭,號召狐狸前來助陣。狐狸回答說:「假如我們不清楚你們是誰,又不知道你們跟誰打起來了,我們一定很願意出手相助。」

◆ 承諾之前,務必弄清楚需要付出多少。 ◆

Townsend 258 = Perry 126

163. The Jackdaw and the Fox

A half-famished Jackdaw seated himself on a fig-tree, which had produced some fruit entirely out of season, and waited in the hope that the figs would ripen. A Fox seeing him sitting so long and learning the reason of his doing so, said to him, "You are indeed, sir, sadly deceiving yourself; you are indulging a hope strong enough to cheat you, but which will never reward you with enjoyment."

♦ Don't deceive yourself. ♦

163. 寒鴉和狐狸

有隻餓得奄奄一息的寒鴉，站在一棵無花果樹上。此時，早已經過了果子豐收的時令，樹上只留著幾個果子。寒鴉抱著無花果可以成熟的希望在那兒等待。一隻狐狸看他久久地站在那兒，問清原委之後，狐狸對寒鴉說：「先生，你這無疑是自欺欺人，真可憐；你滿懷著強烈的希望來欺騙自己，然而回報你的，決不是快樂。」

♦ 不要自欺欺人。 ♦

Townsend 141 = Perry 147

164. The Lion, the Bear, and the Fox

A Lion and a Bear seized a Kid at the same moment, and fought fiercely for its possession. When they had fearfully lacerated each other and were faint from the long combat, they lay down exhausted with fatigue.

A Fox, who had gone round them at a distance several times, saw them both stretched on the ground with the Kid lying untouched in the middle. He ran in between them, and seizing the Kid scampered off as fast as he could. The Lion and the Bear saw him, but not being able to get up, said,"Woe be to us, that we should have fought and belabored ourselves only to serve the turn of a Fox."

♦　　It sometimes happens that one man has all the toil, and another all the profit.　　♦

164. 獅子、熊和狐狸

獅子和熊同時抓住了一隻小羔羊，他們倆為了爭奪小羊激烈地打鬥起來。他們狠撕猛咬對方，經過一場苦鬥之後，有氣無力地躺在地上。

一隻狐狸早已在遠處繞著他們轉了好幾圈了，看到他們都直挺挺地躺在地上，那隻小羔羊躺在他們中間沒人碰。於是，狐狸跑到他們兩個中間，抓住小羔羊飛奔而去。獅子和熊雖然看見了他，可是卻站不起來了，只好說道：「我們都錯了，我們鬥得你死我活，卻便宜了狐狸。」

♦　　有時候，一人全盡其勞，他人盡得其利。　　♦

Townsend 273 = Perry 394

165. The Lion and the Fox

A Fox entered into partnership with a Lion on the pretense

of becoming his servant. Each undertook his proper duty in accordance with his own nature and powers. The Fox discovered and pointed out the prey; the Lion sprang on it and seized it. The Fox soon became jealous of the Lion carrying off the Lion's share, and said that he would no longer find out the prey, but would capture it on his own account. The next day he attempted to snatch a lamb from the fold, but he himself fell prey to the huntsmen and hounds.

♦ Don't attempt more than you can handle. ♦

165. 獅子和狐狸

一隻狐狸和一隻獅子同行，狐狸謊稱要做獅子的僕人。他們根據自己的天性和能力，各擔其職。狐狸發現並指出獵物；獅子撲上去抓獵物。狐狸見獅子拿走了自己的那份食物，便嫉妒起來，於是說自己不再願意搜尋獵物了，只願去捕捉獵物。第二天，他到羊圈裡去抓一隻羔羊，但是他自己卻成了獵人和獵狗的獵物。

♦ 不要奢求自己得不到的。 ♦

Townsend 160 = Perry 149

166. The Lion, the Fox, and the Ass

The Lion, the Fox and the Ass entered into an agreement to assist each other in the chase. Having secured a large booty, the Lion on their return from the forest asked the Ass to allot his due portion to each of the three partners in the treaty. The

Ass carefully divided the spoil into three equal shares and modestly requested the two others to make the first choice. The Lion, bursting out into a great rage, devoured the Ass. Then he requested the Fox to do him the favor to make a division. The Fox accumulated all that they had killed into one large heap and left to himself the smallest possible morsel. The Lion said,"Who has taught you, my very excellent fellow, the art of division? You are perfect to a fraction."He replied,"I learned it from the Ass, by witnessing his fate."

♦ Happy is the man who learns from the misfortunes of others. ♦

166. 獅子、狐狸和驢

獅子、狐狸和驢達成合約,在狩獵時要相互幫助。他們抓到了一個大獵物,從森林回來後,獅子對驢說要分給他三份中應得的一份。驢很小心地把獵物平分成三份,並且很謙讓,請獅子和狐狸先來挑。獅子勃然大怒,吞掉了驢。隨後,他請狐狸來幫忙分配一下。狐狸把全部的獵物堆在一起,只給自己留了極少的一小口。

獅子說道:「這種分配的技術方式是誰教你的,我的好夥伴?」狐狸答道:「我親眼目睹了驢的命運,從他那裡學來的。」

♦ 從別人的不幸中吸取教訓的,才是幸福的人。 ♦

Townsend 235 = Perry 289

167. The Quack Frog

A Frog once upon a time came forth from his home in the

marsh and proclaimed to all the beasts that he was a learned physician, skilled in the use of drugs and able to heal all diseases. A Fox asked him, "How can you pretend to prescribe for others, when you are unable to heal your own lame gait and wrinkled skin?"

♦ Boastful claims end up exposing themselves. ♦

167. 青蛙庸醫

以前，有一隻青蛙住在沼澤地裡。有一天他從家裡出來，大聲地向所有的動物宣佈：「我是一個博學多才、醫術高明的醫生，包治百病。」一隻狐狸問他：「你連自己的腿痛皮皺都治不好，怎麼還可以吹噓能給別人治百病呢？」

♦ 誇大其談會暴露自己的弱點。 ♦

Townsend 39 = Perry 142

168. The Sick Lion

A Lion, unable from old age and infirmities to provide himself with food by force, resolved to do so by artifice. He returned to his den, and lying down there, pretended to be sick, taking care that his sickness should be publicly known. The beasts expressed their sorrow, and came one by one to his den, where the Lion devoured them.

After many of the beasts had thus disappeared, the Fox discovered the trick and presenting himself to the Lion, stood on the outside of the cave, at a respectful distance, and asked him how he was. "I am very middling," replied the Lion, "but why do you stand without? Pray enter within to talk with me." "No, thank you," said the Fox. "I notice that there are many prints of feet entering your cave, but I see no trace of any returning."

♦   He is wise who is warned by the misfortunes of others.   ♦

168. 生病的獅子

　　一隻年老多病的獅子，已經不能靠自己的力量捕獲獵物了，於是他想出了一個狡詐的方法。他回到洞穴裡，躺下裝病，並且設法讓大家都知道他病倒了。動物們對此都很難過，大家都很擔心他，於是一個接一個進到洞裡去看望獅子，結果沒有一隻活著出來，他們全被獅子吃掉了。

　　在很多動物都失蹤了以後，狐狸終於看出了獅子的詭計。他也前去看望獅子，但是只站在洞口並沒有進去，他恭敬地與獅子保持著適當的距離，詢問獅子病情是否好轉。「還過得去吧！」獅子應答說，「但是為什麼你要站在外面呢？請進來和我說說話吧。」、「謝謝您的美意，我看我還是不進去了。我注意到在您洞口有很多腳印，但都是走向洞裡的，而沒有看到有一個是出來的。」

♦   智者懂得借鑒他人的不幸。   ♦

Townsend 134 = Perry 24

169. The Swollen Fox

A very hungry Fox, seeing some bread and meat left by shepherds in the hollow of an oak, crept into the hole and made

FOX 狐狸

a hearty meal. When he finished, he was so full that he was not able to get out, and began to groan and lament his fate. Another Fox passing by heard his cries, and coming up, inquired the cause of his complaining. On learning what had happened, he said to him,"Ah, you will have to remain there, my friend, until you become such as you were when you crept in, and then you will easily get out."

♦　　　　　　　Don't be greedy.　　　　　　　♦

169. 發胖的狐狸

一隻饑腸轆轆的狐狸，看到一棵橡樹洞裡，有牧羊人留下來的麵包和肉，於是他就躡手躡腳地爬進狹小的樹洞裡，美美地飽餐了一頓。可是，當他風捲殘雲般地把所有的美味佳餚一掃而光後，才發現自己的肚皮已經圓滾滾的了，想要出去根本就不可能了。狐狸不由得嚎啕大哭，抱怨著自己悲慘的遭遇。另一隻狐狸路過這裡，聽到了他的哭聲，於是便上前打聽到底是怎麼回事。當瞭解了事情的前因後果後，他笑著對洞裡的同胞說：「老弟，只要你恢復到原來的體形，就能輕而易舉地逃出來了。」

♦　　　　　　　不能貪婪。　　　　　　　♦

Townsend 188 = Perry 344

170. The Wolf and the Fox

At one time a very large and strong Wolf was born among the wolves, who exceeded all his fellow-wolves in strength, size, and swiftness, so that they unanimously decided to call him "Lion."

The Wolf, with a lack of sense proportioned to his enormous size, thought that they gave him this name in earnest, and, leaving his own race, consorted exclusively with the lions. An old sly Fox, seeing this, said, "May I never make myself so ridiculous as you do in your pride and self-conceit; for even though you have the size of a lion among wolves, in a herd of lions you are definitely a wolf."

◆　　　　　Know yourself and your limits.　　　　　◆

170. 狼和狐狸

　　狼群裡曾經出現了一隻強大兇猛的狼，無論在力量、體型還是速度上，他都遠遠勝於狼群中其他的狼，可以稱得上是狼群中的霸主，於是群狼一致決定稱他為「獅子」。但是這隻狼的判斷力卻與他那魁梧的體型不相稱。他以為這個稱呼是名副其實的，於是便離開自己的同類，終日混跡於獅群當中。一隻老奸巨猾的狐狸看到了，就對他說：「希望我永遠都不會變得像你一樣，由於太過驕傲自大，而把自己搞得滑稽可笑；因為即使在狼群裡你像獅子一樣高大魁梧；但是在獅群裡，你仍然還是一隻渺小的狼。」

◆　　　　　　　要有自知之明。　　　　　　　◆

FOX 狐狸

11.
FROGS
青蛙

FROGS 青蛙

Townsend 52

171. The Boys and the Frogs

Some boys, playing near a pond, saw a number of Frogs in the water and began to pelt them with stones. They killed several of them, when one of the Frogs, lifting his head out of the water, cried out,"Pray stop, my boys: what is sport to you, is death to us."

♦　　One man's pleasure may be another's pain.　　♦

171. 男孩和青蛙

幾個小男孩在池塘旁邊玩耍，看見有幾隻青蛙在水裡，就用石頭去砸青蛙。他們一口氣砸死了數隻青蛙，此時，有只青蛙從水裡面鑽出頭來，朝他們喊著：「停下吧，孩子們！你們的遊戲能使我們喪命！」

♦　　一個人的快樂，也許就是別人的痛苦。　　♦

Townsend 51 = Perry 44

172. The Frogs Asking for a King

The Frogs, grieved at having no established Ruler, sent ambassadors to Jupiter entreating for a King. Perceiving their simplicity, he cast down a huge log into the lake. The Frogs were terrified at the splash occasioned by its fall and hid themselves in the depths of the pool. But as soon as they realized that the huge log was motionless, they swam again to the top of the water, dismissed their fears, climbed up, and began squatting on it in contempt.

After some time they began to think themselves ill-treated in the appointment of so inert a Ruler, and sent a second deputation to Jupiter to pray that he would set over them another sovereign. He then gave them an Eel to govern them. When the Frogs discovered his easy good nature, they sent yet a third time to Jupiter to beg him to choose for them still another King. Jupiter, displeased with all their complaints, sent a Heron, who preyed upon the Frogs day by day till there were none left to croak upon the lake.

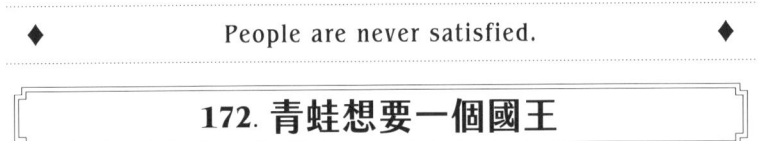

♦　　　　　People are never satisfied.　　　　　♦

172. 青蛙想要一個國王

青蛙為沒有領導者而苦惱，就讓使者去請求朱比特賜予他們一個國王。朱比特考慮到青蛙頭腦簡單，就往湖裡投了一大截木頭來唬弄他們。木頭掉到水裡時濺起的水花把青蛙們嚇了一跳，他們紛紛隱藏到池塘深處。不久，他們就意識到大木頭是靜止不動的，於是就放開膽子浮到水面上，大搖大擺地爬到木頭上了。

一段時間之後，青蛙開始對這個愚鈍的國王不滿了，覺得他們受到了朱比特的捉弄，於是再次派出使者去請求朱比特給他們換一個統治者。於是，朱比特就讓一條鰻魚去統治他們。青蛙發現朱比特好說話，就第三次派出使者，請求朱比特再給他們換一個統治者。青蛙的這些抱怨，使朱比特極為不滿，他派了一隻鷺鷥去當青蛙的國王。鷺鷥每天都捕食青蛙，到最後池塘邊再也沒有他們呱呱的叫聲了。

♦　　　　　★人們總是不滿足。　　　　　♦

FROGS 青蛙

Townsend 139 = Perry 43

173. The Frogs and the Well

Two Frogs lived together in a marsh. But one hot summer the marsh dried up, and they left it to look for another place to live in: for frogs like damp places if they can get them. By and by they came to a deep well, and one of them looked down into it, and said to the other,"This looks a nice cool place. Let us jump in and settle here."But the other, who had a wiser head on his shoulders, replied,"Not so fast, my friend. Supposing this well dried up like the marsh, how should we get out again?"

♦　　　　　Look before you leap.　　　　　♦

173. 青蛙和井

兩隻青蛙一起住在沼澤裡。在一個天氣異常炎熱的夏天，沼澤乾涸了，青蛙只得離開沼澤去尋找其他住的地方，因為青蛙喜歡待在潮濕的地方。他們找啊找啊，最後來到一口深井跟前，其中一隻青蛙往井下望瞭望，對另一隻青蛙說道：「這看起來是個陰涼的好地方，不如我們就跳進去，在這兒安家吧！」另一隻頭腦比較靈活的青蛙回答說：「別著急，朋友，如果這口井跟那個沼澤一樣乾涸了，我們應該怎麼爬出來呢？」

♦　　　　　三思而後行。　　　　　♦

Townsend 187 = Perry 69

174. The Two Frogs

Two Frogs were neighbors. One inhabited a deep pond, far

removed from public view; the other lived in a gully containing little water, and traversed by a country road. The Frog that lived in the pond warned his friend to change his residence and entreated him to come and live with him, saying that he would enjoy greater safety from danger and more abundant food. The other refused, saying that he felt it so very hard to leave a place to which he had become accustomed. A few days afterwards a heavy wagon passed through the gully and crushed him to death under its wheels.

◆ A willful man will have his way to his own hurt. ◆

174. 兩隻青蛙

兩隻青蛙比鄰而居，其中一隻住在很難被人發現的深水塘裡，而另一隻則住在橫穿鄉村小路的淺水溝裡。住在池塘裡的青蛙，好心地勸告住在水溝裡的朋友，要他換個地方住，而且表示希望他能搬來和自己一起住，因為深水塘更安全，食物也更豐富。但是另一隻青蛙拒絕了他的好意，說要他下決心離開住慣了的地方是很困難的。就在幾天之後，一輛沉重的馬車經過水溝，它的車輪無情地把這隻固執的青蛙輾死了。

◆ 固執己見，到頭來只能是自作自受。 ◆

Townsend 312 = Perry 314

175. The Frogs' Complaint Against the Sun

Once upon a time, when the Sun announced his intention to take a wife, the Frogs lifted up their voices in clamor to the sky. Jupiter, disturbed by the noise of their croaking, inquired the cause of their complaint. One of them said,"The Sun, now while he is single, parches up the marsh, and compels us to die miserably in our arid homes. What will be our future condition if he should beget other suns?"

♦   Watch the actions of your enemy.   ♦

175. 青蛙抱怨太陽

有一次,太陽宣佈打算娶個妻子。青蛙聽了以後,扯著嗓子對著天空呱呱地大聲叫。青蛙的叫聲驚擾了朱比特,朱比特詢問他們為何抱怨不迭。其中一隻青蛙回答說:「僅僅有一個太陽,就把我們的沼澤曬乾了,害得我們在乾旱的大地上悲慘地死去。如果他以後生養幾個小太陽,將來我們還能生存下去嗎?」

♦   要注意敵人的一舉一動。   ♦

Chambry 201 = Perry 141

176. The Lion and the Frog

A lion heard a frog croaking loudly and turned towards the sound, thinking that this must be the sound of some huge beast. After a while, the lion saw the frog come up out of the swamp. He went over to the frog and as he crushed him underfoot, the lion said,"No one should be worried about a sound before the thing itself has been examined."

♦   This fable is for a man with a big mouth who talks   ♦
         and talks without accomplishing anything.

176. 獅子和青蛙

青蛙呱呱地叫著，聲音大得引起了獅子的注意。獅子想能發出這聲音的，肯定是某種龐然大物，於是，他就在邊上等了一會兒，卻只看到青蛙從沼澤裡爬出來。獅子走了過去，踩死了青蛙，說道：「在還沒有看到他的真面目之前，我們不該被他的聲音嚇倒。」

♦　　　　**有些人也和青蛙一樣，只會虛張聲勢。**　　　　♦

Townsend 177 = Perry 376

177. The Ox and the Frog

An Ox drinking at a pool trod on a brood of young frogs and crushed one of them to death. The Mother coming up, and missing one of her sons, inquired of his brothers what had become of him. "He is dead, dear Mother; for just now a very huge beast with four great feet came to the pool and crushed him to death with his cloven heel."

The Frog, puffing herself out, inquired, "if the beast was as big as that in size."

"Cease, Mother, to puff yourself out," said her son, "and do not be angry; for you would, I assure you, sooner burst than successfully imitate the hugeness of that monster."

♦　　　　Conceit may lead to self-destruction.　　　　♦

FROGS 青蛙

177. 牛和青蛙

　　一頭在水塘邊飲水的牛，踩到了一窩小青蛙，並且踩死了其中一隻。青蛙媽媽來了，發現她的一個孩子不見了，就問小青蛙的兄弟，那個孩子發生了什麼事情。「他死了，親愛的媽媽，因為剛才一個長著四個大蹄子的巨獸，來到水塘邊，用後蹄踩死了他。」

　　青蛙媽媽鼓起肚子，問道：「那動物，是不是像這麼大個兒。」

　　「媽媽，別再鼓氣了，」她的兒子說，「別生氣。因為我敢肯定，你還沒模仿成那怪物的塊頭，自己就先脹破了。」

◆　　　　　　　**自負會毀了自己。**　　　　　　　◆

12.
GOAT
山羊

Townsend 37 = Perry 280

178. The Goat and the Goatherd

A Goatherd had sought to bring back a stray goat to his flock. He whistled and sounded his horn in vain; the straggler paid no attention to the summons. At last the Goatherd threw a stone, and breaking its horn, begged the Goat not to tell his master. The Goat replied,"Why, you silly fellow, the horn will speak though I be silent."

♦　　Do not attempt to hide things which cannot be hid.　　♦

178. 山羊和牧羊人

牧羊人想把一隻走丟的山羊叫回羊群裡，他又是打口哨，又是吹號角，但都是徒勞。走失的山羊對此毫不理會。最後，牧羊人撿起一塊石頭朝山羊扔去，沒想到一下子把羊角打斷了。牧羊人祈求山羊別告訴他的主人這件事，山羊回答道：「愚蠢的人，即使我保持沉默，羊角也會開口說話的。」

♦　　不要試圖去隱藏根本無法掩蓋的東西。　　♦

Townsend 58 = Perry 6

179. The Goatherd and the Wild Goats

A Goatherd, driving his flock from their pasture at eventide, found some Wild Goats mingled among them, and shut them up together with his own for the night. The next day it snowed very hard, so that he could not take the herd to their usual feeding places, but was obliged to keep them in the fold. He gave his own goats just sufficient food to keep them alive, but fed the strangers more abundantly in the hope of enticing them to stay with him and of making them his own.

When the thaw set in, he led them all out to feed, and the Wild Goats scampered away as fast as they could to the mountains. The Goatherd scolded them for their ingratitude in leaving him, when during the storm he had taken more care of them than of his own herd. One of them, turning about, said to him," That is the very reason why we are so cautious; for if you yesterday treated us better than the Goats you have had so long, it is plain also that if others came after us, you would in the same manner prefer them to ourselves."

◆　　Old friends cannot with impunity be sacrificed for new ones.　　◆

179. 牧羊人和野山羊

薄暮時分，牧羊人驅趕著羊群離開牧場，發現羊群裡混進了幾頭野山羊，就把牠們跟自己的羊一塊關到了羊圈裡。次日，大雪紛紛揚揚，牧羊人不能把羊帶到平日去的草地吃草了，只能把牠們關在羊圈裡。牧羊人僅給自己的羊少量的飼料，讓牠們能維持生命就可以了；但他對那幾頭野山羊卻十分慷慨，給牠們足夠的飼料，讓牠們吃得飽飽的，以便留住牠們，歸自己所有。

天氣變暖之後，牧羊人驅趕著所有的羊去草地上吃草，野山羊借機以最快的速度逃到山裡去了。牧羊人譴責野山羊不知心存感激，暴風雪來臨時自己照料牠們，比照顧自己的羊還要盡心，如今牠們卻離他而去。

一隻野山羊轉過身來對牧羊人說:「這恰恰是我們小心翼翼的原因。那些羊很早就和你在一起了,可是你對待我們比對牠們還要好,假如以後再來了其他的羊,你必然就偏愛新來的羊,把我們撇在一旁。」

◆　　　　**喜新厭舊的人必然會遭到懲罰。**　　　　◆

Townsend 281 = Perry 516

180. The She-Goats and Their Beards

The She-Goats having obtained a beard by request to Jupiter, the He-Goats were sorely displeased and made complaint that the females equaled them in dignity. "Allow them," said Jupiter, "to enjoy an empty honor and to assume the badge of your nobler sex, so long as they are not your equals in strength or courage."

◆　　It matters little if those who are inferior to us in merit should be like us in outside appearances.　　◆

180. 母山羊和鬍子

母山羊請求朱比特也讓她們長鬍子,朱比特答應了。公山羊對此感到非常不滿,向朱比特抱怨母山羊和他們同等高貴。朱比特安撫地說:「就讓她們擁有代表男性高貴身份的標誌好了,讓她們因此虛榮吧!但是她們的力量和勇氣不可能與你們抗衡。」

◆　　　**不要在乎比我們弱小的人在外表上模仿我們。**　　　◆

Townsend 76 = Perry 98

181. The Wolf and the Kid

A Kid was perched up on the top of a house, and looking down saw a Wolf passing under him. Immediately he began to revile and attack his enemy. "Murderer and thief," he cried, "what do you here near honest folks' houses? How dare you make an appearance where your vile deeds are known?"

"Curse away, my young friend," said the Wolf.

♦ It is easy to be brave from a safe distance. ♦

181. 狼和小羊

一隻小羊爬到了屋頂上,他看到有一隻狼從下面經過,馬上破口大罵,用言語來攻擊他的敵人。「你這個兇手、盜賊,」他歇斯底里地喊著,「你到老實人家旁邊幹什麼?有誰不知道你喪盡天良,你居然還有膽子露面?」

「你想罵,就使勁地罵吧!我年輕的朋友。」狼說。

♦ 在明明知道沒有危險的境地,顯示勇敢是件很容易的事。 ♦

GOAT 山羊

13.
GODS
眾神

GODS 眾神

Chambry 291 = Perry 198

182. Apollo and the Snake

A creeping snake who had been stepped on by many people made his way to the temple of Apollo and went inside. Apollo immediately explained to the snake, "If you had simply killed the first person who stepped on you, no one would ever have dared to step on you again!"

◆ The story shows that if people who have previously committed a crime are swiftly punished, then others will become afraid on their account. ◆

182. 阿波羅和蛇

蛇遭受了許多人的踩踏。於是，他一路爬到了阿波羅的神殿，抱怨他所遭受的不公的待遇。阿波羅回答道：「如果當初你把第一個踩你的人殺了，誰還敢再踩你呢？」

◆ 如果罪犯都能及時受到懲罰，別人就不敢輕易犯罪。 ◆

Jacobs 54 = Perry 580

183. Avaricious and Envious

Two neighbours came before Jupiter and prayed him to grant their hearts' desire. Now the one was full of avarice, and the other eaten up with envy. So to punish them both, Jupiter granted that each might have whatever he wished for himself, but only on condition that his neighbour had twice as much. The

Avaricious man prayed to have a room full of gold. No sooner said than done; but all his joy was turned to grief when he found that his neighbour had two rooms full of the precious metal. Then came the turn of the Envious man, who could not bear to think that his neighbour had any joy at all. So he prayed that he might have one of his own eyes put out, by which means his companion would become totally blind.

◆　　　　Vices are their own punishment.　　　　◆

183. 貪婪和嫉妒

互為鄰居的兩個人，其中一個貪婪無比，另一個被嫉妒心所吞噬。這兩人都祈求朱比特滿足他們的願望。為了使他們得到懲罰，朱比特答應了他們的請求，唯一的要求是，不管他們希望得到什麼，他的鄰居都能得到他的雙倍。貪婪的人請求神賜予他整整一屋子的黃金，神立刻如數賜給他金子，但是當他發現他的鄰居居然為此獲得了滿滿兩屋子黃金的時候，全部的喜悅都變成了傷悲。

接下來是愛嫉妒的人，他完全不能忍受鄰居有任何的快樂，於是就請求神弄瞎自己的一隻眼睛，如此一來，他的鄰居就雙目失明了。

◆　　　　這就是惡有惡報。　　　　◆

Townsend 121 = Perry 163

184. The Bee and Jupiter

A Bee from Mount Hymettus, the queen of the hive,

ascended to Olympus to present Jupiter some honey fresh from her combs. Jupiter, delighted with the offering of honey, promised to give whatever she should ask. She therefore besought him, saying, "Give me, I pray thee, a sting, that if any mortal shall approach to take my honey, I may kill him." Jupiter was much displeased, for he loved the race of man, but could not refuse the request because of his promise. He thus answered the Bee, "You shall have your request, but it will be at the peril of your own life. For if you use your sting, it shall remain in the wound you make, and then you will die from the loss of it."

♦　　　Evil wishes, like chickens, come home to root.　　　♦

184. 蜜蜂和朱比特

一隻蜂王從伊米托斯山飛到奧林匹斯山，向朱比特神獻上從蜂房採來的新鮮蜂蜜。朱比特看見貢品很開心，就向蜂王承諾，不管她提出何種願望，都能夠得到滿足。於是，蜂王就懇求說：「神啊，請你賜予我一根能螫人的刺，假如有人膽敢走近我的蜂房，把我的蜂蜜拿走，我就要把他殺掉。」愛護人類的朱比特聞得這番話很不愉快，但是他已經承諾過了，不好回絕蜂王的要求，於是就回答說：「你能夠得到你想要的刺，但是得用你自己的生命來承擔這個後果。一旦你拿刺螫人，刺就會殘留在被螫人的傷口裡面，而你失去了刺，就會死去。」

♦　　　心懷不善的人最終會自食惡果。　　　♦

Townsend 302 = Perry 117

185. The Camel and Jupiter

The Camel, when he saw the Bull adorned with horns, envied him and wished that he himself could obtain the same honors. He went to Jupiter, and besought him to give him horns. Jupiter, vexed at his request because he was not satisfied with his size and strength of body, and desired yet more, not only refused to give him horns, but even deprived him of a portion of his ears.

◆　The Gods will deal with those who do not honor them.　◆

185. 駱駝和朱比特

駱駝看見公牛有著漂亮的牛角作裝飾，非常羨慕，希望自己也能夠獲得一樣的角。他來到朱比特面前，懇求他賜給自己一對角。朱比特對駱駝的請求大為惱火，因為駱駝不滿足於自己的身形和力量，還想得到更多的東西，於是不僅拒絕給駱駝一對角，更把他的耳朵削去了一部分。

◆　老天會懲罰那些不尊重他的人。　◆

Townsend 247 = Perry 274

186. The Goods and the Ills

All the Goods were once driven out by the Ills from that common share which they each had in the affairs of mankind; for the Ills by reason of their numbers had prevailed to possess the earth. The Goods wafted themselves to heaven and asked for a righteous vengeance on their persecutors. They entreated Jupiter that they might no longer be associated with the Ills, as they had nothing in common and could not live together, but were engaged in unceasing warfare; and that an indissoluble law might be laid down for their future protection.

Jupiter granted their request and decreed that henceforth the Ills should visit the earth in company with each other, but that the Goods should one by one enter the habitations of men. Hence it arises that Ills abound, for they come not one by one, but in troops, and by no means singly: while the Goods proceed from Jupiter, and are given, not alike to all, but singly, and separately; and one by one to those who are able to discern them.

◆　　　Vices are their own punishment.　　　◆

186. 好事和壞事

世界上壞事比好事的數量多，壞事憑著勢力大，把全部的好事都從人間趕走了。好事升上了天堂，懇求朱比特神給他們公正還擊的權利。他們保證從今以後再不與壞事為伍，因為他們之間毫無共通之處，如同水火不相容，因此不能再待在一起；還懇求朱比特制定具有約束力的法律，保護他們將來不再被壞事壓迫。

朱比特答應了他們的要求，下令說從今以後，世間壞事必須成群而至，而好事則是一個接一個單獨降臨人間。從那以後，人間一直都是禍不單行，壞事接連而至，因為壞事必須成群結隊，絕不可以單獨行動；好事是由朱比特一件一件地單獨賜給人類，而不是一下子送出，並且只有那些能夠分辨是非的人，才能夠獲得這份恩賜。

◆　　　　　　惡有惡報。　　　　　　◆

Chambry 129 = Perry 316

187. Hercules and Pallas

Hercules, once journeying along a narrow roadway, came across a strange-looking animal that reared its head and threatened him. Nothing daunted, the hero gave him a few lusty blows with his club, and thought to have gone on his way. The monster, however, much to the astonishment of Hercules, was now three times as big as it was before, and of a still more threatening aspect. He thereupon redoubled his blows and laid about him fast and furiously; but the harder and quicker the strokes of the club, the bigger and more frightful grew the monster, and now completely filled up the road. Pallas then appeared upon the scene. "Stop, Hercules," said she. "Cease your blows. The monster's name is Strife. Let it alone, and it will soon become as little as it was at first."

♦   Strife feeds on conflict.   ♦

187. 赫拉克勒斯和帕拉斯

曾經有一次，大力神赫拉克勒斯在一條很狹窄的小路上走著，突然發現有一隻怪物站在對面，高昂著頭，想向自己發起進攻。英雄毫無懼色，抓起棒子奮力地朝怪物打過去，打算把它趕走，好繼續前進；不料，那怪物的身體居然馬上比之前增大了兩倍，模樣也更加恐怖。赫拉克勒斯驚訝之餘，掄起棒子再打，他使出的力氣大出一倍，棒子好似雨點般劇烈地落到那怪物身上。然而棒子打得越快越狠，怪物就變得越大越恐怖。最終，怪物巨大的身體堵住了整條路。就在此刻，智神帕拉斯降臨了，他對赫拉克勒斯說：「停下吧！赫拉克勒斯，不要再打了。這怪物就叫做衝突，隨它去吧！不理睬它，它一會兒就變得像先前那樣小了。」

♦ 　　　　　　爭執是衝突的溫床。　　　　　　♦

Chambry 130 = Perry 111

188. Hercules and Plutus

Thanks to his excellent qualities, Hercules was received into heaven. He saluted the gods who came to congratulate him one after another, but when he was approached by Plutus, the god of wealth and the son of Fortune, Hercules turned his eyes aside. Father Jupiter asked him why he did this. Hercules answered, "I hate the god of riches: he is a friend to the wicked who corrupts the entire world by throwing his money around!"

♦ 　Riches are justly hated by courageous people:
coffers of cash put a stop to honest traffic in praise.　♦

188. 赫拉克勒斯和普魯托斯

赫拉克勒斯由於其出色的德行，而成為天宮的一員。眾神紛紛前來向他祝賀，但是，當財神和命運之子普魯托斯走上前來向他祝賀的時候，赫拉克勒斯卻對他愛搭不理。朱比特問他為什麼這樣做。他回答道：「我討厭財富之神，就因為他四處散財，整個世界才墮落的！」

♦ 　有勇氣之人有很好的理由厭惡財富：存放現金的保
　險箱不會得到真心的讚美。　♦

Townsend 12 = Perry 291

189. Hercules and the Wagoner

A Carter was driving a wagon along a country lane, when the wheels sank down deep into a rut. The rustic driver, stupefied and aghast, stood looking at the wagon, and did nothing but utter loud cries to Hercules to come and help him. Hercules, it is said, appeared and thus addressed him,"Put your shoulders to the wheels, my man. Goad on your bullocks, and never more pray to me for help, until you have done your best to help yourself, or depend upon it you will henceforth pray in vain."

◆　　　　Self-help is the best help.　　　　◆

189. 赫拉克勒斯和馬車夫

車夫趕著四輪馬車走在鄉間小路上，車輪突然陷進了一道深溝之中，笨手笨腳的車夫被眼前的情況驚得呆若木雞，他站在原地看著馬車，手足無措地高聲向大力神赫拉克勒斯求助。據傳說，赫拉克勒斯在馬車夫跟前出現了，對他說：「老兄，拿自己的肩膀扛住輪子，用鞭子去趕馬；要是你還沒有用盡全力幫助你自己，就先別向我尋求援助；如果單單靠祈禱，你會一無所獲。」

◆　　　　最好的幫助就是自助。　　　　◆

Chambry 109 = Perry 102

190. Hermes and the Earth

When Zeus had fashioned man and woman, he ordered

Hermes to take them to Gaia, the Earth, and to show them how to obtain food by digging in the ground. At first, the Earth refused to cooperate in Hermes' mission. Hermes then compelled her, saying that Zeus had ordered her to do so. Earth replied,"Then let them dig as much as they like, but they will pay for it with groans and tears!"

♦ This fable is suitable for those people who casually take out loans but who then find it difficult to pay them back. ♦

190. 赫爾墨斯和大地之神

在人類被創造出來之後,赫爾墨斯奉宙斯之命,帶著他們去見大地之神蓋亞,好教他們如何種地以獲得食物。起初,大地之神拒絕了赫爾墨斯的請求。無奈之下,赫爾墨斯只得告訴她,這是宙斯的命令。大地之神答道:「那麼,他們愛挖多少就挖多少吧!不過,他們要用他們的呻吟和眼淚來償還!」

♦ 有些人草率地借了款之後卻發現自己很難還清。 ♦

Townsend 149 = Perry 285

191. The Image of Mercury and the Carpenter

A very poor man, a Carpenter by trade, had a wooden image of Mercury, before which he made offerings day by day, and begged the idol to make him rich, but in spite of his entreaties he became poorer and poorer. At last, being very angry, he took his image down from its pedestal and dashed it against the wall.

When its head was knocked off, out came a stream of gold, which the Carpenter quickly picked up and said, "Well, I think thou art altogether contradictory and unreasonable; for when I paid you honor, I reaped no benefits: but now that I maltreat you I am loaded with an abundance of riches."

♦ People expect religion to give them profit. ♦

191. 墨丘利木像和木匠

有個木匠很貧窮,於是雕了一尊墨丘利的木像,每天都獻祭,祈求可以發財,但他卻越來越貧窮。最後,他十分氣憤,把木像從座上拿下來,用力地扔到牆上。木像的頭被摔了下來,中間露出一塊金子。木匠趕緊把金子撿起來,說:「啊!我覺得你什麼事情總是唱反調,真是沒道理可言。對你無比恭敬時,我沒得到任何好處;現在虐待你了,你反倒給了我如此豐厚的錢財。」

♦ 人們總是希望神靈給予他們好處。 ♦

L'Estrange 86 = Perry 36

192. An Imposter to the Oracle

There was a certain bantering droll that took a journey to Delphos, a purpose to try if he could put a trick upon Apollo. He carried a sparrow in his hand under his coat, and told the god, I have somewhat in my hand, says he, is it dead or living? If the oracle should say 'twas dead, he could show it alive; if living, 'twas but squeezing it, and then 'twas dead. Now he that saw the malice of his heart gave him this answer: It shall e'en be which of the two you please; for 'tis in your choice to have it either the one or the other.

◆　　　　　　　Do not mock the gods.　　　　　　　◆

192. 到阿波羅神殿去的騙子

從前，有個愛嘲弄人的小丑出發前往特爾斐，想試試能不能使阿波羅上當。他一手抓了隻麻雀藏在外套下面，對阿波羅說：「我手裡的東西是死的還是活的？」如果阿波羅說它是死的，那他就會拿活的給他看；如果阿波羅說它是活的，那他就會把它捏死。阿波羅看穿了他的險惡用心，於是回答說：「隨你高興了，因為只有你才能決定它是死是活。」

◆　　　　　　　別想唬弄神。　　　　　　　◆

Chambry 119 = Perry 107

193. Jupiter and the Fox

Jupiter had turned the fox into the likeness of a human being and had seated her on the throne as his queen. But when the fox happened to notice Aesops FoHeg a beetle creeping out from its hole, she leaped up and began chasing this familiar object of prey. The gods laughed at the fox as she ran, while the great father of the gods blushed and renounced his relations with the fox. As he chased her out of the chamber, Jupiter said, "Live the life you deserve, since you clearly are not worthy of my favours!"

◆　　　No piece of luck can conceal a depraved nature.　　　◆

193. 朱比特和狐狸

朱比特把狐狸變成人形，並讓她以皇后的身份坐在他旁邊。然而，一看到有隻甲蟲從洞裡爬出來，狐狸就從寶座上跳起來，像平時一樣追趕她的獵物。眾神紛紛取笑狐狸，朱比特也羞愧難耐，當場宣佈斷絕關係。朱比特把狐狸趕出了房間，說：「你顯然不值得我厚愛，既然如此，那就去過你應得的生活吧！」

♦　　　　　**運氣再好也藏不住墮落的本性。**　　　　　♦

L'Estrange 182 = Perry 313

194. Jupiter and Fraud

Jupiter appointed Mercury to make him a composition of fraud and hypocrisy, and to give every artifice his dose on't. The medicine was prepared according to the bill, and the proportions duly observed, and divided: only there was a great deal too much of it made, and the overplus remained still in the mortar. Upon examining the whole account, there was a mistake it seems, in the reck'ning; for the tailors were forgotten in the catalogue: so that Mercury, for brevity sake, gave the tailors the whole quantity that was left; and from hence comes the old saying: There's knavery in all trades, but most in tailors.

♦　　　It is natural to be a knave; men must rise above.　　　♦

194. 朱比特和欺騙

朱比特指定墨丘利為他做一種欺騙和虛偽的混合物，並決定各行各業的劑量。藥根據藥單的要求配製好了，並嚴格按照劑量的要求，分成了好幾份；只是藥做得太多了，剩下的仍然放在研缽裡。仔細想想這整件事，似乎還是有考慮不周的地方，比如把裁縫給漏了。於是，墨丘利為了省事，就把剩下的所有劑量都給了裁縫。從那以後，就有了「無商不奸，裁縫尤甚」這句俗語。

◆　　欺騙是人的本性，但人必須超越這一劣根性。　　◆

L'Estrange 185 = Perry 109

195. Jupiter and Modesty

Man was made in such a hurry (according to the old fable) that Jupiter had forgotten to put modesty into the composition, among his other affections; and finding that there was no way of introducing it afterwards, man by man, he proposed the turning of it loose among the multitude. Modesty took her self at first to be a little hardly dealt withal, but in the end, came over to agree to't, upon condition that carnal love might not be suffered to come into the same company; for wherever that comes, says she, I'm gone.

◆　　Modesty and carnal love cannot survive together.　　◆

195. 朱比特和謙遜

朱比特造人的時候太匆忙了（古老的神話中是這麼寫的），以致在注入其他的情感時，忘了把謙遜一起放進去；後來，朱比特發現不可能向人們一個個地推行謙遜的德行，於是他提議讓謙遜在人們中間自生自滅。起初，謙遜對此還有點遲疑，但到最後，他還是同意了,條件是不與淫樂共存。他說:「淫樂一來,我就離開。」

◆ 謙遜和淫樂無法共存。 ◆

Townsend 252 = Perry 100

196. Jupiter, Neptune, Minerva, and Momus

According to an ancient legend, the first man was made by Jupiter, the first bull by Neptune, and the first house by Minerva. On the completion of their labors, a dispute arose as to which had made the most perfect work. They agreed to appoint Momus as judge, and to abide by his decision.

Momus, however, being very envious of the handicraft of each, found fault with all. He first blamed the work of Neptune because he had not made the horns of the bull below his eyes, so he might better see where to strike. He then condemned the work of Jupiter, because he had not placed the heart of man on the outside, that everyone might read the thoughts of the evil disposed and take precautions against the intended mischief, and, lastly, he inveighed against Minerva because she had not contrived iron wheels in the foundation of her house, so its inhabitants might more easily remove if a neighbor proved unpleasant. Jupiter, indignant at such inveterate faultfinding, drove him from his office of judge, and expelled him from the mansions of Olympus.

◆ Judge honestly or not at all. ◆

196. 朱比特、尼普頓、密涅瓦和莫摩斯

有個古老的傳說,說主神朱比特造了第一個人,海神尼普頓造了第一頭牛,智慧女神密涅瓦造了第一座房子。完工後,他們就產生了爭執,都說自己的活幹得最好。最後,他們同意讓非難之神莫摩斯來當裁判官,並一致服從他的決定。

莫摩斯對這三位神的手藝充滿了妒意,因此挑出了一大堆的缺點和不足。他首先指責海神尼普頓的工作,說他未能讓牛的雙角長在牛眼底下,使牛能夠更方便看清楚往哪兒進攻。接下來,他指責朱比特的工作,說他未能讓人的心長在外面,使人人都能發現惡人的想法,提前預防他的陰謀詭計。然後,他譴責密涅瓦,因為她未能發明出裝在屋腳上的鐵輪子,以便等房主發現鄰居不好相處時,更輕而易舉地搬走。朱比特看他如此吹毛求疵,暴怒之下,就把他從裁判席上攆走,剝奪了他進奧林匹斯聖殿的權利。

◆ 　　　　不誠實的人不配做仲裁者。　　　　◆

L'Estrange 140 = Perry 221

197. Jupiter and a Serpent

Jupiter had presents made him upon his wedding-day, greater, or less, from all living creatures. A serpent brought him a rose in his mouth for an offering. The thing was acceptable enough, but not the presenter; for (says Jupiter) though gifts are welcome to me, of themselves, I must not yet receive any from a serpent.

◆ 　　If you receive a gift you must befriend the giver.　　◆

197. 朱比特和蛇

在朱比特結婚的當天，所有的生物都送上了或大或小的禮物。蛇嘴裡含著一朵玫瑰，作為獻給朱比特的賀禮。禮物是不錯，但送禮的卻不怎麼樣。朱比特說：「雖然我很喜歡這些禮物，但是，我一定不會接受蛇的任何禮物。」

♦　　**如果你接受了禮物，你就要和送禮的人做朋友。**　　♦

L'Estrange 184 = Perry 106

198. Jupiter's Wedding

When the toy had once taken Jupiter in the head to enter into a state of matrimony, he resolved for the honour of his celestial lady, that the whole world should keep a festival upon the day of his marriage, and so invited all living creatures, tag-rag and bob-tail, to the solemnity of his wedding. They all came in very good time, saving only the tortoise. Jupiter told him 'twas ill done to make the company stay, and asked him, Why so late? "Why truly," says the tortoise,"I was at home, at my own house, my dearly beloved house, and home is home, let it be never so homely."Jupiter took it very ill at his hands, that he should think himself better in a ditch, then in a palace, and so he passed this judgment upon him; that since he would not be persuaded to come out of his house upon that occasion, he should never stir abroad again from that day forward, without his house upon his head.

♦　　A beggar may be as proud and as happy in a cottage, as a prince in a palace.　　♦

198. 朱比特的婚禮

有一次,朱比特一時興起決定結婚。為了隆重其事,他決定結婚當天要普天同慶,於是,邀請了所有的生物,三教九流都來參加這場莊嚴的婚禮。除了龜之外,所有的動物都準時到了。朱比特告訴龜說,讓大家等他是很不好的,並問他:「為什麼來得這麼遲?」,「哎呀!」龜說,「我在家呢!在我自己的家,我深愛著的家。金窩銀窩不如自己的狗窩啊!」朱比特聽到這話很不高興,他居然認為待在溝渠裡要比待在皇宮好。於是,他下達了對龜的判決:既然他的婚禮都不能使他離開家,那麼,從那天起,他必須頭頂著房子才能出門。

♦ 住在茅屋裡的乞丐,也許和皇宮裡的王子一樣自豪、幸福。 ♦

L'Estrange 111 = Perry 28

199. Large Promises

There was a poor sick man, that according to the course of the world, when physicians had given him over, betook himself to his prayers, and vowed a sacrifice of a thousand oxen ready down upon the nail, to either Apollo, or Aesculapius, which of the two would deliver him from this disease. Ah my dear, (says his wife) have a care what you promise, for where would you have these oxen if you should recover? Sweet heart (says he) thou talks like a fool. Have the gods nothing else to do, dost think, then to leave their bus'ness, and come down to sue me in an action of debt? They restored him however for that bout, to make trial of his honesty and good faith. He was no sooner up, but for want of living oxen, he made out his number upon past, and offered them up in form upon an altar. For this mockery, divine vengeance pursued him, and he had an apparition come to him in a dream, that bad him go and search in such a place near the coast, and he should find a considerable treasure. Away he went, and as he was looking for the mony fell into the hands of pirates. He begged hard for his liberty, and offered a thousand talents of gold for his ransom; but they would not trust him, and so he was carried away, and sold afterwards as a slave for as many groats.

♦　　　　　Do not mock the gods.　　　　　♦

199. 誇大的承諾

　　從前，有個可憐的傢伙病得很重，連醫生都說這世上沒有什麼能救活他了。於是，他誠心地祈禱，並許下誓言，不管是阿波羅還是埃斯柯拉庇俄斯，只要誰能治好他的病，他就獻上一千頭牛做為祭品。他的妻子說：「親愛的，可別輕易做出承諾，要是你真好了，你到哪裡去找一千頭牛呢？」他答道：「親愛的，你說這話可真傻。你想，難道神仙就沒別的事可做了嗎？他們難道會放下手中的事，專程跑下來告我欠債不還嗎？」然而，那一次，神為了考驗他的誠信和信仰，就把他給治好了。他身體康復了之後，由於沒有足夠多的活牛，他就隨便湊了個數，把牠們放在祭壇上作為貢品，裝個樣子。受到這樣的嘲弄，天神開始對他進行報復。有一次他做夢夢見幽靈指示他到海邊某個地方，在那裡會找到寶藏。他出發了，就在他尋找寶藏的時候，他落入了海盜的手裡。他拚命地哀求他們放了他，並提供一千塔蘭特的金子作為贖金；但是，他們不相信他的話，帶走了他，後來把他當作奴隸賤賣了。

◆　　　　　不要和神耍小聰明。　　　　◆

Chambry 131 = Perry 110

200. The Man and the Hero

A man kept a hero shrine in his house and made expensive sacrifices to it. Since he was constantly paying out money and spending great sums on the offerings, the god came to him one night and said,"Look here, stop squandering your wealth: if you spend everything and become poor, you'll put the blame on me!"

◆　Likewise, when people suffer misfortune because of their own foolishness, they often blame the gods.　◆

200. 人和英雄

有個人在自己家裡供了個神龕，並花了許多錢置辦供品。神注意到他一直都花許多錢來準備供品，於是，有一天晚上，神到他家來對他說：「聽著，別再浪費錢了。要是你把錢都花光了，成了窮光蛋，你會怪我的！」

◆　人們在遭遇不幸的時候，經常抱怨上天，卻不想想這是由於他們自己的愚蠢造成的。　◆

Townsend 254 = Perry 35

201. The Man and the Satyr

A Man and a Satyr once drank together in token of a bond of

alliance being formed between them. One very cold wintry day, as they talked, the Man put his fingers to his mouth and blew on them. When the Satyr asked the reason for this, he told him that he did it to warm his hands because they were so cold. Later on in the day they sat down to eat, and the food prepared was quite scalding. The Man raised one of the dishes a little towards his mouth and blew in it. When the Satyr again inquired the reason, he said that he did it to cool the meat, which was too hot.

"I can no longer consider you as a friend" said the Satyr,"a fellow who with the same breath blows hot and cold."

♦　　　　Maintain a single position.　　　　♦

201. 人和薩提

有個男人和森林之神薩提，曾同飲為盟。一個非常寒冷的冬日，他們一塊談話時，那人把手指放在嘴邊上吹。當薩提問他為什麼這樣時，男人告訴薩提，他的手冰涼，這樣是為了暖暖他的手。後來有一天，他們坐下來吃飯，飯很燙，那人把一盤菜稍稍端向嘴邊，對著它吹氣。薩提又問這樣做的原因，他說肉太燙了，這樣做是讓它涼一涼。

「我不能再把你當朋友了！」薩提說，「因為你這種人，一會兒出熱氣，一會兒又出冷氣。」

♦　　　　立場要堅定。　　　　♦

Townsend 132 = Perry 88

202. Mercury and the Sculptor

Mercury once determined to learn in what esteem he was

held among mortals. For this purpose he assumed the character of a man and visited in this disguise a Sculptor's studio having looked at various statues, he demanded the price of two figures of Jupiter and Juno. When the sum at which they were valued was named, he pointed to a figure of himself, saying to the Sculptor,"You will certainly want much more for this, as it is the statue of the Messenger of the Gods, and author of all your gain."The Sculptor replied,"Well, if you will buy these, I'll fling you that into the bargain."

◆　　　　　Don't overvalue yourself.　　　　　◆

202. 墨丘利和雕刻家

　　有一次，墨丘利想知道他在人間受到多大的尊重，便化作一個凡人，去參觀一個雕刻家的畫室。他看到各式各樣的雕像，還問了主神朱比特和天后朱諾兩尊神像的價格。聽了兩尊神像的報價之後，墨丘利指著自己的神像，對雕刻家說：「這尊神像，你的要價肯定要高得多，因為祂是神使的雕像，而且是你的一切收益的創造者。」雕刻家回答說：「啊！假如你買這些的話，我就把這個廉價貨送給你。」

◆　　　　　　　不要自視過高。　　　　　　　◆

L'Estrange 170 = Perry 89

203. Mercury and Tiresias

Mercury had a great mind to try if Tiresias was so famous

a diviner as the world took him for, or not. So he went and stole Tiresias's oxen; and ordered the matter to be in the company with Tiresias, as upon bus'ness by the by, when the news should be brought him of the loss of his oxen. Mercury went to Tiresias in the shape of a man, and the tidings came as Mercury had contrived it: upon this, he took Mercury up to a high tower, hard by, and bad him look well about him, and ten him what birds he saw. Why, says Mercury, I see an eagle upon wing there, that takes her course from the right-hand to the left. That eagle (says Tiresias) is nothing to our purpose; wherefore pray look again once. Mercury stood gazing a while, and then told Tiresias of a crow he had discovered upon a tree, that was one while looking up into the air, and another while down towards the ground: That's enough; (says Tiresias) for this motion of the crow, is as much as to say, I do appeal to heaven, and to earth, that the man that is now with Tiresias, can help him to his oxen again if he pleases.

◆　　　　Vanity lives with fortune-tellers　　　　◆

203. 墨丘利和提瑞西阿斯

墨丘利很想知道，提瑞西阿斯是不是真的像世人認為的那樣，是個出色的占卜者。於是，他跑去偷走了提瑞西阿斯的牛，並讓人假裝不經意地提起這事兒，告訴提瑞西阿斯，他的牛不見了。這時候，墨丘利化成人形跑去找提瑞西阿斯，而提瑞西阿斯已經聽到傳聞說，這是墨丘利做的；於是，他把墨丘利帶到一座高塔上，讓他好好看看四周，告訴他看見了什麼鳥。「嗯！」墨丘利說，「我看見那裡有隻鷹在飛翔，從右邊飛到了左邊。」提瑞西阿斯說：「我們要說的不是那隻鷹，你再好好看看。」墨丘利站著看了一會兒，然後告訴提瑞西阿斯說，他發現樹上有隻烏鴉，一會兒看天，一會兒看地。提瑞西阿斯說：「夠了。因為這隻烏鴉的動作是想說，我上求天，下求地，現在和提瑞西阿斯在一起的那個人，如果他樂意，就能幫助提瑞西阿斯找回他的牛。」

◆　　　算命者只會說些無用的話。　　　◆

L'Estrange 96 = Perry 178

204. Mercury and a Traveller

One that was just entring upon a long journey, took up a fancy of putting a trick upon Mercury. He say'd him a short prayer for the bon voyage, with a promise, that the god should go half with him in whatever he found. Some body had lost a bag of dates and almonds, it seems, and it was his fortune to find it. He fell to work upon them immediately, and when he had eaten up the kernels, and all that was good of them, himself, he lay'd the stones, and the shells upon an altar; and desired Mercury to take notice that he had performed his vow. For, says he, here are the outsides of the one, and the insides of the other, and there's the moiety I promised you.

◆　Peoples' actions toward the gods differ from their words.　◆

204. 墨丘利和旅行者

有個人要出遠門，在他出發的時候，想要捉弄一下墨丘利。他簡短地向墨丘利作了祈禱，祈求旅途平安，並許諾說，不管他在路上找到什麼，墨丘利都能享有其中的一半。他運氣很好，剛好撿到了似乎是有人遺失的一袋子棗和杏。他馬上就開始享用起來，當他自己把果仁和其中能吃的東西都吃掉了，他就把果殼和棗核放在祭壇上，讓墨丘利知道他遵守了自己的誓言。他說：「這些是杏殼和棗核，這就是我答應給你的那一半。」

♦　　　　　**人們在神面前總是言行不一。**　　　　　♦

Townsend 249 = Perry 173

205. Mercury and the Workmen

A Workman, felling wood by the side of a river, let his axe drop - by accident into a deep pool. Being thus deprived of the means of his livelihood, he sat down on the bank and lamented his hard fate. Mercury appeared and demanded the cause of his tears. After he told him his misfortune, Mercury plunged into the stream, and, bringing up a golden axe, inquired if that were the one he had lost. On his saying that it was not his, Mercury disappeared beneath the water a second time, returned with a silver axe in his hand, and again asked the Workman if it were his. When the Workman said it was not, he dived into the pool for the third time and brought up the axe that had been lost. The Workman claimed it and expressed his joy at its recovery. Mercury, pleased with his honesty, gave him the golden and silver axes in addition to his own.

The Workman, on his return to his house, related to his companions all that had happened. One of them at once resolved to try and secure the same good fortune for himself. He ran to the river and threw his axe on purpose into the pool at the same place, and sat down on the bank to weep. Mercury appeared to him just as he hoped he would; and having learned the cause of his grief, plunged into the stream and brought up a golden axe, inquiring if he had lost it. The Workman seized it greedily, and declared that truly it was the very same axe that he had lost. Mercury, displeased at his knavery, not only took away the golden axe, but refused to recover for him the axe he had thrown into the pool.

◆　　　　Truth is the better strategy.　　　　◆

205. 墨丘利和工人

　　有個工人在河邊砍樹時，不小心把斧頭掉進了一個深水池裡去了。他就這樣失去了謀生的工具，於是在河岸上坐下，為自己艱難的命運悲痛。墨丘利出現了，問他為何痛哭流涕。他把自己的不幸告訴了墨丘利，墨丘利就躍入河中，撈上了一把金斧，問是不是他丟的那把斧子。聽他說不是之後，墨丘利又潛到水下一會兒，手裡拿了把銀斧上來，又問工人那是不是他的那把。當工人說不是時，墨丘利第三次跳入深水池中，撈出了他丟的那把斧頭。工人認領了這把斧頭，並為斧頭的失而復得而高興。墨丘利對他的誠實感到非常高興，於是除了他自己的那把斧頭之外，又把金斧和銀斧也都給了他。

　　這個工人回到家中，向自己的夥伴提到了發生的一切。其中的一個人立刻決定試一試，希望得到同樣的好運。他跑到河邊，故意把他的斧頭扔進的深水池的同一處地方，然後坐在岸邊痛哭。墨丘利正如期望的那樣出現在面前，在得知他悲痛的原因之後，墨丘利躍入河中，帶上來一把金斧，問是不是他丟的。這個工人貪婪地抓住金斧頭，宣稱這的確是他丟掉的那把斧子。墨丘利對他的欺詐行為感到很生氣，不僅拿走了金斧頭，並拒絕再去為他撈回他扔進深水池中的斧子。

♦　　　　　　　誠實就是最好的策略。　　　　　　　♦

Chambry 298 = Perry 239

206. The Oath's Punishment

A certain man took a deposit from a friend but intended to keep it for himself. When the depositor then summoned him to swear an oath regarding the deposit, he realized the danger he was in and prepared to leave the city and go to his farm. When he reached the city gates, he saw a lame man who was also on his way out of town. He asked the man who he was and where he was going. The man said that he was the god named Oath and that he was on his way to track down wicked people. The man then asked Oath how often he revisited each city. Oath replied, "I come back after forty years, or sometimes thirty." Accordingly, on the very next day the man did not hesitate to swear an oath that he had never received the deposit. But then the man ran into Oath, who dragged him off to the edge of a cliff. The man asked Oath how he could have said that he wasn't coming back for another thirty years when in fact he didn't even grant him a single day's reprieve. Oath explained, "You also need to know that if somebody intends to provoke me, I am accustomed to come back again the very same day."

♦　　The fable shows that there is no fixed day on which wicked people are punished by the god.　　♦

206. 誓言之神的懲罰

有一次，某人從朋友那裡收到了一筆存款，他抵擋不住金錢的誘惑，決定將其據為己有。當他的朋友想取回存款的時候，他卻矢口否認說，從沒收到過什麼存款。於是，存款人就讓他對此立誓，他意識到自己面臨的危險，就決定逃出城去。走到城門的時候，他看見有個跛子也要出城，就問他是誰，要去哪裡。跛子回答說，他是誓言之神，正在追捕壞人。他接著問誓言之神多久會再回來。「我四十年後，或者三十年後會再回來。」誓言之神回答說。他聽了之後非常滿意，就回家了。第二天，他毫不遲疑地發誓說，他從沒收到過那筆存款。但是，誓言之神隨後就現身了，把他拖到了峭壁邊上。他問誓言之神：「你告訴我說你三十年後才會回來，怎麼你連一天都不讓我緩一下呢？」誓言之神解釋說：「你也應該知道，如果有人故意要激怒我，我一天可以來兩次。」

◆　　　　上天懲罰壞人是不挑日子的。　　　　◆

Townsend 207 = Perry 99

207. The Seller of Images

A certain man made a wooden image of Mercury and offered it for sale. When no one appeared willing to buy it, in order to attract purchasers, he cried out that he had the statue to sell of a benefactor who bestowed wealth and helped to heap up riches. One of the bystanders said to him, "My good fellow, why do you sell him, being such a one as you describe, when you may yourself enjoy the good things he has to give?" "Why," he replied, "I am in need of immediate help, and he is wont to give his good gifts very slowly."

♦ When you lie, you often have to expand the lie. ♦

207. 賣神像的人

有個人雕刻了一尊赫耳墨斯的木像，把祂拿到市場上去賣。可是根本無人問津。於是他就大聲地吆喝以招攬顧客。他聲稱他的雕像能給人帶來財運，誰買去了就會大富大貴，腰纏萬貫。這時旁邊的一個人就問他：「朋友，既然你說得這麼好，你應該自己享用祂帶給你的財富，為什麼還要把祂賣給別人呢？」「啊，」他回答說，「我現在得馬上得到錢，但是祂不可能現在就把財富給我，那是需要很長的時間的。」

♦ 一旦說謊，以後就得繼續說謊。 ♦

Townsend 156 = Perry 174

208. The Traveler and Fortune

A Traveler wearied from a long journey lay down, overcome with fatigue, on the very brink of a deep well. Just as he was about to fall into the water, Dame Fortune, it is said, appeared to him and waking him from his slumber thus addressed him,"Good Sir, pray wake up: for if you fall into the well, the blame will be thrown on me, and I shall get an ill name among mortals; for I find that men are sure to impute their calamities to me, however much by their own folly they have really brought them on themselves."

♦ Everyone is more or less master of his own fate. ♦

208. 旅行者和命運女神

　　一個旅行者經過長途跋涉後疲憊不堪,最後在一口深井邊倒下睡著了。據說,當他馬上就要落到井裡時,命運女神在他面前出現,及時把他從美夢中喚醒。她是這樣喚醒他的:「尊敬的先生,請立刻醒過來吧!如果你掉到井裡去了,我就會受到人們的譴責,而且還會臭名昭彰,因為我發現,儘管大多數人吃苦遭殃都是因為自己做出的愚蠢行為,但是他們卻總是把責任推到我頭上。」

◆　　　　每個人都或多或少掌握著自己的命運。　　　　◆

Townsend 268 = Perry 508

209. The Trees under the Protection of the Gods

　　The Gods, according to an ancient legend, made choice of certain trees to be under their special protection. Jupiter chose the oak, Venus the myrtle, Apollo the laurel, Cybele the pine, and Hercules the poplar. Minerva, wondering why they had preferred trees not yielding fruit, inquired the reason for their choice.

　　Jupiter replied,"It is lest we should seem to covet the honor for the fruit."But said Minerva,"Let anyone say what he will the olive is more dear to me on account of its fruit."Then said Jupiter,"My daughter, you are rightly called wise; for unless what we do is useful, the glory of it is vain."

◆　　　　　　　　Do what is useful.　　　　　　　　◆

209. 受到神靈保護的樹

傳說中，神靈可以選擇一種樹木，給以專門的保護。朱比特選擇了橡樹，維納斯選擇了桃金娘，阿波羅選擇了月桂樹，西布莉選擇了松樹，赫拉克勒斯選擇了白楊。密涅瓦不明白為什麼他們都選擇了不結果實的樹，就問他們選擇的原因。

朱比特說：「是為了防止我覬覦果實帶來的榮譽。」密涅瓦說：「任何人都會覺得橄欖樹因為它的果實而更加珍貴。」朱比特說：「我的女兒，你很有智慧，如果我們做的都沒有用處，那麼榮譽也是徒然的。」

◆　　　　　　做事要選擇有意義的。　　　　　　◆

Chambry 319 = Perry 367

210. War and His Bride

The gods were getting married. One after another, they all got hitched, until finally it was time for War to draw his lot, the last of the bachelors. Hubris, or Reckless Pride, became his wife, since she was the only one left without a husband. They say War loved Hubris with such abandon that he still follows her everywhere she goes. So do not ever allow Hubris to come upon the nations or cities of mankind, smiling fondly at the crowds, because War will be coming right behind her.

◆　This fable, in a simple yet profound way, reminds us that disputes and wars are inseparable, urging　◆
us to cherish peace.

210. 戰爭和他的新娘

眾神一個接一個地結婚了,最後只剩下戰爭這個單身漢。戰爭決定結婚的時候,由於只剩下傲慢還沒找到丈夫,所以,傲慢就成了他的新娘。據說戰爭對傲慢非常迷戀,直到今天,不管她走到哪兒,他還是寸步不離。所以,千萬不要讓傲慢到人類的國度或城市裡來,因為戰爭就緊隨其後。

♦ 提醒人們爭端與戰爭是不可分割的,呼籲珍惜和平。 ♦

Chambry 123 = Perry 312

211. Zeus and the Jar of Good Things

Zeus gathered all the useful things together in a jar and put a lid on it. He then left the jar in human hands. But man had no self-control and he wanted to know what was in that jar, so he pushed the lid aside, letting those things go back to the abode of the gods. So all the good things flew away, soaring high above the earth, and Hope was the only thing left. When the lid was put back on the jar, Hope was kept inside. That is why Hope alone is still found among the people, promising that she will bestow on each of us the good things that have gone away.

Note: Unlike the famous "Pandora's box" version of this story (which is attested as early as the eighth century B.C.E. in the Greek poet Hesiod), this version notably does not blame all the misfortune of the world on a woman.

♦ Greed and dissatisfaction often lead to loss, and even result in losing valuable things. ♦

211. 宙斯和存放好東西的罐子

宙斯把他收集到的所有好東西都放進一個罐子裡，並用蓋子蓋上，然後把它作為禮物送給了人類。但是，人類非常好奇裡面放的到底是什麼，就把它打開了。於是，所有的好東西都飛走了，又飛回到眾神那裡。只有希望還在，因為當蓋子被重新蓋上的時候，希望還在罐子裡面。這就是為什麼希望仍然留在人間，以使每個人都懷著會得到那些飛走的好東西的希望。

注：這個故事還有另一個版本，即《潘朵拉魔盒》，這個版本最早是由古希臘詩人赫西埃德，於西元前八世紀寫成的。二者的區別在於，該版本並不把不幸歸罪於女人。

◆ 貪婪和不滿足常常會帶來損失，甚至導致失去寶貴的東西。 ◆

Chambry 57 = Perry 311

212. Zeus and Man

They say that in the beginning, when the animals were being formed, they received their endowments from Zeus. To some he gave strength, and to some speed, and to others wings. Man, however, was still naked so he said to Zeus, "I am the only one that you have left without a gift" Zeus replied, "You are unaware of the gift you have obtained, but it is the greatest gift of all: you have received the gift of speech and the ability to reason, which has power both among the gods and among mortals; it is stronger than the strong and swifter than the swift" Man then recognized the gift he had been given and bowed down before Zeus, offering him thanks.

♦ The fable shows that while we have all been honoured by God with the gift of speech and reason, there are some who are unaware of this great honour and are instead jealous of the animals even though the animals lack both speech and sense. ♦

212. 宙斯和人

宙斯在造動物的時候，賜予每種動物不同的天分。有些動物得到了力量，有些得到了速度，而有些得到了翅膀。人發現自己還是赤身裸體，身上什麼都沒有，就去找宙斯並對他說：「只有我還沒有收到您的禮物。」宙斯回答道：「你已經得到了最好的禮物，只是你還沒有意識到。我賜予了你語言的天賦和人神共有的理性思考能力，它力量最為強大，反應也最為迅速。」人這才意識到自己得到了什麼樣的才能，對宙斯鞠了一個躬，表示感謝。

♦ 雖然上天賜予我們每個人言語和思考的天賦，但是有些人不但還沒有意識到這個天賦，相反，還對那些既不會說話又不會思考的動物心生嫉妒。 ♦

Chambry 322 = Perry 240

213. Zeus and Prometheus

Following Zeus's orders, Prometheus fashioned humans and animals. When Zeus saw that the animals far outnumbered the humans, he ordered Prometheus to reduce the number of the animals by turning them into people. Prometheus did as he was told, and as a result those people who were originally animals have a human body but the soul of an animal.

♦   This fable is suitable for a man who is rough and brutal.   ♦

213. 宙斯和普羅米修斯

宙斯命普羅米修斯造人和動物。宙斯注意到動物的數量遠遠超過了人的數量,就下令把動物變成人,以減少它們的數目。普羅米修斯照做了,結果,那些從動物變成的人,雖然有了人形,卻獸性難改。

♦   這個故事適用於那些粗魯又殘忍的人。   ♦

GODS 众神

14.
HARE
野兎

HARE 野兔

Chambry 192 = Perry 333

214. The Hare and the Fox

The hare said to the fox,"They say you are very artful, fox. What art is it that you practice exactly?"The fox replied,"If you don't know my arts, I will have you to dinner so that you can get a taste of my art."The hare followed the fox to her den but the fox had nothing there to eat except for the hare himself. The hare exclaimed,"I have learned to my cost that your name does not derive from any kind of artistry but from fraud!"

Note: The Greek fable relies on wordplay involving a nickname for the fox, kerdo, which is related to trickery and profit-making.

◆ The fable shows that overly curious people often pay a very high price for recklessly indulging their curiosity. ◆

214. 野兔和狐狸

野兔對狐狸說：「別人都說你足智多謀。你到底是用了什麼手段呢？」狐狸回答道：「你如果想知道，就請來我家吃晚飯吧！我會讓你見識見識的。」野兔同意了狐狸的提議，跟她回了家，沒想到自己卻成了狐狸的晚餐。野兔悲呼：「現在我知道你根本沒有什麼聰明才智，你耍的都是一些坑蒙拐騙的伎倆！」

注：希臘版的寓言巧妙地運用了雙關，狐狸的暱稱 kerdo，意為欺詐、謀利。

◆ 　　　　好奇害死貓。　　　　 ◆

Townsend 155 = Perry 331

215. The Hare and the Hound

A Hound started a Hare from his lair, but after a long run, gave up the chase. A goat-herd seeing him stop, mocked him, saying "The little one is the best runner of the two."The Hound replied,"You do not see the difference between us: I was only running for a dinner, but he for his life?"

◆ Motivation is everything. ◆

215. 野兔和獵狗

獵狗把野兔追出了洞,並且窮追不捨。追了很長一段距離後,獵狗突然停下來,放棄了追逐。牧羊人看見獵狗停住了,就嘲諷他道:「看起來,你們兩個相比,還是那個小兔子跑得比較快。」獵狗回答說:「你沒有發現我們兩者之間的不同嗎?我跑僅僅是為了一頓飯,而他跑是為了他的命。」

◆ 動機決定一切。 ◆

Townsend 18 = Perry 226

216. The Hare and the Tortoise

A Hare one day ridiculed the short feet and slow pace of the Tortoise, who replied, laughing,"Though you be swift as the wind, I will beat you in a race."The Hare, believing her assertion to be simply impossible, assented to the proposal; and they agreed that the Fox should choose the course and fix the goal. On the

HARE 野兔

day appointed for the race the two started together. The Tortoise never for a moment stopped, but went on with a slow but steady pace straight to the end of the course. The Hare, lying down by the wayside, fell fast asleep. At last waking up, and moving as fast as he could, he saw the Tortoise had reached the goal, and was comfortably dozing after her fatigue.

◆　　　　Slow but steady wins the race.　　　　◆

216. 龜兔賽跑

　　有一天，兔子譏諷烏龜腿又短，速度又慢，烏龜大笑著回答說：「儘管你跑得像風一樣快，但我仍然能夠在比賽中打敗你。」兔子認為這根本不可能，就建議舉行一場比賽，比賽路線和終點由狐狸來選擇確定。

　　比賽如期而至，龜兔在同一時刻衝出了起跑線。烏龜儘管走得慢，但是朝著終點一步一步、鍥而不捨地堅定前行；兔子卻在半路時，躺在路邊呼呼地睡起覺來。結果等到兔子醒來，奮不顧身往前衝時，卻發現烏龜早已到達了終點，筋疲力盡之後，正舒適地打盹呢！

◆　　　　雖然慢但只要堅持就是勝利。　　　　◆

Jacobs 70 = Perry 102

217. The Hare with Many Friends

A Hare was very popular with the other beasts who all claimed to be her friends. But one day she heard the hounds approaching and hoped to escape them by the aid of her many

Friends. So, she went to the horse, and asked him to cany her away from the hounds on his back. But he declined, stating that he had important work to do for his master. "He felt sure, "he said,"that all her other friends would come to her assistance."

She then applied to the bull, and hoped that he would repel the hounds with his horns. The bull replied,"I am very sorry, but I have an appointment with a lady; but I feel sure that our friend the goat will do what you want." The goat, however, feared that his back might do her some harm if he took her upon it. The ram, he felt sure, was the proper friend to apply to. So she went to the ram and told him the case. The ram replied,"Another time, my dear friend. I do not like to interfere on the present occasion, as hounds have been known to eat sheep as well as hares."

The Hare then applied, as a last hope, to the calf, who regretted that he was unable to help her, as he did not like to take the responsibility upon himself, as so many older persons than himself had declined the task. By this time the hounds were quite near, and the Hare took to her heels and luckily escaped.

♦　　　　He that has many friends, has no friends.　　　　♦

217. 朋友眾多的野兔

野兔很受其他動物的歡迎，大夥都聲稱自己是兔子的朋友。但是有一天，野兔聽說獵狗逐漸逼近了，滿心希望她的眾多夥伴能幫助她逃過此劫。野兔去找馬，懇求他能馱著自己離開，避免獵狗的攻擊，但是馬拒絕了兔子的請求，說他還有重要的工作要替主人做，馬說：「我敢肯定，你別的朋友一定會過來幫助你的。」

HARE 野兔

野兔又去求公牛,希望牛能用角抵抗獵狗的進攻。牛回答說:「十分抱歉,我跟一位夫人有個約會,我敢肯定,我們的朋友山羊一定會 幫助你的。」然而,山羊說如果野兔坐到他背上,恐怕野兔會受傷,他覺得野兔去求公羊相助更為妥適。於是,野兔就跑到公羊跟前,把情況告訴了他,公羊說:「下次吧,親愛的夥伴。我不想插手這件事,正如大家所知,獵狗不僅吃兔子,同時也吃羊。」

窮途末路的野兔,懷著最後一絲希望,向小牛求助。但是小牛說,既然那些年長的動物都拒絕擔負這個責任,恐怕他也是愛莫能助了。這時,獵狗已經逼得很近了,野兔拔腿便逃,並且幸運地擺脫了追擊。

◆　　　　　朋友太多就等於沒有朋友。　　　　　◆

Townsend 294 = Perry 138

218. The Hares and the Frogs

The Hares, oppressed by their own exceeding timidity and weary of the perpetual alarm to which they were exposed, with one accord determined to put an end to themselves and their troubles by jumping from a lofty precipice into a deep lake below. As they scampered off in large numbers to carry out their resolve, the Frogs lying on the banks of the lake heard the noise of their feet and rushed helter-skelter to the deep water for safety. On seeing the rapid disappearance of the Frogs, one of the Hares cried out to his companions, "Stay, my friends, do not do as you intended; for you now see that there are creatures who are still more timid than ourselves."

◆　　There is always someone worse off than yourself.　　◆

218. 野兔和青蛙

野兔膽子很小，成天提心吊膽。終於有一天，野兔們厭倦了這種整日膽戰心驚的生活，達成一致決定，打算從高高的懸崖跳到下面的深湖中，徹底結束自己的生命，擺脫這些煩惱。一群群的野兔結伴去自殺，正在湖邊躺著的青蛙聽見野兔的腳步聲，嚇得趕緊遊進了深深的湖水中。看到青蛙急急忙忙地藏身，其中的一隻野兔對夥伴喊道：「先別動，朋友們，別自殺了！大家瞧，世界上還有比我們更膽小的動物呢！」

◆　　　　**總會有人不如你的。**　　　　◆

HARE 野兔

15.
HORSE
馬

Townsend 67 = Perry 549

219. The Charger and the Miller

A Charger, feeling the infirmities of age, was sent to work in a mill instead of going out to battle. But when he was compelled to grind instead of serving in the wars, he bewailed his change of fortune and called to mind his former state, saying, "Ah! Miller, I had indeed to go campaigning before, but I was barbed from counter to tail, and a man went along to groom me; and now I cannot understand what ailed me to prefer the mill before the battle." "Forbear," said the Miller to him, "harping on what was of yore, for it is the common lot of mortals to sustain the ups and downs of fortune."

♦　　　　　Fortune has its ups and downs.　　　　　♦

219. 軍馬和磨坊主

有一匹年老體衰的軍馬不能再出去戰鬥了，就被送到磨坊裡。軍馬被迫拉磨而不是在戰場上服役，不禁為命運無常而哀歎，他說道：「噢！磨坊主啊！我從前馳騁沙場，從前胸到尾巴都傷痕累累，但是有人照料我。我現在不明白自己為什麼放棄戰場來到這裡。」、「忍著吧！」磨坊主對他說，「別老拿陳年舊事喋喋不休的，因為命運的起伏是世間的常情。」

♦　　　　　人生總有起起伏伏。　　　　　♦

Townsend 40 = Perry 319

220. The Horse and Groom

A Groom used to spend whole days in currycombing and rubbing down his Horse, but at the same time stole his oats and sold them for his own profit. "Alas!" said the Horse,"if you really wish me to be in good condition, you should groom me less, and feed me more."

♦ Appearances aren't everything. ♦

220. 馬和馬夫

馬夫時常花費整天的時間,來給他的馬梳理毛髮,把馬全身上下擦洗得一乾二淨。但是同時,他卻偷走馬的燕麥去賣錢供自己花費。馬說道:「唉!如果你真願意我過得好,就少給我梳洗幾次,多餵我點飼料。」

♦ 光看表相是不夠的。 ♦

Townsend 193 = Perry 269

221. The Horse and the Stag

At one time the Horse had the plain entirely to himself. Then a Stag intruded into his domain and shared his pasture. The Horse, desiring to revenge himself on the stranger, asked a man if he were willing to help him in punishing the Stag. The man replied that if the Horse would receive a bit in his mouth and agree to carry him, he would contrive effective weapons against

HORSE 馬

the Stag. The Horse consented and allowed the man to mount him. From that hour he found that instead of obtaining revenge on the Stag, he had enslaved himself to the service of man.

◆ If you allow men to use you for your own purposes, they will use you for theirs. ◆

221. 馬和鹿

很多年前,馬獨占據著整片平原,之後鹿侵占了馬的地盤,跟他共用草場。馬決定向這個陌生人報仇,就向一個人詢問是否樂意替他給鹿一個教訓。這人回答道,要是馬願意在嘴裡放上一塊馬銜,並且允許他騎在馬背上,他就能想出一個好辦法來對付鹿。馬答應了,就讓這人坐到了自己的背上。從此馬不但沒能夠報復鹿,自己反倒淪為奴隸,為人服務。

◆ 如果為了自己的目的願意被別人利用,就會幫助別人達到目的。 ◆

16.
INSECT
昆蟲

INSECT 昆蟲

Perry 409

222. The Ant and the Chrysalis

An Ant nimbly running about in the sunshine in search of food came across a Chrysalis that was very near its time of change. The Chrysalis moved its tail, and thus attracted the attention of the Ant, who then saw for the first time that it was alive. "Poor, pitiable animal! "cried the Ant disdainfully. "What a sad fate is yours! While I can run hither and hither, at my pleasure, and, if I wish, ascend the tallest tree, you lie imprisoned here in your shell, with power only to move a joint or two of your scaly tail." The Chrysalis heard all this, but did not try to make any reply.

A few days after, when the Ant passed that way again, nothing but the shell remained. Wondering what had become of its contents, he felt himself suddenly shaded and fanned by the gorgeous wings of a beautiful Butterfly. "Behold in me, "said the Butterfly,"your much-pitied friend! Boast now of your powers to run and climb as long as you can get me to listen."So saying, the Butterfly rose in the air, and, borne along and aloft on the summer breeze, was soon lost to the sight of the Ant forever.

◆　　　　　Appearances are deceptive.　　　　　◆

222. 螞蟻和蛹

太陽下一隻螞蟻來回奔波，到處尋找食物，突然碰見一隻將要蛻變的蛹。那蛹扭動著尾巴，引起了螞蟻的注意，他這才第一次看到，原來這傢伙是個活物。「可憐的東西！」螞蟻故作驕傲地大喊一聲,「你的命運是何等地淒慘!我可以隨心所欲地東逛逛西走走,如果我願意,我還能爬到最高的那棵大樹上,可是你卻被囚禁在你的殼裡,至多也只是活動活動你那條醜陋的尾巴上的一兩個關節。」蛹聽了螞蟻的這些話,卻沒有做出任何回答。

數天後,螞蟻又路過這兒,看到只剩下一個空殼。螞蟻正想知道蛹變成什麼時,忽然覺得有什麼東西遮住了頭頂上的陽光,緊跟著一對華麗的蝴蝶翅膀,在他眼前扇起一陣風。「好好看看我!」蝴蝶說,「我就是你的可憐的朋友。只要你有本事讓我留下來聽你誇耀,你就接著吹噓你那四處奔走和爬樹的技能吧!」蝴蝶說著,就飛到了天上,伴著夏日的風,他越飛越高,很快就從螞蟻的視線中,永遠地消失了。

♦ **外表是具有欺騙性的。** ♦

Townsend 288 = Perry 235

223. The Ant and the Dove

An Ant went to the bank of a river to quench its thirst, and being carried away by the rush of the stream, was on the point of drowning. A Dove sitting on a tree overhanging the water plucked a leaf and let it fall into the stream close to her. The Ant climbed onto it and floated in safety to the bank. Shortly afterwards a birdcatcher came and stood under the tree, and laid his lime-twigs for the Dove, which sat in the branches. The Ant, perceiving his design, stung him in the foot. In pain the birdcatcher threw down the twigs, and the noise made the Dove take wing.

♦ Return favors given to you. ♦

INSECT 昆蟲

223. 螞蟻和鴿子

　　螞蟻來到河邊喝水，不幸被激流沖走，馬上就要被淹死了。這時，在岸邊的樹上正好有一隻鴿子，他採下一片葉子，扔在螞蟻身旁。螞蟻爬上了樹葉，安全地漂回到岸邊。過了不久，來了個捕鳥人，他站在樹下，將抹了膠水的小樹枝伸向了樹上的鴿子。螞蟻看穿了捕鳥人的居心，狠狠地在他腳上叮了一口。捕鳥人因為疼痛，手中的樹枝掉到地上，鴿子被聲音驚動，拍了拍翅膀，飛走了。

◆　　　　　　好心終有好報。　　　　　　◆

L'Estrange 188 = Perry 166

224. An Ant Formerly a Man

　　The ant, or pismire, was formerly a husband-man, that secretly filched away his neighbour's goods and corn, and stored all up in his own barn. He drew a general curse upon his head for't, and Jupiter, as a punishment, and for the credit of mankind, turned him into a pismire; but this change of shape wrought no alteration, either of mind or of manners; for he keeps the same humour and nature to this very day.

◆　　At the root, people stay the same even if they look like they are changing.　　◆

224. 由人演變成的螞蟻

　　螞蟻以前是個農夫。他當時悄悄地把鄰居的貨物和玉米偷走，把它們全儲藏在自己的穀倉裡，為此，他受到了詛咒。朱比特為了維護人類的名譽，決定罰他變成螞蟻。但是，雖然外形改變了，他的思想、行為卻沒有改變，直到今天，他還是死性不改。

◆ 儘管人們表面上看起來有所改變，但骨子裡卻還是一樣。 ◆

Townsend 13 = Perry 373

225. The Ants and the Grasshopper

The Ants were spending a fine winter's day drying grain collected in the summertime. A Grasshopper, perishing with famine, passed by and earnestly begged for a little food. The Ants inquired of him,"Why did you not treasure up food during the summer?" He replied,"I had not leisure enough. I passed the days in singing." They then said in derision,"If you were foolish enough to sing all the summer, you must dance supperless to bed in the winter."

◆ It is thrifty to prepare today for the wants of tomorrow. ◆

225. 螞蟻和蚱蜢

在一個晴朗的冬日，螞蟻們正忙於翻曬夏天儲藏的糧食。一隻饑腸轆轆的蚱蜢走過來，懇求螞蟻給些吃的。螞蟻問蚱蜢：「你為什麼不在夏天存儲些食物呢？」蚱蜢回答說：「夏天我在唱歌呢！沒空做事。」螞蟻於是不無嘲諷地說：「你太愚蠢了，整個夏天都在歌唱中度過了，那麼到冬天，你就一天到晚空著肚子跳舞吧！」

◆ ★未雨綢繆，才能防患於未然。 ◆

INSECT 昆蟲

Chambry 335 = Perry 241

226. The Cicada and the Fox

A cicada was singing on top of a tall tree. The fox wanted to eat the cicada, so she came up with a trick. She stood in front of the tree and marvelled at the cicada's beautiful song. The fox then asked the cicada to come down and show himself, since the fox wanted to see how such a tiny creature could be endowed with such a sonorous voice. But the cicada saw through the fox's trick. He tore a leaf from the tree and let it fall to the ground. Thinking it was the cicada, the fox pounced and the cicada then said, "Hey, you must be crazy to think I would come down from here! I've been on my guard against foxes ever since I saw the wings of a cicada in the spoor of a fox."

♦ The fable shows that a discerning person is made wise by the misfortunes of his neighbours. ♦

226. 蟬和狐狸

蟬停在高高的枝頭上唱歌。狐狸聽見了，就走過去對他說：「多美妙的聲音啊！你能下來讓我有這個榮幸瞻仰一下，如此偉大的歌唱家嗎？因為我真的很好奇，這麼小的個子，怎麼能有這麼宏亮的嗓音」但是，蟬看穿了狐狸的詭計，就從樹上扯下一片葉子，扔了下去。狐狸誤以為是蟬飛下來了，猛地跳起來咬上一口。於是，蟬說道：「你一定是瘋了，才會指望我從這裡下去！自從我在一隻狐狸的足跡邊發現了蟬翼之後，我就無時無刻不在提防你們。」

♦ 能辨別是非的人，能從鄰居的不幸中吸取教訓。 ♦

Life of Aesop 135 = Perry 3

227. The Dung Beetle and the Eagle

As he was being chased by an eagle, the hare ran to the dung beetle, begging the beetle to save him. The beetle implored the eagle to respect the hare's asylum, solemnly compelling him by the sacred name of Zeus and pleading with the eagle not to disregard him simply because of his small size. But the eagle brushed the beetle aside with a flick of his wing and grabbed the hare, tearing him to pieces and devouring him. The beetle was enraged and flew off together with the eagle to find the nest in which the eagle kept his eggs. After the eagle was gone, the beetle smashed all the eggs. When the eagle came back, he was dreadfully upset and looked for the creature who had smashed the eggs, intending to tear him to pieces. When it was time for the eagle to nest again, he put his eggs in an even higher place, but the beetle flew all the way up to the nest, smashed the eggs, and went away. The eagle grieved for his little ones and said that this must be the result of some angry plot of Zeus to exterminate the eagle race. When the next season came, the eagle did not feel secure keeping the eggs in his nest and instead went up to Olympus and placed the eggs in Zeus's lap. The eagle said to Zeus,"Twice my eggs have been destroyed; this time, I am leaving them here under your protection."When the beetle found out what the eagle had done, he stuffed himself with dung and went straight up to Zeus and flew right into his face. At the sight of this filthy creature, Zeus was startled and leaped to his feet, forgetting that he held the eagle's eggs inside his lap. As a result, the eggs were broken once again. Zeus then learned of the wrong that had been done to the beetle, and when the eagle returned, Zeus said to him, "It is only right that you have lost your little ones, since you mistreated the beetle!" The beetle said, " The eagle treated me badly, but he also acted very impiously towards you, O Zeus! The eagle did not fear to violate your sacred name, and he killed the one who had taken refuge with me. I will not cease until I have punished the eagle completely!" Zeus did not want the race of eagles to be wiped out, so he urged the beetle to relent. When his efforts to persuade the beetle failed, Zeus changed the breeding season of the eagles, so that it would take place at a time when the beetles were not found above ground.

◆　　　False confidence often leads into danger.　　　◆

227. 金龜子和老鷹

　　有隻兔子正在被老鷹追趕，就在他走投無路、危在旦夕的時候，他碰見了金龜子，並向金龜子求救。於是金龜子就懇求老鷹看在宙斯的份上不要再追了，不要因為他個子小就瞧不起他，不把他的話當回事。然而，老鷹展翅一揮就把金龜子掃到一邊，抓住了兔子，還當著金龜子的面把他撕成了碎片，飽餐了一頓。

　　金龜子被激怒了，他跟著老鷹飛回了他的巢穴，並趁他外出的時候，把老鷹的蛋都弄碎了。老鷹回來後，看到這情景非常難過，他四處尋找兇手，發誓要將他碎屍萬段。

　　這一次，老鷹找了一個更高的地方築巢，可是，金龜子又飛到他的巢裡，把他的蛋弄碎了。老鷹傷心欲絕，向宙斯求助。宙斯說：「在下次交配季節到來的時候，你可以把蛋放在我的膝蓋上。有我的保護，他們會很安全的。」老鷹向宙斯表達了謝意，並照宙斯的話做了。

金龜子知道後，在自己身上黏滿了糞便，徑直朝宙斯的臉飛去。宙斯被這突然襲擊弄得措手不及，忘了老鷹的蛋還在他的雙膝之間，馬上從寶座上跳了起來，於是，老鷹的蛋又破了。

　　宙斯瞭解了事情的原委之後，希望金龜子能寬宏大量一點，原諒老鷹，不要把老鷹趕盡殺絕。但是，宙斯的勸告對金龜沒有發揮任何作用，於是，宙斯只好改變老鷹的交配季節，讓他們在金龜子還在地底下的時候趕緊交配。

◆　　　　　　　錯誤的自信常常導致危險。　　　　　　　◆

Townsend 290 = Perry 272

228. The Flea and the Man

　　A Man, very much annoyed with a Flea, caught him at last, and said, "Who are you who dare to feed on my limbs, and to cost me so much trouble in catching you?" The Flea replied, "O my dear sir, pray spare my life, and destroy me not, for I cannot possibly do you much harm." The Man, laughing, replied, "Now you shall certainly die by mine own hands, for no evil, whether it be small or large, ought to be tolerated."

◆　　　　　　　Tolerate no evil.　　　　　　　◆

228. 跳蚤和人

　　有個人終於抓住了把他惹得心煩意亂的跳蚤，他對跳蚤說：「你算什麼東西，竟敢吸我的血，還讓我費了這麼大的力氣才抓到你？」跳蚤說：「親愛的先生，求您放我一條生路吧！千萬不要殺我,我對你的傷害並不大啊!」這人笑著回答說:「我一定要親手捏死你,凡是罪惡,無論大小,都不會得到寬恕。」

◆ 　　　　　不能輕饒邪惡之人。　　　　　◆

Townsend 138 = Perry 231

229. The Flea and the Wrestler

A Flea settled upon the bare foot of a Wrestler and bit him, causing the man to call loudly upon Hercules for help. When the Flea a second time hopped upon his foot, he groaned and said,"o Hercules! if you will not help me against a Flea, how can I hope for your assistance against greater antagonists?"

◆ 　We petition gods far minor matters, yet take offence if such petitions are not granted.　◆

229. 跳蚤和摔角手

一隻跳蚤停在一名摔角手的赤腳上,咬了他一口,痛得摔角手大聲向大力神赫拉克勒斯求助。當跳蚤再次跳到他腳上咬他的時候,他呻吟著說道:「唉,赫拉克勒斯啊!如果你不肯幫我對付一隻跳蚤,還叫我怎麼指望你,幫我對付更強大的對手呢?」

◆ 　我們因為小事請求上天,如果得不到幫助就會感到憤怒。　◆

Townsend 28 = Perry 80

230. The Flies and the Honey-Pot

A number of Flies were attracted to a jar of honey which had been overturned in a housekeeper's room, and placing their feet in it, ate greedily. Their feet, however, became so smeared with the honey that they could not use their wings, nor release themselves, and were suffocated. Just as they were expiring, they exclaimed,"O foolish creatures that we are, for the sake of a little pleasure we have destroyed ourselves."

♦　　　　Pleasure bought with pains, hurts.　　　　♦

230. 蒼蠅和蜂蜜罐

女管家的屋子裡有一罐蜂蜜被打翻了，一群蒼蠅被吸引過來，他們叮在蜂蜜上貪婪地吃了起來。但是蒼蠅的腳被蜂蜜黏住了，飛不起來也動不了。最後蒼蠅都被蜂蜜淹死了。快要斷氣的蒼蠅大叫道：「我們真是愚蠢啊！為了這麼一點點享受，斷送了自己的性命。」

♦　　　　享樂的代價往往是痛苦和傷害。　　　　♦

Townsend 218 = Perry 498

231. The Fly and the Draught-Mule

A Fly sat on the axle-tree of a chariot, and addressing the Draught-Mule said,"How slow you are! Why do you not go faster? See if I do not prick your neck with my sting."The Draught-Mule replied,"I do not heed your threats; I only care for him who sits above you, and who quickens my pace with his whip, or holds me back with the reins. Away, therefore, with your insolence, for I know well when to go fast, and when to go slow."

♦　　　Ignore complaines who have no influence.　　　♦

231. 蒼蠅和拉車的騾子

　　一隻蒼蠅停在一輛四輪馬車的車軸上，對拉車的騾子說：「你走得可真慢啊！為什麼你就不能跑快一點呢？看來是我沒叮你脖子的緣故！」騾子回答說：「我根本不在乎你的威脅，我只聽從坐在上面那個人的命令，只要他揮一揮鞭子，我就加快速度；他拉住韁繩，我就停下來。所以收起你那副傲慢的嘴臉滾吧！因為我自己非常清楚，什麼時候該快，什麼時候該慢。」

♦　　　　　不要理睬沒有影響力的抱怨者。　　　　　♦

Townsend 260 = Perry 137

232. The Gnat and the Bull

　　A Gnat settled on the horn of a Bull, and sat there a long time. Just as he was about to fly off, he made a buzzing noise, and inquired of the Bull if he would like him to go. The Bull replied,"I did not know you had come, and I shall not miss you when you go away."

♦　　Some men are of more consequence in their own
      eyes than in the eyes of their neighbors.　　♦

232. 蚊子和公牛

有隻蚊子落到一隻公牛的角上,停留了好久。要走的時候,他嗡嗡地邊飛邊問,公牛是否願意他離開。公牛回答說:「我不知道你什麼時候來的,你走了以後,我也不會想念你。」

◆ 有些人總是覺得自己很重要,但是他人卻不以為然。 ◆

Townsend 190 = Perry 255

233. The Gnat and the Lion

A Gnat came and said to a Lion, "I do not in the least fear you, nor are you stronger than I am. For in what does your strength consist? You can scratch with your claws and bite with your teeth as a woman in her quarrels. I repeat that I am altogether more powerful than you; and if you doubt it, let us fight and see who will conquer." The Gnat, having sounded his horn, fastened himself upon the Lion and stung him on the nostrils and the parts of the face devoid of hair. While trying to crush him, the Lion tore himself with his claws, until he punished himself severely. The Gnat thus prevailed over the Lion, and, buzzing about in a song of triumph, flew away. But shortly afterwards he became entangled in the meshes of a cobweb and was eaten by a spider. He greatly lamented his fate, saying, "Woe is me! that I, who can wage war successfully with the hugest beasts, should perish myself from this spider, the most inconsiderable of insects !"

◆ No matter how you brag, you can be undone. ◆

INSECT 昆蟲

233. 蚊子和獅子

　　蚊子飛到獅子跟前對他說：「我一點都不害怕你，你比我強不到哪去！你有什麼本領呢？不過是用爪子抓，用牙齒咬，就像女人打架一樣。我再說一遍，我哪兒都比你強，如果你不服氣，我們就打一架，看誰是勝者。」蚊子奏響了號角，飛快地朝獅子猛衝過去，專挑他鼻子上和臉上沒長毛髮的地方叮。獅子想去拍蚊子，就拿爪子向自己臉上戳去，結果自己的臉被抓得到處是傷，只好承認被打敗。蚊子戰勝了獅子，高唱著凱歌，嗡嗡地飛走了。然而沒多久，蚊子就撞到一張蜘蛛網上 被黏住，馬上就被蜘蛛吃掉了。蚊子為自身的命運感慨道：「真悲哀啊！我戰勝了最強大的野獸，卻死在這最不起眼的蜘蛛手裡。」

◆　　　　不管人怎麼吹噓，最後還還是會被消滅。　　　　◆

234. The Scorpion and the Frog

　　A scorpion and a frog meet on the bank of a stream and the scorpion asks the frog to carry him across on its back. The frog asks, "How do I know you won't sting me?" The scorpion says, "Because if I do, I will die too."

　　The frog is satisfied, and they set out, but in midstream, the scorpion stings the frog. The frog feels the onset of paralysis and starts to sink, knowing they both will drown, but has just enough time to gasp "Why?"

　　Replies the scorpion, "It's my nature…"

◆　　　　Inherent nature cannot be changed.　　　　◆

234. 蠍子和青蛙

　　蠍子和青蛙在河邊相遇，蠍子請求青蛙背他過河。青蛙問：「我憑什麼相信你不會螫我呢？」蠍子回答說：「要是我螫了你的話，你死了我也活不了。」於是青蛙就放心了，他背起蠍子開始渡河。可當他們游到河的中央時，蠍子還是用他的尾巴螫了青蛙，青蛙頓時感到全身麻痺，四肢不能動彈，身子也緩緩地往下沉。青蛙心知他倆都難逃被淹死的命運，在彌留之際，青蛙掙扎著質問蠍子：「為什麼要這麼做？」

　　蠍子無可奈何地答道：「江山易改，本性難移……」

　　◆　　　一個人的天性或本質行為，很難改變。　　　◆

235. The Silkworm and Spider

　　Having received an order for twenty yards of silk from Princess Lioness, the Silkworm sat down at her loom and worked away with zeal. A Spider soon came around and asked to hire a web-room near by. The Silkworm acceded, and the Spider commenced her task and worked so rapidly that in a short time the web was finished.

　　"Just look at it," she said,"and see how grand and delicate it is. You cannot but acknowledge that I'm a much better worker than you. See how quickly I perform my labors." " Yes," answered the Silkworm,"but hush up, for you bother me. Your labors are designed only as base traps, and are destroyed whenever they are seen, and brushed away as useless dirt; while mine are stored away, as ornaments of Royalty."

♦　　True art is thoughtful, delights and endures.　　♦

235. 蠶和蜘蛛

　　獅子公主向蠶下了二十碼絲的訂單，蠶在織機前興致盎然地織起來。一會兒一隻蜘蛛爬過來，她請求蠶把旁邊的紡織屋借給她。蠶立刻允許了。蜘蛛一進屋便開始快速結網，一會兒工夫就織完了。「睜大眼睛好好看看吧！」她說，「多麼壯觀精緻的一張網！看我織得有多快，這下你不得不承認，在紡織方面我比你厲害多了吧！」「嗯，的確挺快的。」蠶回答道，「不過還是請你免開尊口，不要打擾我工作。你織的網不過是卑鄙而又令人討厭的陷阱，一旦被發現就會被捅破，最後你的網會被當作毫無用處的塵土掃走；而我精心織出來的是，要作為王室的裝飾品被收藏起來的。」

♦　　藝術品的真諦在於意蘊深長、情趣豐富、亙古不變。　　♦

Townsend 175 = Perry 216

236. The Wasp and the Snake

　　A Wasp seated himself upon the head of a Snake and, striking him unceasingly with his stings, wounded him to death. The Snake, being in great torment and not knowing how to rid himself of his enemy, saw a wagon heavily laden with wood, and went and purposely placed his head under the wheels, saying, "At least my enemy and I shall perish together."

♦　　As a last resort take your enemy with you.　　♦

236. 馬蜂和蛇

一隻馬蜂落到一條蛇的頭上，用自己的蜂針在蛇頭上到處亂螫，想要將蛇置於死地。蛇痛不欲生，卻不知如何才能趕走敵人。蛇看見一輛滿載木材的大車疾馳而至，便立即迎著車爬過去，將自己的頭塞到了車輪底下，憤憤地說：「至少我可以跟我的敵人同歸於盡。」

♦　　**萬不得已的時候，可以選擇和敵人同歸於盡。**　　♦

INSECT 昆蟲

17.
LAMB
小羊

LAMB 小羊

L'Estrange 29 = Perry 478

237. A Dog, a Sheep, and a Wolf

A Dog brought an Action of the Case against a Sheep, for some certain Measures of Wheat, that he had lent him. The Plaintiff proved the Debt by three positive Witnesses, the Wolf, the Kite, and the Vulture. The Defendant was cast in Costs and Damages, and forced to sell the Wool off his Back to satisfy the Creditor.

◆ Tis not a Straw matter whether the main Cause be right or wrong, or the Charge true or false; where the Bench, Jury and Witnesses are in a Conspiracy against the Prisoner. ◆

237. 狗、綿羊和狼

狗起訴山羊，要求山羊歸還欠他的一些小麥。原告方提供了三位證人，證明山羊確實向狗借過小麥還沒還，他們分別是：狼、鳶和禿鷹。被告被裁定要承擔所有的費用和損失，為了還債，山羊不得不把羊毛賣給了狼。

◆ 如果陪審團、法官和證人合夥起來要定你的罪，那麼事情的是非對錯，以及指控是否有效，根本就不重要。 ◆

Townsend 178 = Perry 477

238. The Stag, the Wolf, and the Sheep

A Stag asked a Sheep to lend him a measure of wheat, and said that The Wolf would be his surety. The Sheep, fearing some fraud was intended, excused herself, saying,"The Wolf is accustomed to seize what he wants and to run off; and you, too, can quickly outstrip me in your rapid flight. How then shall I be able to find you, when the day of payment comes?"

◆　　　　Two blacks do not make one white.　　　◆

238. 雄鹿、狼和羊

雄鹿跑去懇請羊借給他一斗麥子,並且說狼可以為他擔保。羊懷疑他是存心欺騙,就為自己找了個藉口說:「狼常常是看中什麼搶什麼,搶了就跑;而你呢?比我跑得快多了,到了還麥子那天,我又怎麼能找到你呢?」

◆　　　　　黑加黑不可能變成白。　　　　　◆

Townsend 99 = Perry 212

239. The Widow and the Sheep

A certain poor widow had one solitary Sheep. At shearing time, wishing to take his fleece and to avoid expense, she sheared him herself, but used the shears so unskillfully that with the fleece she sheared the flesh. The Sheep, writhing with pain, said,"Why do you hurt me so, Mistress? What weight can my blood add to the wool? If you want my flesh, there is the butcher, who will kill me in an instant; but if you want my fleece and wool, there is the shearer, who will shear and not hurt me."

◆　　The least outlay is not always the greatest gain.　　◆

283

LAMB 小羊

239. 寡婦和綿羊

有一個寡婦很窮,唯一的財產就是一隻羊。到了剪羊毛的時節,她既想要羊毛,同時又捨不得花錢僱人,於是她就決定自己動手剪。但是由於她剪羊毛的技藝太不熟練,結果連毛帶肉都給剪下來了。羊疼得滿地打滾,哭訴道:「女主人,你為什麼要這樣傷害我?剪下肉,能增加羊毛的分量嗎?如果你是想要我的肉的話,把屠夫叫來就行了,他只需要一刀能把我給殺了;如果是想要我的毛的話,還是應該找剪毛工來,他既能很好地剪下我的羊毛,又不會傷害我。」

♦ 最少的開支不一定可以獲得最大的回報。 ♦

L'Estrange 60

240. A Wolf, a Lamb, and a Goat

As a lamb was following a goat, up comes a wolf wheedling, to get him aside, and make a breakfast of him. "Why what a fool are you," says the wolf, "that may'st have your belly full of sweet milk at home, to leave your mother for a nasty stinking goat!" "Well," says the lamb, "but my mother has placed me here for my security; and you'd fain get me into a corner, to worry me. Pray'e, which of the two am I to trust to now?"

♦ Trust your parents over your enemy. ♦

240. 狼、羔羊和山羊

狼看見一隻小羔羊跟在山羊的後面,就走上前來哄騙他,想把他騙到一邊，當早餐吃掉。「你怎麼這麼傻呢！」狼說，「不在家好好享受你的羊奶，卻要離開母親，跟著一隻又髒又臭的山羊！」「嗯，」小羔羊說，「可是我媽媽是為了我的安全，才把我放在這兒的；你一定很想把我騙到角落，然後把我吃了。天啊，現在我該相信誰呢？」

◆　　　　要相信你的父母，不要相信你的敵人。　　　　◆

LAMB 小羊

18.
LION
獅子

LION 獅子

Jacobs 23 = Perry 563

241. Androcles

A slave named Androcles once escaped from his master and fled to the forest. As he was wandering about there he came upon a Lion lying down moaning and groaning. At first he turned to flee, but finding that the Lion did not pursue him, he turned back and went up to him. As he came near, the Lion put out his paw, which was all swollen and bleeding, and Androcles found that a huge thorn had got into it, and was causing all the pain. He pulled out the thorn and bound up the paw of the Lion, who was soon able to rise and lick the hand of Androcles like a dog. Then the Lion took Androcles to his cave, and every day used to bring him meat from which to live. But shortly afterwards both Androcles and the Lion were captured, and the slave was sentenced to be thrown to the Lion, after the latter had been kept without food for several days. The Emperor and all his Court came to see the spectacle, and Androcles was led out into the middle of the arena. Soon the Lion was let loose from his den, and rushed bounding and roaring towards his victim. But as soon as he came near to Androcles he recognised his friend, and fawned upon him, and licked his hands like a friendly dog. The Emperor, surprised at this, summoned Androcles to him, who told him the whole story. Whereupon the slave was pardoned and freed, and the Lion let loose to his native forest.

♦   Gratitude is the sign of noble souls.   ♦

241. 安德羅克勒斯

　　有個叫安德羅克勒斯的奴隸從主人家逃掉了，躲進了森林。當他在森林裡徘徊時，突然看見地上躺著一頭獅子，正在痛苦地呻吟著。安德羅克勒斯先是轉身就想逃，但是發現獅子並沒有追他，就轉過身來走上前去。當他走近時，獅子伸出了紅腫流血的爪子，安德羅克勒斯發現一根大刺紮在上面，為此獅子才痛苦萬分。安德羅克勒斯把刺拔出，幫獅子把傷口包紮好。一會兒獅子就能夠站起來了，舔著安德羅克勒斯的手，像一條馴良的狗一樣。傷好後的獅子把安德羅克勒斯帶到洞中，每天帶肉給他吃，這樣安德羅克勒斯才能夠繼續生存下來。

　　然而不久之後，安德羅克勒斯和獅子都被捉住了。逃跑的安德羅克勒斯被判決扔給數天未進食的獅子。皇帝陛下攜全體大臣前來觀看獅子吃人的場面。安德羅克勒斯被領到了鬥獸場的中央。不久，獅子也從牢籠裡被放了出來，怒吼著奔向這個可憐的人。但是獅子一走近安德羅克勒斯，就馬上認出了牠的朋友，獅子停下來，像和善的狗一樣，諂媚似地去舔安德羅克勒斯的手。皇帝看了，十分吃驚，連忙召見安德羅克勒斯前來問個究竟。皇帝聽完安德羅克勒斯的整個故事後，赦免了他的罪，並賜他自由，獅子也被放回森林。

◆　　　　　心存感激是高尚靈魂的標誌。　　　　　◆

Townsend 173 = Perry 340

242. The Bowman and Lion

　　A very skillful Bowman went to the mountains in search of game, but all the beasts of the forest fled at his approach. The

LION 獅子

Lion alone challenged him to combat. The Bowman immediately shot out an arrow and said to the Lion,"I send thee my messenger, that from him thou mayest learn what I myself shall be when I assail thee. "The wounded Lion rushed away in great fear, and when a Fox who had seen it all happen told him to be of good courage and not to back off at the first attack he replied,"You counsel me in vain; for if he sends so fearful a messenger, how shall I abide the attack of the man himself?"

◆　　Be on guard against men who can strike from a distance.　　◆

242. 射手和獅子

一個箭不虛發的射手身背弓箭進山打獵，森林裡的百獸聽說他要來，都紛紛逃跑了，只有獅子留下來和他對戰。射手看見獅子，當即射出一箭，並對獅子說：「這就是我的信使，你會從他那兒得知，我會在什麼時間、什麼地點對付你。」受傷的獅子嚇得落荒而逃。看到這一切的狐狸勸告獅子振作一些，不能第一個回合就退縮。獅子回答說：「你講什麼都沒有意義。他派出的信使都如此令人生畏，假如他親自來，我怎能抵擋得住他的進攻？」

◆　　一定要留心那些從遠處發起進攻的人。　　◆

Townsend 142 = Perry 76

243. The Doe and the Lion

A Doe hard pressed by hunters sought refuge in a cave belonging to a Lion. The Lion concealed himself on seeing her approach, but when she was safe within the cave, sprang upon her and tore her to pieces. "Woe is me," exclaimed the Doe,"who have escaped from man, only to throw myself into the mouth of a wild beast?"

♦ In avoiding one evil, care must be taken not to fall into another. ♦

243. 母鹿和獅子

一隻母鹿被獵人緊緊追趕，在一個屬於獅子的洞穴尋找避難之地。獅子看見母鹿過來了，就躲了起來，直到母鹿以為自己在洞裡是安全的了，才撲上去把她撕成了碎片。「我真不幸！」母鹿歎道，「才逃開了人類的追捕，又把自己送到了野獸的嘴中。」

♦ 避難的人一定要當心，不要陷入另一場劫難。 ♦

Townsend 241 = Perry 409

244. The Fox and the Lion

A Fox saw a Lion confined in a cage, and standing near him, bitterly reviled him. The Lion said to the Fox,"It is not thou who reviles me; but this mischance which has befallen me."

♦ Chance sometimes rules. ♦

244. 狐狸和獅子

狐狸看見一頭獅子被困在籠子裡，於是走過來對獅子大聲謾罵。獅子就對狐狸說：「要不是我身陷困境，還輪不到你對我出言不遜。」

◆ 有時某種偶然的情況決定一切。 ◆

Townsend 201 = Perry 450

245. The Hares and the Lions

The Hares harangued the assembly, and argued that all should be equal. The Lions made this reply, "Your words, O Hares! are good; but they lack both claws and teeth such as we have."

◆ Be prepared to defend your position. ◆

245. 野兔和獅子

野兔在動物聚會上發表演講,指出所有的動物都應該一律平等。獅子回答說:「兔子啊!你的話沒錯,但是你沒有像我們這樣強有力爪子和鋒利的牙齒。」

◆ 捍衛自己的地位前要有所準備。 ◆

Townsend 9 = Perry 334

246. The Kingdom of the Lion

The beasts of the field and forest had a Lion as their king. He was neither wrathful, cruel, nor tyrannical, but just and gentle as a king could be. During his reign he made a royal proclamation for a general assembly of all the birds and beasts, and drew up conditions for a universal league, in which The Wolf and the Lamb, the Panther and the Kid, the Tiger and the Stag, the Dog and the Hare, should live together in perfect peace and amity. The Hare said,"Oh, how I have longed to see this day, in which the weak shall take their place with impunity by the side of the strong."and after the Hare said this, he ran for his life.

◆ Nature will out. ◆

246. 獅子的王國

田野和森林中的百獸以獅子為王。他既不憤怒、殘忍，也不暴虐，而是正派、溫和的，正像君主的樣子。在他當政期間，他發佈了一道聖旨，召集全體鳥獸們開集會，並且制訂了一個大家遵守的公約。公約中規定，狼和綿羊、豹子和山羊、老虎和鹿、狗和野兔，應該和睦地共同生活在一起。野兔說道：「噢，我是多麼期盼著看到這一天啊！到那時，弱者在強者身邊也不用擔驚受怕了。」兔子說完之後，就逃命去了。

◆ 本性決定一切。 ◆

Townsend 26 = Perry 191

247. The Ass, the Fox, and the Lion

The Ass and the Fox, having entered into partnership together for their mutual protection, went out into the forest to hunt. They had not proceeded far when they met a Lion. The Fox, seeing imminent danger, approached the Lion and promised to contrive for him the capture of the Ass if the Lion would pledge his word not to harm the Fox. Then, upon assuring the Ass that he would not be injured, the Fox led him to a deep pit and arranged that he should fall into it. The Lion, seeing that the Ass was secured, immediately clutched the Fox, and attacked the Ass at his leisure.

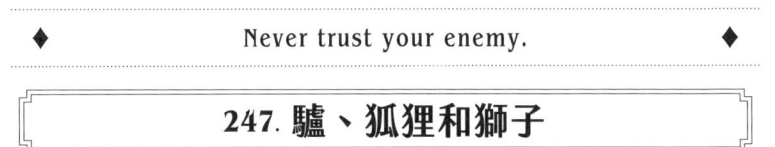

♦　　　　　　Never trust your enemy.　　　　　　♦

247. 驢、狐狸和獅子

　　驢和狐狸到森林裡打獵，約定要相互保護對方。他們剛走不遠就遇到了獅子。狐狸見災難即將降臨，就走到獅子跟前承諾說，只要獅子能保證不傷害他，他就會想法子抓到驢並交給獅子。獅子答應了狐狸，不會讓他受到傷害，狐狸騙驢說他不會受到傷害，然後把驢引到了一個深深的陷阱裡。獅子知道驢逃不掉了，就一下子先把狐狸捉住，然後再去捉驢。

♦　　　　　　永遠別信任你的敵人。　　　　　　♦

Townsend 131 = Perry 144

248. The Lion in a Farmyard

A Lion entered a farmyard. The Farmer, wishing to catch him, shut the gate. When the Lion found that he could not escape, he flew upon the sheep and killed them, and then attacked the oxen. The Farmer, beginning to be alarmed for his own safety, opened the gate and released the Lion. On his departure the Farmer grievously lamented the destruction of his sheep and oxen, but his wife, who had been a spectator to all that took place, said,"On my word, you are rightly served, for how could you for a moment think of shutting up a Lion along with you in your farmyard when you know that you shake in your shoes if you only hear his roar at a distance?"

◆　　Do not take on more than you can handle.　　◆

248. 農場裡的獅子

　　有隻獅子闖到農夫家的宅院裡。農夫想要捉住獅子，就馬上把院子的大門緊緊關上了。獅子發現自己無法脫身，便攻擊綿羊，咬死了牠們，隨後又去攻擊那些牛。農夫害怕自身難保，便打開大門放走了獅子。獅子走後，農夫為自己失去了很多牛羊而悲痛萬分。他妻子看到剛才發生的一切，便說：「要我說的話，你這是自作自受。你明知自己在平時遠遠聽見一聲獅吼，便會嚇得發抖，怎麼會一時頭腦發昏，把獅子和自己一起關在宅院裡呢？」

◆　　不要嘗試自己無法掌控的事。　　◆

Townsend 47 = Perry 140

249. The Lion in Love

　　A Lion demanded the daughter of a woodcutter in marriage. The Father, unwilling to grant, and yet afraid to refuse his request, hit upon this expedient to rid himself of his importunities. He expressed his willingness to accept the Lion as the suitor of his daughter on one condition: that he should allow him to extract his teeth, and cut off his claws, as his daughter was fearfully afraid of both. The Lion cheerfully assented to the proposal. But when the toothless, clawless Lion returned to repeat his request, the Woodman, no longer afraid, set upon him with his club, and drove him away into the forest.

◆　　　　Love can blind even the wildest.　　　　◆

249. 戀愛中的獅子

　　一隻獅子向一個樵夫的女兒求婚。樵夫不想答應，可是又不敢拒絕。為擺脫獅子的胡攪蠻纏，他急中生智，表示願意獅了娶他女兒，但是有一個條件：要獅子拔了牙，砍去爪子，因為他的女兒非常懼怕這兩樣東西。獅子高興地答應了。然而當沒了牙和爪子的獅子再來求婚時，樵夫不再害怕，用棍將他趕回森林裡了。

◆　　　　愛可以讓最野蠻的人變得盲目。　　　　◆

L'Estrange 11 = Perry 484

250. The Lion and an Ass

An ass was so hardy once, as to fall a mopping and braying at a lion. The lion began at first to show his teeth, and to stomach the affront; but upon second thoughts; well! (says he) jeer on, and be an ass still. Take notice only by the way, that 'tis the baseness of your character that has saved your carcass.

◆　　　　Don't bother fighting with fools.　　　　◆

250. 獅子和驢

驢有一次非常勇敢,居然向獅子嘶鳴示威。起初,獅子也開始齜牙咧嘴,容忍了驢的挑釁,但是仔細想想,獅子說:「好了!接著譏笑我吧!你再怎麼譏笑我,你還是一頭驢。順便說一下,要不是你這麼下賤,不值得我動手,你的小命早就沒了。」

♦　　　　不要浪費力氣與傻瓜打架。　　　　♦

Townsend 104 = Perry 338

251. The Lion and the Boar

On a summer day, when the great heat induced a general thirst among the beasts, a Lion and a Boar came at the same moment to a small well to drink. They fiercely disputed which of them should drink first, and were soon engaged in the agonies of a mortal combat. When they stopped suddenly to catch their breath for a fiercer renewal of the fight, they saw some Vultures waiting in the distance to feast on the one that should fall first. They at once made up their quarrel, saying, "It is better for us to make friends, than to become the food of Crows or Vultures."

♦　　　Better to be friends than fight.　　　♦

251. 獅子和野豬

夏日,因天氣太過炎熱,百獸口渴難耐,獅子和野豬同時到一口小井邊來喝水。他們為誰先喝爭執不休,很快就打得你死我活。當他們停下來喘口氣,預備恢復好精神接著再拚一場時,看

LION 獅子

見有幾隻禿鷲等在遠處,看誰先倒下,然後飽餐一頓。他們即刻和解了,說:「比起當烏鴉或禿鷲的食物,我們還是做朋友比較好。」

◆　　　　　　做朋友總比做敵人好。　　　　　　◆

Townsend 214 = Perry 143

252. The Lion and the Bull

A Lion, greatly desiring to capture a Bull, and yet afraid to attack him on account of his great size, resorted to a trick to ensure his destruction. He approached the Bull and said, "I have slain a fine sheep, my friend; and if you will come home and partake of him with me, I shall be delighted to have your company." The Lion said this in the hope that, as the Bull was in the act of reclining to eat, he might attack him to advantage, and make his meal on him.

The Bull, on approaching the Lion's den, saw the huge spits and giant caldrons, and no sign whatever of the sheep, and, without saying a word, quietly took his departure. The Lion inquired why he went off so abruptly without a word of salutation to his host, who had not given him any cause for offense. "I have reasons enough," said the Bull. "I see no indication whatever of your having slaughtered a sheep, while I do see very plainly every preparation for your dining on a bull."

◆　　When a man has both an interest and an
　　inclination to betray us, there's no trusting him.　　◆

252. 獅子和公牛

　　有一隻獅子很想抓一頭公牛,可是因公牛塊頭太大又不敢攻擊他,只好施展詭計來將公牛置於死地。他靠近公牛,說道:「我殺了一隻綿羊,我的朋友,如果你肯光臨寒舍和我分享他,我將感到非常愉快。」獅子說這話,是希望在公牛臥下吃東西時,趁機去襲擊他,讓他成為自己的美餐。

　　公牛走近獅子的洞穴,看見巨大的烤肉叉和大鍋,卻不見綿羊的半根寒毛,於是就一聲不響悄然離開了。獅子責問公牛為什麼都沒問候一下主人就走開了,而且主人並沒有冒犯他。「我有足夠的理由。」公牛說,「你殺死了一隻綿羊我是一點也沒看出來,倒清清楚楚地看到,你要吃公牛肉的種種準備。」

◆　　如果看出了一個人背叛的動機和跡象,就不要相信他。　　◆

Townsend 274 = Perry 335

253. The Lion and the Eagle

An Eagle stayed his flight and entreated a Lion to make an alliance with him to their mutual advantage. The Lion replied, "I have no objection, but you must excuse me for requiring you to find surety for your good faith, for how can I trust anyone as a friend who is able to fly away from his bargain whenever he pleases?"

◆　　　　　　　Try before you trust.　　　　　　　◆

253. 獅子和鷹

一隻鷹停止飛行，請獅子與他結盟，這樣能互惠互利。獅子回答道：「我不反對。但請你原諒，我要請你找一個人來擔保你的信用，因為一個可以隨時違約飛走的人，我如何能信任他做朋友呢？」

♦　　　　　要試過了再相信。　　　　　♦

Townsend 147 = Perry 148

254. The Lion and the Hare

A Lion came across a Hare, who was fast asleep. He was just in the act of seizing her, when a fine young Hart trotted by, and he left the Hare to follow him. The Hare, scared by the noise, awoke and scudded away. The Lion was unable after a long chase to catch the Hart, and returned to feed upon the Hare. On finding that the Hare also had run off, he said, "I am rightly served, for having let go of the food that I had in my hand for the chance of obtaining more."

♦　　　　Take the opportunity at hand.　　　　♦

254. 獅子和兔子

獅子碰到了一隻正在酣睡的兔子。獅子正要捉她的時候，突然看見一隻漂亮年輕的公鹿正從他身邊慢慢跑過，就丟下兔子去追公鹿。兔子被他的聲音嚇醒，飛快地跑走了。獅子追鹿追了好久都沒有追上，便回來吃兔子。發現兔子也逃走了，他說：「我真是自作自受,為了得到更多,將已經到手的食物丟掉了。」

◆　　　　　及時抓住身邊的機會。　　　　　◆

Townsend 295 = Perry 259

255. The Lion, Jupiter, and the Elephant

The Lion wearied Jupiter with his frequent complaints. "It is true, O Jupiter!" he said, "that I am gigantic in strength, handsome in shape, and powerful in attack. I have jaws well provided with teeth, and feet furnished with claws, and I lord it over all the beasts of the forest, and what a disgrace it is, that being such as I am, I should be frightened by the crowing of a cock."

Jupiter replied, "Why do you blame me without a cause? I have given you all the attributes which I possess myself, and your courage never fails you except in this one instance."

On hearing this the Lion groaned and lamented very much and, reproaching himself with his cowardice, wished that he might die. As these thoughts passed through his mind, he met an Elephant and came close to hold a conversation with him. After a time he observed that the Elephant shook his ears very often, and he inquired what was the matter and why his ears moved with such a tremor every now and then. Just at that moment a Gnat settled on the head of the Elephant, and he replied, "Do you see that, little buzzing insect? If it enters my ear, my fate is sealed. I should die presently?"

The Lion said, "Well, since so huge a beast is afraid of a

tiny gnat, I will no more complain, nor wish myself dead. I find myself, even as I am, better off than the Elephant."

◆ There is always someone else worse off than you. ◆

255. 獅子、朱比特和大象

獅子常常訴苦，朱比特對此感到不耐煩。「的確，朱比特！」他說，「我力大無窮，形貌英俊，攻擊力強。我的下顎有銳利的牙齒，腳上有利爪，統領森林中的一切野獸，但是我卻害怕聽到雞鳴，這是多麼大的恥辱啊！」

朱比特回答說：「你為什麼無緣無故地責怪我？我已經把我所有的一切特質賦予了你，而你除了這一點外，做什麼都很勇敢。」

聽了這番話，獅子呻吟著悲痛不已，責怪自己膽怯並恨不得死掉。他正這麼想著的時候，遇見了大象，就走過去與他攀談。過了一陣，他看到大象總是不停地扇著耳朵，就問大象是怎麼回事，為什麼一刻不停地搖晃耳朵。這時恰好有隻蚊子落在大象頭上。大象說：「你瞧見那隻嗡嗡叫的小東西沒有？假如他鑽進了我的耳朵裡，我的命就完了。我立刻就會死去。」

獅子說道：「啊，既然這樣龐大的動物也怕一隻小小的蚊子，我就不用再抱怨，不用再尋死了。我發現自己即便像現在這樣，也比大象好得多。」

◆ 總有人不如你的。 ◆

Townsend 56 = Perry 146

256. The Lion, the Mouse, and the Fox

A Lion, fatigued by the heat of a summer's day, fell fast asleep in his den. A Mouse ran over his mane and ears and woke him from his slumbers. He rose up and shook himself in great wrath, and searched every corner of his den to find the Mouse. A Fox seeing him said, "A fine Lion you are, to be frightened of a Mouse."

"Tis not the Mouse I fear," said the Lion; "I resent his familiarity and ill-breeding."

◆　　　Little liberties are great offenses.　　　◆

256. 獅子、老鼠和狐狸

酷熱的天氣使獅子疲憊不堪，他躺在洞中酣睡。一隻老鼠從他的鬃毛和耳朵上跑過，將他從夢中吵醒了。獅子爬起來，大怒，搖擺著身子四處尋找那隻老鼠。一隻狐狸看見後說：「你是一隻威嚴的獅子，也被老鼠嚇怕了。」

「我並不是怕老鼠⋯⋯」獅子說，「只是恨他的放肆無禮。」

◆　　　小小的失禮，便是大大的冒犯。　　　◆

Townsend 301 = Perry 563

257. The Lion and the Shepherd

A Lion, roaming through a forest, trod upon a thorn. Soon

LION 獅子

afterward he came up to a Shepherd and fawned upon him, wagging his tail as if to say, "I am a suppliant, and seek your aid." The Shepherd boldly examined the beast, discovered the thorn, and placing his paw upon his lap, pulled it out; thus relieved of his pain, the Lion returned into the forest. Some time after, the Shepherd, being imprisoned on a false accusation, was condemned "to be cast to the Lions" as the punishment for his imputed crime. But when the Lion was released from his cage, he recognized the Shepherd as the man who healed him, and instead of attacking him, approached and placed his foot upon his lap. The King, as soon as he heard the tale, ordered the Lion to be set free again in the forest, and the Shepherd to be pardoned and restored to his friends.

♦ Return favors and favors will be bestowed on you. ♦

257. 獅子和牧羊人

一頭獅子走過樹林時，不小心踩到一根刺。他連忙跑到牧羊人面前，對著他搖尾獻媚，好像在說：「我想求你幫忙。」牧羊人壯著膽子，仔細檢查一番，發現了那根刺，就把獅子的爪子放在自己膝上，將刺拔了出來，解除了獅子的痛苦。獅子返回森林中去了。不久以後，牧羊人遭人誣告被關進了牢房，並被判決「丟去餵獅子」。那獅子從籠子裡被放出來時，認出牧羊人是曾經醫治過自己人，不但沒撲過去，反而慢慢走近他，把爪子放在牧羊人的膝上。國王聽說了這件事情後，便下令把獅子重放山林，赦免牧羊人，牧羊人又回到朋友的身邊。

♦ 好心有好報。 ♦

Townsend 236 = Perry 258

258. The Lion, the Wolf, and the Fox

A Lion, growing old, lay sick in his cave. All the beasts came to visit their king, except the Fox. The Wolf therefore, thinking that he had a capital opportunity, accused the Fox to the Lion of not paying any respect to him who had the rule over them all and of not coming to visit him. At that very moment the Fox came in and heard these last words of The Wolf. The Lion roaring out in a rage against him, the Fox sought an opportunity to defend himself and said, "and who of all those who have come to you have benefited you so much as I, who have traveled from place to place in every direction, and have sought and learnt from the physicians the means of healing you?"

The Lion commanded him immediately to tell him the cure, when he replied, "You must flay a wolf alive and wrap his skin yet warm around you." The Wolf was at once taken and flayed; whereon the Fox, turning to him, said with a smile, "You should have moved your master not to ill, but to good, will."

♦　　　　The first liar doesn't stand a chance.　　　　♦

258. 獅子、狼和狐狸

一隻獅子老了，生病躺在洞中。除了狐狸之外，百獸們都去探望他們的國王。狼心想這可是大好機會，便向獅子控訴狐狸，說狐狸對統治他們的獅子毫不尊敬，也不來探望他。正在這時候，狐狸走進來，聽到狼說的最後幾句話。獅子一見到狐狸就怒吼起來，狐狸伺機為自己開脫說：「在所有探望大王的動物之中，

LION 獅子

誰像我對你這麼好呢？我四處奔走，遍訪名醫，好不容易從醫生那裡問到醫治你的方法。」

獅子命令他立刻說出藥方，狐狸回答說：「你得活剝一隻狼，將他的皮趁熱裹在你身上。」狼立刻被抓住剝了皮。這時狐狸轉身向狼，笑著說：「你不應當慫恿主人起惡念，而應該誘導他發善心才對。」

♦ 說謊者是不會得逞的。 ♦

Townsend 140 = Perry 339

259. The Lion's Share

The Lion went once a hunting along with the Fox, the Jackal and the Wolf. They hunted and they hunted till at last they surprised a Stag, and soon took its life. Then came the question how the spoil should be divided. "Quarter me this Stag" roared the Lion; so the other animals skinned it and cut it into four parts. Then the Lion took his stand in front of the carcass and pronounced judgment: " The first quarter is for me in my capacity as King of Beasts; the second is mine as arbiter; another share comes to me for my part in the chase; and as for the fourth quarter, well, as for that, I should like to see which of you will dare to lay a paw upon it."

"Humph," grumbled the Fox as he walked away with his tail between his legs; but he spoke in a low growl.

♦ You may share the labours of the great, but you will not share the spoil. ♦

259. 獅子的份額

　　有一次，獅子跟狐狸、豺和狼一起去打獵。他們不停地追捕，最後終於逮住了一隻成年雄鹿，並很快就將牠殺死了，接著就是如何分戰利品的問題了。「把這隻雄鹿的四分之一分給我。」獅子吼道，於是其他的幾個動物就剝了雄鹿的皮，並把鹿分成四份。然後獅子站在鹿的屍體前面，宣佈了他的裁決：「第一個四分之一歸我，因為我是百獸之王；第二份歸我，因為我是仲裁者；再一份也歸我，因為我也參與了狩獵；至於第四份嘛，嗯……至於這一份，我看你們誰敢動牠。」

　　「哼！」狐狸不滿的嘟噥著，夾著尾巴走開了，不過他嘟噥的聲音很小。

◆　　你可以與強者共患難，卻無法與他們同享福。　　◆

Townsend 42 = Perry 257

260. The Lioness

　　A controversy prevailed among the beasts of the field as to which of the animals deserved the most credit for producing the greatest number of whelps at a birth. They rushed clamorously into the presence of the Lioness and demanded of her the settlement of the dispute. "and you," they said, "how many sons have you at a birth?" The Lioness laughed at them, and said, "Why! I have only one; but that one is altogether a thoroughbred Lion."

◆　　The value is in the worth, not in the number.　　◆

LION 獅子

260. 母獅子

田野間的野獸在爭論,哪一種動物一胎生的數量最多,生的最多的應該得到最高的榮譽。他們喧鬧地衝到母獅子前面,要求她來解決爭端。「那麼你……」他們說,「你一胎生多少個幼獅呢?」母獅嘲笑他們說:「啊!我只生一個,可是這一個便是純種的獅子。」

◆ 　　　　　價值在於質,而不在於量。　　　　　◆

Townsend 29 = Perry 284

261. The Man and the Lion

A Man and a Lion traveled together through the forest. They soon began to boast of their respective superiority to each other in strength and prowess. As they were disputing, they passed a statue carved in stone, which represented "a Lion strangled by a Man." The traveler pointed to it and said, "See there! How strong we are, and how we prevail over even the king of beasts." The Lion replied, " This statue was made by one of you men. If we Lions knew how to erect statues, you would see the Man placed under the paw of the Lion."

◆ 　　One story is good, till another is told.　　◆

261. 人和獅子

有個人與獅子同行趕路,穿越森林。他們很快就開始互相吹噓自己比對方有力、比對方勇敢。他們正在爭辯的時候,經過一尊石像，那石像刻的是「人掐死獅子」的情形。

行人指著石像說：「瞧呀！我們人類多強壯啊！我們征服了百獸之王呢 The Old Lion」獅子回答說：「這石像是你們人做的。如果我們獅子懂得如何雕刻石像，你就會看到人被踩在獅子的腳下了。」

♦ 　　當只有一個故事時，這個故事是好的，可是當說出另一個故事來時，它就相形見絀了。　　♦

Townsend 119 = Perry 481

262. The Old Lion

A Lion, worn out with years and powerless from disease, lay on the ground at the point of death. A Boar rushed upon him, and avenged with a stroke of his tusks a long-remembered injury. Shortly afterwards the Bull with his horns gored him as if he were an enemy. When the Ass saw that the huge beast could be assailed with impunity, he let drive at his forehead with his heels. The expiring Lion said, "I have reluctantly brooked the insults of the brave, but to be compelled to endure such treatment from thee, a disgrace to Nature, is indeed to die a double death."

♦ 　　Only cowards insult dying majesty.　　♦

262. 老獅子

一隻獅子因為年老體衰、病弱無力，而倒在地上，馬上就要死了。一頭野豬朝獅子衝過來，用獠牙撕咬他，以報復很久以前受到的傷害。不久之後，公牛用角去頂獅子，好像獅子是敵人一

LION 獅子

樣。當驢看到這個龐大的野獸被攻擊不會反擊時,他就用蹄子踢獅子的額頭。奄奄一息的獅子說:「我不情願地忍受了勇者的侮辱,但還要被迫忍受你這樣對待我,而你不過是自然的棄兒,這簡直等於叫我死了兩回。」

◆ 只有懦夫會侮辱將死的君主。 ◆

Townsend 100 = Perry 339

263. The Wild Ass and the Lion

A wild Ass and a Lion entered into an alliance so that they might capture the beasts of the forest with greater ease. The Lion agreed to assist the Wild Ass with his strength, while the Wild Ass gave the Lion the benefit of his greater speed. When they had taken as many beasts as their necessities required, the Lion undertook to distribute the prey, and for this purpose divided it into three shares. "I will take the first share," he said, "because I am King: and the second share, as a partner with you in the chase: and the third share (believe me) will be a source of great evil to you, unless you willingly resign it to me, and set off as fast as you can."

◆ Might makes right. ◆

263. 野驢和獅子

為了更容易捕捉森林中的動物,野驢和獅子結成了同盟。獅子的力氣大,野驢的速度快,因此可以相互協助進行狩獵。捉了足夠多的獵物之後,獅子把它們分成了三份。「第一份應該是我拿。」獅子說,「因為我是森林之王;作為你的合作夥伴,第二份也是我所應得的;至於這第三份,除非你自願放棄並馬上離開逃命,否則我想厄運會降臨到你身上的。」

◆　　　　　　力量即真理。　　　　　　◆

Townsend 286 = Perry 347

264. The Wolf and the Lion I

A Wolf, having stolen a lamb from a fold, was carrying him off to his lair. A Lion met him in the path, and seizing the lamb, took it from him. Standing at a safe distance, The Wolf exclaimed,"You have unrighteously taken that which was mine from me!" To which the Lion jeeringly replied,"It was righteously yours, eh? The gift of a friend?"

◆　　　　　　The strong prevail.　　　　　　◆

264. 狼和獅子(版本一)

狼從羊圈裡偷了一隻小羔羊,大搖大擺地叼著往洞裡走去。但是在路上碰到了獅子,獅子一下把小羔羊從他口中搶了過去。狼跑到安全的距離之外,對著獅子大聲喊:「你這個蠻不講理的傢伙,你搶走本該屬於我的東西!」獅子卻不以為然地回答道:「那理所當然是你的嗎?還是你的朋友送你的禮物?」

◆　　　　　　有力量才能獲勝。　　　　　　◆

311

LION 獅子

Townsend 238 = Perry 260

265. The Wolf and the Lion II

Roaming by the mountainside at sundown, a Wolf saw his own shadow become greatly extended and magnified, and he said to himself,"Why should I, being of such an immense size and extending nearly an acre in length, be afraid of the Lion? Ought I not to be acknowledged as King of all the collected beasts?" While he was indulging in these proud thoughts, a Lion fell upon him and killed him. He exclaimed with a too late repentance,"Wretched me! this overestimation of myself is the cause of my destruction."

◆ Do not merely envy others while ignoring your own abilities. ◆

265. 狼和獅子（版本二）

日落西山之時，狼正在山腳下徘徊，突然，他發現自己的影子，在夕陽的映照下顯得又大又長，於是他自言自語道：「我的身材高大魁梧，從頭到尾快有一畝地那麼長了，我還有什麼理由懼怕獅子呢？所有的動物都必須尊我為王，難道不是這樣嗎？」就在狼想入非非之際，一隻獅子撲過來將他殺死了。在彌留之際，狼後悔莫及，歎道：「我真是太不幸了！我對自己的評價過高，到頭來只是枉送了自己的性命。」

◆ 不要只羨慕他人，不顧自身實力。 ◆

19.
MEN
人

MEN 人

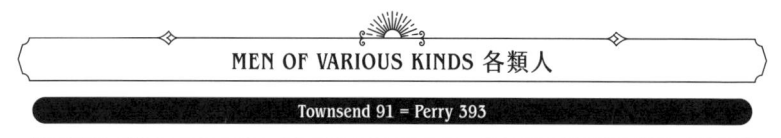

MEN OF VARIOUS KINDS 各類人

Townsend 91 = Perry 393

266. The Aethiop

The purchaser of a black servant was persuaded that the color of his skin arose from dirt contracted through the neglect of his former masters. On bringing him home he resorted to every means of cleaning, and subjected the man to incessant scrubbings. The servant caught a severe cold, but he never changed his color or complexion.

◆　　What's bred in the bone will stick to the flesh.　　◆

266. 黑僕人

黑僕的買主聽人說，黑僕之所以皮膚黑，都是因為之前的主人忽略了他的衛生問題，才搞得他渾身污垢，皮膚黑黑的。買主一把黑僕帶回家，就想盡各種辦法給他清洗。黑僕一直洗啊洗啊，直到凍得患上了重感冒，但是他身上或臉的顏色卻從未曾變白。

◆　　深植於骨子之中的東西是無法改變的。　　◆

Townsend 306 = Perry 525

267. The Bald Man and the Fly

A Fly bit the bare head of a Bald Man who, endeavoring to destroy it, gave himself a heavy slap. Escaping, the Fly said mockingly,"You who have wished to revenge, even with death, the Prick of a tiny insect, see what you have done to yourself to add insult to injury?" The Bald Man replied,"I can easily make peace with myself, because I know there was no intention to hurt. But you, an ill-favored and contemptible insect who delights in sucking human blood, I wish that I could have killed you even if I had incurred a heavier penalty."

◆　　　　Revenge will hurt the avenger.　　　　◆

267. 禿子和蒼蠅

禿子的頭被蒼蠅叮了一下，禿子就想把那隻蒼蠅打死，卻狠狠地給了自己一巴掌。逃掉的蒼蠅不無嘲笑地說：「一隻小蟲子叮你一下，你就想報仇，甚至於還想弄死這隻小蟲子，可最終竟然自己既被挨打又丟了面子。」禿子回答說：「我打自己幾下有什麼關係？因為我不會故意傷害自己。但是你這隻可惡卑鄙的小蟲子，專門以吸別人的血為樂，我真想一下子拍爛你，即使是吃再多的苦我也願意！」

◆　　　　報復他人的人，自己也會受到傷害。　　　　◆

L'Estrange 166 = Perry 72

268. A Bee-Master

There came a thief into a bee-garden in the absence of the master, and robbed the hives. The owner discovered it upon his return, and stood pausing a while to be-think himself, how this should come to pass. The bees, in this interim, came laden home out of the fields from feeding, and missing their combs, they fell powdering in swarms upon their master. Well (says he) you are a company of senseless and ungrateful wretches, to let a stranger go away quietly that has rifled ye, and to bend all your spite against your master, that is at this instant beating his brains how he may repair and preserve ye.

♦ Don't take your friends for foes. ♦

268. 養蜂人

小偷趁主人不在的時候溜進了養蜂園，偷走了蜂箱。主人回來後發現蜂箱被偷了，站著想了一會兒，怎麼會發生這種事。就在這時，蜜蜂從野外採滿了花蜜回來找他們的蜂巢，一看見他們的主人，就一起圍攻他。「哦！」他說，「你們這群冷血、忘恩負義的傢伙！陌生人搶了你們的東西，你們卻讓他一聲不響地走了；現在，你們的主人正絞盡腦汁想著怎麼修復、保護你們的蜂巢，你們卻把我當成了眾矢之的。」

♦ 不要把朋友誤當成敵人。 ♦

Townsend 229 = Perry 499

269. The Brother and the Sister

A Father had one son and one daughter, the former remarkable for his good looks, the latter for her extraordinary ugliness. While they were playing one day as children, they happened by chance to look together into a mirror that was placed on their mother's chair. The boy congratulated himself on his good looks; the girl grew angry, and could not bear the self-praises of her Brother, interpreting all he said (and how could she do otherwise?) into reflection on herself. She ran off to her father, to be avenged on her Brother, and spitefully accused him of having, as a boy, made use of that which belonged only to girls. The father embraced them both, and bestowing his kisses and affection impartially on each, said, "I wish you both would look into the mirror every day: you, my son, that you may not spoil your beauty by evil conduct; and you, my daughter, that you may make up for your lack of beauty by your virtues."

♦　　　Inner beauty is better than outer Beauty.　　　♦

269. 兄妹

　　一個父親有一個兒子和一個女兒，前者英俊不凡，後者卻出奇地醜。當這對兄妹還是孩子時，有一天他們在玩耍，無意中一起向放在母親椅子上的一面鏡子裡看。男孩為自己的漂亮容貌而慶幸，女孩生起氣來，並且受不了哥哥的自誇，以為哥哥的每句話都是在反襯她的醜（她又能怎麼做呢？）。

　　為了報復她的哥哥，女孩跑到父親面前狠狠地告了他一狀，說他作為一個男孩子，卻用那種只屬於女孩子的東西。父親擁抱了他們倆，並且把親吻和慈愛公平地分給了他們兩個，然後說道：「我希望你們倆每天都照照鏡子。我的兒子啊，那樣你就不會因為罪惡的行徑而毀壞自己的美麗；而你，我的女兒，那樣你就會用美德來彌補你美貌的不足。」

♦　　　　　　內在美比外在美重要。　　　　　　♦

Townsend 276 = Perry 527

270. The Buffoon and the Countryman

A rich Nobleman once opened the theaters without charge to the people, and gave a public notice that he would handsomely reward any person who invented a new amusement for the occasion.

Various public performers contended for the prize. Among them came a Buffoon well known among the populace for his jokes, and said that he had a kind of entertainment which had never been brought out on any stage before. This report being spread about made a great stir, and the theater was crowded in every part. The Buffoon appeared alone upon the platform, without any apparatus or confederates, and the very sense of expectation caused an intense silence. He suddenly bent his head towards his bosom and imitated the squeaking of a little pig so admirably with his voice that the audience declared he had a porker under his cloak, and demanded that it should be shaken out. When that was done and nothing was found, they cheered the actor, and loaded him with the loudest applause.

A Countryman in the crowd, observing all that has passed, said, "So help me, Hercules, he shall not beat me at that trick!" and at once proclaimed that he would do the same thing on the next day, though in a much more natural way.

On the morrow a still larger crowd assembled in the theater, but now partiality for their favorite actor very generally prevailed, and the audience came rather to ridicule the Countryman than to see the spectacle. Both of the performers appeared on the stage.

The Buffoon grunted and squeaked away first, and obtained, as on the preceding day, the applause and cheers of the spectators. Next the Countryman commenced, and pretending that he concealed a little pig beneath his clothes (which in truth he did, but not suspected by the audience) contrived to take hold of and to pull his ear causing the pig to squeak. The Crowd, however, cried out with one consent that the Buffoon had given a far more exact imitation, and clamored for the Countryman to be kicked out of the theater.

On this the rustic produced the little pig from his cloak and showed by the most positive proof the greatness of their mistake. "Look here," he said,"this shows what sort of judges you are."

◆　　Men often applaud an imitation and hiss the real thing.　　◆

270. 小丑和鄉下人

　　有一次，一個富有的貴族開了一個戲院，對大家免費，還貼出告示，說重金獎賞臨時創造出新鮮娛樂活動的人。

　　各式各樣的大眾演員都來角逐這個獎項。這些人之中，有一個在老百姓中間因為會講笑話而出名的小丑，他說有一種以前從來沒有在任何舞臺上表演過的娛樂表演。消息傳開後，引起了一陣巨大的騷動，戲院的每一個角落都擠滿了觀眾。小丑獨自出現在臺上，沒有任何工具或者幫手，整個戲院的觀眾由於期待而鴉雀無聲。忽然間，小丑低下頭，把頭朝向胸脯，學著小豬吱吱叫了起來。他學得如此的惟妙惟肖，以至於觀眾們都以為他的斗篷下面藏了一隻小豬，並且紛紛要求小丑把斗篷打開。小丑照著大家的話做了，但是在斗篷裡面沒有任何東西，觀眾為表演者大聲歡呼,並且給了他最熱烈的掌聲。

人群裡有個鄉下人看到了發生的一切,說道:「幫幫我吧!大力神啊!他這種把戲可騙不了我!」並且他立刻大聲宣佈,明天他將會表演同樣的節目,只是用一種更自然的方式。

次日,更多的人聚集在了劇場裡,但是只是為他們喜愛的演員捧場。他們不是來看奇觀的,而是來取笑農夫的。兩名演員都出現在了舞臺上,小丑先學豬哼哼吱吱的叫,與前一天一樣,他獲得了觀眾們的掌聲和歡呼。接下來那個鄉下人開始表演了,他假裝在衣服下面藏了一隻小豬(實際上,他的確是這樣做的,只是觀眾們沒有猜到),握住並扯豬的耳朵,使得小豬吱吱叫了起來。然而,觀眾們異口同聲地大喊,說小丑的模仿要比鄉下人像得多,並且大聲要求把鄉下人趕出戲院。

聽到這裡,這個鄉下人把小豬從斗篷裡拿出來,用這最不容置疑的證據說明了他們巨大的錯誤。「看這兒!」他說道,「它說明了你們的判斷力究竟如何。」

◆　　　人們常常為仿製品鼓掌,卻忽略了原來的事物。　　　◆

Townsend 161 = Perry 414

271. The Bull, the Lioness, and the Wild-Boar Hunter

A Bull finding a lion's cub asleep gored him to death with his horns. The Lioness came up, and bitterly lamented the death of her whelp. A wild-boar Hunter, seeing her distress, stood at a distance and said to her, "Think how many men there are who have reason to lament the loss of their children, whose deaths have been caused by you."

♦ Don't complain about things you yourself have done. ♦

271. 公牛、母獅和打野豬的獵人

公牛發現了一隻熟睡的幼獅,用牛角頂死了他。母獅走過來,為自己孩子的死悲痛不已。打野豬的獵人看見了不幸的母獅,站在遠處對她說:「想想有多少人的孩子因你而死去,想想有多少人因此而哭吧!」

♦ 不要抱怨自己犯過的罪行。 ♦

Townsend 5 = Perry 29

272. The Charcoal-Burner and the Fuller

A Charcoal-burner carried on his trade in his own house. One day he met a friend, a Fuller, and entreated him to come and live with him, saying that they should be far better neighbors and that their housekeeping expenses would be lessened. The Fuller replied, " The arrangement is impossible as far as I am concerned, for whatever I should whiten, you would immediately blacken again with your charcoal."

♦ Like will draw like. ♦

272. 燒炭人和漂洗工

有個燒炭人在家裡工作。有一天,他遇到一個漂洗工朋友,就請他搬來和自己住在一起,並說兩人不僅可以成為好鄰居,還

可以省下一筆管理家務的費用。漂洗工答覆道：「就我個人而言，我覺得這個安排不太可能，因為凡是我漂白了的，你馬上就會用木炭把它變黑。」

◆　　　　　　物以類聚，人以群分。　　　　　　◆

Townsend 227 = Perry 475

273. The Cobbler Turned Doctor

A Cobbler unable to make a living by his trade and made desperate by poverty, began to practice medicine in a town in which he was not known. He sold a drug, pretending that it was an antidote to all poisons, and obtained a great name for himself by long-winded puffs and advertisements.

When the Cobbler happened to fall sick himself of a serious illness, the Governor of the town determined to test his skill. For this purpose he called for a cup, and while filling it with water, pretended to mix poison with the Cobbler's antidote, commanding him to drink it on the promise of a reward. The Cobbler, under the fear of death, confessed that he had no knowledge of medicine, and was only made famous by the stupid clamors of the crowd. The Governor then called a public assembly and addressed the citizens, "Of what folly have you been guilty? You have not hesitated to entrust your heads to a man, whom no one could employ to make even the shoes for their feet."

Note: The punch line in Latin depends on the dual meaning of caput, both "head" but also "life": the king makes fun of the people for having trusted their heads (lives) to the very man to whom they would not even trust their feet. Cobblers were proverbially incapable of taking up other professions,"don't let the cobbler make pronouncements on anything above the sole".

◆　　　Beware of those not trained in their craft.　　　◆

273. 補鞋匠改行當醫生

有個補鞋匠靠做鞋無法養活自己，窮得走投無路了，就跑到一個沒有人認識他的小鎮裡當起了醫生。他賣一種藥，謊稱它是世上所有毒藥的解藥。靠著沒完沒了的宣傳和廣告，他聲名大振。

有一次，補鞋匠偶然得了重病並且變得很虛弱，鎮長決定試探一下他的醫術，為此他讓人拿來一隻杯子，倒水的時候，他假裝把毒藥和補鞋匠的解藥混合在一起倒在水裡，讓鞋匠喝了它，還說喝下去有賞。補鞋匠怕死，只好承認自己一點醫術都不懂，是眾人愚蠢的喧鬧使他成了名。於是鎮長把公眾都召集起來，對市民們說：「看看你們犯了多麼愚蠢的錯誤啊！你們毫不猶豫地把自己的性命託付給這個人，可是他連給你們做鞋子都不配。」

注：文中巧妙地運用了拉丁文中 caput 的意思，既是「頭」也是「性命」，國王嘲笑大家把腦袋（性命）託付給一個連腳都不能託付的人，眾所周知，補鞋匠是做不了其他行業的：關於腳以上的事物，補鞋匠是沒有發言權的。

◆　　　要小心那些沒有受過專門訓練的人。　　　◆

Townsend 48 = Perry 51

274. The Laborer and the Snake

A Snake, having made his hole close to the porch of a cottage, inflicted a mortal bite on the Cottager's infant son. Grieving over his loss, the Father resolved to kill the Snake. The next day, when it came out of its hole for food, he took up his axe, but by swinging too hastily, missed its head and cut off only the end of its tail. After some time the Cottager, afraid that the Snake would bite him also, endeavored to make peace, and placed some bread and salt in the hole. The Snake, slightly hissing, said," There can henceforth be no peace between us; for whenever I see you I shall remember the loss of my tail, and whenever you see me you will be thinking of the death of your son."

◆ No one truly forgets injuries in the presence of him who caused the injury. ◆

274. 工人和蛇

一條蛇在緊靠著一個茅屋的門口挖了洞,並把茅屋主人的幼子狠狠地咬了一口。那孩子死了,他的父親非常傷心,決定要殺死這條蛇。第二天在蛇出洞覓食的時候,他拿起斧頭向蛇砍去,但砍得太急促,沒有砍下蛇的頭,只砍下了尾巴尖。

不久,茅屋主人怕蛇也會咬自己,極力求和,將一些麵包和鹽放到蛇洞裡去。蛇發出微微的嘶嘶聲,說:「我們之間休想再有和平,因為我一看見你,便會想起我失去的尾巴;你一瞧見我,便會想起你死去的兒子。」

◆ 在傷害我們的人面前,沒有人會真正忘記所受到的傷害。 ◆

L'Estrange 89 = Perry 56

275. A Cunning Woman

A certain dame that passed in the world under the name of a cunning woman, took upon her to avert divine judgments, and to foretell strange things to come. She played the counterfeit witch so long, till in the conclusion, she was taken up, arraign'd, try'd, convicted, condemned to dye, and at last executed for a witch indeed. D'ye hear, good woman (says one to her, as she was upon the way to her execution) are the gods so much easier then the judges, that you should be able to make them do any thing for ye, and yet could not prevail with the bench for the saving of your own life?

♦   Pretend to be something and pay the consequences.   ♦

275. 狡猾的女人

從前有一位女士，世人都稱她為「狡猾的女人」。她向人們傳達神的旨意，並預言即將發生的怪事。她假扮女巫裝如此之久，以致到最後，她真被當成女巫抓了起來。在經過審判後，她被判定為死刑，最後被處死了。「聽我說，善良的女人，」就在她被押往刑場的路上，有人 對她說，「難道神比法官更好對付嗎？你可以讓神為你做任何事，卻不能使陪審團赦免你的死刑嗎？」

♦   任何偽裝都要付出代價。   ♦

L'Estrange 95 = Perry 170

276. A Doctor and His Patient

Pray, Sir, how d'ye find yourself? Says the Dr. to his patient. Why truly, says the Patient, I have had a violent Sweat; oh the best Sign in the World, quoth the Dr. and then a little while after he is at it again, with a pray how d'ye find your Body? Alas, says t'other, I have just now had such a terrible Fit of horror and shaking upon me! Why this is all as it should be, says the Physician, it shows a mighty Strength of Nature. and then he comes over him a third time with the same Question again; why I am all swell'd, says t'other, as if I had a Dropsy; best of all, quoth the Doctor, and goes his way. Soon after this, comes one of the sick Man's Friends to him with the same Question, how he felt himself; why truly so well, says he, that I am e'en ready to die, of I know not how many good Signs and Tokens.

◆   A death-bed Flattery is the worst of Treacheries.   ◆

276. 醫生和他的病人

「先生，請告訴我，你覺得自己怎麼樣？」醫生對他的病人說。「哎呀！」病人說，「我剛剛冒汗冒得很厲害。」「哦，這可是最好的徵兆了。」醫生說。過了一會兒，醫生又過來詢問病情，問病人覺得怎麼樣。「唉！」病人說，「我剛剛很害怕，渾身哆嗦！」「哎呀，本來就是會這樣的。」 醫生說，「這是因為自然的力量太強大了。」接著，他第三次問了病人同樣的問題。「我為什麼全身浮腫？」病人說，「好像得了水腫一樣？」「這最好不過了。」醫生說完就逕自走開了。在這之後不久，那個病人的一個朋友來看他，同樣問他覺得怎麼樣。「哎呀！我覺得太好了，」他說，「我死而無憾了，你瞧我知道了這麼多正常的體徵和跡象。」

◆　　對垂死之人的奉承是最惡劣的背叛。　　◆

Chambry 134 = Perry 114

277. The Doctor at the Funeral

As a doctor was following the funeral cortege of one of his relatives, he remarked to the mourners in the procession that the man would not have died if he had stopped drinking wine and used an enema. Someone in the crowd then said to the doctor, "Hey! This is hardly the time to offer such advice, when it can't do him any good. You should have given him the advice when he still could have used it!"

Note: Compare the Latin joke in Propertius, Elegies 2.14: "medicine is now being administered to the ashes" (i.e. after the cremation of the body). Compare also the English proverb, "after death, the doctor" (e.g., Shakespeare, Henry VIII 3.2.41: "he brings his physic after the patient's death").

◆　The fable shows that friends should offer their helep when there is need of it, and not play the wise man after the fact.　◆

277. 醫生和葬禮

醫生出席了一個親戚的葬禮。在葬禮上，他對前來悼唁的人說，如果死者能夠把酒戒掉，接受治療，那他就不會死了。有人聽到了他的話，就對醫生說：「你說這些還有什麼用呢？說什麼都救不了他了。你為什麼不在他還有救的時候，建議他戒酒、接受治療呢？」

注：對照普羅佩提烏斯的《頌》第二章第十四節：「現在藥被給予了骨灰。」（比如，在屍體被火葬之後）。也可參照英國的諺語，「病人死了之後，醫生才出現。」（比如，莎士比亞的《亨利八世》第三章第二節四：「醫生在病人死了之後才來為他看病。」）。

◆　**朋友應該及時地提供幫助，而不應該扮演事後諸葛。**　◆

Townsend 233 = Perry 68

278. The Two Men Who Were Enemies

Two men, deadly enemies to each other, were sailing in the same vessel. Determined to keep as far apart as possible, the one seated himself in the stem, and the other in the prow of the ship. A violent storm arose, and with the vessel in great danger of sinking, the one in the stern inquired of the pilot which of the two ends of the ship would go down first. On his replying that he supposed it would be the prow, the Man said,"Death would not be grievous to me, if I could only see my Enemy die before me."

◆　Ultimate satisfaction is seeing your enemy perish before you.　◆

278. 兩個仇敵

兩個死對頭要同乘一艘船出海航行。為了儘量遠離對方，他們兩個人一個坐在船尾,一個坐在船頭。一場猛烈的暴風雨來臨了,船隨時都有沉到海裡的危險,坐在船尾的那個人問舵手,船的哪頭會先沉沒,舵手回答說,他覺得船頭應該會先沉下去的。聽了舵手的話,那個人說:「只要能讓我看到我的敵人比我先死去,就算是我死了,也不會感到痛苦了。」

◆　　　　臨死前的滿足就是看到敵人先死去。　　　　◆

Townsend 80 = Perry 42

279. The Farmer and His Sons

A farmer, being on the point of death, wished to be sure that his sons would give the same attention to his farm as he himself had given it. He called them to his bedside and said, "My sons, there is a great treasure hid in one of my vineyards." The sons, after his death, took their spades and mattocks and carefully dug over every portion of their land. They found no treasure, but the vines repaid their labor by an extraordinary and superabundant crop.

◆　　　　Good counsel is the best legacy.　　　　◆

279. 農夫和他的兒子們

一位臨死的農夫,希望自己的兒子們能像他一樣精心料理農場。他把兒子們叫到床邊,對他們說:「孩子們,在我的葡萄園裡藏著很多財寶。」他的兒子們在農夫死後就用鐵鍬和鋤頭仔仔細細地翻遍了葡萄園裡的角落,結果什麼財寶都沒找到,但是他們的勞動還是得到了回報——這一年的葡萄收成異常好。

◆　　　　好的建議是最好的遺產。　　　　◆

Townsend 6 = Perry 53

280. The Father and His Sons

A father had a family of sons who were perpetually quarreling among themselves. When he failed to heal their disputes by his exhortations, he determined to give them a practical illustration of the evils of disunion; and for this purpose he one day told them to bring him a bundle of sticks. When they had done so, he placed the faggot into the hands of each of them in succession, and ordered them to break it in pieces. They tried with all their strength, and were not able to do it. He next opened the faggot, took the sticks separately, one by one, and again put them into his sons' hands, upon which they broke them easily. He then addressed them in these words,"My sons, if you are of one mind, and unite to assist each other, you will be as this faggot, uninjured by all the attempts of your enemies; but if you are divided among yourselves, you will be broken as easily as these sticks.",

♦   There is strength in union.   ♦

280. 父與子

一位父親有好幾個兒子，兄弟之間經常吵架。父親多次勸告還是未能讓他們平息爭端，於是他就決定用實例來告訴他們兄弟不團結的後果。一天，父親叫兒子們給他拿一捆木棍來，之後讓他們輪流把這捆木棍折斷。兄弟幾人用盡了全力，依舊無法折斷木棍。接著父親解開繩子，又給每個兒子一根木棍，這一次，他們輕而易舉地就把木棍折斷了。然後父親語重心長地對兒子們說：「孩子們，如果你們幾個能同心協力，相互扶持，就會像這捆木棍一樣，任何敵人都傷害不了你們；可是，如果你們自己四分五裂，就會像這一根根的木棍一樣，輕而易舉就被人折斷了。」

◆　　　　　團結就是力量。　　　　　◆

Townsend 79 = Perry 94

281. The Father and His Two Daughters

A man had two daughters, the one married to a gardener, and the other to a tile-maker. After a time he went to the daughter who had married the gardener, and inquired how she was and how all things went with her. She said,"All things are prospering with me, and I have only one wish, that there may be a heavy fall of rain, in order that the plants may be well watered."

Not long after, he went to the daughter who had married the tilemaker, and likewise inquired of her how she fared; she replied,"I want for nothing, and have only one wish, that the dry weather may continue, and the sun shine hot and bright, so that the bricks might be dried."He said to her,"If your sister wishes for rain, and you for dry weather, with which of the two am I to join my wishes?"

◆　　　　You cannot please everyone.　　　　◆

281. 父親和兩個女兒

一位父親有兩個女兒，一個嫁給了花匠，另一個嫁給了瓦匠。過了些日子，他去探望那個嫁給花匠的女兒，問她過得如何。女兒說：「一切都順心如意，只希望老天爺能多下點雨，好好澆灌一下這些植物。」

過沒多久，他又去探望那個嫁給瓦匠的女兒，同樣問她過得如何。女兒回答道：「我什麼都不缺，只希望天氣能一直這麼晴朗，陽光能更燦爛些，這樣磚瓦就能快點乾。」父親對他女兒說：「如果你姐姐希望下雨，而你又盼著天晴，那我應該為誰祈禱呢？」

◆　　　　　不可能讓每個人都滿意。　　　　　◆

Townsend 279 = Perry 363

282. The King's Son and the Painted Lion

A King, whose only son was fond of martial exercises, had a dream in which he was warned that his son would be killed by a lion. Afraid the dream should prove true, he built for his son a pleasant palace and adorned its walls for his amusement with all kinds of life-sized animals, among which was the picture of a lion.

When the young Prince saw this, his grief at being thus confined burst out afresh, and, standing near the lion, he said, "O you most detestable of animals! through a lying dream of my father's, which he saw in his sleep, I am shut up on your account in this palace as if I had been a girl: what shall I now do to you?" With these words he stretched out his hands toward a thorn-tree, meaning to cut a stick from its branches so that he might beat the lion. But one of the tree's prickles pierced his finger and caused great pain and inflammation, so that the young Prince fell down in a fainting fit. A violent fever suddenly set in, from which he died not many days later.

♦ We had better bear our troubles bravely than try to escape them. ♦

282. 國王的兒子與畫上的獅子

　　國王有個喜歡軍事的獨生子。國王做了一個夢，夢見自己被警告說，兒子會被獅子給殺死。他害怕夢會應驗，就為兒子造了座漂亮的宮殿，並且，為了讓兒子高興，還在牆上掛著各式各樣逼真的動物畫像，其中有一幅就是獅子的。

　　年輕的王子看到這幅畫像，突然為自己被這麼關起來而感到悲傷。他站在獅子畫像的旁邊，說道：「喂，你這最可惡的動物！我父親做了一個荒唐的夢，就是因為你，我才像個女孩一樣被關在這裡，我現在該拿你怎麼辦？」說著，他爬上一棵帶刺的樹，打算折下一根樹枝作棍子，這樣他就可以打那獅子了。可是他的手指給樹刺紮破了，非常疼，還感染了。就這樣，年輕的王子一陣眩暈倒下了。他發了高燒，沒過幾天就死了。

♦ 人們要勇敢地去面對困難，而不要試圖去迴避它。 ♦

Townsend 62 = Perry 31

283. The Man and His Two Sweethearts

　　A middle-aged man, whose hair had begun to turn gray, courted two women at the same time. One of them was young, and the other well advanced in years. The elder woman, ashamed to be courted by a man younger than herself, made a point, whenever her admirer visited her, to pull out some portion of his black hairs. The younger, on the contrary, not wishing to become the wife of an old man, was equally zealous in removing every gray hair she could find. Thus it came to pass that between them both he very soon found that he had not a hair left on his head.

♦　　Those who seek to please everybody please nobody.　♦

283. 男人和兩個情人

一個頭髮已經開始變白的中年人，同時追求兩個女人，一個年輕，另一個年老。那年老的女人覺得被比自己年輕的男人追求面子上不好看，於是她打定主意，每逢她的愛慕者一來，就拔掉他一些黑髮。恰好相反，那年輕的女人不想成為一個老頭的妻子，於是也同樣拔掉她能找到的每一根白髮。兩個人輪流拔著，結果他很快就發現，自己頭上一根頭髮也不剩了。

♦　　　　想使人人滿意，必定無人滿意。　　　　♦

Townsend 209 = Perry 95

284. The Man and His Wife

A man had a Wife who made herself hated by all the members of his household. Wishing to find out if she had the same effect on the persons in her father's house, he made some excuse to send her home on a visit to her father.

After a short time she returned, and when he inquired how she had got on and how the servants had treated her, she replied, "The herdsmen and shepherds cast on me looks of aversion."

He said, "O Wife, if you were disliked by those who go out early in the morning with their flocks and return late in the evening, what must have been felt towards you by those with whom you passed the whole day!"

♦   Straws show how the wind blows.   ♦

284. 男人和他的妻子

一個男人的妻子與他家裡的所有人都相處不好。丈夫想知道她與娘家的人是否也是如此,就找個藉口把她送回了娘家去探望她的父親。

不久妻子回來了,就問她過得怎麼樣,那些僕人待她又怎麼樣。她回答說:「那些放牛和牧羊的人都不給我好臉色看。」

他說:「噢!老婆,如果連那些早出晚歸的牧人都不喜歡你,那麼整天和你在一起過日子的人又該作何感想呢?」

♦   看草知風向。   ♦

Chambry 10 = Perry 5

285. The Man, the Pig and the Miracle

In Athens, there was a man who had taken out a loan and was now being asked by the creditor to pay back the money. At first he asked the creditor to give him an extension, since he said he couldn't manage to find the cash. But he could not get the creditor to agree, so he brought the only pig that he had, a sow, and put it up for sale as the creditor was looking on. A buyer approached and asked if the sow was a good breeder. The man replied that she was indeed; in fact, her litters were miraculous: for the Mysteries she gave birth only to female piglets, while for the Panathenaea Festival she gave birth only to males. When the buyer was dumbfounded by this story, the creditor added,"That's nothing! For the Festival of Dionysus, she gives birth to baby goats."

◆ This story shows that when it serves their purposes, people commonly do not hesitate to swear to the most incredible fabrications. ◆

285. 人、豬和奇蹟

從前在雅典，有個人借了債未能如期歸還。債主向他討債的時候，他沒有錢來還，於是，只好在債主的監視下，把他唯一的一隻母豬賣掉。有個買家過來問他，這隻母豬是不是很能生養。「當然了！」那人回答說，「事實上，她產的小豬都太不可思議了！有些時候，她生出來的都是小母豬，而在另一些時候，她生出來的都是小公豬。」買主驚訝得無言以對，債主又接著說：「這沒什麼！她有時候甚至還能生出小山羊呢！」

◆ 為了達到目的，即使是最荒唐的事情，人們也會毫不猶豫地斷言。 ◆

Townsend 272 = Perry 32

286. The Manslayer

A man committed a murder, and was pursued by the relations of the man whom he murdered. On his reaching the river Nile he saw a Lion on its bank and being fearfully afraid, climbed up a tree. He found a serpent in the upper branches of the tree, and again being greatly alarmed, he threw himself into the river, where a crocodile caught him and ate him. Thus the earth, the air, and the water alike refused shelter to a murderer.

♦   Murderers have no place to hide.   ♦

286. 殺人兇手

有個人殺了人,被受害者的親屬追捕。他跑到尼羅河邊,看見岸上有頭獅子,非常害怕,就爬到一棵樹上。他發現樹枝上有一條大蛇懸在他頭上,又驚恐萬分,於是跳到了河裡,結果被鱷魚抓住並吃掉了。可見,土、空氣、水都不會庇護殺人犯。

♦   天網恢恢,疏而不漏。   ♦

Townsend 122 = Perry 927

287. The Milk-Woman and Her Pail

A farmer's daughter was carrying her Pail of milk from the field to the farmhouse, when she fell a-musing. " The money for which this milk will be sold, will buy at least three hundred eggs. The eggs, allowing for all mishaps, will produce two hundred and fifty chickens. The chickens will become ready for the market when poultry will fetch the highest price, so that by the end of the year I shall have money enough from my share to buy a new gown. In this dress I will go to the Christmas parties, where all the young fellows will propose to me, but I will toss my head and refuse them every one."At this moment she tossed her head in unison with her thoughts, when down fell the milk pail to the ground, and all her imaginary schemes perished in a moment.

◆　　Do not count your chickens before they are hatched.　　◆

287. 擠奶姑娘和她的桶子

　　一個農夫的女兒頭頂著一桶牛奶從農地裡向家走去，這時她想起了件美妙的事。「將來賣掉這牛奶的錢至少可以買三百個雞蛋。這些雞蛋，除去意外損失，將來能孵出二百五十隻小雞。當雞的價格漲到最高價時，這些雞就可以到市場上賣了，這樣到年底，我所得的錢就夠買一套新禮服了。我要穿著這件禮服去聖誕晚會，在那兒，所有的小夥子都會來向我求婚，但是我要搖頭拒絕他們每一個人。」這時，她邊想邊搖頭，牛奶桶掉在了地上，她想像的所有計畫，頓時都破滅了。

◆　　小雞還沒孵出來不要急著數有多少隻。　　◆

Townsend 283 = Perry 721

288. The Miller, His Son, and Their Ass

　　A Miller and his son were driving their Ass to a neighboring fair to sell him. They had not gone far when they met with a troop of women collected round a well, talking and laughing. "Look there," cried one of them,"did you ever see such fellows, to be trudging along the road on foot when they might ride?" The old man hearing this, quickly made his son mount the Ass, and continued to walk along merrily by his side. Presently they came up to a group of old men in earnest debate. " There," said one of them,"it proves what I was a-saying. What respect is shown to old age in these days? Do you see that idle lad riding while his old father has to walk? Get down, you young scapegrace, and let the old man rest his weary limbs."Upon this the old man made his son dismount, and got up himself. In this manner they had not proceeded far when they met a company of women and children,"Why, you lazy old fellow" cried several tongues at once,"how can you ride upon the beast, while that poor little lad there can hardly keep pace by the side of you?" The good-natured Miller immediately took up his son behind him. They had now almost reached the town. "Pray, honest friend" said a citizen,"is that Ass your own?" "Yes," replied the old man. "O, one would not have thought so," said the other,"by the way you load him. Why, you two fellows are better able to carry the poor beast than he you.""Anything to please you," said the old man; "we can but try."So, alighting with his son, they tied the legs of the Ass together and with the help of a pole endeavored to carry him on their shoulders over a bridge near the entrance to the town. This entertaining sight brought the people in crowds to laugh at it, till the Ass, not liking the noise nor the strange handling that he was subject to, broke the cords that bound him and, tumbling off the pole, fell into the river. Upon this, the old man, vexed and ashamed, made the best of his way home again, convinced that by endeavoring to please everybody he had pleased nobody, and lost his Ass in the bargain.

♦ You can't please everyone. ♦

288. 磨坊主、他的兒子和他們的驢

一位磨坊主和他的兒子＜

正趕驢到附近的集市去賣。沒走多遠，他們就遇見一群女人圍著一口井，正說笑著。「看那兒！」其中一個婦女叫道，「你們見過這樣的人嗎？有驢可以騎的時候卻要徒步跋涉？」

老人聽了這話，立即讓兒子騎上驢，自己繼續愉快地走路。不久，他們遇見一群正激烈爭論著的老人。「看那兒！」其中一位老人說，「這證明了我說的話。現在對老年人還有什麼尊重？你們看見了嗎？那懶傢伙騎驢，他老爹卻必須走路。下來，你這個小壞蛋，讓老人歇歇他疲勞的腿。」聽到這話，老人讓兒子下驢來，自己騎上去了。就這樣，他們還沒走出多遠，碰見了一群婦女和孩子：「哎呀！你這懶惰的老傢伙。」大家不約而同地喊，「這可憐的小傢伙都快跟不上你了，你怎麼還騎著驢？」好脾氣的磨坊主立即讓兒子坐在自己身後，他們現在就要到鎮上了。

「請問，誠實的朋友。」一個人說，「那驢是你自己的嗎？」「是。」。老人回答。「噢，別人可不會這麼想。」另一個人說，「因為你這樣騎著他。哎呀！你們兩個傢伙最好能馱著這可憐的畜牲，這樣總比讓牠馱著你們強。」「都聽你的。」老人說，「我們只好試試了。」

因此，磨坊主和兒子一起下驢，把驢的腿綁在一根桿子上，然後擔在肩上，走過城門附近的一座橋。這有趣的場面使人群發笑；而驢不喜歡這笑聲，也不喜歡主人這樣奇怪地對待牠，牠掙斷了綁著牠的繩子，從桿上摔下來，掉進了河裡。看到這情景，老人又羞又惱，走最近的路回到家中。他明白了，極力想取悅每個人，最終不能取悅任何一個人，而且自己還丟了驢。

◆　　　　　不可能讓每個人都滿意。　　　　　◆

Townsend 38 = Perry 225

289. The Miser

A Miser sold all that he had and bought a lump of gold, which he buried in a hole in the ground by the side of an old wall and went to look at daily. One of his workmen observed his frequent visits to the spot and decided to watch his movements. He soon discovered the secret of the hidden treasure, and digging down, came to the lump of gold, and stole it. The Miser, on his next visit, found the hole empty and began to tear his hair and to make loud lamentations. A neighbor, seeing him overcome with grief and learning the cause, said,"Pray do not grieve so; but go and take a stone, and place it in the hole, and fancy that the gold is still lying there. It will do you quite the same service; for when the gold was there, you had it not, as you did not make the slightest use of it."

♦　　Wealth not used is wealth that does not exist.　　♦

289. 守財奴

一個守財奴賣掉他所有的東西，買了一塊金子。他把金子埋在一堵舊牆邊一個地洞裡，天天去看。他的一個工人發現他經常去那個地方，就決定觀察他的行動。他很快發現了這藏寶的祕密，於是往下挖，找到並且偷走了金子。守財奴下一次去看的時候，發現洞空了，於是扯著頭髮，大聲哭起來。一位鄰居看見他悲痛欲絕，知道了原因後，說：「你別太難過了，只要去拿一塊石頭，把它放在洞裡，假想著金子還在那兒。它在那兒和金子在那兒是一樣的，因為金子在那兒的時候，你也等於是沒有金子，因為你根本沒有用過它。」

♦　　財富不加以利用，就失去了存在的價值。　　♦

L'Estrange 176 = Perry 221

290. A Musician

A man that had a very course voice, but an excellent musique-room, would be still practicing in that chamber, for the advantage of the echo. He took such a conceit upon't, that he must needs be showing his parts upon a public theatre, where he performed so very ill, that the auditory hissed him off the stage, and threw stones at him.

♦　　We rarely see ourselves as others see us.　　♦

290. 音樂家

有這樣一個人,他的聲音不怎麼樣,但練歌房卻很好,他經常在房間裡練歌,因為房間裡的回音使他的歌聲顯得非常好聽。他對此誤以為真,覺得自己必須在劇院裡向公眾一展他的歌喉。但是,他演唱得非常糟糕,觀眾把他噓下了台,還向他扔石頭。

♦　　我們對自己的瞭解程度遠不及別人對我們的瞭解。　　♦

Townsend 85 = Perry 60

291. The Old Man and Death I

An old man was employed in cutting wood in the forest, and, in carrying the faggots to the city for sale one day, became very wearied with his long journey. He sat down by the wayside, and throwing down his load, besought "Death" to come. "Death" immediately appeared in answer to his summons and asked for what reason he had called him. The old Man hurriedly replied, "That, lifting up the load, you may place it again upon my shoulders."

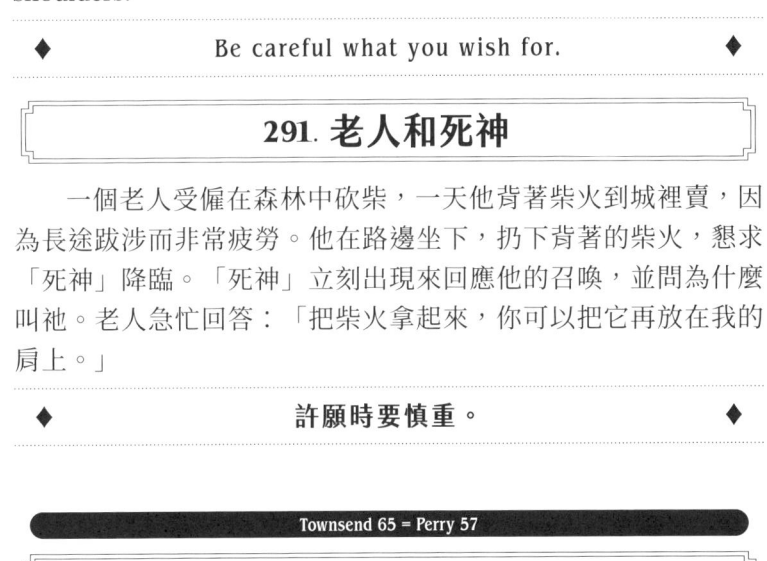

♦　　　　　　Be careful what you wish for.　　　　　　♦

291. 老人和死神

　　一個老人受僱在森林中砍柴,一天他背著柴火到城裡賣,因為長途跋涉而非常疲勞。他在路邊坐下,扔下背著的柴火,懇求「死神」降臨。「死神」立刻出現來回應他的召喚,並問為什麼叫祂。老人急忙回答:「把柴火拿起來,你可以把它再放在我的肩上。」

♦　　　　　　　　許願時要慎重。　　　　　　　　♦

Townsend 65 = Perry 57

292. The Old Woman and the Physician

　　An Old Woman having lost the use of her eyes, called in a Physician to heal them, and made this bargain with him in the presence of witnesses:that if he should cure her blindness, he should receive from her a sum of money; but if her infirmity remained, she should give him nothing. This agreement being made, the Physician, time after time, applied his salve to her eyes, and on every visit took something away, stealing all her property little by little, and when he had got all she had, he healed her and demanded the promised payment.

　　The old woman, when she recovered her sight and saw none

of her goods in her house, would give him nothing. The Physician insisted on his claim, and. as she still refused, summoned her before the Judge. The Old Woman, standing up in the Court, argued, " This man here speaks the truth in what he says; for I did promise to give him a sum of money if I should recover my sight: but if I continued blind, I was to give him nothing. Now he declares that I am healed. I on the contrary affirm that I am still blind; for when I lost the use of my eyes, I saw in my house various chattels and valuable goods: but now, though he swears I am cured of my blindness, I am not able to see a single thing in it."

◆ That fable shows that by their own actions, wicked people can unwittingly serve as witnesses against themselves in a court of law. ◆

292. 老婦人和醫生

一位老婦人雙目失明，叫了一位醫生來治療，並且在有證人在場的情況下與醫生達成了協定：如果醫生治好了她的眼睛，就能從她那裡得到一筆錢；可如果她的病不見好轉，她就一分錢都不給。協議達成後，醫生一次又一次地給她的眼睛塗藥膏，而且每次來訪，他都拿走一些東西，就這樣一點一點地偷走了她所有的財產。當他得到了老婦人所有的東西時，他治好了老婦人，並要求她支付約定好的報酬。

恢復視力並看到屋裡一無所有的老婦人，一分錢也不給醫生。醫生堅持他的要求，但是老婦人始終拒絕，於是醫生把她告到了法官那裡。站在法庭上，老婦人辯解說：「這個人在這兒說的話是事實，因為我確實答應過，如果我恢復了視力，就給他一筆錢；但是如果我繼續失明，我什麼都不給他。現在他宣佈我痊癒了。而相反，我認定我仍然看不見，因為我的眼睛看不見的時候，我還能知道我屋裡有各種家當和貴重物品；可現在，儘管他發誓說治好了我的眼睛，可我看不見屋裡有任何東西。」

◆ 　　這則寓言告訴我們，惡人在法庭上會不由自主地證明自己的罪行。　　◆

Townsend 94 = Perry 493

293. The Old Woman and the Wine-Jar

　　An old woman found an empty jar which had lately been full of prime old wine and which still retained the fragrant smell of its former contents. She greedily placed it several times to her nose, and drawing it backwards and forwards said," O most delicious! How nice must the Wine itself have been, when it leaves behind in the very vessel which contained it so sweet a perfume !"

◆ 　　The memory of a good deed lives. 　　◆

293. 老婦人和酒罈

　　一個老婦人發現了一個空酒罈，這個酒罈剛剛裝過上等的陳酒，仍然留有盛過之酒的芳香。她幾次貪婪地把酒罈拿到鼻子旁邊，來回地嗅著，說：「一定很香！裝過酒的罐子都留著這麼香的味道，那酒本身得有多香呀！」

◆ 　　美好的行為能夠流芳百世。　　◆

Townsend 297 = Perry 204

294. The Rich Man and the Tanner

A rich man lived near a Tanner, and not being able to bear the unpleasant smell of the tan-yard, he pressed his neighbor to go away. The Tanner put off his departure from time to time, saying that he would leave soon. But as he still continued to stay, as time went on, the rich man became accustomed to the smell, and feeling no manner of inconvenience, made no further complaints.

◆ One can get used to most anything. ◆

294. 富人和皮匠

一個住在皮匠隔壁的富人,因難以忍受皮革場中難聞的氣味,就強迫這位鄰居搬走。皮匠一次次地推遲搬走的時間,總說他馬上就會離開,可是卻仍然待在那兒。隨著時間的推移,富人對這種難聞的氣味也漸漸習慣了,不再感到任何不便,也就不再抱怨了。

◆ 時間長了對一切都會習慣。 ◆

Townsend 182 = Perry 419

295. The Thief and the Innkeeper

A Thief hired a room in a tavern and stayed a while in the hope of stealing something which should enable him to pay his reckoning. When he had waited some days in vain, he saw the

Innkeeper dressed in a new and handsome coat and sitting before his door. The Thief sat down beside him and talked with him. As the conversation began to flag, the Thief yawned terribly and at the same time howled like a wolf. The Innkeeper said,"Why do you howl so fearfully?" "I will tell you," said the Thief,"but first let me ask you to hold my clothes, or I shall tear them to pieces. I know not, sir, when I got this habit of yawning, nor whether these attacks of howling were inflicted on me as a judgment for my crimes, or for any other cause; but this I do know, that when I yawn for the third time, I actually turn into a wolf and attack men."

With this speech he commenced a second fit of yawning and again howled like a wolf, as he had at first. The Innkeeper, hearing his tale and believing what he said, became greatly alarmed and, rising from his seat, attempted to run away. The Thief laid hold of his coat and entreated him to stop, saying,"Pray wait, sir, and hold my clothes, or I shall tear them to pieces in my fury, when I turn into a wolf."At the same moment he yawned the third time and set up a terrible howl. The Innkeeper, frightened lest he should be attacked, left his new coat in the Thief's hand and ran as fast as he could into the inn for safety. The Thief made off with the coat and did not return again to the inn.

◆   Every tale is not to be believed.   ◆

295. 賊和客棧老闆

賊在旅館租了一間房，一住就是好幾天。他希望能偷點東西來支付房租。可是白白等了幾天，仍然是一無所獲。一天，他看到旅館老闆穿著一件很氣派的新外套坐在門口，便走上前去坐下來，和他閒聊起來。聊著聊著，賊突然就使勁地打了個哈欠，並像狼一樣大吼起來。店老闆不解地問：「你的叫聲怎麼那麼嚇人呢？」、「我願意告訴你。」賊說，「但是，我得先請你把我的衣服抓緊，不然的話，我會把它撕得粉碎。先生，我自己也不知道，我什麼時候有了打哈欠的習慣，也不知道這種可怕的嚎叫，傳染到我身上是懲罰我的罪孽，還是其他別的原因；我只知道，當我第三次打哈欠的時候，我就會變成狼去襲擊別人。」

　　說了這番話之後，他又開始打第二個哈欠，並且和上次一樣，發出了狼一般的嚎叫聲。客棧老闆聽了他的故事，信以為真，非常害怕，趕緊站起來想逃走。賊拽著他的外套讓他留步，說：「先生，請等一等，務必要抓著我的衣服，不然我變成狼時，就會暴怒地撕破它。」話音剛落，賊又開始打第三個哈欠，嘴裡還發出讓人心驚膽戰的嚎叫。旅館的老闆生怕他會真的撲過來咬他，便使勁掙脫出來，也顧不上那件新外套還抓在賊手裡，飛快地跑進旅館裡保命。賊如願得到了大衣，就再也不回那家旅館了。

◆　　　　　　不應該輕易地相信別人。　　　　　　◆

Townsend 291 = Perry 122

296. The Thieves and the Cock

　　Some Thieves broke into a house and found nothing but a Cock, whom they stole, and got off as fast as they could. Upon arriving at home they prepared to kill the cock, who thus pleaded for his life,"Pray spare me; I am very serviceable to men. I wake them up in the night to their work." " That is the very reason why we must the more kill you," they replied; "for when you wake your neighbors, you entirely put an end to our business."

◆ The safeguards of virtue are hateful those with evil intentions. ◆

296. 小偷和公雞

幾個小偷悄悄溜進一戶人家，可是除了一隻公雞什麼也沒找到。他們把雞偷了就趕快逃跑了。一到家，他們就準備殺掉公雞。公雞為了能保住自己的性命，苦苦央求道：「求求你們放過我吧！我對人類有很大的用處。我能在深夜把人們叫醒起來工作。」「就憑這一點，你就非死不可！」小偷們答道，「當你叫醒鄰居們時，也是我們偷盜結束之時！」

◆ 美德的捍衛者正是那些惡徒的敵人。 ◆

Townsend 113 = Perry 432

297. The Three Tradesmen

A great city was besieged, and its inhabitants were called together to consider the best means of protecting it from the enemy. A Bricklayer earnestly recommended bricks as affording the best material for an effective resistance. A Carpenter, with equal enthusiasm, proposed timber as a preferable method of defense. Upon which a Currier stood up and said, "Sirs, I differ from you altogether: there is no material for resistance equal to a covering of hides; and nothing so good as leather?"

◆ Every man for himself ◆

297. 三個工匠

一座大城市被敵軍包圍了。城裡的居民被聚集到一起，共同商議對抗敵人的辦法。熱心的砌磚匠主張用磚來抵禦敵人。懷著同樣熱情的木匠提議用木頭會更有效。這時一個皮匠站出來說：「先生們，你們的意見我都不同意。我認為要抵禦敵人的話，沒有一樣東西比獸皮更好了。」

◆　　　　每一個人首先想到的都是自己。　　　　◆

Townsend 243 = Perry 370

298. The Trumpeter Taken Prisoner

A Trumpeter, bravely leading on the soldiers, was captured by the enemy. He cried out to his captors, "Pray spare me, and do not take my life without cause or without inquiry. I have not slain a single man of your troop. I have no arms, and carry nothing but this one brass trumpet." " That is the very reason for which you should be put to death," they said; "for, while you do not fight yourself, your trumpet stirs all the others to battle."

◆　　　　　　　Words may be deeds.　　　　　　　◆

298. 被俘的號兵

一個號兵帶著戰士勇敢地衝鋒，被敵人俘獲了。他朝著抓住他的人大喊：「求求你放了我吧！請不要無緣無故地殺我，我沒有傷害你方任何人。我除了這個銅號，身上沒有任何武器。」「正因為這樣，你才更應該死。」敵人回答，「你雖然不親自衝鋒陷陣，但是你的號角卻召集所有的士兵來攻打我們。」

◆ 　　　　　有時候言語就是行動。　　　　　◆

L'Estrange 58 = Perry 66

299. Two Young Men and a Cook

Two young fellows slipped into a cooks shop, and while the master was busy at his work, one of them stole a piece of flesh, and conveyed it to the other. The master missed it immediately, and challenged them with the theft. He that took it, swore he had none on't. and he that had it, swore as desperately that he did not take it. The cook reflecting upon the conceit: Well, my masters, (says he) these frauds and fallacies may pass upon men; but there's an eye above that sees thorough them.

◆ 　　　　You can trick man but not God.　　　　◆

299. 兩個年輕人和一個廚師

兩個年輕人溜進了廚師的店裡，趁著廚師在忙的時候，其中一人偷走了一塊肉，把它交給另外一個人。店長馬上就覺察到了，並指責他們偷了他的肉。偷肉的那人發誓說他沒有偷，而藏肉的人也同樣發誓沒有偷。廚師想了想，「哦，年輕人！」，他說，「這些欺騙的伎倆或許騙得過世人，但是騙不了舉頭三尺的神明。」

◆ 　　　你可以騙得過世人，但騙不了神明。　　　◆

Townsend 73 = Perry 55

300. The Widow and Her Little Maidens

A widow who was fond of cleaning had two little maidens to wait on her. She was in the habit of waking them early in the morning, at cockcrow. The maidens, aggravated by such excessive labor, resolved to kill the cock who roused their mistress so early. When they had done this, they found that they had only prepared for themselves greater troubles, for their mistress, no longer hearing the hour from the cock, woke them up to their work in the middle of the night.

◆ Be careful what you ask for. ◆

300. 寡婦和她的小女僕

有個有潔癖的寡婦，雇了兩個女僕來伺候她。寡婦習慣在早上公雞鳴叫的時候叫醒僕人，這樣就可以讓她們多做些事。女僕對如此繁重的勞役感到憤憤不平，於是決定殺了那隻公雞。殺掉公雞後，她們發現自己的日子反而更加艱難了，因為她們的女主人聽不到公雞的打鳴聲，半夜就開始催促她們起來工作了。

◆ 請求之前要慎重考慮。 ◆

L'Estrange 157 = Perry 246

301. A Wife and a Drunken Husband

A woman that lay under the mortification of a fuddling husband, took him once when he was dead drunk; and had his body laid in a charnel-house. By the time that she thought he might be come to himself again, away goes she, and knocks at the door. Who's there (says the toper). One, says the woman, that brings meat for the dead. Friend, (says he), bring me drink rather. I wonder any body that knows me, should bring me one without t'other. Nay then, (says she), the humour I perceive has taken possession of him; he has gotten a habit, and his case is desperate.

♦ It's hard to give up bad habits. ♦

301. 妻子和喝醉酒的丈夫

有個女人嫁給了個嗜酒如命的丈夫。有一次，她的丈夫喝得酩酊大醉，她就把他帶到了停屍房。在覺得他差不多該醒來的時候，她走過去敲了敲門。「是誰啊？」裡面的人說。女人回答：「我是來給死人送肉的。」、「朋友……」他說，「還是給我點酒吧！如果是認識我的人，怎麼會只給我帶肉，而沒有帶酒呢？」「那就不要了。」她說，「他已經完全被酒控制了；這是他的習慣，他的情況已經無藥可救了。」

♦ 陋習難改。 ♦

L'Estrange 198 = Perry 205

302. A Woman and Her Two Daughters

A woman that had two daughters, buried one of them, and mourners were provided to attend the funeral. The surviving daughter wondered to see strangers so much concerned at the loss of her sister, and her nearest relations so little. Pray mother, says she, what's the reason of this? Oh, says the mother, we that are a-kin to her, are never the better for crying, but the strangers have money for't.

♦   Professional mourners serve those who pay the most.   ♦

302. 一個女人和她的兩個女兒

有個女人生了兩個女兒，其中一個死了，她把她安葬了之後，邀請了哀悼者來參加葬禮。還活著的那個女兒，看見陌生人對他姐姐的去世感到這麼悲傷，而她的至親卻很平靜。「媽媽！」她說，「這到底是為什麼？」，「噢！」母親回答道，「我們雖然是她的親人，卻不會哭得比他們更悲傷，因為這些陌生人是為了錢才哭的。」

♦   給的錢越多，職業弔唁者哭得越悲痛。   ♦

BOY 男孩

Townsend 205 = Perry 211

303. The Boy Bathing

A boy bathing in a river was in danger of being drowned. He called out to a passing traveler for help, but instead of holding out a helping hand, the man stood by unconcernedly, and scolded the boy for his imprudence. "Oh, sir!" cried the youth, "pray help me now and scold me afterwards."

♦   Counsel without help is useless.   ♦

303. 洗澡的男孩

一個男孩在河裡洗澡，就要被河水淹死了。他對著岸上經過的路人大聲求救，那人不但不伸出援助之手，反倒漠不關心地站在那兒，責怪男孩太不小心。小男孩大喊：「先生，求你現在先把我救上來，以後再罵我也不晚！」

◆　　不願伸出援助之手，再多的說教也毫無用處。　◆

L'Estrange 165 = Perry 54

304. A Boy and Cockles

Some people were roasting of cockles, and they hissed in the fire. Well (says a block-headed boy) these are villainous creatures sure, to sing when their houses are a-fire over their heads.

◆　　Obtain facts before making an opinion.　　◆

304. 男孩和文蛤

有些人在烤文蛤，文蛤在火裡發出咻咻的聲音。「嗯！」一個笨笨的小男孩說，「這些傢伙肯定是瘋了，頭頂的房子都著火了居然還在唱歌！」

◆　　要瞭解事實之後，才能下結論。　　◆

Townsend 46 = Perry 18

305. The Boy and the Filberts

A boy put his hand into a pitcher full of filberts. He grasped as many as he could possibly hold, but when he tried to pull out his hand, he was prevented from doing so by the neck of the pitcher. Unwilling to lose his filberts, and yet unable to withdraw his hand, he burst into tears and bitterly lamented his disappointment. A bystander said to him,"Be satisfied with half the quantity, and you will readily draw out your hand."

◆　　　　　Do not attempt too much at once.　　　　　◆

305. 男孩和榛子

　　有個男孩把手伸到裝滿榛子的罐子裡，抓了滿滿一大把榛子，當他打算從罐子裡把手拿出來的時候，手卻被卡在罐口了。男孩不願意放棄手中的榛子，但是手又被卡在罐子裡拿不出來，因此嚎啕大哭，一面哭，一面抱怨自己真不走運。一個旁觀者對他說：「如果你只抓半把榛子，你早就把手從罐裡拿出來了。」

◆　　　　　　　　切忌急功近利。　　　　　　　　◆

Townsend 61 = Perry 209

306. The Boy and the Nettles

　　A boy was stung by a Nettle. He ran home and told his Mother, saying,"Although it hurts me very much, I only touched it gently." " That was just why it stung you," said his Mother. "The next time you touch a Nettle, grasp it boldly, and it will be soft as silk to your hand, and not in the least hurt you."

◆　　　Whatever you do, do with all your might.　　　◆

306. 男孩和蕁麻

一個男孩被蕁麻的刺扎到了,他跑到家對他媽媽說:「我不過是輕輕地摸了摸蕁麻,但卻被扎得好疼啊!」男孩的媽媽回答道:「正是因為你很輕地撫摸它,蕁麻才會扎到你。下次,你必須把蕁麻使勁地握在手心裡,它才會變得如同絲綢那樣柔軟,完全不會傷害到你。」

♦ 不管做什麼事情都必須全力以赴。 ♦

Townsend 84 = Perry 200

307. The Thief and His Mother

A boy stole a lesson-book from one of his schoolfellows and took it home to his Mother. She not only abstained from beating him, but encouraged him. He next time stole a cloak and brought it to her, and she again commended him. The Youth, advanced to adulthood, proceeded to steal things of still greater value. At last he was caught in the very act, and having his hands bound behind him, was led away to the place of public execution.

His Mother followed in the crowd and violently beat her breast in sorrow, whereupon the young man said,"I wish to say something to my Mother in her ear."She came close to him, and he quickly seized her ear with his teeth and bit it off. The Mother upbraided him as an unnatural child, whereon he replied,"Ah! if you had beaten me when I first stole and brought to you that lesson-book, I should not have come to this, nor have been thus led to a disgraceful death"

♦　　　We are made by our teachings in youth.　　　♦

307. 賊和他的母親

　　一個男孩把他同學的課本偷回家給他媽媽，他媽媽不僅沒有打他，而且還誇獎他。於是男孩把斗篷又偷回家，再次得到了媽媽的表揚。這個年輕人長大成人之後，便開始偷更貴重的東西，終於有一次在行竊中被人當場抓獲，結果他被五花大綁地帶到刑場，準備公開處死。

　　他的媽媽跟在人群中，搥胸頓足，哭天喊地。那位青年說：「我想跟我媽私下裡說幾句話。」誰知當他媽媽走到他身邊，他卻一口咬下了她的耳朵。他媽責怪他說他不可理喻，他卻講道：「啊！想當初，我第一次把偷來的課本帶回去給你的時候，你如果打了我，我也就不至於落到現在這種境地，也更不會這麼恥辱地死去了。」

♦　　　年輕時受到的教導決定了人的一生。　　　♦

FARMER/HERDSMAN 農夫 / 牧人
Townsend 143 = Perry 283

308. The Farmer and the Fox

　　A Farmer, who bore a grudge against a Fox for robbing his poultry yard, caught him at last, and being determined to take an ample revenge, tied some rope well soaked in oil to his tail, and set it on fire. The Fox by a strange fatality rushed to the fields of the Farmer who had captured him. It was the time of the wheat harvest; but the Farmer reaped nothing that year and returned home grieving sorely.

♦   Be careful lest revenge backfire.   ♦

308. 農夫和狐狸

有一隻狐狸常常來偷農夫的家禽,農夫恨透了他,最後終於抓住了這隻狐狸,決定要好好教訓他一頓來解恨。於是他把一根浸滿了油的繩子綁在狐狸的尾巴上,然後點燃了繩子。狐狸被這突如其來的火嚇得東逃西竄,跑進了這位農夫的莊稼地裡,燒光了所有莊稼。那正是小麥的收成時節,而農夫顆粒無收,傷心欲絕地回家了。

♦   小心不要讓復仇的行為害了自己。   ♦

Townsend 21 = Perry 176

309. The Farmer and the Snake

One winter a Farmer found a Snake stiff and frozen with cold. He had compassion on it, and taking it up, placed it in his bosom. The Snake was quickly revived by the warmth, and resuming its natural instincts, bit its benefactor, inflicting on him a mortal wound. "Oh," cried the Farmer with his last breath, "I am rightly served for pitying a scoundrel."

♦   The greatest kindness will not bind the ungrateful.   ♦

309. 農夫和蛇

有一年冬天,一位農夫發現了一條被凍僵的蛇,他很同情這條蛇,就把牠撿起來,放在自己懷裡。蛇暖和後很快甦醒過來,並恢復了牠的本性,咬了恩人一口,給農夫造成了致命的傷害。農夫臨死前啜泣道:「我真是活該啊!要去同情這種惡人。」

◆　　　心地再善良的人也無法感化忘恩負義的人。　　　◆

Townsend 20 = Perry 194

310. The Farmer and the Stork

A Farmer placed nets on his newly-sown plowlands and caught a number of Cranes, which came to pick up his seed. With them he trapped a Stork that had fractured his leg in the net and was earnestly beseeching the Farmer to spare his life. "Pray save me, Master" he said, "and let me go free this once. My broken limb should excite your pity. Besides, I am no Crane, I am a Stork, a bird of excellent character; and see how I love and slave for my father and mother. Look too, at my feathers— they are not the least like those of a Crane." The Farmer laughed aloud and said, "It may be all as you say, I only know this: I have taken you with these robbers, the Cranes, and you must die in their company."

◆　　　Birds of a feather flock together.　　　◆

310. 農夫和鸛

農夫在剛剛播過種的農田上裝了網,抓住了很多來偷吃種子的鶴。這其中還有一隻鸛,他的腳被網折斷了,拚命地哀求農夫饒他一命:「求您救救我,老爺,這次就放了我吧!求您看在我斷腿的份上,可憐可憐我吧!而且我不是一般的鶴,我是一隻品德高尚的鶴,您看我是多麼孝敬自己的父母啊!為他們辛勤勞作。看看我的羽毛,和鶴的根本就不一樣。」農夫聽了哈哈大笑,說:「或許你說得沒錯,但我只知道,你和那些偷吃的鶴一起被我抓住,你就要和他們一起受死。」

◆　　　　　　　**物以類聚,人以群分。**　　　　　　　◆

Townsend 17 = Perry 49

311. The Herdsman and the Lost Bull

A Herdsman tending his flock in a forest lost a Bull-calf from the fold. After a long and fruitless search, he made a vow that, if he could only discover the thief who had stolen the Calf, he would offer a lamb in sacrifice to Hermes, Pan, and the Guardian Deities of the forest. Not long afterwards, as he ascended a small hillock, he saw at its foot a Lion feeding on the Calf. Terrified at the sight, he lifted his eyes and his hands to heaven, and said, "Just now I vowed to offer a lamb to the Guardian Deities of the forest if I could only find out who had robbed me; but now that I have discovered the thief I would willingly add a full-grown Bull to the Calf I have lost, if I may only secure my own escape from him in safety."

◆　　　Be careful what you wish for; your wish may be granted.　　　◆

311. 牧人和走失的公牛

牧人在森林中丟了一頭小公牛，他找了很久都沒找到，他發誓假如能發現偷牛的賊，他將會給赫耳墨斯、潘神和森林守護神獻上一隻小羔羊。不久，牧人爬上一座小山丘看見有頭獅子在山腳下正吃著他的小牛。看到這種情景牧人嚇得魂都丟了，趕緊抬起頭，伸出雙手，向著天空說道：「我剛才發誓說，要是找著了偷牛賊就向森林守護神貢獻一隻羔羊。此時，我已經找到了這個賊，假如我能安全地從他那兒逃脫，我情願再添上一頭大公牛作為獻禮。」

◆　　　　許願時要小心，願望是會成真的。　　　　◆

Townsend 106 = Perry 207

312. The Shepherd and the Sea

A Shepherd, keeping watch over his sheep near the shore, saw the Sea very calm and smooth, and longed to make a voyage with a view to commerce. He sold all his flock, invested it in a cargo of dates, and set sail. But a very great tempest came on, and the ship being in danger of sinking, he threw all his merchandise overboard, and barely escaped with his life in the empty ship. Not long afterwards when someone passed by and observed the unruffled calm of the Sea, he interrupted him and said,"It is again in want of dates, and therefore looks quiet."

◆　　　Understand what you are doing before you do it.　　　◆

312. 牧羊人和海

　　有個牧羊人在海邊放羊，看見大海如此寧靜祥和，便渴望能航海去做生意。於是，他賣掉了羊群，買了烏龜船裝滿，就啟航了。不料，突來的暴風雨在海上瘋狂肆虐，眼看船有下沉的危險，牧羊人只好將所有的貨物拋進海裡，這才乘坐著空空的航船倖免於難。事過不久，有人路過海邊，看見大海如此風平浪靜，大為讚歎。牧羊人卻打斷了他：「大海又想要棗子吃了，所以才會顯得如此寧靜。」

◆　　　　　**有所行動前要充分瞭解情況。**　　　　◆

Townsend 263 = Perry 208

313. The Shepherd and the Sheep

　　A Shepherd driving his Sheep to a wood, saw an oak of unusual size full of acorns, and spreading his cloak under the branches, he climbed up into the tree and shook them down. The Sheep eating the acorns inadvertently frayed and tore the cloak. When the Shepherd came down and saw what was done, he said, "O you most ungrateful creatures! You provide wool to make garments for all other men, but you destroy the clothes of him who feeds you."

◆　　　An appetite blinds men to their surrounds.　　　◆

313. 牧羊人和羊

　　一個牧羊人趕著他的羊群來到一片橡樹林裡，他看到一棵巨大無比的橡樹上長滿了橡子,便高興地脫下外衣,把它鋪在橡樹下,接著牧羊人爬上樹去,使勁把橡子搖下來。羊跑過來盡情享受這些橡子,在衣服上來回走動,最後把牧羊人的外衣磨破了。牧羊人從樹上下來,見到如此情形,生氣地說道:「你們這些忘恩負義的畜牲!你們把自己的羊毛給別人做衣服,可我辛辛苦苦餵養你們,你們卻毀了我的衣服!」

◆　　　　貪欲會使人忘記周遭的情況。　　　　◆

Townsend 230 = Perry 215

314. The Wasps, the Partridges, and the Farmer

The Wasps and the Partridges, overcome with thirst, came to a Farmer and besought him to give them some water to drink. They promised amply to repay him the favor which they asked. The Partridges declared that they would dig around his vines and make them produce finer grapes. The Wasps said that they would keep guard and drive off thieves with their stings. But the Farmer interrupted them, saying, "I have already two oxen, who, without making any promises, do all these things. It is surely better for me to give the water to them than to you."

◆　　This fable is appropriate for a man who is ungrateful.　　◆

314. 黃蜂、鷓鴣和農夫

黃蜂和鷓鴣口乾舌燥,央求農夫給點兒水解渴。他們還保證一定會好好地報答農夫。鵐鳩信誓旦旦地表示，他可以幫農夫的葡萄鬆土，好讓它們結出更加甘甜爽口的果實。黃蜂則保證，他們可以守衛農夫的葡萄園，防止賊把果實偷走。

但是農夫卻打斷了他們的話說道：「我已經有兩頭牛了，他們從沒保證過什麼，就做了這些工作。我覺得把水留給他們喝要比給你們喝更好。」

◆　　　這個故事適用於那些不知感激的人。　　　◆

HUNTER/FISHER 獵人 / 漁夫

Townsend 7 = Perry 199

315. The Boy Hunting Locusts

A boy was hunting for locusts. He had caught a goodly number, when he saw a Scorpion, and mistaking him for a locust, reached out his hand to take him. The Scorpion, showing his sting, said: If you had but touched me, my friend, you would have lost me, and all your locusts too!"

◆　　　　　　　Caution is important.　　　　　　　◆

315. 捉蝗蟲的男孩

有個男孩捉了很多很多蝗蟲。突然他發現了一隻蠍子，誤認為那是蝗蟲，就伸出手想去捉。蠍子亮出了毒刺，說道：「朋友，如果你敢碰我一下，你不僅得不到我，還會丟掉你全部的蝗蟲！」

◆　　　　　　　凡事都要小心謹慎。　　　　　　　◆

MEN 人

Townsend 128 = Perry 18

316. The Fisherman and the Little Fish

A fisherman who lived on the produce of his nets, one day caught a single small Fish as the result of his day's labor. The Fish, panting convulsively, thus entreated for his life, "O Sir, what good can I be to you, and how little am I worth? I am not yet come to my full size. Pray spare my life, and put me back into the sea. I shall soon become a large fish fit for the tables of the rich, and then you can catch me again, and make a handsome profit of me." The Fisherman replied, "I should indeed be a very simple fellow if, for the chance of a greater uncertain profit, I were to forego my present certain gain."

♦ A little thing in hand is worte more than a great thing in prospect. ♦

316. 漁夫和小魚

有位漁夫靠撒網捕魚為生。有一天，在經過一天勞頓之後，他只抓到了一條小魚。小魚拚命地喘著氣，懇求漁夫饒自己一命：「先生，我對您來說有什麼用呢？我這樣的小魚根本就值不了幾個錢。我還沒長大呢！求您饒了我，把我放回大海吧！很快我就會長成一條大魚，可以做成美味佳餚，到那時您再抓我，就可以賺一大筆錢了。」漁夫答道：「如果為了說不定的利益，而放走現在擁有的，那我可真是太天真了。」

♦ 把握在手的東西就算再小，也比幻想中的東西好。 ♦

Townsend 278 = Perry 402

317. The Hunter and the Horseman

A certain Hunter, having snared a hare, placed it upon his shoulders and set out homewards. On his way he met a man on horseback who begged the hare of him, under the pretense of purchasing it. However, when the Horseman got the hare, he rode off as fast as he could. The Hunter ran after him, as if he was sure of overtaking him, but the Horseman increased more and more the distance between them. The Hunter, sorely against his will, called out to him and said, "Get along with you! for I will now make you a present of the hare."

♦　　A fool will make excuses for foolish behavior.　　♦

317. 獵人和騎馬者

有個獵人抓到一隻野兔,把牠放在肩上扛到家裡。在路上他碰見了一個騎馬的人,那人假意說想買獵人手裡的兔子。他一拿住兔子,就騎馬飛快地跑了。獵人在馬後窮追不捨,覺得自己肯定能追上那匹馬。然而,眼看騎馬的那人愈跑愈遠,獵人只能違心地朝他的背影高喊:「快滾蛋吧!那兔子就當是我白送給你的!」

♦　　蠢人會為自己的行為找藉口。　　♦

Townsend 129 = Perry 326

318. The Hunter and the Woodman

A hunter, not very bold, was searching for the tracks of a Lion. He asked a man felling oaks in the forest if he had seen any marks of his footsteps or knew where his lair was. "I will," said the man, "at once show you the Lion himself." The Hunter, turning very pale and chattering with his teeth from fear, replied, "No, thank you. I did not ask that; it is his track only I am in search of, not the Lion himself."

♦ The hero is brave in deeds as well as words. ♦

318. 獵人和伐木工

有個獵人膽子不大,到森林裡去尋找獅子的足跡。他向正在砍伐橡樹的工人詢問是否看到過獅子的腳印,是否知道獅子的老窩在哪兒。「當然清楚!」伐木工說,「我馬上就帶你去尋找獅子。」獵人聞聽此言,嚇得面色慘白,牙齒直打顫,戰戰兢兢地說:「多謝,不用了。我想找的是獅子的蹤跡,而非獅子。」

♦ 英雄是在言語和行動上都很勇敢的人。 ♦

Townsend 93 = Perry 327

319. The Huntsman and the Fisherman

A Huntsman, returning with his dogs from the field, fell in by chance with a Fisherman who was bringing home a basket well laden with fish. The Huntsman wished to have the fish, and their owner experienced an equal longing for the contents of the game-bag. They quickly agreed to exchange the produce of their day's sport. Each was so well pleased with his bargain that they made for some time the same exchange day after day. Finally a neighbor said to them,"If you go on in this way, you will soon destroy by frequent use the pleasure of your exchange, and each will again wish to retain the fruits of his own sport."

♦ Abstain and enjoy. ♦

319. 獵人和漁夫

獵人帶著獵狗打獵回來,在路上遇見了漁夫。他看到漁夫提著滿滿的一籃子魚,非常羨慕,正好漁夫也對獵人袋中的獵物非常感興趣,兩人馬上表示願意交換他們這一天的勞動果實。這個交易使獵人跟漁夫都很歡喜,於是在之後的一段時間裡,每天他們都會做這樣的交換。後來,有個鄰居對他們說:「要是你們繼續這樣下去,就會因為太頻繁而失去交換所帶來的樂趣,那個時候,你們二位都會想保有自己的獵物。」

♦ 節制也是快樂。 ♦

MILITARY MEN 軍隊人員

Townsend 157 = Perry 375

320. The Bald Knight

A bald Knight, who wore a wig, went out to hunt. A sudden puff of wind blew off his hat and wig, at which a loud laugh rang forth from his companions. He pulled up his horse, and with great glee joined in the joke by saying,"What a marvel it is that hairs which are not mine should fly from me, when they have forsaken even the man on whose head they grew."

♦ It's good to be able to laugh at yourself. ♦

320. 禿頭騎士

一個禿頭騎士戴著假髮出去打獵。突然一陣風吹來,把他的帽子跟假髮都吹掉了,他的夥伴們禁不住大笑起來。騎士勒住了馬,笑呵呵地說:「這頭髮本來就不是我的,居然從我的頭上掉下來,多麼令人驚奇啊!腦袋長出這頭髮的人,不也被它拋棄了嗎?」

♦ 人要懂得適時自嘲。 ♦

Townsend 69 = Perry 320

321. The Horse and His Rider

A Horse Soldier took the utmost pains with his charger. As long as the war lasted, he looked upon him as his fellow-helper in all emergencies and fed him carefully with hay and corn. But when the war was over, he only allowed him chaff to eat and made him carry heavy loads of wood, subjecting him to much slavish drudgery and ill-treatment.

War was again proclaimed, however, and when the trumpet summoned him to his standard, the Soldier put on his charger its military trappings, and mounted, being clad in his heavy coat of mail. The Horse fell down straightway under the weight, no longer equal to the burden, and said to his master, "You must now go to the war on foot, for you have transformed me from a Horse into an Ass; and how can you expect that I can again turn in a moment from an Ass to a Horse?"

♦ Care defines ability. ♦

321. 馬和騎兵

有個騎兵十分愛惜他的戰馬。在戰爭期間,不管情況如何緊急,他都視馬為自己的親密戰友,拿乾草跟穀子精心地餵養他。但是戰爭結束之後,他卻只餵馬一些穀糠,讓他背重重的木頭,做各樣繁重的勞動工作,還隨意地虐待他。

沒過多久,戰爭再次爆發,號角聲召喚著騎兵歸隊,他替戰馬配好戰時裝備,自己也穿上沉重的盔甲,一躍騎到馬上。但他剛剛坐到馬背上,馬隨即就被壓得倒在地上。再也背不動重擔的馬向他的主人說:「你只好走上疆場了,我早已被你由一匹馬變成了一頭驢,你總不能希望我瞬間又由驢變成馬吧!」

♦ 養兵千日,用兵一時。 ♦

Townsend 267 = Perry 524

322. The Two Soldiers and the Robber

Two soldiers traveling together were set upon by a Robber. The one fled away; the other stood his ground and defended himself with his stout right hand. The Robber being slain, the timid companion ran up and drew his sword, and then, throwing back his traveling cloak said," I'll at him, and him, and "I'll take care he shall learn whom he has attacked."

On this, he who had fought with the Robber made answer, "I only wish that you had helped me just now, even if it had been only with those words, for I should have been the more encouraged, believing them to be true; but now put up your sword in its sheath and hold your equally useless tongue, till you can deceive others who do not know you. I, indeed, who have experienced with what speed you run away, know right well that no dependence can be placed on your valor."

♦　　　　　Actions speak louder than words.　　　　　♦

322. 兩個士兵和強盜

兩個士兵在一起趕路，途中他們遭到強盜突襲。其中一個士兵立刻逃到一邊，而另一個勇敢地迎上去，用他強壯的右手頑強地與強盜進行殊死的搏鬥。強盜被殺死了，膽小的同伴跑過來從鞘裡抽出劍，脫掉披風說：「讓我來對付他，我要讓他知道，他搶的是什麼人。」

聽到他的話，剛才和強盜搏鬥的士兵說：「我只願你剛才能來幫助我，即使只說這兩句話，我都會當成是真的，就更有勇氣去和強盜對抗。而現在還是請你把劍插回劍鞘裡，並且管好你同樣沒用的舌頭，留著去欺騙那些不瞭解你的人吧！我已經領教了你逃跑的速度，十分清楚你的勇氣，是靠不住的。」

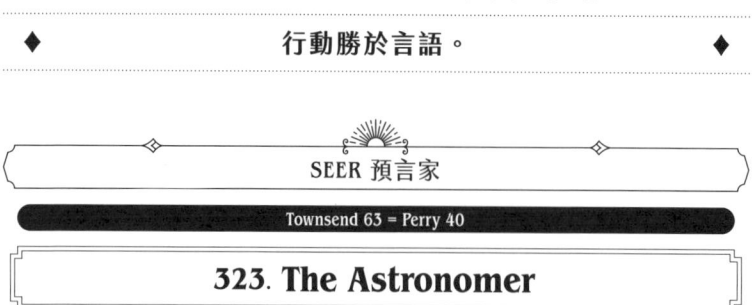

♦　　　　　　　行動勝於言語。　　　　　　　♦

SEER 預言家

Townsend 63 = Perry 40

323. The Astronomer

An Astronomer used to go out at night to observe the stars.

One evening, as he wandered through the suburbs with his whole attention fixed on the sky, he fell accidentally into a deep well. While he lamented and bewailed his sores and bruises, and cried loudly for help, a neighbor ran to the well, and learning what had happened said,"Hark ye, old fellow, why, in striving to pry into what is in heaven, do you not manage to see what is on earth?"

♦ Keep one eye on the ground. ♦

323. 天文學家

有一個天文學家，經常晚上到室外觀察星象。一天晚上，天文學家到郊外漫步，正聚精會神地盯著星空看時，突然一不小心掉進了一口深井，身上碰撞得青一塊紫一塊。他一邊呻吟，一邊高聲求救。一個鄰居跑到井邊問清原因，跟他說道：「老兄，當你滿心注意天上的時候，怎麼就不留心地上發生的事情呢？」

♦ 要注意身邊發生的一切。 ♦

Townsend 145 = Perry 306

324. The Philosopher, the Ants, and Mercury

A Philosopher witnessed from the shore the shipwreck of a vessel, of which the crew and passengers were all drowned. He inveighed against the injustice of Providence, which would for the sake of one criminal perchance sailing in the ship allow so many innocent persons to perish. As he was indulging in these reflections, he found himself surrounded by a whole army of Ants, near whose nest he was standing. One of them climbed up and stung him, and he immediately trampled them all to death with his foot. Mercury presented himself, and striking the Philosopher with his wand, said,"and are you indeed to make yourself a judge of the dealings of Providence, who hast thyself in a similar manner treated these poor Ants?"

♦　　　　　Act as you profess to believe.　　　　　♦

324. 哲學家、螞蟻和墨丘利

一位哲學家在海岸上目睹了一艘船的失事，船員和乘客都淹死了。他痛斥上帝的不公平，因為有一名罪犯偶然乘坐這條船，就讓這麼多無辜的人喪命。

在他沉浸在這些思索中的時候，他發現自己被大批螞蟻包圍著，他正站在這些螞蟻的巢穴旁邊。其中有隻螞蟻爬上來咬了他一口，他立刻用腳把牠們都踩死了。墨丘利出現了，用他的魔杖打了哲學家一下，說：「你以同樣的方式對待這些可憐的螞蟻，你真的要裁決上帝的行為嗎？」

♦　　　　　　　要言行一致。　　　　　　　♦

Townsend 195 = Perry 161

325. The Prophet

A Wizard, sitting in the marketplace, was telling the fortunes of the passers-by when a person ran up in great haste, and announced to him that the doors of his house had been broken open and that all his goods were being stolen. He sighed heavily and hastened away as fast as he could run. A neighbor saw him running and said,"Oh! you fellow there! you say you can foretell the fortunes of others; how is it you did not foresee your own?"

♦ This is a fable for people who do a poor job of managing their own lives but who nevertheless make pronouncements about things that are none of their business. ♦

325. 預言家

一位術士坐在市場裡，正在給過路的行人算命。這時一個人急匆匆地跑來，對術士通報說，他房間的門被撬開了，他所有的東西正被往外偷走。他重重歎了一口氣，飛快地跑開了。一位鄰居看見他在跑，說：「哦！你這個傢伙！你說能預測別人的命運，怎麼沒有預見你自己的呢？」

♦ 這個故事說的是，有些人管不好自己的事，還去瞎指揮別人。 ♦

TRAVELER 旅行者

Townsend 43 = Perry 33

326. The Boasting Traveler

A man who had traveled in foreign lands boasted very much, on returning to his own country, of the many wonderful and heroic feats he had performed in the different places he had visited. Among other things, he said that when he was at Rhodes he had leaped to such a distance that no man of his day could leap anywhere near him as to that, there were in Rhodes many persons who saw him do it and whom he could call as witnesses. One of the bystanders interrupted him, saying,"Now, my good man, if this be all true there is no need of witnesses. Suppose this to be Rhodes, and leap for us."

◆　　He Who does a thing well does not need to boast.　　◆

326. 吹牛的旅行者

　　有個人曾到國外旅行，回來後，逢人就炫耀自己在國外立下無數卓越功勳。他揚言自己在羅德島上曾經奮力一躍，當世無人能比他跳得遠，羅德島上當時在場的很多人都能夠做他的證人。此時，有個旁觀者打斷他，說道：「能幹的人，假如你說的都屬實的話，也就沒有什麼找證人的必要了。假設這裡就是羅德島，你就跳給我們看吧！」

◆　　　　　真正成功的人沒必要自我吹噓。　　　　　◆

Townsend 123 = Perry 177

327. The Seaside Travelers

　　Some travelers, journeying along the seashore, climbed to the summit of a tall cliff, and looking over the sea, saw in the distance what they thought was a large ship. They waited in the hope of seeing it enter the harbor, but as the object on which they looked was driven nearer to shore by the wind, they found that it could at the most be a small boat, and not a ship. When however it reached the beach, they discovered that it was only a large faggot of sticks, and one of them said to his companions, "We have waited for no purpose, for after all there is nothing to see but a load of wood."

◆　　Our mere anticipations af life outrun its realities.　　◆

327. 海邊的旅行者

　　幾個旅行者沿著海邊旅行，他們爬到一座高聳的峭壁的最頂處，放眼遠眺，在海天相接的地方看到一個東西，便以為是艘大船。他們充滿希望地等著，希望那艘船能駛進海灣。可是當它隨風進入海灣時，他們卻發現那不過是艘小船。最後當它靠岸時，他們終於看清楚，那只是一大捆木棍。其中一個人對他的同伴說：「我們白等了，到最後只等了一捆木頭。」

◆　　　**在生活中，現實往往比我們所期盼的更殘酷。**　　◆

Townsend 298 = Perry 168

328. The Shipwrecked Man and the Sea

　　A shipwrecked man, having been cast upon a certain shore, slept after his buffetings with the deep. After a while he awoke, and looking upon the Sea, loaded it with reproaches. He argued that it enticed men with the calmness of its looks, but when it had induced them to plow its waters, it grew rough and destroyed them. The Sea, assuming the form of a woman, replied to him,"Blame not me, my good sir, but the winds, for I am by my own nature as calm and firm even as this earth; but the winds suddenly falling on me create these waves, and lash me into fury."

◆　　Use care to place your blame on the right person.　　◆

328. 落水的人和海

　　有個人乘坐的船失事了，被海水沖到了岸上。和海浪搏鬥的他筋疲力盡,在岸邊沉沉地睡去。過了一會兒他醒了過來,看著海面波濤不驚,就開始怒斥大海。他責備大海用寧靜的外表欺騙人們,而當人們為之所動,駕船到海上航行時,大海就變了臉,變得狂暴不羈,掀起驚濤駭浪吞噬掉航海的船隻。大海以一個婦人的模樣出現在他面前,說道:「尊敬的先生,這不能怪我,該受責備的應該是風啊!其實,我跟大地一樣是寧靜祥和的,可是風肆虐地抽打我,他掀起層層巨浪,把我弄得勃然大怒。」

◆　　　　　責備人之前要弄清狀況。　　　　　◆

Townsend 293 = Perry 175

329. The Travelers and the Plane-Tree

Two Travelers, worn out by the heat of the summer's sun, laid themselves down at noon under the widespreading branches of a Plane-Tree. As they rested under its shade, one of the Travelers said to the other, "What a singularly useless tree is the Plane! It bears no fruit, and is not of the least service to man." The Plane-Tree, interrupting him, said, " You ungrateful fellows! Do you, while receiving benefits from me and resting under my shade, dare to describe me as useless, and unprofitable?"

◆　　　Some men underrate their best blessings.　　　◆

329. 兩個旅行者和梧桐樹

夏日中午的太陽異常炎熱,兩個旅行者頭頂烈日,被曬得精疲力竭,倒在一棵枝繁葉茂的梧桐樹下乘涼。他們在濃密的樹蔭底下休息的時候,其中一個對他的同伴說:「梧桐樹真是太沒用啦,一點兒果實都不結,對人來說完全沒有用處。」梧桐樹生氣地打斷了他:「你們這些忘恩負義不知好歹的傢伙!你們現在正享受著我的恩惠,在我的樹蔭底下乘涼,怎麼還敢譭謗我,說我不結果實毫無用處?」

◆　　　　有些人常忽視了上帝給予的恩賜。　　　　◆

Townsend 271 = Perry 355

330. Truth and the Traveler

A wayfaring man, traveling in the desert, met a woman standing alone and terribly dejected. He inquired of her, "Who art thou?" "My name is Truth," she replied. "and for what cause," he asked, "have you left the city to dwell alone here in the wilderness?" She made answer, "Because in former times, falsehood was with few, but is now with all men."

◆　　　　Falsehood is with all men.　　　　◆

330. 真理和旅行者

一個旅行者在穿越大沙漠時,看到一個女人形單影隻、極度沮喪地站在那裡。他問道:「你是誰?」「我的名字叫做真理。」女人回答道。他繼續問道:「你為什麼不住在繁華熱鬧的城市,而獨自來到這荒無人煙的沙漠?」女人說:「因為以前謊言只能在少數人那裡聽到,可是現在謊言無處不在,所有的人都在說謊。」

◆　　　　謊言無處不在。　　　　◆

Townsend 118 = Perry 67

331. The Two Travelers and the Axe

Two men were journeying together. One of them picked up an axe that lay upon the path, and said, " I have found an axe." " Nay, my friend," replied the other,"do not say 'I', but 'We' have found an axe. " They had not gone far before they saw the owner of the axe pursuing them, and he who had picked up the axe said,"We are undone." " Nay," replied the other," keep to your first mode of speech, my friend; what you thought right then, think right now. Say 'I', not 'We' are undone."

♦ He who shares the danger ought to share the prize. ♦

331. 兩個旅行者和斧頭

兩個人一起結伴同行，其中的一個人撿起路邊的一把斧頭說道：「我發現了一把斧頭。」「不應該這麼說，我的朋友，」另一個人回答道，「不能說『我』，而應該說是『我們』發現了一把斧頭。」還沒走多遠，他們就發現斧頭的主人追了過來。撿斧頭的那個人說：「我們要倒楣了。」「錯了！」另一個人趕忙糾正他說，「還是像你上次那樣說吧！我的朋友，你那時是怎麼想的，現在還那樣想好了。所以，應該說是『我』倒楣了，千萬不要說是『我們』倒楣了。」

♦ 能和你共患難的人才可和你同享福。 ♦

20.
MONKEY
猴子

Townsend 199 = Perry 569

332. The Apes and the Two Travelers

Two men, one who always spoke the truth and the other who told nothing but lies, were traveling together and by chance came to the land of Apes. One of the Apes, who had raised himself to be king, commanded them to be seized and brought before him, that he might know what was said of him among men. He ordered at the same time that all the Apes be arranged in a long row on his right hand and on his left, and that a throne be placed for him, as was the custom among men.

After these preparations he signified that the two men should be brought before him, and greeted them with this salutation, "What sort of a king do I seem to you to be, O strangers?" The Lying Traveler replied, "You seem to me a most mighty king." " and what is your estimate of those you see around me?" "These," he made answer, "are worthy companions of yourself, fit at least to be ambassadors and leaders of armies." The Ape and all his court, gratified with the lie, commanded that a handsome present be given to the flatterer.

On this the truthful Traveler thought to himself, "If so great a reward be given for a lie, with what gift may not I be rewarded, if, according to my custom, I tell the truth?" The Ape quickly turned to him. "and pray how do I and these my friends around me seem to you?" " Thou art," he said, " a most excellent Ape, and all these thy companions after thy example are excellent Apes too." The King of the Apes, enraged at hearing these truths, gave him over to the teeth and claws of his companions.

◆ The truth often hurts. ◆

332. 猴子和兩個旅行者

以前有兩個人，其中一個人總是講真話，而另一個人總是撒謊。兩人一同外出旅遊，意外地闖入猴子的領地。有隻自立為王的猴子，下令讓手下捉住這兩人，並把他們帶到自己面前，想藉此瞭解，人類怎麼評價自己。猴王同時又命令眾猴站成長長的兩排，分列在自己的左右，並且按著人類的習慣，給自己放置了一張寶座。

一切都已安排妥當，猴王吩咐把那兩個人帶進來。一看見他們，猴王就問道：「陌生人，在你們看來，我這個國王當得怎麼樣？」愛撒謊的人說道：「依我之見，您是權力最大的君主。」「那麼，你怎麼評價我身邊的這群猴子呢？」「您的夥伴個個都配得上替您效勞，起碼稱得上是大使或者將軍。」眾猴聽聞得這番諛言，個個樂不可支，送了一份十分豐厚的禮品給這個愛拍馬屁的人。

見此，那個向來講真話的人暗自想到：「幾句謊言就換得如此多的禮物，如果我依照自己的習慣講了真話，什麼樣的禮物我得不到呢？」猴王馬上就轉向了他：「你是如何看待我，以及我周圍的這些朋友的？」這人說道：「你是最聰明的一隻猴子，你的這些夥伴以你為楷模，也都是些很出色的猴子。」聽到這些實話，猴王暴怒，下令讓手下眾猴對這可憐的人連抓帶咬。

◆　　　　　　真話總是帶來傷害。　　　　　　◆

Townsend 151 = Perry 463

333. The Dancing Monkeys

A Prince had some Monkeys trained to dance. Being naturally great mimics of men's actions, they showed themselves most apt pupils, and when arrayed in their rich clothes and masks, they danced as well as any of the courtiers. The spectacle was often repeated with great applause,till on one occasion a courtier, bent on; mischief, took from his pocket a handful of nuts and threw them upon the stage. The Monkeys at the sight of the nuts forgot their dancing and became (as indeed they were) Monkeys instead of actors. Pulling off their masks and tearing their robes, they fought with one another for the nuts. The dancing spectacle thus came to an end amidst the laughter and ridicule of the audience.

◆　　　Not everyting you see is what it appears to be.　　　◆

333. 跳舞的猴子

　　有一個王子訓練一些猴子學跳舞。猴子天生就很會模仿人類的行為，他們就像是最靈巧的學生，穿戴上華麗的衣服和面具，就跟弄臣跳得一樣好。表演常常因為熱烈的掌聲而重複進行。直到有一次，一個喜歡惡作劇的弄臣，從他口袋裡掏出一把堅果扔到了舞臺上。猴子們一見到堅果，就忘記了自己在跳舞，又從演員變回了猴子（他們確實也就是猴子），紛紛拉下面具，撕開禮服，互相爭搶著堅果。因此，舞蹈表演就在觀眾們的哄笑和嘲諷聲中，匆匆結束了。

◆　　　　　　　　眼見未必為實。　　　　　　　　◆

Townsend 72 = Perry 364

334. Jupiter and the Monkey

　　Jupiter issued a proclamation to all the beasts of the forest and promised a royal reward to the one whose offspring should be deemed the handsomest. The Monkey came with the rest and presented, with all a mother's tenderness, a flat-nosed, hairless, ill-featured young Monkey as a candidate for the promised reward. A general laugh saluted her on the presentation of her son. She resolutely said,"I know not whether Jupiter will allot the prize to my son, but this I do know, that he is at least in the eyes of me his mother, the dearest, handsomest, and most beautiful of all."

◆　　　　Beauty is in the eyes of the beholder.　　　　◆

334. 朱比特和猴子

　　朱比特對樹林中的百獸發表聲明說，百獸中誰的後代被公認是最英俊瀟灑的，誰就能夠得到重重的賞賜。一隻猴子跟其他動物一道前來，出於母愛的本能，推舉一隻相貌醜陋、沒有毛髮、鼻子塌陷的小猴，作為這項大獎的候選人。大家都對她的推薦感到好笑。她則毅然地說：「我不清楚朱比特是不是同意把這項獎授予我的兒子，但是有一點我很確定，作為他的母親，起碼在我眼中他是最可愛、最英俊、最美麗的。」

◆　　　　　　　　情人眼裡出西施。　　　　　　　　◆

Townsend 265 = Perry 83

335. The Monkey and the Camel

The Beasts of the forest gave a splendid entertainment at which the Monkey stood up and danced. Having vastly delighted

MONKEY 猴子

the assembly, he sat down amidst universal applause. The Camel, envious of the praises bestowed on the Monkey and desiring to divert to himself the favor of the guests, proposed to stand up in his turn and dance for their amusement. He moved about in so utterly ridiculous a manner that the Beasts, in a fit of indignation, set upon him with clubs and drove him out of the assembly.

◆　　　　It is absurd to ape our betters.　　　　◆

335. 猴子和駱駝

　　森林中的野獸們，舉行一次盛大的表演，表演中猴子起來跳舞。他把大家逗得非常開心，在一片掌聲中坐了下來。駱駝羨慕猴子得到的稱讚，也希望能夠得到賓客的喜愛，輪到他時，也提出要站起來給大家跳舞助興。他用極度可笑的方式扭來扭去，野獸們一陣憤怒，都用棍子打他，將他趕出了集會。

◆　　　　模仿別人比自己好的地方是很可笑的。　　　　◆

Townsend 137 = Perry 203

336. The Monkey and the Fishermen

　　A Monkey perched upon a lofty tree saw some Fishermen casting their nets into a river, and narrowly watched their proceedings. The Fishermen after a while gave up fishing, and on going home to dinner left their nets upon the bank. The Monkey, who is the most imitative of animals, descended from the treetop and endeavored to do as they had done. Having handled the net, he threw it into the river, but became tangled in the meshes and

386

drowned. With his last breath he said to himself,"I am rightly served; for what business had I who had never handled a net to try and catch fish?"

◆　　　Imitation is no substitute for knowledge.　　　◆

336. 猴子和漁夫

一隻猴子待在一棵大樹上，看見幾個漁夫在河中撒網，並仔細觀察他們的動作。過了一會兒，漁夫捕完魚了，在回家吃飯的時候，把他們的網留在了岸上。猴子，這最會模仿的動物，從樹梢上下來，竭力像漁夫剛才那樣做。拿起網後，他把網扔進了河裡，但是自己被纏在網裡淹死了。臨死時，他對自己說：「我真是自作自受，我從沒動過漁網，為什麼要試著去捕魚呢？」

◆　　　　　模仿並不能學到真本事。　　　　　◆

Townsend 68 = Perry 81

337. The Monkey and the Fox

A Monkey once danced in an assembly of the Beasts, and so pleased them all by his performance that they elected him their King. A Fox, envying him the honor, discovered a piece of meat lying in a trap, and leading the Monkey to the place where it was, said that she had found a store, but had not used it, she had kept it for him as treasure trove of his kingdom, and counseled him to lay hold of it. The Monkey approached carelessly and was caught in the trap; and on his accusing the Fox of purposely leading him into the snare, she replied,"O Monkey, and are you, with such a

MONKEY 猴子

mind as yours, going to be King over the Beasts?"

♦   A ruler needs many talents.   ♦

337. 猴子和狐狸

在一次百獸的聚會上，猴子的舞蹈博得了大家的喝彩，於是大家就推舉他為王。有隻狐狸發現陷阱裡有一塊肉，因為她覬覦猴子的王位，就把猴子帶到了陷阱處，說她發現了一處寶藏，但還沒有動它，因為她想把它作為猴子的王國的財庫，並勸猴子去取這些寶藏。猴子毫無防範地走了過去，掉進了陷阱裡，於是他指責狐狸故意讓他掉入陷阱。狐狸回答說：「哦！猴子，憑你這樣的腦袋，還想要當百獸之王嗎？」

♦   統治者需要具備多種才能。   ♦

Townsend 153 = Perry 218

338. The Monkeys and Their Mother

The Monkey, it is said, has two young ones at each birth. The Mother fondles one and nurtures it with the greatest affection and care, but hates and neglects the other. It happened once that the young one which was caressed and loved was smothered by the too great affection of the Mother, while the despised one was nurtured and reared in spite of the neglect to which it was exposed.

♦   The best intentions will not always ensure success.   ♦

338. 猴子和牠們的媽媽

據說,猴子們每胎生兩隻小猴。媽媽喜歡其中一個,撫養他時投入了更多的感情和關注;但是卻恨另一個,對他不理不睬。結果,受到愛撫和疼愛的小猴,因為媽媽的過分疼愛窒息而死;而沒有得到照料,被忽視的那個,卻在風雨中順利成長。

♦　　　　有最好的打算不一定總是能成功。　　　　♦

MONKEY 猴子

21.
MOUSE
老鼠

MOUSE 老鼠

Jacob 67 = Perry 613

339. Belling the Cat

Long ago, the mice had a general council to consider what measures they could take to outwit their common enemy, the Cat. Some said this, and some said that; but at last a young mouse got up and said he had a proposal to make, which he thought would meet the case. "You will all agree," said he, "that our chief danger consists in the sly and treacherous manner in which the enemy approaches us. Now, if we could receive some signal of her approach, we could easily escape from her. I venture, therefore, to propose that a small bell be procured, and attached by a ribbon round the neck of the Cat. By this means we should always know when she was about, and could easily retire while she was in the neighbourhood."

This proposal met with general applause, until an old mouse got up and said, " That is all very well, but who is to bell the Cat?" The mice looked at one another and nobody spoke. Then the old mouse said, "It is easy to propose impossible remedies."

♦　　A good plan without practical action is useless.　　♦

339. 給貓繫鈴鐺

很多年以前，老鼠舉行大會，商量採取什麼措施來戰勝大夥共同的敵人—貓。大家你一句，我一句，最終，一隻小老鼠挺身而出，說自己有個妙主意：「我們大家都很清楚，對我們而言，最危險的情況是，貓靠近我們時總是無聲無息的，而且是趁我們沒戒備時發起偷襲。假如在貓接近時，我們能接收到有關信號，就能及時逃跑。所以，我斗膽建議，找個小的鈴鐺，拿繩子拴住，繫到貓的脖子上。如此一來，我們就可以掌握貓的行蹤，一旦貓靠近，我們就有時間撤退了。」

小老鼠提出的建議，得到了大夥兒熱烈的掌聲。一隻年老的老鼠起身問道：「主意是很不錯的，但是讓誰去給貓繫鈴鐺呢？」眾鼠面面相覷，全都不言不語。那隻上了年紀的老鼠感歎道：「提出不可能實現的建議，是件容易的事！」

◆　　　　沒有實際行動的好計畫是無用的。　　　　◆

Townsend 140 = Perry 79

340. The Cat and the Mice

A certain house was overrun with Mice. A Cat, discovering this, made her way into it and began to catch and eat them one by one. Fearing for their lives, the Mice kept themselves close in their holes. The Cat was no longer able to get at them and perceived that she must tempt them forth by some device. For this purpose she jumped upon a peg, and suspending herself from it, pretended to be dead. One of the Mice, peeping stealthily out, saw her and said,"Ah, my good madam, even though you should turn into a meal-bag, we will not come near you."

◆　　　He who is once deceived is doubly cautious.　　　◆

340. 貓和老鼠

某幢房子裡老鼠氾濫成災。一隻貓發現後，就跑來把老鼠一隻隻的捉住並吃掉。因為擔心性命，老鼠都把自己關在洞裡。貓

MOUSE 老鼠

就不能再捉到老鼠，貓也察覺到了，必須用些策略把他們引誘出來。為此，貓假裝吊死在一棵木樁子上。一隻老鼠悄悄地向外窺視，看見了貓，說道：「啊！我的好女士，就算你把自己變成一個裝著食物的口袋，我們也不會走近你的。」

◆　　　　　受過一次欺騙的人會加倍小心。　　　　　◆

Townsend 4 = Perry 150

341. The Lion and the Mouse

A Lion was awakened from sleep by a Mouse running over his face. Rising up angrily, he caught him and was about to kill him, when the Mouse piteously entreated, saying,"If you would only spare my life, I would be sure to repay your kindness." The Lion laughed and let him go. It happened shortly after this that the Lion was caught by some hunters, who bound him by strong ropes to the ground. The Mouse, recognizing his roar, came and gnawed the rope with his teeth, and set him free, exclaiming: " You ridiculed the idea of my ever being able to help you, not expecting to receive from me any repayment of your favor; now you know that it is possible for even a Mouse to confer benefits on a Lion."

◆　　　　　Everyone has need of the other.　　　　　◆

341. 獅子和老鼠

一隻老鼠從一隻獅子的臉上跑過，將他從睡夢中驚醒。獅子大怒，猛然站起來把他抓住，要殺死他。

老鼠哀求道：「只要你肯饒了我的性命，我必定會報答你的大恩大德。」獅子笑了笑，放了他。過了不久，獅子被幾個獵人抓住了，用結實的繩子捆倒在地上。老鼠聽出了獅子的吼聲，用牙齒咬斷了繩索放走了獅子，然後大聲說道：「你當時嘲笑我想幫你的忙，不相信能得到我的報答。現在你知道了吧！就算是小老鼠，也能給獅子以幫助。」

◆　　　　　每個人都是有價值的。　　　　　◆

Townsend 108 = Perry 165

342. The Mice and the Weasels

The Weasels and the Mice waged a perpetual war with each other, in which much blood was shed. The Weasels were always the victors. The Mice thought that the cause of their frequent defeats was that they had no leaders set apart from the general army to command them, and that they were exposed to dangers from lack of discipline. They therefore chose as leaders Mice that were most renowned for their family descent, strength, and counsel, as well as those most noted for their courage in the fight, so that they might be better marshaled in battle array and formed into troops, regiments, and battalions. When all this was done, and the army disciplined, and the herald Mouse had duly proclaimed war by challenging the Weasels, the newly chosen generals bound their heads with straws, that they might be more conspicuous to all their troops. Scarcely had the battle begun, when a great rout overwhelmed the Mice, who scampered off as fast as they could to their holes. The generals, not being able to get in on account of the ornaments on their heads, were all captured and eaten by the Weasels.

♦   The more honor the more danger.   ♦

342. 老鼠和黃鼬

黃鼬與老鼠之間展開了一場持久戰，戰爭中傷亡慘重。黃鼬總是勝利的一方。老鼠認為他們總失敗，是因為沒有將帥來指揮，而且士兵們缺乏訓練，容易遭受危險。因此，他們選出了幾隻老鼠將軍，這些將軍是家族血統、力量和智謀方面最出色的老鼠，還有那些在戰鬥中以英勇而著稱的老鼠，將他們排成比較有利的陣法，組成軍、團和營。當所有這些都完成，軍隊也訓練完畢的時候，老鼠傳令兵向黃鼬發出挑戰，正式宣戰。新選出來的將軍們把稻草綁在頭上，這樣他們的隊伍就能更容易地認出他們。戰鬥剛剛開始，老鼠們就遭到重創，都拚命地逃往洞中。這些將軍們，因為頭上的裝飾物，不能鑽進洞中，全部被黃鼬抓住吃掉了。

♦   越多的榮譽會帶來越多的危險。   ♦

Townsend 146 = Perry 353

343. The Mouse and the Bull

A Bull was bitten by a Mouse and, angered by the wound, tried to capture him. But the Mouse reached his hole in safety. Though the Bull dug into the walls with his horns, he tired before he could rout out the Mouse, and crouching down, went to sleep outside the hole. The Mouse peeped out, crept furtively up his flank, and again biting him, retreated to his hole. The Bull rising up, and not knowing what to do, was sadly perplexed. At which the Mouse said, " The great do not always prevail. There are times when the small and lowly are the strongest to do mischief."

◆　　　　The great do not always prevail.　　　　◆

343. 老鼠和公牛

一頭公牛被老鼠咬傷了，所以發起火來，竭力想抓住老鼠。可是老鼠安全地回到了洞裡。儘管，公牛用角向牆裡面挖，可是在掘出老鼠之前他就累了，趴下來在洞外睡著了。老鼠偷偷向外看，然後悄悄爬到牛肋上，再次咬了公牛，並溜回洞中。公牛站起身，痛苦得不知所措。這時老鼠說：「大個子不會總是贏。有時候，卑微的小東西搗起蛋來才最厲害。」

◆　　　　個頭大不一定占上風。　　　　◆

Townsend 87 = Perry 384

344. The Mouse, the Frog, and the Hawk

A Mouse who always lived on the land, by an unlucky chance formed an intimate acquaintance with a Frog, who lived for the most part in the water. The Frog, one day intent on mischief, bound the foot of the Mouse tightly to his own. Thus joined together, the Frog first of all led his friend the Mouse to the meadow where they were accustomed to find their food. After this, he gradually led him towards the pool in which he lived, until reaching the very brink, he suddenly jumped in, dragging

MOUSE 老鼠

the Mouse with him. The Frog enjoyed the water amazingly, and swam croaking about, as if he had done a good deed. The unhappy Mouse was soon suffocated by the water, and his dead body floated about on the surface, tied to the foot of the Frog. A Hawk observed it, and, pouncing upon it with his talons, carried it aloft. The Frog, being still fastened to the leg of the Mouse, was also carried off a prisoner, and was eaten by the Hawk.

♦　　　　Harm hatch, harm catch.　　　　♦

344. 老鼠、青蛙和鷹

一隻住在陸地上的老鼠，偶然間與常住在水中的青蛙成了親密朋友。一天，青蛙惡作劇，把老鼠的一條腿緊緊地綁在了自己的腿上。之後，青蛙帶著他的老鼠朋友到他們常去的草地尋找食物。然後，他慢慢地領著老鼠朝他住的池塘走去，到了池塘邊上，他突然拖著老鼠一起跳了下去。青蛙非常喜歡水，在水中一邊游一邊叫，好像他剛做了件好事。不幸的老鼠很快被水嗆死了，屍體漂在水面上，但他仍然和青蛙的腿綁在一起。一隻鷹看到了老鼠的屍體，突然用鷹爪撲向老鼠，抓住他飛到空中。和老鼠綁在一起的青蛙也成了獵物，被鷹吃掉了。

♦　　　　　　害人反害己。　　　　　　♦

Townsend 216 = Perry 352

345. The Town Mouse and the Country Mouse

A Country Mouse invited a Town Mouse, an intimate friend, to pay him a visit and partake of his country fare. As they were on

398

the bare plowlands, eating there wheat-stocks and roots pulled up from the hedgerow, the Town Mouse said to his friend, "You live here the life of the ants, while in my house is the horn of plenty. I am surrounded by every luxury, and if you will come with me, as I wish you would, you shall have an ample share of my dainties."

The Country Mouse was easily persuaded, and returned to town with his friend. On his arrival, the Town Mouse placed before him bread, barley, beans, dried figs, honey, raisins, and, last of all, brought a dainty piece of cheese from a basket. The Country Mouse, being much delighted at the sight of such good cheer, expressed his satisfaction in warm terms and lamented his own hard fate. Just as they were beginning to eat, someone opened the door, and they both ran off squeaking, as fast as they could, to a hole so narrow that two could only find room in it by squeezing.

They had scarcely begun their repast again when someone else entered to take something out of a cupboard, whereupon the two Mice, more frightened than before, ran away and hid themselves. At last the Country Mouse, almost famished, said to his friend, "Although you have prepared for me so dainty a feast, I must leave you to enjoy it by yourself. It is surrounded by too many dangers to please me. I prefer my bare plowlands and roots from the hedgerow, where I can live in safety, and without fear."

◆ Better beans and bacon in peace than cakes and ale in fear. ◆

345. 城裡老鼠和鄉下老鼠

MOUSE 老鼠

　　鄉下老鼠邀請他住在城裡的好朋友來家裡做客，品嚐一下鄉村的風味。城裡的老鼠來到貧瘠的荒地裡，吃著麥稈和從灌木叢裡掘出來的根塊。城裡老鼠對他的朋友說：「在這裡，你過著像螞蟻一樣寒酸的生活，我家的食物可豐富多了，各種好吃的應有盡有，你跟我到我家去吧！跟我一起享用那些美味佳餚。」

　　很快，鄉下老鼠就被說動了，於是跟著他的朋友一起進城了。一到家，城裡老鼠就在鄉下老鼠面前堆滿了麵包、燕麥、豆子、乾棗、蜂蜜、葡萄等美味佳餚，最後，他竟然還從籃子裡掏出一大塊精製的乳酪。看到這麼多的美味佳餚，鄉下老鼠不由得心花怒放，他一邊滔滔不絕地表達他的滿意之情，同時也感到了自己生活的艱辛。

　　當他們正準備大快朵頤時，突然聽見有人把門打開了，兩隻老鼠頓時嚇得魂不附體，連忙以最快的速度拚命地擠進一個狹小的洞裡。一會兒，當他們返回宴席準備重新開始吃東西時，又有另外一個人進來打開碗櫃拿東西，這下兩隻老鼠更是嚇得魂飛天外，慌忙逃走並藏了起來。這麼一折騰，鄉下老鼠覺得自己都快要餓死了，他對他朋友說：「即使你給我準備了這麼多美味佳餚，但是我還是無福消受。因為這裡實在太危險，我根本就吃不消。與其這樣，我更願意待在荒地上，繼續吃灌木叢裡的根塊，至少不用擔驚受怕，可以過著平平安安的日子」。

◆　　**平平安安地過簡樸的生活，好過戰戰兢兢地過奢侈的生活。**　　◆

Townsend 204 = Perry 511

346. The Weasel and the Mice

　　A Weasel, inactive from age and infirmities, was not able to catch mice as he once did. He therefore rolled himself in flour and lay down in a dark corner. A Mouse, supposing him to be food, leaped upon him, and was instantly caught and squeezed to death. Another perished in a similar manner, and then a third, and still others after them.

A very old Mouse, who had escaped many a trap and snare, observed from a safe distance the trick of his crafty foe and said,"Ah! you that lie there, may you prosper just in the same proportion as you are what you pretend to be!"

♦ Where strength fails, guile may succeed. ♦

346. 黃鼠狼和老鼠

有隻黃鼠狼已經是風燭殘年了,他現在是舉步維艱,早已不能像以前那樣捕捉老鼠。於是,他在麵粉裡打了一個滾,然後躲在一個黑暗的角落裡,縮成一團。一隻老鼠誤以為他是食物,於是就跳到他身上,結果馬上被抓住,成為他的一頓美餐。不久,另一隻老鼠上了同樣的當。陸陸續續有第三隻、第四隻,乃至更多的老鼠,接連不斷地落入了圈套。

一隻曾無數次從鼠套和陷阱裡死裡逃生的上了年紀的老鼠,在黃鼠狼鞭長莫及的地方,冷眼旁觀這位狡詐敵人的把戲,而後對他說:「喂!躺在那裡縮成一團的那位,希望你能和你所假扮的角色一樣獲得成功。」

♦ 強攻不行,只有智取。 ♦

MOUSE 老鼠

22.
OBJECTS
各種物體

OBJECTS 物體

Townsend 70 = Perry 130

347. The Belly and the Members

The members of the Body rebelled against the Belly, and said, "Why should we be perpetually engaged in administering to your wants, while you do nothing but take your rest, and enjoy yourself in luxury and self-indulgence?" The Members carried out their resolve and refused their assistance to the Belly. The whole Body quickly became debilitated, and the hands, feet, mouth, and eyes, when too late, repented of their folly.

◆ As in the body, so in the state, each member in his proper sphere must work for the common good. ◆

347. 肚子和身體器官

身體上的各個器官一起反對肚子，他們說：「我們為什麼要不斷地滿足你的要求，而你自己卻無所事事，只顧著休息，整天過著奢華放縱的生活？」身體上的所有器官決定不再幫助肚子了。不久之後，整個身體就開始變得十分虛弱，手、腳、嘴和眼睛為曾經的愚蠢感到懊悔，可是已經太晚了。

◆ 不管是身體也好，整個國家也好，所有的組成部分都必須各盡其職，為共同的利益而工作。 ◆

Townsend 159 = Perry 349

348. The Lamp

A Lamp, soaked with too much oil and flaring brightly, boasted that it gave more light than the sun. Then a sudden puff of wind arose, and the Lamp was immediately extinguished. Its owner lit it again, and said, "Boast no more, but henceforth be content to give thy light in silence. Know that not even the stars need to be relit."

♦ Do not boast lest you be taken down. ♦

348. 燈

一盞燈吸太多油，發出很亮的光，就吹噓自己的光比太陽還亮得多。突然一陣風吹來，燈馬上被吹滅了。他的主人又把燈點著，說：「別再瞎吹了，今後靜靜地發光就是了。要知道，就是小星星，也用不著重新點燃的。」

♦ 不要總是吹噓，以免將來倒楣。 ♦

Townsend 25 = Perry 520

349. The Mountain in Labor

A Mountain was once greatly agitated. Loud groans and noises were heard, and crowds of people came from all parts to see what was the matter. While they were assembled in anxious expectation of some terrible calamity, out came a Mouse.

♦ Don't make much ado about nothing. ♦

349. 大山異動

有一次，一座大山發生了異動。人們都聽到了很大的呻吟和喧嚷的聲音，於是，人群從各處湧來，想看個究竟。他們焦慮地

OBJECTS 物體

聚集在一起，以為會有可怕的災難發生，這時跑出來一隻老鼠。

♦ 　　　　　　不要小題大做。　　　　　　♦

Townsend 232 = Perry 46

350. The North Wind and the Sun

The North Wind and the Sun disputed as to which was the most powerful, and agreed that he should be declared the victor who could first strip a wayfaring man of his clothes. The North Wind first tried his power and blew with all his might, but the keener his blasts, the closer the Traveler wrapped his cloak around him, until at last, resigning all hope of victory, the Wind called upon the Sun to see what he could do. The Sun suddenly shone out with all his warmth. The Traveler no sooner felt his genial rays than he took off one garment after another, and at last, fairly overcome with heat, undressed and bathed in a stream that lay in his path.

♦ 　　　Persuasion is better than Force.　　　♦

350. 北風和太陽

北風和太陽爭論誰更強大，說誰能脫去行人的衣服，就宣佈誰是勝利者。北風先使出他的本事，用盡全力來颳風，可是風刮得越厲害，行人就把大衣裹得越緊。一直到最後，北風放棄了一切取勝的希望，叫太陽來，要看看太陽能做什麼。太陽突然把他所有的熱量都放射出來。行人一感受到太陽溫暖的光芒，就立刻把衣服一件一件脫了,最後實在太熱了,就脫光了衣服,到路邊的小溪中洗了個澡。

♦ 勸服勝於暴力。 ♦

Townsend 111 = Perry 412

351. The Rivers and the Sea

The Rivers joined together to complain to the Sea, saying,"Why is it that when we flow into your tides so potable and sweet, you work in us such a change, and make us salty and unfit to drink?" The Sea, perceiving that they intended to throw the blame on him, said,"Pray cease to flow into me, and then you will not be made briny."

♦ Do not blame others. ♦

351. 河與海

河流匯集到一起向大海抱怨:「我們在注入大海前,是甘甜爽口的;而注入你後,我們卻發生了變化,變得又鹹又澀,難以入口,為什麼會這樣?」大海心裡十分清楚,河流有意要把所有的責任都推給他,便說:「那就請你們不要流到我這裡來了,這樣你們就不會再變鹹了」

♦ 不要總是推卸責任。 ♦

OBJECTS 物體

Townsend 256 = Perry 266

352. The Two Bags

Every man, according to an ancient legend, is born into the world with two bags suspended from his neck: a small bag in front full of his neighbors' faults, and a large bag behind filled with his own faults. Hence it is that men are quick to see the faults of others, and yet are often blind to their own failings.

◆　　　Men see other's faults but not their own.　　　◆

352. 兩個袋子

古代有個傳說，所有人降臨到這個世界上時，脖子上都會掛著兩個袋子，在他前面的小袋子裡，裝滿了鄰居的過失；而掛在後面的大袋子裡，裝的全是自己的缺陷。因此，人們往往先看到別人的毛病，而常常忽視自己的缺點。

◆　　　人們總盯著別人的缺點，卻忽視了自己的缺點。　　　◆

Townsend 89 = Perry 378

353. The Two Pots

A river carried down in its stream two Pots, one made of earthenware and the other of brass. The Earthen Pot said to the Brass Pot, "Pray keep at a distance and do not come near me, for if you touch me ever so slightly, I shall be broken in pieces, and besides, I by no means wish to come near you."

◆　　　Equals make the best friends.　　　◆

353. 兩個罐子

　　兩個罐子正在隨波逐流，一隻是陶罐，而另一個是銅罐。陶罐對銅罐說：「請千萬注意要與我保持距離，不要離我太近，因為你只要輕輕地碰我一下，我馬上就會粉身碎骨。話說回來，我也根本不想跟你套關係。」

◆　　　　水準相當的人才有可能成為親密的朋友。　　　　◆

OBJECTS 物體

23.
ODDS/ENDS
雜七雜八

Townsend 33 = Perry 65

354. The Bear and the Two Travelers

Two men were traveling together, when a Bear suddenly met them on their path. One of them climbed up quickly into a tree and concealed himself in the branches. The other, seeing that he must be attacked, fell flat on the ground, and when the Bear came up and felt him with his snout, and smelt him all over, he held his breath, and feigned the appearance of death as much as he could. The Bear soon left him, for it is said he will not touch a dead body. When he was quite gone, the other Traveler descended from the tree, and jocularly inquired of his friend what it was the Bear had whispered in his ear. "He gave me this advice," his companion replied. "Never travel with a friend who deserts you at the approach of danger."

♦　　　Misfortune tests the sincerity of friends.　　　♦

354. 熊與兩個旅人

很久以前，有兩個好朋友約好一塊去旅行，偶然誤入森林中熊的領地，發現一頭大黑熊正咆哮著向他們逼近。其中的一個人敏捷地爬上一棵大樹，躲在樹葉中間，把另外一個不會爬樹的人留在地上。

在地上的那個人，看見熊正要朝他撲過來，趕緊往地上一倒，屏住呼吸裝死。結果熊湊近他聞了聞，就走開了，因為熊不吃沒有生命的東西。

等熊離開之後，在樹上的那人爬下來，笑著問他的朋友：「熊聞了你那麼長時間，牠在你耳邊說了什麼悄悄話呢？」「熊讓我別和那種遇難就逃、見死不救的朋友一起旅行！」這個人回答道。

◆　　　**艱難的處境最能檢驗朋友之間的感情！**　　　◆

L'Estrange 91 = Perry 118

355. A Hunted Beaver

The beaver is a kind of an amphibious creature, but he lives mostly in the water. His testicles, they say, are medicinal; and it is principally for their sake he knows, that people seek his life; and therefore when he finds himself hard pinch'd, he bites them off, and by leaving them to his pursuers, he saves himself.

◆　　Sometimes a small sacrifice results in a greater good.　　◆

355. 被抓住的海狸

海狸是一種兩棲動物，但他大多數時間生活在水中。據說，他的睪丸是可以藥用的，人們為了這個就想取他的性命，所以當海狸發現自己被緊緊抓住時，他會把睪丸咬下來，留給捕捉的人，自己逃命。

◆　　　　**有時候，小的犧牲能換來大局的利益。**　　　　◆

Townsend 16 = Perry 214

356. The Mole and His Mother

A Mole, a creature blind from birth, once said to his

413

Mother,"I am sure than I can see, Mother !" In the desire to prove to him his mistake, his Mother placed before him a few grains of frankincense, and asked,"What is it?" The young Mole said,"It is a pebble."His Mother exclaimed,"My son, I am afraid that you are not only blind, but that you have lost your sense of smell."

◆　　Nobody would notice imperfections if people did
　　　　　not try to conceal them.　　　　◆

356. 田鼠和牠的媽媽

有隻田鼠一生下來就看不見，一次他對他的媽媽說：「我肯定我能看見，媽媽！」為了向小田鼠證明他錯了，他媽媽在他面前放了幾顆乳香，問：「這是什麼？」小田鼠說，「這是一顆小卵石。」他的媽媽叫道：「我的兒子，恐怕你不僅是失明，而且還喪失了嗅覺。」

◆　　如果人不刻意掩飾他的缺點，就沒有人會發現。　　◆

Townsend 303 = Perry 494

357. The Panther and the Shepherds

A Panther, by some mischance, fell into a pit. The Shepherds discovered him, and some threw sticks at him and pelted him with stones, while others, moved with compassion towards one about to die even though no one should hurt him, threw in some food to prolong his life. At night they returned home, not dreaming of any danger, but supposing that on the morrow they would find him dead. The Panther, however, when he had recruited his feeble strength, freed himself with a sudden bound from the pit, and hastened to his den with rapid steps.

After a few days he came forth and slaughtered the cattle, and, killing the Shepherds who had attacked him, raged with angry fury.Then they who had spared his life, fearing for their safety, surrendered to him their flocks and begged only for their lives. To them the Panther made this reply,"I remember alike those who sought my life with stones, and those who gave me food aside, therefore, your fears. I return as an enemy only to those who injured me."

♦ Enemies are made by injury not kindness. ♦

357. 豹子和牧羊人

一隻豹子不幸落入一個深坑中。一群牧羊人發現了他,一些人朝他扔棍子,用石頭砸他;而其他人想就算沒有人傷害他,豹子也會死,所以心生憐憫,扔進些食物來延長他的生命。到了晚上,他們回家了,沒有想到有任何危險,只是猜想第二天豹子就會死了。但是豹子聚集了僅有的氣力,猛然一躍,從深坑中逃了出來,快步趕回了他的巢穴。

幾天以後,豹子回來了,因為憤怒而變得瘋狂,殺死了牛和曾經襲擊過他的牧羊人。那些饒過豹子性命的牧羊人擔心自己的安全,便向豹子獻出牲畜,只求能夠活命。對他們,豹子給出了這樣的答覆:「我記得那些想用石頭砸死我的人,也記得那些給我食物的人;所以,不要害怕。我回來,只是報復那些曾經傷害我的人。」

♦ 傷害而非善心會帶來敵人。 ♦

ODDS/ENDS 雜七雜八

24.
PIG
豬

PIG 豬

Townsend 45 = Perry 85

358. The Piglet, the Sheep, and the Goat

A young Pig was shut up in a fold-yard with a Goat and a Sheep. On one occasion when the shepherd laid hold of him, he grunted and squeaked and resisted violently. The Sheep and the Goat complained of his distressing cries, saying, "He often handles us, and we do not cry out." To this the Pig replied, "Your handling and mine are very different things. He catches you only for your wool, or your milk, but he lays hold on me for my very life."

♦　　　Sometimes complaining is justified.　　　♦

358. 小豬、綿羊和山羊

一頭小豬、一隻山羊和綿羊，一起被關在羊欄裡。有一次，當牧羊人抓住小豬時，他又是哼哼又是尖叫，劇烈地反抗。綿羊和山羊抱怨小豬那令人煩躁的叫聲，說：「他經常抓我們，我們都沒有大叫。」聽了這句話，小豬回答道：「抓你們和抓我是完全不同的事。他抓你們只是為了剪羊毛或者擠羊奶，但是他抓我是為了要我的命。」

♦　　　有時候，抱怨是有道理的。　　　♦

L'Estrange 153 = Perry 223

359. A Sow and a Bitch

A sow and a bitch had a dispute once, which was the fruitfuller of the two. The sow yielded it at last to the bitch;

but you are to take notice at the same time, says she, that your puppies are all blind.

♦ The competitor who does the best wins, not the one who does the most. ♦

359. 母豬和母狗

有一次母豬和母狗在爭論，她們兩個誰更能生養。最後母豬不得不承認母狗生的更多。「可是，同時你也要注意。」她說，「你生的小狗都是瞎的。」

♦ 做得最好而不是做得最多的人，才是贏家。 ♦

L'Estrange 151 = Perry 222

360. A Sow and a Dog

There passed some hard words between a sow and a dog, and the sow swore by Venus, that she'd tear his guts out, if he did not mend his manners. Ay, says the dog, you do well to call upon her for your patroness, that will not so much as endure any creature about her that eats swines flesh. Well (says the sow) and that's a token of her love, to hate any thing that hurts me; but for dogs flesh, 'tis good neither dead, nor living.

♦ When you can't argue, confound. ♦

360. 母豬和狗

有一次母豬和狗吵了起來，母豬對著維納斯起誓，如果狗不檢點自己的行為，她會把他的內臟都挖出來。「哎！」狗說，「維納斯不允許任何吃過豬肉的人靠近她，你居然還敢稱她為你的守護神。」母豬說：「那表現了她對我的愛，她憎惡會傷害我的一切事物；不過，至於狗肉，活的和死的都沒什麼用處。」

◆　　　　　**無從爭辯時，要能自圓其說。**　　　　　◆

Townsend 130 = Perry 224

361. The Wild Boar and the Fox

A Wild Boar stood under a tree and rubbed his tusks against the trunk. A Fox passing by asked him why he thus sharpened his teeth when there was no danger threatening from either huntsman or hound. He replied, "I do it advisedly; for it would never do to have to sharpen my weapons just at the time I ought to be using them."

◆　　　　　Be prepared.　　　　　◆

361. 野豬和狐狸

有頭野豬在路旁的樹幹上霍霍地磨他的牙齒。一隻路過的狐狸看見了，就問野豬：「現在平安無事，既沒有獵人的威脅，也沒有獵犬的追捕，你還磨牙幹什麼呢？」野豬回答道：「我這樣做是未雨綢繆啊！等到要用的時候再臨陣磨槍，是絕對來不及的。」

◆　　　　　**要懂得未雨綢繆。**　　　　　◆

25.
SNAKE
蛇

Townsend 221 = Perry 115

362. The Fowler and the Viper

A Fowler, taking his bird-lime and his twigs, went out to catch birds. Seeing a thrush sitting upon a tree, he wished to take it, and fitting his twigs to a proper length, watched intently, having his whole thoughts directed towards the sky. While thus looking upwards, he unknowingly trod upon a Viper asleep just before his feet. The Viper, turning about, stung him, and falling into a swoon, the man said to himself, "Woe is me! that while I purposed to hunt another, I am myself fallen unawares into the snares of death."

◆ Concentrate on one thing to the exclusion of others at your own peril. ◆

362. 捕鳥人和毒蛇

捕鳥人帶黏鳥膠和捕鳥桿出門抓鳥。他看見一隻畫眉停在樹上，就想要抓住牠。他把手裡的捕鳥桿調到合適的長度，目不轉睛地盯著那隻鳥。就在他一心一意地看著上面的時候，不小心踩到了一條在他腳邊熟睡的毒蛇。毒蛇立刻轉過來咬了他一口，捕鳥人昏倒在地上，自言自語道：「我真是不幸啊！一心想著捉鳥，自己卻不知不覺丟了性命。」

◆ 專心做事時也要留心自己的安危。 ◆

Townsend 112 = Perry 60

363. The Serpent and the File

A Serpent in the course of its wanderings came into an armourer's shop. As he glided over the floor he felt his skin pricked by a file lying there. In a rage he turned round upon it and tried to dart his fangs into it;but he could do no harm to heavy iron and had soon to give over his wrath.

♦　　　It is useless attacking the insensible.　　　♦

363. 蛇和銼刀

一條毒蛇到處閒逛，悄悄溜進了一家軍械修理店。當他在地上蜿蜒爬行時，卻被放在那裡的銼刀弄傷了。蛇勃然大怒，轉過身來，張牙舞爪地向銼刀咬過去，可是這個笨重堅硬的鐵傢伙，卻毫髮未傷，最後，他只能自認倒楣，悻悻而去。

♦　　　攻擊沒有感覺的東西，絕對是徒勞的。　　　♦

L'Estrange 154 = Perry 196

364. A Snake and a Crab

There was a familiarity contracted between a snake and a crab. The crab was a plain dealing creature that advised his companion to give over shuffling and doubling, and to practice good faith. The snake went on in his old way: so that the crab finding that he would not mend his manners, set upon him in his sleep, and strangled him; and then looking upon him as he lay dead at his length: This had never befall's ye, says he, if you had but lived as straight as you dy'd.

♦ Be frank and open in your dealings. ♦

364. 蛇和螃蟹

蛇和螃蟹之間，形成了契約關係。螃蟹做生意非常坦率正直，他建議他的夥伴不要再推諉搪塞、表裡不一，而要講求誠信。蛇依舊我行我素，螃蟹發現蛇一點改過的意思都沒有，就趁他熟睡的時候跳到他身上，夾死了他。然後，看著直挺挺躺著的死蛇，他說：「你要是能像你死了的時候，那樣直挺挺地活著，就不會死了。」

♦ 做生意要開誠佈公。 ♦

Townsend 115 = Perry 176

365. The Woodman and the Serpent

One wintry day a Woodman was tramping home from his work when he saw something black lying on the snow. When he came closer he saw it was a Serpent to all appearance dead. But he took it up and put it in his bosom to warm while he hurried home. As soon as he got indoors he put the Serpent down on the hearth before the fire. The children watched it and saw it slowly come to life again. Then one of them stooped down to stroke it, but the Serpent raised its head and put out its fangs and was about to sting the child to death. So the Woodman seized his axe, and with one stroke cut the Serpent in two. "Ah," said he, "No gratitude from the wicked."

♦ This story reminds us to be grateful to those who have helped us, rather than harming them. ♦

365. 樵夫和蛇

在一個寒風凜冽的冬日，樵夫完工後，拖著疲倦的身子往家走。在途中，他看到有一個黑東西躺在雪地裡，走上前去一看，是一條蛇，不過看起來已經死了。可是樵夫仍然把蛇抱了起來，放到胸口來給蛇取暖，同時加快速度匆匆忙忙往家趕。一進家門，他就把蛇放在火爐前的爐臺上，孩子們都簇擁在旁邊觀看。蛇逐漸恢復了知覺。有一個孩子俯下身去撫摸它。蛇馬上抬起頭，露出鋒利的毒牙，想要把孩子一口咬死。樵夫一把拿起斧頭，把蛇劈成兩半。「呸！」他說，「作惡多端的人，永遠不會心存感激。」

♦ 這個故事提醒我們，要感恩那些幫助過我們的人，而不是傷害他們。 ♦

Townsend 300 = Perry 93

366. The Viper and the File

A viper entered a blacksmith's workshop and bit the file, testing it to if this was something she could eat. The file protested fiercely, "You fool! Why are you trying to wound me with your teeth, when I am able to gnaw through every sort of iron?"

♦ If you have ever tried to take a bite out of someone whose fangs are even sharper than yours, you will recognize yourself in this story. ♦

425

SNAKE 蛇

366. 毒蛇和銼刀

　　一條毒蛇爬進鐵匠鋪，咬了銼刀一口，看看能不能吃。銼刀惡狠狠地說：「你這笨蛋！什麼樣的鋼鐵我都能咬動，你還妄想用牙齒咬傷我？」

　　◆　如果你想過，從比你更兇狠的人那裡索取點什麼，
　　　　從這個故事裡，就能看到自己的影子。　　◆

26.
TREES/PLANTS
樹/植物

TREES/PLANTS 樹 / 植物

L'Estrange 135 = Perry 527

367. Apples and Horse-Turds

Upon a very great fall of rain, the current carried away a huge heap of apples, together with a dunghill that lay in the watercourse. They floated a good while together like brethren and companions; and as they went thus dancing down the stream, the horse-turds would be every foot crying out still. Alack a day! How we apples swim!

◆ People will often think more of themselves than warranted. ◆

367. 蘋果和馬糞

有一次，雨下得非常大，雨水把一大堆蘋果連同河道裡的糞堆一起沖走了。他們像兄弟夥伴一樣一起隨波逐流了好久，就這樣一路順流而下，每前進一步，馬糞就會哀歎：「多悲慘的一天啊！像我們這樣的蘋果，怎麼能這麼游泳呢？」

◆ 人們常會高估自己。 ◆

Townsend 86 = Perry 304

368. The Fir-Tree and the Bramble

A Fir-tree said boastingly to the Bramble, "You are useful for nothing at all; while I am everywhere used for roofs and houses." The Bramble answered, "You poor creature, if you would only call to mind the axes and saws which are about to hew you down, you would have reason to wish that you had grown up a Bramble, not a Fir-Tree."

♦　　　Better poverty without care, than riches with.　　　♦

368. 杉樹和荊棘

一棵杉樹對荊棘吹噓道：「你一點用處都沒有，而我呢！到處都在用杉樹蓋房頂、造房子。」荊棘回答說：「你這個可憐的傢伙，如果你想一想，那些把你砍倒的斧頭和鋸子，就會有理由希望自己是一棵荊棘，而不是一棵杉樹了。」

♦　　　沒人在意的貧困勝過被人覬覦的富有。　　　♦

Townsend 184 = Perry 77

369. The Hart and the Vine

A Hart, hard pressed in the chase, hid himself beneath the large leaves of a Vine. The huntsmen, in their haste, overshot the place of his concealment. Supposing all danger to have passed, the Hart began to nibble the tendrils of the Vine. One of the huntsmen, attracted by the rustling of the leaves, looked back, and seeing the Hart, shot an arrow from his bow and struck it. The Hart, at the point of death, groaned, "I am rightly served, for I should not have maltreated the Vine that saved me."

♦　　　Do not mistreat those who help you.　　　♦

TREES/PLANTS 樹／植物

369. 鹿和藤蔓

鹿為逃開獵人的追擊，躲在一大叢茂盛的藤蔓下面。獵人們只顧著匆匆往前追趕，忽略了鹿的避身之地。鹿覺得萬事大吉了，就開始啃咬藤蔓上的小嫩枝。啃噬時，沙沙的響聲吸引了一個獵人的注意力，他轉過頭來發現了鹿，一箭就射中了牠。奄奄一息的鹿痛苦地哀歎：「藤救我一命，我反而虐待它，現在丟了性命，也是自作自受。」

◆　　　　　　不要恩將仇報。　　　　　　◆

Townsend 223 = Perry 278

370. The Man and the Wood

A Man came into a Wood one day with an axe in his hand, and begged all the Trees to give him a small branch which he wanted for a particular purpose. The Trees were good-natured and gave him one of their branches. What did the Man do but fix it into the axe head, and soon set to work cutting down tree after tree. Then the Trees saw how foolish they had been in giving their enemy the means of destroying themselves.

◆　When helping others, consider whether it might　◆
put yourself in a difficult situation.

370. 人和樹林

一天一個人走進樹林，手裡拿著一把斧頭，向所有的樹請求說他想要一根小樹枝，他有特殊的用處。樹都很和善並給了他。

那個人做的是把樹枝裝在斧頭上,然後很快就開始一棵接一棵地把樹都砍倒了。這時樹才明白,給敵人工具來毀滅自己是多麼愚蠢。

◆　　　　幫助別人時,要考慮是否會讓自己陷入困境。　　　◆

Townsend 127 = Perry 70

371. The Oak and the Reeds

A very large Oak was uprooted by the wind and thrown across a stream. It fell among some Reeds, which it thus addressed, "I wonder how you, who are so light and weak, are not entirely crushed by these strong winds." They replied, "You fight and contend with the wind, and consequently you are destroyed; while we on the contrary bend before the least breath of air, and therefore remain unbroken, and escape."

◆　　　　　　　　Stoop to conquer.　　　　　　　　◆

371. 橡樹和蘆葦

一天晚上,森林裡起了一場暴風。很多樹都被刮倒了,枝葉散落在四周。一棵長在河邊的橡樹,被吹到了水中,並順流而下到了下游。在橡樹順水漂流時,它驚奇地注意到岸上仍然佈滿了蘆葦。

「你們怎樣設法活下來的?」它問,「你們這麼瘦弱,而我,一棵大樹,卻倒下來死了。」

「這不奇怪!」蘆葦低聲說,「你被摧毀了,因為你與暴風

TREES/PLANTS 樹／植物

抗爭。我們活了下來，因為我們給暴風讓路，有一點風就趕緊彎下腰來。」

◆ **忍辱求勝。** ◆

Townsend 162 = Perry 303

372. The Oak and the Woodcutters

The Woodcutter cut down a Mountain Oak and split it in pieces, making wedges of its own branches for dividing the trunk. The Oak said with a sigh,"I do not care about the blows of the axe aimed at my roots, but I do grieve at being torn in pieces by these wedges made from my own branches."

◆ Misfortunes springing from ourselves are the hardest to bear. ◆

372. 橡樹和伐木工

伐木工砍倒了一棵山橡樹，要把它劈開，用它的樹枝做成斧頭，來劈開樹幹。橡樹歎息說：「我不介意我的根被斧頭砍，可是被用我自己的樹枝做成的這些斧頭劈成碎片，卻真的讓我傷心。」

◆ **自己造成的不幸最難忍受。** ◆

Townsend 154 = Perry 302

373. The Oaks and Jupiter

The Oaks presented a complaint to Jupiter, saying,"We bear

for no purpose the burden of life, as of all the trees that grow we are the most continually in peril of the axe."Jupiter made answer,"You have only to thank yourselves for the misfortunes to which you are exposed: for if you did not make such excellent pillars and posts, and prove yourselves so serviceable to the carpenters and the farmers, the axe would not so frequently be laid to your roots."

♦　　　　　Men make their own fate.　　　　　♦

373. 橡樹和朱比特

　　橡樹向朱比特抱怨，說：「我們無緣無故地忍受著生命的重負，因為在所有樹中，我們是最頻繁地遭遇斧頭砍伐的危險。」朱比特回答：「你們遭受不幸只能怨自己。因為，如果你們做不成這麼好的柱子和路標，向木匠和農夫證明自己這樣有用，斧頭也不會這麼頻繁地落到你們身上。」

♦　　　　　　命運由自己來掌握。　　　　　　♦

L'Estrange 78 = Perry 264

374. An Old Tree Transplanted

A certain farmer had one choice apple-tree in his orchard that he valued above all the rest, and he made his landlord every year a present of the fruit on't. He liked the apples so very well, that nothing would serve him but transplanting the tree into his own grounds. It withered presently upon the removal, and so there was an end of both fruit and tree together. The news was no sooner brought to the landlord, but he brake out into this reflexion upon it: This comes, says he, of transplanting an old tree, to gratify an extravagant appetite: whereas if I could have contented my self with the fruit, and left my tenant the tree still, all had been well.

◆　　　Greed often results in calamity.　　　◆

374. 被移種的老樹

　　農夫在他的果園裡，種了一棵蘋果樹。在所有的果樹裡面，農夫最喜歡這棵蘋果樹，每年都把這樹上結的果子作為禮物送給他的地主。地主非常喜歡這棵樹長的蘋果，一定要把這株樹移種到自己的土地上才甘心。一被搬走，這株樹馬上就枯了，樹沒了，蘋果也沒了。地主一聽到這個消息，就開始反省整件事。他說：「這都是我貪得無厭，移種了老樹的結果；如果我吃蘋果就感到滿足，而讓我的佃戶接著照料那株樹，那就什麼事都沒有了。」

◆　　　貪婪通常會帶來災難。　　　◆

Townsend 307 = Perry 413

375. The Olive-Tree and the Fig-Tree

　　The Olive-Tree ridiculed the Fig-Tree because, while she was green all the year round, the Fig-Tree changed its leaves with the seasons. A shower of snow fell upon them, and, finding the Olive full of foliage, it settled upon its branches and broke them down with its weight, at once despoiling it of its beauty and killing the tree. But finding the Fig-Tree denuded of leaves, the snow fell through to the ground, and did not injure it at all.

♦   Brag and nature may bring you down.   ♦

375. 橄欖樹和無花果樹

橄欖樹嘲笑無花果樹,因為她終年常青,而無花果樹的葉子卻隨季節而變化。一陣雪落在她們身上,橄欖樹上滿是葉子,雪就落在它的樹枝上,壓斷了樹枝,頓時剝奪了橄欖樹的美麗,橄欖樹死了。但是因為無花果樹的葉子都落光了,雪就穿過樹枝落到了地上,一點兒都沒有傷害無花果樹。

♦   自大會帶來災難。   ♦

Townsend 266 = Perry 299

376. The Peasant and the Apple-Tree

A peasant had in his garden an Apple-Tree which bore no fruit but only served as a harbor for the sparrows and grasshoppers. He resolved to cut it down, and taking his axe in his hand, made a bold stroke at its roots. The grasshoppers and sparrows entreated him not to cut down the tree that sheltered them, but to spare it, and they would sing to him and lighten his labors. He paid no attention to their request, but gave the tree a second and a third blow with his axe. When he reached the hollow of the tree, he found a hive full of honey. Having tasted the honeycomb, he threw down his axe, and looking on the tree as sacred, took great care of it.

♦   Self-interest alone moves some men.   ♦

TREES/PLANTS 樹 / 植物

376. 農夫和蘋果樹

一個農夫發現園中的蘋果樹不結果實,而成了麻雀和蚱蜢的家,決定砍掉這棵樹。他拿起斧頭狠狠砍了樹根一下,蚱猛和麻雀都懇求他不要砍倒這棵樹,為了報答他,他們會為他唱歌,解除一天勞動所帶來的疲乏。他沒有聽取這個建議,繼續砍樹。砍了三下之後,他發現樹幹中有個洞,裡面有個裝滿蜂蜜的蜂房。嚐過了蜂蜜之後,農夫扔掉了斧頭,把樹當作寶物好好看護了起來。

♦　　　　　自身的利益驅動人的行為。　　　　　♦

Townsend 19 = Perry 213

377. The Pomegranate, Apple-Tree, and Bramble

The Pomegranate and Apple-Tree disputed as to which was the most beautiful. When their strife was at its height, a Bramble from the neighboring hedge lifted up its voice, and said in a boastful tone, "Pray, my dear friends, in my presence at least cease from such vain disputes."

♦　　　Everyone thinks themselves the best.　　　♦

377. 石榴樹、蘋果樹和荊棘

石榴樹和蘋果樹爭論誰更美。他們爭論得最激烈的時候,鄰近籬笆的一叢荊棘大聲地自吹自擂:「我親愛的朋友,在我面前,請停止這種無聊的爭論。」

◆　　　　　每個人都覺得自己最好。　　　　　◆

Townsend 311 = Perry 369

378. **The Rose and the Amaranth**

An Amaranth planted in a garden near a Rose-Tree, thus addressed it,"What a lovely flower is the Rose, a favorite alike with Gods and with men. I envy you your beauty and your perfume." The Rose replied, " I indeed, dear Amaranth, flourish but for a brief season! If no cruel hand pluck me from my stem, yet I must perish by an early doom. But thou art immortal and dost never fade, but blooms for ever in renewed youth."

◆　　　　　Accept your own fate.　　　　　◆

378. 玫瑰和不凋花

花園裡一棵不凋花種在玫瑰叢旁，因而就對玫瑰說：「玫瑰花你真可愛，上帝喜歡你，人也喜歡你。你如此美麗芬芳，我真的好羨慕你。」玫瑰答道：「親愛的不凋花，我的確很繁茂，但是卻稍縱即逝！就算沒有殘酷的手將我折斷，我也難逃夭折的厄運。可是你卻能永保青春，永不凋謝，一直盛開下去。」

◆　　　　　人要接受自己的命運。　　　　　◆

TREES/PLANTS 樹 / 植物

Townsend 166 = Perry 302

379. The Trees and the Axe

A man came into a forest and asked the Trees to provide him a handle for his axe. The Trees consented to his request and gave him a young ash-tree. No sooner had the man fitted a new handle to his axe from it, than he began to use it and quickly felled with his strokes the noblest giants of the forest.

An old oak, lamenting when too late the destruction of his companyions, said to a neighboring cedar, " The first step has lost us all. If we had not given up the rights of the ash, we might yet have retained our own privileges and have stood for ages."

◆ Nothing bothers a man more than to see he has aided his own undoing. ◆

379. 樹和斧頭

一個人來到森林裡，請求樹給他一根木頭做斧柄。樹答應了他的請求，給了他一棵小枝樹。他用小枝樹做成斧柄，剛裝到斧頭上，就掄起斧頭砍倒了森林中最粗最高的一棵樹。

一棵老橡樹痛惜地看著自己的同伴慘遭荼毒，卻無能為力。他悲傷地對他旁邊的雪松說：「我們在第一步就把自己給葬送了。如果我們不把小枝樹給他，也許我們還能維護自己生存的權利，長久地站在這裡。」

◆ 沒有什麼比看到自己親手造成大錯更痛心。 ◆

Townsend 71 = Perry 374

380. The Vine and the Goat

A Vine was luxuriant in the time of vintage with leaves and grapes. A Goat, passing by, nibbled its young tendrils and its leaves. The Vine addressed him and said, "Why do you thus injure me without a cause, and crop my leaves? Is there no young grass left? But I shall not have to wait long for my just revenge; for if you now should crop my leaves, and cut me down to my root, I shall provide the wine to pour over you when you are led as a victim to the sacrifice."

♦ Ingratitude is dangerous. ♦

380. 葡萄和山羊

豐收時節，一棵枝繁葉茂的藤蔓樹，結出了累累的葡萄。一隻山羊大搖大擺地過來啃吃葡萄的嫩蔓和綠葉。葡萄斥責他：「你為什麼無緣無故地傷害我，吃掉我剛長出的新芽？難道地上就沒有嫩草了嗎？還好等不了多久，我就會看到你是如何遭報應的。你現在吃光我的枝葉，我保證，到了你被屠宰後，拿去祭祀的時候，傾倒在你身上的，正是用我的果實釀成的酒。」

♦ 不知感激是很危險的。 ♦

Townsend 189 = Perry 250

381. The Walnut-Tree

A Walnut Tree standing by the roadside bore an abundant

439

crop of fruit. For the sake of the nuts, the passers-by broke its branches with stones and sticks. The Walnut-Tree piteously exclaimed,"O wretched me! that those whom I cheer with my fruit should repay me with these painful requitals!"

♦　　　　You always hurt the one you love.　　　　♦

381. 核桃樹

有棵核桃樹長在路旁，結滿了累累的碩果。過路人覬覦樹上美味的核桃，就用石頭和木棍將樹枝打斷。核桃樹哀歎道；「為什麼我如此不幸呢？我把自己的果實獻給過往的行人，可是到頭來，他們竟然用傷痛來回報我！」

♦　　　　人們往往傷害他們的所愛。　　　　♦

27.
WOLF
狼

WOLF 狼

Townsend 225 = Perry 37

382. The Blind Man and the Whelp

A Blind Man was accustomed to distinguishing different animals by touching them with his hands. The whelp of a Wolf was brought him, with a request that he would feel it, and say what it was. He felt it, and being in doubt, said, "I do not quite know whether it is the cub of a Fox, or the whelp of a Wolf, but this I know full well. It would not be safe to admit him to the sheepfold."

♦　　　Evil tendencies are shown in early life.　　　♦

382. 盲人和幼狼

有個盲人，不管是什麼動物，他只需一摸，就能分辨出牠的種類。有人把一隻幼狼送給他，讓他摸一摸，看看是哪種動物。盲人摸了一下，慢慢地說道：「我還無法肯定這是一隻小狐狸，還是一頭小狼。但有一點無需懷疑，就是絕對不能把牠放進羊群裡去。」

♦　　　兇狠的本性在年幼時就顯現出來。　　　♦

Townsend 194 = Perry 97

383. The Kid and the Wolf

A Kid, returning without protection from the pasture, was pursued by a Wolf. Seeing he could not escape, he turned round, and said, "I know, friend Wolf that I must be your prey, but before

I die I would ask of you one favor you will play me a tune to which I may dance." The Wolf complied, and while he was piping and the Kid was dancing, some hounds hearing the sound ran up and began chasing The Wolf. Turning to the Kid, he said, "It is just what I deserve; for I, who am only a butcher, should not have turned piper to please you."

♦ In the time of dire need, clever thinking is key. ♦

383. 小羊和狼

有隻小羊從草原回來，沒有受到任何的護衛，遭到了狼的追擊。眼看著無法逃脫，小羊就回轉身來對狼說道：「我明白，狼兄，我必然要成為你的盤中飧了。但是臨死之前，我有個不情之請，請你為我吹奏一曲，好讓我能伴著它跳個舞。」狼答應了。正在他吹奏，小羊跳舞之際，幾隻獵狗聽見聲音，紛紛跑過來驅趕狼。狼回過身，對小羊說：「我這是自食其果；我本來只是個屠夫，不應該吹奏曲子來取悅你的。」

♦ 身處絕境的時候，最關鍵的是必須得有智謀。 ♦

Townsend 296 = Perry 261

384. The Lamb and the Wolf

A Wolf pursued a Lamb, which fled for refuge to a certain Temple. The Wolf called out to him and said, " The Priest will slay you in sacrifice, if he should catch you."On which the Lamb replied,"It would be better for me to be sacrificed in the Temple than to be eaten by you."

♦ Better to honor the God than fall to your enemy. ♦

384. 羔羊和狼

狼追趕小羔羊,小羔羊逃到一座神廟裡躲藏。狼大聲對他叫喊:「和尚如果捉住了你,他會殺了你拿去祭神的。」羔羊聽了回答道:「我寧願被祭神犧牲,也不願讓你吃掉。」

♦　　　**尊敬神靈好過落到敵人手中。**　　　♦

Townsend 269 = Perry 158

385. The Mother and the Wolf

A famished Wolf was prowling about in the morning in search of food. As he passed the door of a cottage built in the forest, he heard a Mother say to her child, "Be quiet, or I will throw you out of the window, and The Wolf shall eat you." The Wolf sat all day waiting at the door. In the evening he heard the same woman fondling her child and saying, " You are quiet now, and if The Wolf should come, we will kill him." The Wolf, hearing these words, went home, gasping with cold and hunger. When he reached his den, Mistress Wolf inquired of him why he returned wearied and supperless, so contrary to his wont. He replied, "Why, forsooth! use I gave credence to the words of a woman!"

♦　　　**Enemies' promises were made to be broken.**　　　♦

385. 母親和狼

一天早晨,一隻餓狼四處遊蕩尋找食物。當他經過森林中的一所小屋門口時,他聽到一個母親對她的孩子說:「安靜點,要不我就把你扔到窗戶外頭去, 讓狼把你吃了。」狼在門口坐著等了一天。 晚上他又聽到那個女人安撫她的孩子,說:「你現在安靜了,如果狼來了,我們就殺了他。」聽到這話,狼回了家,又冷又餓地喘著氣。當他到了他的洞穴的時候,狼夫人問他為什麼沒吃晚飯就回來了,還這麼累,和他平時完全相反。他回答:「哎呀,真是的,我居然把一個女人的話當真了!」

◆ 敵人的承諾是不可信的。 ◆

Townsend 78 = Perry 366

386. The Shepherd and the Wolf

A Shepherd once found the whelp of a Wolf and brought it up, and after a while taught it to steal lambs from the neighboring flocks. The Wolf, having shown himself an apt pupil, said to the Shepherd,"Since you have taught me to steal, you must keep a sharp lookout, or you will lose some of your own flock."

◆ Fales men cannot be trusted. ◆

386. 牧羊人和狼

牧羊人發現一隻小狼,便把牠帶回家養起來。過了一段日子,牧羊人就教牠去鄰家的羊群裡偷小羊。小狼顯示出極高的天賦,很快就成了偷羊高手。訓練有素的小狼對牧羊人說:「你讓我學會偷搶,那你最好看緊自己的羊群,否則你的羊也會被偷走的。」

◆ 不可相信惡人。 ◆

WOLF 狼

L'Estrange 155 = Perry 267

387. A Shepherd and a Wolf's Whelp

A Shepherd took a Sucking Whelp of a Wolf, and trained it up with his Dogs. This Whelp fed with them, grew up with them, and whensoever they went out upon the Chace of a Wolf, the Whelp would be sure to make One. It fell out sometimes that the Wolf 'escaped, and the Dogs were forced to go Home again: But this domestic Wolf would be still Hunting on,'till he came up to his Brethren, where he took part of the Prey with them; and so back again to his Master. It happened now and then, that the Wolves abroad were pretty quiet for a Fit, so that this Whelp of a Wolf was fain to make Bold ever and anon with a Sheep in Private by the Bye; but in the Conclusion, the Shepherd came to find out the Roguery, and Hang'd him up for his Pains.

♦ False Men are no more to be Reclaim'd than Wolves, and the Leven of the Predecessors Soures the Blood, in the very Veins of the Whole family. ♦

387. 牧羊人和小狼

牧羊人帶走了一頭還在吃奶的小狼，和他的狗一起進行訓練。這頭小狼和他們一起進食，一起長大，只要他們一出去追狼，這隻小狼也一定會參與。他們有時候會讓狼給逃脫，狗就只好回家，但這隻家養的狼還會繼續追趕；直到他趕上他的兄弟們，從他們那裡分一杯羹，再回到他主人那裡。外頭的狼群會時不時地安靜一會兒，這隻小狼也就越來越大膽，不久就會自己悄悄地吃掉一隻羊。但是，最後，他的行徑還是漸漸地被牧羊人發現了，為了懲罰他,牧羊人就把他吊死了。

◆ **虛偽的人和狼一樣是無法被感化的,祖先的基因融化在血液裡,流淌在整個家族的血脈裡。** ◆

Townsend 74 = Perry 210

388. The Shepherd's Boy and the Wolf

A Shepherd-boy, who watched a flock of sheep near a village, brought out the villagers three or four times by crying out,"Wolf ! Wolf !" and when his neighbors came to help him, laughed at them for their pains. The Wolf, however, did truly come at last. The Shepherd-boy, now really alarmed, shouted in an agony of terror,"Pray, do come and help me; The Wolf is killing the sheep"; but no one paid any heed to his cries, nor rendered any assistance. The Wolf having no cause of fear, at his leisure lacerated or destroyed the whole flock.

◆ There is no believing a liar, even when he speaks the truth. ◆

388. 牧童和狼

一個牧童在村子附近放羊,他總是突然大喊:「狼來了!狼來了!」欺騙村裡的人跑出來,幫助他打狼。看到他們中了自己圈套的狼狽樣子,男孩哈哈大笑。男孩戲弄了村民三四次。結果到最後狼真的來了,男孩這下真的驚慌失措了,他驚恐地高聲呼救:「求求你們,快來幫我啊!狼把羊吃啦!」可是對於他的哀求大家都充耳不聞,更不用說去幫助他了。因此,狼肆無忌憚地獵殺了整個羊群。

◆ 說謊者即使說了真話也不會有人相信。 ◆

Townsend 10 = Perry 156

389. The Wolf and the Crane

A Wolf who had a bone stuck in his throat hired a Crane, for a large sum, to put her head into his mouth and draw out the bone. When the Crane had extracted the bone and demanded the promised payment, The Wolf, grinning and grinding his teeth, exclaimed, "Why, you have surely already had a sufficient recompense, in having been permitted to draw out your head in safety from the mouth and jaws of a wolf."

◆ In serving the wicked, expect no reward, and be thankful if you escape Injury for your pains. ◆

389. 狼和鶴

狼的喉嚨裡卡了一塊骨頭，於是他花了很多錢雇來一隻鶴，讓他把頭伸進自己的嘴裡，把喉嚨裡的那塊骨頭給叼出來。鶴取出了骨頭後，向狼要事先約定好的報酬。狼呲牙裂嘴笑著，惡狠狠地叫囂起來：「什麼報酬？你把你的腦袋伸到我的嘴裡，最後還能毫髮無傷地出來，那全都是我手下留情的緣故。這就已經是最好的酬勞了。」

◆ 為壞人辦事情，千萬別奢望能獲得回報，做完事情後不受傷害就已經謝天謝地了。 ◆

L'Estrange 39 = Perry 568

390. A Wolf and a Fox

　　A wolf that had a mind to take his ease, stored himself privately with provisions, and so kept close a while. Why, how now friend says a fox to him, we haven't seen you abroad at the chase this many a day! Why truly says the wolf, I have gotten an indisposition that keeps me much at home, and I hope I shall have your prayers for my recovery. The fox had a fetch in't, and when he saw it would not fadge; away goes he presently to a shepherd, and tells him where he might surprise a wolf if he had a mind to't. The shepherd followed his directions, and destroyed him. The fox immediately, as his next heir, repairs to his cell, and takes possession of his stores; but he had little joy of the purchase, for in a very short time, the same shepherd did as much for the fox, as he had done before for the wolf.

◆　　Take pleasure when thieves destroy themselves.　　◆

390. 狼和狐狸

　　狼決定要安逸地休息一陣，於是就悄悄地儲藏了些糧食，一段時間都閉門不出。「怎麼了？現在怎麼樣，朋友？」狐狸對他說，「我們這些天都沒見你外出捕獵。」「哎呀，」狼說，「我身體有點不舒服，所以大部分時間都待在家裡。我希望能得到你的祝福。」狐狸試圖從狼那裡偷點糧食，但沒有得逞。狐狸馬上跑去找牧羊人，告訴他狼的住處，說只要他願意，就可以對狼進行突襲。牧羊人按照狐狸指給他的方向，殺死了狼。而狐狸隨即變成狼的繼任者，回到了狼窩，把狼的食物據為己有。但是，他還沒來得及慶祝，牧羊人就又回來了，用他之前對付狼的方法，結果了狐狸的性命。

♦　　　　看著盜賊們自取滅亡，真是大快人心。　　　　♦

Townsend 217 = Perry 474

391. The Wolf, the Fox, and the Ape

A Wolf accused a Fox of theft, but the Fox entirely denied the charge. An Ape undertook to adjudge the matter between them. When each had fully stated his case the Ape announced this sentence,"I do not think you, Wolf, ever lost what you claim; and I do believe you, Fox, to have stolen what you so stoutly deny."

♦　　The dishonest, if they act honestly, get no credit.　　♦

391. 狼、狐狸和猿

狼指控狐狸偷竊，但是狐狸卻死不承認。猿猴被請來做裁判。當雙方都振振有詞地陳述了自己的觀點之後，猿裁決道：「狼，儘管你說你的東西被偷了，但是我相信，其實你並沒丟東西；狐狸，即便你死不認帳，可是我仍然認為，你是小偷。」

♦　　不誠實的人即使是做了誠實的事，也不會得到人們的信任。　　♦

Townsend 213 = Perry 157

392. The Wolf and the Goat

A Wolf saw a Goat feeding at the summit of a steep precipice, where he had no chance of reaching her. He called to her and earnestly begged her to come lower down, lest she fall by some mishap; and he added that the meadows lay where he was standing, and that the herbage was most tender. She replied, "No, my friend, it is not for the pasture that you invite me, but for yourself, who are in want of food."

♦　　　Be careful when you enemy invites you.　　　♦

392. 狼和山羊

狼看見山羊在陡峭的懸崖上吃草，卻無法靠近他。於是他就跟羊打招呼，假裝好意地請她往下走一些，免得一不小心掉下來，他還補充說他站的地方也有極其柔嫩可口的青草。山羊回答說：「免了吧！我的朋友，你請我下去哪裡是想讓我吃草，分明是你自己嘴饞想吃肉了吧。」

♦　　　收到敵人的邀請時要小心。　　　♦

L'Estrange 31 = Perry 572

393. A Wolf, Kid, and Goat

A goat that was going out one morning for a mouthful of fresh grass, charged her kid upon her blessing, not to open the door till she came back, to any creature that had not a beard. The goat was no sooner out of sight, but up comes a wolf to the door, that had over-heard the charge; and in a small pipe calls to the kid to let her mother come in. The kid smelt out the roguery, and had the wolf show his beard, and the door should be open to him.

♦　　　A hypocrite can usually be found out.　　　♦

451

WOLF 狼

393. 狼、孩子和山羊

一天早上，山羊要外出吃青草，囑咐她的孩子，在她回來之前，不要給沒有長鬍子的動物開門。狼聽到了山羊的囑咐，等山羊一走遠，他就走到門前，從一根很小的管道裡叫孩子開門讓她的媽媽進來。孩子看穿了他的詭計，叫狼給他看看他的鬍子，他才會給他開門。

♦ 偽裝者通常都會被識破。 ♦

Townsend 228 = Perry 154

394. The Wolf and the Horse

A Wolf coming out of a field of oats met a Horse and thus addressed him, "I would advise you to go into that field. It is full of fine oats, which I have left untouched for you, as you are a friend whom I would love to hear enjoying good eating." The Horse replied, "If oats had been the food of wolves, you would never have indulged your ears at the cost of your belly."

♦ Men of evil reputation, when they perform a good deed, fail to get credit for it. ♦

394. 狼和馬

狼從一片燕麥田裡走出來時遇到一匹馬，於是就對他說：「我建議你現在趕快到地裡去。那裡的燕麥長勢驚人，可是我一點都沒捨得吃，全給你留著呢！因為，我把你當成是我的好朋友，我就喜歡聽你津津有味地吃東西時發出的聲音。」馬回答道：「如果你會把燕麥當成你的食物的話，你是絕對不會只讓耳朵享福，而讓肚子忍饑挨餓的。」

♦ **惡名昭彰的人，即使是做好事也不會得到別人的信任。** ♦

Townsend 110 = Perry 346

395. The Wolf and the Housedog

A Wolf, meeting a big well-fed Mastiff with a wooden collar about his neck asked him who it was that fed him so well and yet compelled him to drag that heavy log about wherever he went. "The master," he replied. Then said The Wolf, "May no friend of mine ever be in such a plight; for the weight of this chain is enough to spoil the appetite."

♦ Bettre starve free than be a fat slave. ♦

395. 狼和看家狗

狼看到獒犬雖然長得身強體壯，但是脖子上卻戴著無比沉重的項圈，於是便問他，是誰把他餵養得龐大腰圓，可是又迫使他無論到哪裡，都必須拖著那沉重的枷鎖。「是我的主人。」獒犬回答道。狼對他說：「希望我的朋友們不會經受這樣的痛苦！因為那塊沉重的枷鎖，足以讓人失去食慾。」

♦ **飢餓的自由者好過餵飽的奴隸。** ♦

Townsend 1 = Perry 155

396. The Wolf and the Lamb

Wolf, meeting with a Lamb astray from the fold, resolved not to lay violent hands on him, but to find some plea to justify to the Lamb The Wolf's right to eat him. He thus addressed him, "Sirrah, last year you grossly insulted me." "Indeed," bleated the Lamb in a mournful tone of voice, " I was not then born." Then said The Wolf, " You feed in my pasture." " No, good sir," replied the Lamb, " I have not yet tasted grass." Again said The Wolf,"You drink of my well." " No," exclaimed the Lamb, " I never yet drank water, for as yet my mother's milk is both food and drink to me." Upon which The Wolf seized him and ate him up, saying, "Well! I won't remain supperless, even though you refute every one of my imputations."

◆ The tyrant will always find a pretext for his tyranny. ◆

396. 狼和小羊

狼遇見了一隻離群的小羔羊，決定不採用任何暴力手段，而是找出理由向小羊證明，吃他是完全正確的。於是他對小羊吼道：「小傢伙，去年你深深地傷害了我。」小羊可憐地哀叫著：「實在是冤枉啊！去年我還沒生出來呢！」於是，狼改口說道：「你曾經跑到我的草地上偷吃青草。」「沒有啊！好先生，」小羊解釋說，「迄今為止，我還沒有品嚐過青草的滋味呢！」狼又說：「那你就是把我井裡的水給喝了。」「絕對沒有啊！」小羊叫起來，「我從來也沒有喝過水，時至今日，我全部的食物和飲料，就是我媽媽的奶水。」聽了小羊的話，狼還是把他抓住然後一口吃掉了，「去你的！就算我的每一個理由你都能駁倒，但是我總不能沒有東西當晚飯吃吧！」

◆　　　　殘暴的人總能為其殘暴的行為辯護。　　　　◆

L'Estrange 130 = Perry 149

397. A Wolf and a Lion

As a wolf and a lion were abroad upon adventure together, Heark, (says the wolf) don't you hear the bleating of sheep? My life for yours sir, I'll go fetch you a purchase. Away he goes, and follows his ear, till he came just under the sheepfold: but it was so well fortified, and the dogs asleep so near it, that back he comes sneaking to the lion again, and tells him, There are sheep yonder (says he) 'tis true, but they are as lean as carrion, and we had e'en as good let them alone 'till they have more flesh on their backs.

◆　　　　Indifference hides promises unkept.　　　　◆

397. 狼和獅子

狼和獅子一起外出冒險，「聽！」狼說，「難道你沒有聽見羊的叫聲嗎？我可以為您赴湯蹈火，先生，我要幫您抓隻羊回來。」於是，狼出發了，沿著聲音傳來的方向，剛好走到了羊圈下面。但是，羊圈非常堅固，而狗就睡在邊上，見此情景，狼就偷偷溜回了獅子那裡，還告訴獅子說：「那裡確實是有羊，不過，他們都瘦得皮包骨頭，我們還是等他們多長點肉，再來捉他們吧。」

◆　　　　無動於衷的背後，隱藏著未實現的承諾。　　　　◆

WOLF 狼

Townsend 90 = Perry 160

398. The Wolf and the Sheep

A Wolf, sorely wounded and bitten by dogs, lay sick and maimed in his lair. Being in want of food, he called to a Sheep who was passing, and asked him to fetch some water from a stream flowing close beside him. "For," he said, "if you will bring me drink, I will find means to provide myself with meat." "Yes," said the Sheep, "if I should bring you the draught, you would doubtless make me provide the meat also."

♦　　Hypocritical speeches are easily seen through.　　♦

398. 狼和羊

狼被狗咬得遍體鱗傷，只能一動不動地躺在窩裡。饑腸轆轆的他好不容易等到一隻羊從他窩前經過，趕緊把羊叫住，乞求他幫忙從旁邊的小溪裡取點水。狼說：「如果你能幫忙打點水給我喝，我就能為自己找到肉吃。」「你想得倒挺美的！」羊說，「如果我打水給你喝，毫無疑問，你必定會把我當肉吃了。」

♦　　　　虛偽的謊言很容易被戳穿。　　　　♦

Townsend 49 = Perry 451

399. The Wolf in Sheep's Clothing I

Once upon a time a Wolf resolved to disguise his appearance in order to secure food more easily. Encased in the skin of a sheep, he pastured with the flock deceiving the shepherd by his costume. In the evening he was shut up by the shepherd in the fold; the gate was closed, and the entrance made thoroughly secure. But the shepherd, returning to the fold during the night to obtain meat for the next day, mistakenly caught up The Wolf instead of a sheep, and killed him instantly.

♦ Harm seek, harm find. ♦

399. 披著羊皮的狼（版本一）

從前有隻狼，為了更容易地獲得食物，決定將自己偽裝起來。他把羊皮披在自己身上，騙過了牧羊人，混到羊群裡與他們一起「吃草」。到了晚上，他和其他的羊一起被牧羊人關進羊圈，大門也被緊鎖，出口也堵得密不透風的。可是當晚牧羊人又返回了羊圈，想宰隻羊作為第二天的食物。結果他誤把那隻不幸的狼當成羊，可憐的狼就這樣一命嗚呼了。

♦ 害人不成，反誤了自己的性命。 ♦

Townsend 263 = Perry 952

400. The Wolf in Sheep's Clothing II

A Wolf found great difficulty in getting at the sheep owing to the vigilance of the shepherd and his dogs. But one day it found the skin of a sheep that had been flayed and thrown aside, so it put it on over its own pelt and strolled down among the sheep. The Lamb that belonged to the sheep, whose skin the Wolf was wearing, began to follow the Wolf in the Sheep's clothing; so, leading the Lamb a little apart, he soon made a meal off her, and for some time he succeeded in deceiving the sheep, and enjoying hearty meals.

♦ Appearances are deceptive. ♦

400. 披著羊皮的狼（版本二）

狼發現牧羊人和他的牧羊狗非常警惕，因此很難有機會靠近羊群。但是有一天，牠在野外發現了一隻剛剛被宰殺了的母羊的皮，於是狼便把那張皮披到自己的身上混入羊群。母羊的孩子們看到了，以為是他們的媽媽，便全都跟在狼的後面走。就這樣狼把那些小羔羊帶出了羊群，美美地飽餐了一頓。狼後來又重施故技，每天都享受著美味佳餚。

♦ 表象是能騙人的。 ♦

Townsend 200 = Perry 234

401. The Wolf and the Shepherd I

A Wolf followed a flock of sheep for a long time and did not attempt to injure one of them. The Shepherd at first stood on his guard against him, as against an enemy, and kept a strict watch over his movements.

But when The Wolf, day after day, kept in the company of the sheep and did not make the slightest effort to seize them, the Shepherd began to look upon him as a guardian of his flock rather than as a plotter of evil against it; and when occasion called him one day into the city, he left the sheep entirely in his charge. The Wolf, now that he had the opportunity, fell upon the sheep, and destroyed the greater part of the flock. When the Shepherd returned to find his flock destroyed, he exclaimed, "I have been rightly served; why did I trust my sheep to a Wolf?"

◆　　Don't trust your enemy to guard your valuables.　　◆

401. 狼和牧羊人（版本一）

狼尾隨著羊群走了很長的一段路，可是自始至終卻沒有吃到一隻羊。一開始，牧羊人把狼看得緊緊的，就像對待敵人一樣，謹慎地注意著狼的一舉一動。

時間一天天過去了，狼仍然與羊相處得十分融洽，絲毫看不出任何想對羊下手的意思。於是牧羊人不再把狼看作是兇殘陰險的傢伙，相反把他當成是羊群的守衛者。一天，牧羊人要進城辦事，就把羊群整個託付給狼看管。狼一看到這個天賜的良機終於到了，就開始肆無忌憚地捕殺羊群。牧羊人回來後發現自己的羊已經差不多損失殆盡，他後悔莫及：「我真是咎由自取，為什麼我，竟然會把羊群託付給一隻狼？」

◆　　決不可讓敵人替你保管貴重的財產。　　◆

Townsend 115 = Perry 453

402. The Wolf and the Shepherds II

A Wolf passing by, saw some Shepherds in a hut eating a haunch of mutton for their dinner. Approaching them, he said, "What a clamor you would raise if I were to do as you are doing!"

◆　　Circumstances dictate how actions are seen.　　◆

WOLF 狼

402. 狼和牧羊人（版本二）

一隻狼路過一座小屋，看到屋裡有幾個牧羊人，在津津有味地啃著羊腿，於是他便走上前去，對他們說：「如果我要是做跟你們一樣的事情，你們說不定會扯著嗓子高聲叫罵呢！」

◆ 　　　環境決定了行為的正確與錯誤。　　　◆

L'Estrange 22 = Perry 547

403. A Wolf and a Sow

A wolf came to a sow that was just lying down, and very kindly offered to take care of her litter. The sow as civilly thanked her for her love, and desired she would be pleased to stand off a little, and do her the good office at a distance.

◆ 　An enemy is most dangerous when offering you help.　◆

403. 狼和母豬

母豬剛剛躺下來，狼就走過來，非常好心地要幫她，照顧她的孩子。母豬非常有禮貌地對她的關心表示了感謝，並希望她能站遠一點，在遠處幫她照看孩子就可以了。

◆ 　當敵人向你提供幫助的時候，就是最危險的時候。　◆

Townsend 64 = Perry 153

404. The Wolves and the Sheep

"Why should there always be this fear and slaughter between us?" said the Wolves to the Sheep. " Those evil-disposed Dogs have much to answer for. They always bark whenever we approach you and attack us before we have done any harm. If you would only dismiss them from your heels, there might soon be treaties of peace and reconciliation between us." The Sheep, poor silly creatures, were easily beguiled and dismissed the Dogs, whereupon the Wolves destroyed the unguarded flock at their own pleasure.

◆　　A foolish peace is more destructive than a bloody war.　　◆

404. 狼和綿羊

「為什麼我們之間，總是有那麼多的恐懼和廝殺？」狼對羊說，「這全怪那些脾氣暴躁的狗。每當我們靠近你們，還沒做任何事時，他們就開始狂吠著，張牙舞爪地撲過來要咬我們。如果你們可以讓他們不再跟著你們的話，我們之間就可以永享和平了。」可憐而又愚蠢的羊，輕而易舉地就中了圈套，把牧羊犬給趕走了。於是，狼便開始肆無忌憚地捕殺沒有牧羊犬護衛的羊。

◆　　愚蠢的求和比血腥的戰鬥還有毀滅性。　　◆

WOLF 狼

Townsend 171 = Perry 342

405. The Wolves and the Sheepdogs

The Wolves thus addressed the Sheepdogs, "Why should you, who are like us in so many things, not be entirely of one mind with us, and live with us as brothers should? We differ from you in one point only. We live in freedom, but you bow down to and slave for men, who in return for your services flog you with whips and put collars on your necks. They make you also guard their sheep, and while they eat the mutton throw only the bones to you. If you will be persuaded by us, you will give us the sheep, and we will enjoy them in common, till we all are surfeited." The Dogs listened favorably to these proposals, and, entering the den of the Wolves, they were set upon and torn to pieces.

◆　　　　Don't be take in by your enemy.　　　　◆

405. 狼和牧羊狗

狼對牧羊狗說：「我們之間有這麼多相似之處，你們為什麼不站在我們這一邊，和我們像兄弟一樣相親相愛呢？我們唯一的不同之處就是，我們無拘無束，你們卻要服從人類的奴役，你們辛勤勞動，但是得到的卻只是鞭打和脖套。你們替人們守護羊群，但是他們有肉吃時，卻只把吃剩下的骨頭留給你們。如果你聽從我們的勸告把羊趕到我們那邊去，我們就可以大快朵頤，直至吃得心滿意足為止。」牧羊狗覺得這個主意挺不錯，就跟著狼走了，結果他們一進狼窩，就立刻被狼撕得粉碎。

◆　　　　　　不要被敵人收買。　　　　　　◆

Aesop's Fables: Townsend (1867)

Townsend 1.	The Wolf and the Lamb	Townsend 27.	The Tortoise and the Eagle
Townsend 2.	The Bat and the Weasels	Townsend 28.	The Flies and the Honey-Pot
Townsend 3.	The Ass and the Grasshopper	Townsend 29.	The Man and the Lion
Townsend 4.	The Lion and the Mouse	Townsend 30.	The Farmer and the Cranes
Townsend 5.	The Charcoal-Burner and the Fuller	Townsend 31.	The Dog in the Manger
Townsend 6.	The Father and His Sons	Townsend 32.	The Fox and the Goat
Townsend 7.	The Boy Hunting Locusts	Townsend 33.	The Bear and the Two Travelers
Townsend 8.	The Cock and the Jewel	Townsend 34.	The Oxen and the Axle-Trees
Townsend 9.	The Kingdom of the Lion	Townsend 35.	The Thirsty Pigeon
Townsend 10.	The Wolf and the Crane	Townsend 36.	The Raven and the Swan
Townsend 11.	The Fisherman Piping	Townsend 37.	The Goat and the Goatherd
Townsend 12.	Hercules and the Wagoner	Townsend 38.	The Miser
Townsend 13.	The Ants and the Grasshopper	Townsend 39.	The Sick Lion
Townsend 14.	The Traveler and his Dog	Townsend 40.	The Horse and Groom
Townsend 15.	The Dog and the Shadow	Townsend 41.	The Ass and the Lapdog
Townsend 16.	The Mole and his Mother	Townsend 42.	The Lioness
Townsend 17.	The Herdsman and the Lost Bull	Townsend 43.	The Boasting Traveler
Townsend 18.	The Hare and the Tortoise	Townsend 44.	The Cat and the Cock
Townsend 19.	The Pomegranate, Apple-Tree, and Bramble	Townsend 45.	The Piglet, the Sheep, and the Goat
Townsend 20.	The Farmer and the Stork	Townsend 46.	The Boy and the Filberts
Townsend 21.	The Fanner and the Snake	Townsend 47.	The Lion in Love
Townsend 22.	The Fawn and his Mother	Townsend 48.	The Laborer and the Snake
Townsend 23.	The Bear and the Fox	Townsend 49.	The Wolf in Sheep's Clothing
Townsend 24.	The Swallow and the Crow	Townsend 50.	The Ass and the Mule
Townsend 25.	The Mountain in Labor	Townsend 51.	The Frogs Asking for a King
Townsend 26.	The Ass, the Fox, and the Lion	Townsend 52.	The Boys and the Frogs
		Townsend 53.	The Sick Stag

Townsend 54. The Salt Merchant and his Ass
Townsend 55. The Oxen and the Butchers
Townsend 56. The Lion, the Mouse, and the Fox
Townsend 57. The Vain Jackdaw
Townsend 58. The Goatherd and the Wild Goats
Townsend 59. The Mischievous Dog
Townsend 60. The Fox Who Had Lost His Tail
Townsend 61. The Boy and the Nettles
Townsend 62. The Man and His Two Sweethearts
Townsend 63. The Astronomer
Townsend 64. The Wolves and the Sheep
Townsend 65. The Old Woman and the Physician
Townsend 66. The Fighting Cocks and the Eagle
Townsend 67. The Charger and the Miller
Townsend 68. The Fox and the Monkey
Townsend 69. The Horse and His Rider
Townsend 70. The Belly and the Members
Townsend 71. The Vine and the Goat
Townsend 72. Jupiter and the Monkey
Townsend 73. The Widow and Her Little Maidens
Townsend 74. The Shepherd's Boy and the Wolf
Townsend 75. The Cat and the Birds
Townsend 76. The Kid and the Wolf
Townsend 77. The Ox and the Frog
Townsend 78. The Shepherd and the Wolf
Townsend 79. The Father and His Two Daughters
Townsend 80. The Farmer and His Sons
Townsend 81. The Crab and Its Mother
Townsend 82. The Heifer and the Ox

Townsend 83. The Swallow, the Serpent, and the Court of Justice
Townsend 84. The Thief and His Mother
Townsend 85. The Old Man and Death
Townsend 86. The Fir-Tree and the Bramble
Townsend 87. The Mouse, the Frog, and the Hawk
Townsend 88. The Man Bitten by a Dog
Townsend 89. The Two Pots
Townsend 90. The Wolf and the Sheep
Townsend 91. The Aethiop
Townsend 92. The Fisherman and His Nets
Townsend 93. The Huntsman and the Fisherman
Townsend 94. The Old Woman and the Wine-Jar
Townsend 95. The Fox and the Crow
Townsend 96. The Two Dogs
Townsend 97. The Stag in the Ox-Stall
Townsend 98. The Hawk, the Kite, and the Pigeons
Townsend 99. The Widow and the Sheep
Townsend 100. The Wild Ass and the Lion
Townsend 101. The Eagle and the Arrow
Townsend 102. The Sick Kite
Townsend 103. The Lion and the Dolphin
Townsend 104. The Lion and the Boar
Townsend 105. The One-Eyed Doe
Townsend 106. The Shepherd and the Sea
Townsend 107. The Ass, the Cock, and the Lion
Townsend 108. The Mice and the Weasels
Townsend 109. The Mice in Council
Townsend 110. The Wolf and the Housedog

Townsend 111. The Rivers and the Sea

Townsend 112. The Playful Ass

Townsend 113. The Three Tradesmen

Townsend 114. The Master and His Dogs

Townsend 115. The Wolf and the Shepherds

Townsend 116. The Dolphins, the Whales, and the Sprat

Townsend 117. The Ass Carrying the Image

Townsend 118. The Two Travelers and the Axe

Townsend 119. The Old Lion

Townsend 120. The Old Hound

Townsend 121. The Bee and Jupiter

Townsend 122. The Milk-Woman and Her Pail

Townsend 123. The Seaside Travelers

Townsend 124. The Brazier and His Dog

Townsend 125. The Ass and His Shadow

Townsend 126. The Ass and His Masters

Townsend 127. The Oak and the Reeds

Townsend 128. The Fisherman and the Little Fish

Townsend 129. The Hunter and the Woodman

Townsend 130. The Wild Boar and the Fox

Townsend 131. The Lion in a Farmyard

Townsend 132. Mercury and the Sculptor

Townsend 133. The Swan and the Goose

Townsend 134. The Swollen Fox

Townsend 135. The Fox and the Woodcutter

Townsend 136. The Birdcatcher, the Partridge, and the Cock

Townsend 137. The Monkey and the Fishermen

Townsend 138. The Flea and the Wrestler

Townsend 139. The Two Frogs

Townsend 140. The Cat and the Mice

Townsend 141. The Lion, the Bear, and the Fox

Townsend 142. The Doe and the Lion

Townsend 143. The Farmer and the Fox

Townsend 144. The Seagull and the Kite

Townsend 145. The Philosopher, the Ants, and Mercury

Townsend 146. The Mouse and the Bull

Townsend 147. The Lion and the Hare

Townsend 148. The Peasant and the Eagle

Townsend 149. The Image of Mercury and the Carpenter

Townsend 150. The Bull and the Goat

Townsend 151. The Dancing Monkeys

Townsend 152. The Fox and the Leopard

Townsend 153. The Monkeys and Their Mother

Townsend 154. The Oaks and Jupiter

Townsend 155. The Hare and the Hound

Townsend 156. The Traveler and Fortune

Townsend 157. The Bald Knight

Townsend 158. The Shepherd and the Dog

Townsend 159. The Lamp

Townsend 160. The Lion, the Fox, and the Ass

Townsend 161. The Bull, the Lioness, and the Wild-Boar Hunter

Townsend 162. The Oak and the Woodcutters

Townsend 163. The Hen and the Golden Eggs

Townsend 164. The Ass and the Frogs

Townsend 165. The Crow and the Raven

- Townsend 166. The Trees and the Axe
- Townsend 167. The Crab and the Fox
- Townsend 168. The Woman and Her Hen
- Townsend 169. The Ass and the Old Shepherd
- Townsend 170. The Kites and the Swans
- Townsend 171. The Wolves and the Sheepdogs
- Townsend 172. The Hares and the Foxes
- Townsend 173. The Bowman and Lion
- Townsend 174. The Camel
- Townsend 175. The Wasp and the Snake
- Townsend 176. The Dog and the Hare
- Townsend 177. The Bull and the Calf
- Townsend 178. The Stag, the Wolf, and the Sheep
- Townsend 179. The Peacock and the Crane
- Townsend 180. The Fox and the Hedgehog
- Townsend 181. The Eagle, the Cat, and the Wild Sow
- Townsend 182. The Thief and the Innkeeper
- Townsend 183. The Mule
- Townsend 184. The Hart and the Vine
- Townsend 185. The Serpent and the Eagle
- Townsend 186. The Crow and the Pitcher
- Townsend 187. The Two Frogs
- Townsend 188. The Wolf and the Fox
- Townsend 189. The Walnut-Tree
- Townsend 190. The Gnat and the Lion
- Townsend 191. The Monkey and the Dolphin
- Townsend 192. The Jackdaw and the Doves
- Townsend 193. The Horse and the Stag
- Townsend 194. The Kid and the Wolf
- Townsend 195. The Prophet
- Townsend 196. The Fox and the Monkey
- Townsend 197. The Thief and the Housedog
- Townsend 198. The Man, the Horse, the Ox, and the Dog
- Townsend 199. The Apes and the Two Travelers
- Townsend 200. The Wolf and the Shepherd
- Townsend 201. The Hares and the Lions
- Townsend 202. The Lark and Her Young Ones
- Townsend 203. The Fox and the Lion
- Townsend 204. The Weasel and the Mice
- Townsend 205. The Boy Bathing
- Townsend 206. The Ass and the Wolf
- Townsend 207. The Seller of Images
- Townsend 208. The Fox and the Grapes
- Townsend 209. The Man and His Wife
- Townsend 210. The Peacock and Juno
- Townsend 211. The Hawk and the Nightingale
- Townsend 212. The Dog, the Cock, and the Fox
- Townsend 213. The Wolf and the Goat
- Townsend 214. The Lion and the Bull
- Townsend 215. The Goat and the Ass
- Townsend 216. The Town Mouse and the Country Mouse
- Townsend 217. The Wolf, the Fox, and the Ape
- Townsend 218. The Fly and the Draught-Mule
- Townsend 219. The Fishermen
- Townsend 220. The Lion and the Three Bulls
- Townsend 221. The Fowler and the Viper

Townsend 222. The Horse and the Ass

Townsend 223. The Fox and the Mask

Townsend 224. The Geese and the Cranes

Townsend 225. The Blind Man and the Whelp

Townsend 226. The Dogs and the Fox

Townsend 227. The Cobbler Turned Doctor

Townsend 228. The Wolf and the Horse

Townsend 229. The Brother and the Sister

Townsend 230. The Wasps, the Partridges, and the Farmer

Townsend 231. The Crow and Mercury

Townsend 232. The North Wind and the Sun

Townsend 233. The Two Men Who Were Enemies

Townsend 234. The Gamecocks and the Partridge

Townsend 235. The Quack Frog

Townsend 236. The Lion, the Wolf, and the Fox

Townsend 237. The Dog's House

Townsend 238. The Wolf and the Lion

Townsend 239. The Birds, The Beasts, and the Bat

Townsend 240. The Spendthrift and the Swallow

Townsend 241. The Fox and the Lion

Townsend 242. The Owl and the Birds

Townsend 243. The Trumpeter Taken Prisoner

Townsend 244. The Ass in the Lion's Skin

Townsend 245. The Sparrow and the Hare

Townsend 246. The Flea and the Ox

Townsend 247. The Goods and the Ills

Townsend 248. The Dove and the Crow

Townsend 249. Mercury and the Workmen

Townsend 250. The Eagle and the Jackdaw

Townsend 251. The Fox and the Crane

Townsend 252. Jupiter, Neptune, Minerva, and Momus

Townsend 253. The Eagle and the Fox

Townsend 254. The Man and the Satyr

Townsend 255. The Ass and His Purchaser

Townsend 256. The Two Bags

Townsend 257. The Stag at the Pool

Townsend 258. The Jackdaw and the Fox

Townsend 259. The Lark Burying Her Father

Townsend 260. The Gnat and the Bull

Townsend 261. The Bitch and Her Whelps

Townsend 262. The Dogs and the Hides

Townsend 263. The Shepherd and the Sheep

Townsend 264. The Grasshopper and the Owl

Townsend 265. The Monkey and the Camel

Townsend 266. The Peasant and the Apple-Tree

Townsend 267. The Two Soldiers and the Robber

Townsend 268. The Trees Under the Protection of the Gods

Townsend 269. The Mother and the Wolf

Townsend 270. The Ass and the Horse

Townsend 271. Truth and the Traveler

Townsend 272. The Manslayer

Townsend 273. The Lion and the Fox

Townsend 274. The Lion and the Eagle

Townsend 275. The Hen and the Swallow

Townsend 276. The Buffoon and the Countryman

Townsend 277. The Crow and the Serpent

Townsend 278. The Hunter and the Horseman

Townsend 279. The King's Son and the Painted Lion

Townsend 280. The Cat and Venus

Townsend 281. The She-Goats and Their Beards

Townsend 282. The Camel and the Arab

Townsend 283. The Miller, His Son, and Their Ass

Townsend 284. The Crow and the Sheep

Townsend 285. The Fox and the Bramble

Townsend 286. The Wolf and the Lion

Townsend 287. The Dog and the Oyster

Townsend 288. The Ant and the Dove

Townsend 289. The Partridge and the Fowler

Townsend 290. The Flea and the Man

Townsend 291. The Thieves and the Cock

Townsend 292. The Dog and the Cook

Townsend 293. The Travelers and the Plane-Tree

Townsend 294. The Hares and the Frogs

Townsend 295. The Lion, Jupiter, and the Elephant

Townsend 296. The Lamb and the Wolf

Townsend 297. The Rich Man and the Tanner

Townsend 298. The Shipwrecked Man and the Sea

Townsend 299. The Mules and the Robbers

Townsend 300. The Viper and the File

Townsend 301. The Lion and the Shepherd

Townsend 302. The Camel and Jupiter

Townsend 303. The Panther and the Shepherds

Townsend 304. The Ass and the Charger

Townsend 305. The Eagle and His Captor

Townsend 306. The Bald Man and the Fly

Townsend 307. The Olive-Tree and the Fig-Tree

Townsend 308. The Eagle and the Kite

Townsend 309. The Ass and His Driver

Townsend 310. The Thrush and the Fowler

Townsend 311. The Rose and the Amaranth

Townsend 312. The Frogs' Complaint Against the Sun

附錄 2

Perry's Index to the Aesopica

Perry 1.	Eagle and Fox	Perry 27.	The Fox looks at the Actor's Mask
Perry 2.	Eagle, Jackdaw and Shepherd	Perry 28.	The Cheater
Perry 3.	Eagle and Beetle	Perry 29.	The Charcoal Dealer and the Fuller
Perry 4.	Hawk and Nightingale	Perry 30.	The Shipwrecked Man
Perry 5.	The Athenian Debtor	Perry 31.	The Middle-aged Man and his Two Mistresses
Perry 6.	The Goatherd and the Wild Goats	Perry 32.	The Murderer
Perry 7.	Cat as Physician and the Hens	Perry 33.	The Braggart
Perry 8.	Aesop at the Shipyard	Perry 34.	Impossible Promises
Perry 9.	The Fox and the Goat in the Well	Perry 35.	The Man and the Satyr
Perry 10.	Fox and Lion	Perry 36.	Evil-wit
Perry 11.	The Fisherman Pipes to the Fish	Perry 37.	A Blind Man
Perry 12.	Fox and Leopard	Perry 38.	The Ploughman and the Wolf
Perry 13.	The Fisherman	Perry 39.	The Wise Swallow
Perry 14.	The Ape boasting to the Fox about his Ancestry	Perry 40.	The Astrologer
Perry 15.	The Fox and the Grapes out of Reach	Perry 41.	Fox and Lamb
Perry 16.	The Cat and the Cock	Perry 42.	The Farmer's Bequest to his Sons
Perry 17.	The Fox without a Tail	Perry 43.	Two Frogs
Perry 18.	The Fisherman and the Little Fish	Perry 44.	The Frogs ask Zeus for a King
Perry 19.	The Fox and the Thornbush	Perry 45.	The Oxen and the Squeaking-Axle
Perry 20.	Fox and Crocodile	Perry 46.	The North Wind and the Sun
Perry 21.	The Fishermen and the Tunny	Perry 47.	The Boy with the Stomach-Ache
Perry 22.	The Fox and the Woodcutter	Perry 48.	The Nightingale and the Bat
Perry 23.	Cocks and Partridge	Perry 49.	The Herdsman who lost a Calf
Perry 24.	The Fox with the Swollen Belly	Perry 50.	The Weasel and Aphrodite
Perry 25.	The Halcyon	Perry 51.	The Farmer and the Snake
Perry 26.	A Fisherman	Perry 52.	The Farmer and his Dogs

- Perry 53. The Farmer's Sons
- Perry 54. The Snails in the Fire
- Perry 55. The Woman and her Overworked Maidservants
- Perry 56. The Witch
- Perry 57. The Old Woman and the Thieving Physician
- Perry 58. The Overfed Hen
- Perry 59. Weasel and File
- Perry 60. The Old Man and Death
- Perry 61. Fortune and the Farmer
- Perry 62. The Dolphins at War and the Gudgeon (or Crab)
- Perry 63. Demades the Orator
- Perry 64. The Wrong Remedy for Dog-bite
- Perry 65. The Travellers and the Bear
- Perry 66. The Youngsters in the Butcher's Shop
- Perry 67. The Wayfarers who Found an Axe
- Perry 68. The Enemies
- Perry 69. Two Frogs were Neighbours
- Perry 70. The Oak and the Reed
- Perry 71. The Timid and Covetous Man who found a Lion made of Gold
- Perry 72. The Beekeeper
- Perry 73. The Ape and the Dolphin
- Perry 74. The Stag at the Fountain
- Perry 75. The One-eyed Stag
- Perry 76. The Stag and the Lion in a Cave
- Perry 77. The Stag and the Vine
- Perry 78. The Passengers at Sea
- Perry 79. Cat and Mice
- Perry 80. The Flies in the Honey
- Perry 81. The Ape and the Fox
- Perry 82. Ass, Cock, and Lion
- Perry 83. The Ape and the Camel
- Perry 84. The Two Beetles
- Perry 85. The Pig and the Sheep
- Perry 86. The Thrush
- Perry 87. The Goose that laid the Golden Eggs
- Perry 88. Hermes and the Statuary
- Perry 89. Hermes and Tiresias
- Perry 90. Viper and Watersnake
- Perry 91. The Ass who would be Playmate to his Master
- Perry 92. The Two Dogs
- Perry 93. The Viper and the File
- Perry 94. The Father and his Two Daughters
- Perry 95. The Ill-tempered Wife
- Perry 96. Viper and Fox
- Perry 97. The Young Goat and the Wolf as Musicians
- Perry 98. The Kid on the House-top and the Wolf
- Perry 99. A Statue of Hermes on Sale
- Perry 100. Zeus, Prometheus, Athena and Momus
- Perry 101. The Jackdaw in Borrowed Feathers
- Perry 102. Hermes and Earth
- Perry 103. Hermes and the Artisans
- Perry 104. Zeus and Apollo, a Contest in Archery
- Perry 105. Man's Years
- Perry 106. Zeus and the Turtle
- Perry 107. Zeus and the Fox

Perry 108. Zeus and Man
Perry 109. Zeus and Shame
Perry 110. The Hero
Perry 111. Heracles and Plutus
Perry 112. Ant and Beetle
Perry 113. The Tunny and the Dolphin
Perry 114. The Physician at the Funeral
Perry 115. The Fowler and the Asp
Perry 116. The Crab and the Fox
Perry 117. The Camel who wanted Horns
Perry 118. The Beaver
Perry 119. The Gardener watering his Vegetables
Perry 120. The Gardener and his Dog
Perry 121. The Cithara Player
Perry 122. The Thieves and the Cock
Perry 123. The Jackdaw and the Crows
Perry 124. Fox and Crow
Perry 125. The Crow and the Raven
Perry 126. Jackdaw and Fox
Perry 127. The Crow and the Dog
Perry 128. Crow and Snake
Perry 129. The Jackdaw and the Pigeons
Perry 130. The Stomach and the Feet
Perry 131. The Jackdaw fleeing from Captivity
Perry 132. The Dog who would chase a Lion
Perry 133. The Dog with the Meat and his Shadow
Perry 134. The Sleeping Dog and the Wolf
Perry 135. The Famished Dogs
Perry 136. The Dog and the Hare

Perry 137. The Gnat and the Bull
Perry 138. The Hares and the Frogs
Perry 139. The Sea-gull and the Kite
Perry 140. The Lion in Love
Perry 141. The Lion and the Frog
Perry 142. The Aged Lion and the Fox
Perry 143. The Lion and the Bull invited to Dinner
Perry 144. The Lion in the Farmer's Yard
Perry 145. Lion and Dolphin
Perry 146. The Lion startled by a Mouse
Perry 147. Lion and Bear
Perry 148. The Lion and the Hare
Perry 149. The Lion, Ass, and Fox
Perry 150. Lion and Mouse
Perry 151. The Lion and the Ass Hunting
Perry 152. The Brigand and the Mulberry Tree
Perry 153. The Wolves and the Sheep
Perry 154. The Wolf and the Horse
Perry 155. The Wolf and the Lamb
Perry 156. The Wolf and the Heron
Perry 157. The Wolf and the Goat
Perry 158. The Wolf and the Old Woman Nurse
Perry 159. Wolf and Sheep
(Three True Statements)
Perry 160. The Disabled Wolf and the Sheep
Perry 161. The Fortune-teller
Perry 162. The Baby and the Crow
Perry 163. Zeus and the Bees
Perry 164. The Mendicant Priests

Perry 165. Battle of the Mice and Cats
Perry 166. The Ant
Perry 167. The Fly
Perry 168. The Shipwrecked Man
Perry 169. The Prodigal Young Man and the Swallow
Perry 170. Physician and Sick Man
Perry 171. Bat, Thorn Bush, and Gull
Perry 172. The Bat and the Two Weasels
Perry 173. Hermes and the Woodcutter
Perry 174. Fortune and the Traveller by the Well
Perry 175. The Travellers and the Plane Tree
Perry 176. The Man who warmed a Snake
Perry 177. The Driftwood on the Sea
Perry 178. The Traveller's Offering to Hermes
Perry 179. The Ass and Gardener
Perry 180. The Ass with a Burden of Salt
Perry 181. The Ass and the Mule
Perry 182. The Ass carrying the Image of a God
Perry 183. The Wild Ass and the Tame Ass
Perry 184. The Ass and the Cicadas
Perry 185. The Donkeys make a Petition to Zeus
Perry 186. The Ass and his Driver
Perry 187. The Wolf as Physician
Perry 188. Ass in Lion's Skin
Perry 189. The Ass and the Frogs
Perry 190. Ass, Crow, and Wolf
Perry 191. The Fox betrays the Ass
Perry 192. The Hen and the Swallow

Perry 193. The Fowler and the Lark
Perry 194. The Fowler and the Stork
Perry 195. The Camel seen for the First Time
Perry 196. The Snake and the Crab
Perry 197. Snake, Weasel and Mice
Perry 198. Zeus and the Downtrodden Snake
Perry 199. The Boy and the Scorpion
Perry 200. The Thief and his Mother
Perry 201. The Pigeon and the Picture
Perry 202. The Pigeon and the Crow
Perry 203. The Ape and the Fisherman
Perry 204. The Rich Man and the Tanner
Perry 205. The Hired Mourners
Perry 206. Shepherd and Dog
Perry 207. The Shepherd and the Sea
Perry 208. The Shepherd and his Sheep
Perry 209. The Shepherd and the Young Wolves
Perry 210. The Shepherd who cried "Wolf!" in Jest
Perry 211. The Boy bathing in the River
Perry 212. The Sheep unskillfully Sheared
Perry 213. Pomegranate, Apple Tree, and Bramble
Perry 214. The Mole
Perry 215. The Wasps and the Partridges
Perry 216. The Wasp and the Snake
Perry 217. The Bull and the Wild Goats
Perry 218. The Ape's Twin Offspring
Perry 219. The Peacock and the Jackdaw
Perry 220. Camel and Elephant, Candidates for King

Perry 221. Zeus and the Snake

Perry 222. The Sow and the Bitch

Perry 223. A Dispute concerning Fecundity

Perry 224. The Wild Boar and the Fox

Perry 225. The Miser

Perry 226. The Tortoise and the Hare

Perry 227. The Swallow nesting on the Courthouse

Perry 228. The Geese and the Cranes

Perry 229. The Swallow and the Crow

Perry 230. The Turtles takes Lessons from the Eagle

Perry 231. The Athlete and the Flea

Perry 232. The Foxes at the Meander River

Perry 233. The Swan and his Owner

Perry 234. The Wolf and the Shepherd

Perry 235. The Ant and the Dove

Perry 236. The Travellers and the Crow

Perry 237. A Donkey Bought on Approval

Perry 238. The Fowler and the Pigeons

Perry 239. The Depostiary and the god Horkos (Oath)

Perry 240. Prometheus and Men

Perry 241. Cicada and Fox

Perry 242. The Hyena and the Fox

Perry 243. The Hyenas

Perry 244. The Parrot and the Cat (Partridge and Cat)

Perry 245. The Timid Soldier and the Crows

Perry 246. The Wife and her Drunken Husband

Perry 247. Diogenes on a Journey

Perry 248. Diogenes and the Bald Man

Perry 249. The Dancing Camel

Perry 250. The Nut Tree

Perry 251. The Lark

Perry 252. The Dog, the Rooster, and the Fox

Perry 253. Dog and Shellfish

Perry 254. Dog and Butcher

Perry 255. Mosquito and Lion

Perry 256. Hares and Foxes

Perry 257. Lioness and Fox

Perry 258. The Sick Lion, the Wolf, and Fox

Perry 259. The Lion, Prometheus and the Elephant

Perry 260. The Wolf admiring his Shadow

Perry 261. The Wolf and the Lamb

Perry 262. The Trees and the Olive

Perry 263. The Ass and the Mule

Perry 264. The Ass and his Fellow Traveller the Dog

Perry 265. The Fowler and the Partridge

Perry 266. The Two Wallets

Perry 267. The Shepherd and the Wolf that he brought up with his Dogs

Perry 268. The Caterpillar and the Snake

Perry 269. The Wild Boar, the Horse, and the Hunter

Perry 270. The Wall and the Stake

Perry 271. Winter and Spring

Perry 272. Man and Flea

Perry 273. The Flea and the Ox

Perry 274. Good Things and Evil

473

Perry 275. The Eagle who had his Wings Cropped

Perry 276. The Wounded Eagle

Perry 277. The Nightingale and the Swallow

Perry 278. The Athenian and the Theban

Perry 279. The Goat and the Ass

Perry 280. Goat and Goatherd

Perry 281. The Fighting Cocks

Perry 282. Little Fish escape the Net

Perry 283. The Fire-Bearing Fox

Perry 284. The Man and the Lion travelling together

Perry 285. The Man who broke a Statue of Hermes

Perry 286. Spider and Lizard

Perry 287. The Arab and his Camel

Perry 288. The Bear and the Fox

Perry 289. The Frog Physician

Perry 290. The Oxen and the Butchers

Perry 291. The Ox-driver and Heracles

Perry 292. Ox and Ass Ploughing

Perry 293. The Weasel Caught

Perry 294. The Crane and the Peacock

Perry 295. The Farmer who lost his Mattock

Perry 296. The Farmer and the Eagle

Perry 297. Farmer and Cranes

Perry 298. Farmer and Starlings

Perry 299. The Farmer and the Tree

Perry 300. The Steer and the Bull

Perry 301. The Slave Girl and Aphrodite

Perry 302. The Oak Trees and Zeus

Perry 303. The Woodcutters and the Pine

Perry 304. The Fir Tree and the Thistle

Perry 305. The Sick Stag and his Friends

Perry 306. Hermes and a Man bitten by an Ant

Perry 307. Hermes and the Sculptor

Perry 308. The Dog and the Square-hewn Statue of Hermes

Perry 309. Hermes with a Wagon full of Lies among the Arabs

Perry 310. The Eunuch and the Soothsayer

Perry 311. Zeus, the Animals, and Men

Perry 312. Zeus and the Jar full of Good Things

Perry 313. The Judgments of Zeus

Perry 314. The Sun and the Frogs

Perry 315. The Mule

Perry 316. Heracles and Athena

Perry 317. The Unskilled Physician

Perry 318. The Old Race Horse in the Mill

Perry 319. The Horse and his Groom

Perry 320. The Soldier and his Horse

Perry 321. The Camel in the River

Perry 322. The Crab and his Mother

Perry 323. The Crow and Hermes

Perry 324. The Sick Crow and his Mother

Perry 325. The Lark and the Farmer

Perry 326. The Timid Hunter

Perry 327. The Hunter and the Fisherman

Perry 328. The Dog at the Banquet

Perry 329. The Hunting Dog

Perry 330. The Dog and his Master

Perry 331. Dog and Hare

Perry 332. The Dog with a Bell on his Neck

Perry 333. The Rabbit and the Fox

Perry 334. The Lion's Reign

Perry 335. The Lion and the Eagle

Perry 336. Sick Lion, Fox, and Stag

Perry 337. Lion, Fox, and Ape

Perry 338. The Lion and the Boar

Perry 339. Lion and Wild Ass, Partners in the Hunt

Perry 340. The Lion and the Bowman

Perry 341. The Mad Lion

Perry 342. The Wolves and the Dogs

Perry 343. The Wolves and the Dogs at War

Perry 344. A Wolf among the Lions

Perry 345. The Wolf and the Fox at a Trap

Perry 346. The Wolf and the Well-fed Dog

Perry 347. Wolf and Lion

Perry 348. The Wolf as Governor and the Ass

Perry 349. The Lamp

Perry 350. Adulterer and Husband

Perry 351. The Calf and the Deer

Perry 352. The Country Mouse and the City Mouse

Perry 353. The Mouse and the Bull

Perry 354. The Mouse and the Blacksmiths

Perry 355. The Wayfarer and Truth

Perry 356. The Sheep and the Dog

Perry 357. The Ass that envied the Horse

Perry 358. The Ass in the Lion's Skin

Perry 359. The Donkey on the Tiles

Perry 360. The Ass eating Thorns

Perry 361. The Fowler, the Partridge and the Cock

Perry 362. The Snake's Tail and the Other Members

Perry 363. The Boy and the Painted Lion

Perry 364. The Ape Mother and Zeus

Perry 365. The Shepherd about to enclose a Wolf in the Fold

Perry 366. The Shepherd who reared a Wolf

Perry 367. War and Insolence

Perry 368. The Hide in the River

Perry 369. The Rose and the Amaranth

Perry 370. The Trumpeter

Perry 371. The Lizard and the Amaranth

Perry 372. Three Bulls and a Lion

Perry 373. The Cicada and the Ant

Perry 374. The Goat and the Vine

Perry 375. The Baldheaded Horseman

Perry 376. The Toad puffing herself up to equal Ox

Perry 377. The Boasting Swallow and the Crow

Perry 378. The Two Pot

Perry 379. The Man enamoured of his own Daughter

Perry 380. The Man who evacuated his own Wits

Perry 381. The Aged Farmer and the Donkeys

Perry 382. The Ancestors of the Delphians

Perry 383. The Two Roads

Perry 384. The Mouse and the Frog

Perry 385. The Dreams

Perry 386. The Foolish Girl

Perry 387. The Poor Man Catching Insects

Perry 388. The Widow and the Ploughman
Perry 389. The Cat's Birthday Dinner
Perry 390. The Crow and the Pitcher
Perry 391. The Landlord and the Sailors
Perry 392. The Sick Donkey and the Wolf Physician
Perry 393. The Aethiopian
Perry 394. The Fox as Helper to the Lion
Perry 395. The Serpent and the Eagle
Perry 396. The Kites and the Swans
Perry 397. The Fowler and the Cicada
Perry 398. The Crow and the Swan
Perry 399. The Swan that was caught instead of a Goose
Perry 400. The Bees and the Shepherd
Perry 401. The Foal
Perry 402. The Hunter and the Horseman
Perry 403. The Hunter and the Dog
Perry 404. Hunter and Wolf
Perry 405. Cyclops
Perry 406. Dog tearing a Lion's Skin
Perry 407. A Dog, chasing a wolf
Perry 408. A Thirsty Rabbit descended into a well
Perry 409. The Fox and the Lion in a Cage
Perry 410. The Youth and the Woman
Perry 411. The Onager and the ASS
Perry 412. The Rivers and the Sea
Perry 413. The Fig and the Olive
Perry 414. The Bull, Lioness, and the wild Boar
Perry 415. The Dog and the Smiths

Perry 416. A Bear, a Fox, and a Lion hunted together
Perry 417. A Wolf and Lycophron
Perry 418. The Ostrich
Perry 419. The Thief and the Innkeeper
Perry 420. The Two Adulterers
Perry 421. The Sailor and his Son
Perry 422. The Eagle once a Man
Perry 423. Aesop and the Bitch
Perry 424. Aesop to the Corinthians
Perry 425. The Fisherman and the Octopus
Perry 426. Fox and Crane
Perry 427. Fox and Hedgehog
Perry 428. The Sybarite and the Chariot
Perry 429. The Man who tried to count the Waves
Perry 430. The Creation of Man
Perry 431. Man's Loquacity
Perry 432. Apollo, the Muses and the Dryads
Perry 433. Aphrodite and the Merchant
Perry 434. The Wren on the Eagle's Back
Perry 435. The Black Cat
Perry 436. The Priest of Cybele and the Lion
Perry 437. The Owl and the Birds
Perry 438. The Sybarite Woman and the Jug
Perry 439. The Laurel and the Olive
Perry 440. The Runaway Slave
Perry 441. The Feast Day and the Day After
Perry 442. The Origin of Blushes
Perry 443. Heron and Buzzard

Perry 444. Eros among Men

Perry 445. Pleasure and Pain

Perry 446. The Cuckoo and the Little Birds

Perry 447. The Crested Lark, burying her Father

Perry 448. The Musical Dogs

Perry 449. The Dog's House

Perry 450. The Lions and the Hares

Perry 451. The Wolf in Sheep's Clothing

Perry 452. The Wolf and the Ass on Tria

Perry 453. The Wolf and the Shepherds

Perry 454. The Mouse and the Oyster

Perry 455. Momus and Aphrodite

Perry 456. The Fool and the Sieve

Perry 457. The Boy on the Wild Horse

Perry 458. The Ass and the Snake called Dipsas

Perry 459. The Peeping of an Ass

Perry 460. The Shadow of an Ass

Perry 461. The Eyes and the Mouth

Perry 462. The Privilege of Grief

Perry 463. The Dancing Apes

Perry 464. The Apes Founding a City

Perry 465. The Shepherd and the Butcher

Perry 466. Plenty and Poverty

Perry 467. The Satyr and Fire

Perry 468. The Moon and her Mother

Perry 469. The Bull deceived by the Lion

Perry 470. The Cicadas

Perry 471. The Lice and the Farmer

Perry 472. The Vainglorious Jackdaw and the Peacock

Perry 473. The Sparrow gives Advice to the Hare

Perry 474. The Wolf and the Fox before Judge Ape

Perry 475. From Cobbler to Physician

Perry 476. What the Ass said to the Old Shepherd

Perry 477. Sheep, Stag, and Wolf

Perry 478. Sheep, Dog, and Wolf

Perry 479. Woman in Childbirth

Perry 480. Dog and her Puppies

Perry 481. The Old Lion, the Boar, the Bull, and the Ass

Perry 482. The Dogs and the Crocodiles

Perry 483. The Dog, the Treasure and the Vulture

Perry 484. The Ass insults the Boar

Perry 485. The Frogs Dread the Battle of the Bulls

Perry 486. The Kite and the Doves

Perry 487. The Bullock, the Lion, and the Robber

Perry 488. The Eagle, the Cat, and the Wild Sow

Perry 489. Caesar to a Flunkey

Perry 490. The Eagle and the Crow

Perry 491. The Two Mules and the Robbers

Perry 492. The Stag and the Oxen

Perry 493. What the Old Woman said to the Wine Jar

Perry 494. The Panther and the Shepherds

Perry 495. Aesop and the Farmer

Perry 496. The Butcher and the Ape

Perry 497. Aesop and the Saucy Fellow

Perry 498. The Fly and the Mule

Perry 499. Brother and Sister

Perry 500. Socrates to his Friends

Perry 501. On Believing and Not Believing

Perry 502. The Eunuch's Reply to the Scurrilous Person

Perry 503. The Cockerel and the Pearl

Perry 504. The Bees and the Drones get Judgment from the Easp

Perry 505. Concerning Relaxation and Tension

Perry 506. The Dog to the Lamb

Perry 507. The Cicada and the Owl

Perry 508. Trees under the Patronage of the Gods

Perry 509. The Peacock complains to Juno about his Voice

Perry 510. Aesop's Reply to an Inquisitive Fellow

Perry 511. The Weasel and the Mice

Perry 512. The Enigmatic Will

Perry 513. The Thief and his Lamp

Perry 514. The Rule of King Lion

Perry 515. Prometheus

Perry 516. The Bearded She-Goats

Perry 517. The Dogs send an Embassy to Jupiter

Perry 518. The Fox and the Dragon

Perry 519. About Simonides

Perry 520. The Mountain in Labor

Perry 521. The Ant and the Fly

Perry 522. How Simonides was saved by the Gods

Perry 523. King Demetrius and the Poet Menander

Perry 524. Two Soldiers and a Robber

Perry 525. The Bald Man and the Fly

Perry 526. The Ass and the Pig's Barley

Perry 527. The Buffoon and the Country Fellow

Perry 528. Two Bald Men

Perry 529. Prince, the Fluteplayer

Perry 530. Time (Opportunity)

Perry 531. The Bull and the Calf

Perry 532. The Old Dog and the Hunter

Perry 533. The Ape and the Fox

Perry 534. Mercury and the Two Women

Perry 535. Prometheus and Guile

Perry 536. On Apollo's Oracle

Perry 537. Aesop and the Writer

Perry 538. Pompey and his Soldier

Perry 539. Juno, Venus, and the Hen

Perry 540. The Bullock and the Old Ox

Perry 541. Aesop and the Victorious Athlete

Perry 542. The Ass and the Lyre

Perry 543. The Widow and the Soldier

Perry 544. The Two Suitors

Perry 545. Aesop and the his Mistress

Perry 546. The Cock carried in a litter by Cats

Perry 547. The Sow giving birth and the Wolf

Perry 548. Aesop and the Runaway Slave

Perry 549. The Race Horse

Perry 550. When the Bear gets Hungry

Perry 551. The Traveller and the Raven

Perry 552. The Snake and the Lizard

Perry 553. The Crow and the Sheep

Perry 554. Socrates and a Worthless Servant

Perry 555. The Harlot and the Young Man

Perry 556. The Butterfly and the Wasp

Perry 557. The Ground-Swallow and the Fox

Perry 558. Two Cocks and a Hawk

Perry 559. The Snail and the Mirror

Perry 560. The Bald Man and the Gardener

Perry 561. The Owl, the Cat, and the Mouse

Perry 562. The Partridge and the Fox
(The Rooster and the Fox)

Perry 563. The Lion and the Shepherd

Perry 564. The Gnat and the Bull

Perry 565. The Disdainful Horse

Perry 566. The Bat

Perry 567. The Nightingale and the Hawk

Perry 568. The Envious Fox and the Wolf

Perry 569. The King of the Apes

Perry 570. The Goose and the Stork

Perry 571. The Obliging Horse

Perry 572. The Kid and the Wolf

Perry 573. The Domestic Snake

Perry 574. The Eagle and the Kite

Perry 575. The Wethers and the Butcher

Perry 576. The Fowler and the Birds

Perry 577. The Crow and the other Birds at Dinner

Perry 578. The Horse, the Lion and the Goats

Perry 579. The Sword and the Passer-by

Perry 580. The Covetous Man and the Envious Man

Perry 581. The Boy and the Thief

Perry 582. The Farmer and his Ox

Perry 583. The Pig without a Heart

Perry 584. The River-fish and the Sea-fish

國家圖書館出版品預行編目(CIP)資料

伊索寓言裡的人生真相：405則故事,讀懂世道人心(中英對照)/伊索著；盛世教育譯.
-- 初版. -- 新北市：笛藤出版圖書有限公司, 2025.03
　　面；　公分
中英對照
ISBN 978-957-710-963-7(平裝)

1.CST: 寓言

871.36　　　　　　　　　　114002331

伊索寓言裡的人生真相 405則故事，讀懂世道人心(中英對照)

定價450元　2025年3月27日　初版第1刷

著　　　者	伊　索
總 編 輯	洪季楨
編輯協力	陳珏琪
封面設計	王舒玗
編輯企劃	笛藤出版
發 行 所	八方出版股份有限公司
發 行 人	林建仲
地　　址	231新北市新店區寶橋路235巷6弄6號4樓
電　　話	(02) 2777-3682
傳　　真	(02) 2777-3672
總 經 銷	聯合發行股份有限公司
地　　址	新北市新店區寶橋路235巷6弄6號2樓
電　　話	(02) 2917-8022．(02) 2917-8042
製 版 廠	造極彩色印刷製版股份有限公司
地　　址	新北市中和區中山路二段380巷7號1樓
電　　話	(02) 2240-0333．(02) 2248-3904
郵撥帳戶	八方出版股份有限公司
郵撥帳號	19809050

●本書經合法授權，請勿翻印●
(本書裝訂如有漏印、缺頁、破損，請寄回更換。)